GODSENT

A THRILLER BY
RICHARD BURTON

ARCADE PUBLISHING • NEW YORK

"For as the lightning cometh out of the east, and shineth even unto the west; so shall also the coming of the Son of Man be." Matthew 24:27

All Rights Reserved. No part of this book may be reproduced in any manner without the express written consent of the publisher, except in the case of brief excerpts in critical reviews or articles. All inquiries should be addressed to Arcade Publishing, 307 West 36th Street, 11th Floor, New York, NY 10018.

Arcade Publishing books may be purchased in bulk at special discounts for sales promotion, corporate gifts, fund-raising, or educational purposes. Special editions can also be created to specifications. For details, contact the Special Sales Department, Arcade Publishing, 307 West 36th Street, 11th Floor, New York, NY 10018 or arcade@skyhorsepublishing.com.

Arcade Publishing® is a registered trademark of Skyhorse Publishing, Inc. ®, a Delaware corporation.

Visit our website at www.arcadepub.com

10 9 8 7 6 5 4 3 2 1

Library of Congress Cataloging-in-Publication Data is available on file.

ISBN: 978-1-61145-706-3

Printed in the United States of America.

PROLOGUE

2016

Kate huddled shivering on the bare steel bunk, a cold, hard slab without a mattress or blanket. A metal toilet and sink sat in one corner, both gleaming like sterilized operating-room equipment in the glare of bright fluorescent lights set in a high ceiling that was also steel. In the center of the floor was a grated drain; somehow, that drain was the most ominous thing about the place. It could have only one purpose she could think of: the easy disposal of blood and other bodily fluids.

Speaking of which, her bladder felt like it was about to burst. But without a shred of privacy to mask her from the unseen eyes she felt sure were watching her every move, Kate couldn't bring herself to use the toilet. It wasn't a question of modesty. No, it felt like an act of surrender, as if she would be acquiescing in her own debasement, cooperating with whoever had broken into the compound and kidnapped her and brought her here . . . wherever "here" was. A cold metal room smaller than her bathroom at home. A cell.

She'd been awakened from a sound sleep to find a flashlight shining into her eyes, blinding her. When she'd opened her mouth to scream, a gag had been thrust roughly in. Then she'd been hooded and trussed up, all with a practiced, impersonal efficiency that, even in the midst of her terror, amazed her. These people, whoever they were, knew what they were doing. Not a word was spoken. She'd felt a sharp prick in her arm and realized she'd been injected with something.

Where were her bodyguards, Wilson and Trey? The former Navy SEALS were pushovers for nobody. But her attackers had gotten past them somehow, as well as the other guards patrolling the seaside resort. And they'd gotten past the top-of-the-line AEGIS security system, the same high-tech security system Papa Jim used in his prisons and immigrant detention facilities, which, he'd told her, more to boast than reassure, was as close to military grade as a civilian could get . . . and maybe (he'd added with a sly wink) just a tad bit closer.

God, what about Ethan?

Had they kidnapped him too? *Please let him be okay!* she prayed. *Please . . .*

As the injection took hold and she lost consciousness, Kate had felt herself lifted, and the sensation was like floating in a dream, as if she were drifting upward, lighter than air, right up through the ceiling.

✠   ✠   ✠

When she opened her eyes again, it had been to find herself here, alone in this cold, antiseptic, metal box of a cell. She was no longer wearing her pajamas but instead an orange jumpsuit and hospital-style slippers, also orange, as if she were a captured terrorist facing interrogation. Underneath she was wearing a bra and panties . . . which wouldn't have been so strange except for the fact that she hadn't worn a bra to bed. She didn't feel bruised or violated in any way beyond the gross violation of just being here, but even so, the realization that she'd been stripped and then dressed in prisoner's garb while she lay unconscious and helpless, utterly exposed, made her sick to her stomach.

There were no windows to the cell, not even a door that she could see. For all she knew, she was buried deep underground. Nor did she have any idea how long she'd been here. Hours, surely. Perhaps days. She'd never been so frightened in her life. Yet the fear was distant somehow, muffled, and Kate guessed that whatever she'd been injected with had yet to fully wear off. Or maybe she'd been given something else to keep her calm. Sedated. Numb.

She was almost grateful for it. She wasn't chained or tied up or anything; she could climb off the bunk if she wanted to and pace the dimensions of her cell. But she couldn't summon the will. Besides, the idea was repugnant, as if they'd already reduced her to nothing more than an animal in a cage.

"Who are you?" she called in a voice that came out sounding more like a plea than a demand. "What do you want?"

No answer.

The only sounds were her own breathing, a faint, continuous buzz from the overhead lights, and a whisper of air from a vent located high on one wall. In that hush, more profound than any silence, the beating of her heart was like thunder in her ears.

Ethan had warned her more than once that she was in danger. Tried to send her away. Just last week he'd brought it up again. But as always, she'd refused. "I'm not going anywhere," she told him firmly. "Not after all we've been through. Besides, I have faith in you, and faith moves mountains, right?"

"But does it stop bullets? Does it stop bombs?"

She hadn't had an answer for that.

"I don't want you to get hurt," he pressed on, looking down at her with concern. How handsome he was, this tall, strong son of hers, this miracle who had given her life meaning when she had all but given up on life. "Things are getting crazy now. Take Trey and Wilson and make the old man fly you somewhere for a week or so. Think of it as a vacation."

"What, just when things are getting interesting?" she joked weakly. "No way, José."

His smile was tinged with sadness, and his eyes seemed to hold a knowledge far beyond his twenty years as he opened his arms and gathered her into a warm hug. "I'm sorry," he said.

"For what?"

She felt him shrug. "I don't know. Everything you've been through. I know it hasn't been easy."

"I don't have any regrets," she said. She drew away, holding him at arm's length and staring into his eyes, rich brown flecked with gold. "How could I? I'm so proud of you, Ethan."

"I hope you always will be."

Not by any means for the first time, and she knew not for the last, either, Kate felt afraid. Afraid of what others might do to her son.

Afraid of what he might do.

Now, shivering on the steel bunk, she wondered if he was all right. The thought that he might be dead didn't occur to her. She had no doubt whatsoever that she would have known immediately if he were. His absence from the world would have been apparent to her senses; even in the depths of whatever drugged sleep they'd imposed upon her, she would have known. The very molecules of her body would have cried out in anguish and loss. No, her son was alive, of that she was sure.

But only that.

Had he been kidnapped too? Was he nearby, lying on an identical bunk, in an identical cell, wondering about her? Was he afraid? Hurt? Or had he escaped as only he could do? Maybe she had been the solitary victim, the sole target. Ethan had many enemies . . . and even those who thought of themselves as friends could be dangerous. They would not hesitate to use her to attack or manipulate him. This, she realized, was what Ethan had been afraid of. Why he'd wanted her to go away. Had insisted and insisted, until finally she'd agreed.

And yet, if she'd known what was going to happen, had somehow caught a glimpse of her future, seen herself in this ridiculous orange jumpsuit, in this stark icebox of a room, waiting apprehensively for her mysterious captors to show themselves and begin whatever process of torture or interrogation they had in mind, it wouldn't have changed anything. She still wouldn't have been able to refuse him.

Finally, despite her determination, Kate realized that her trip to the toilet could be postponed no longer. She swung her legs over the side of the bunk and placed her feet cautiously on the metal floor, half expecting that she would receive an electric shock for her trouble. But the only thing that transmitted itself from the floor through the thin paper soles of her slippers was an intense cold that made her toes curl and her jaw clench. God, what she wouldn't give for a thick sweater and a pair of woolen socks!

Not until reaching the toilet did she consider the logistical difficulties presented by the orange jumpsuit. A zipper ran from the neckline to the waist; there was no choice but to unzip it and let the whole garment fall to her ankles, leaving her in bra and panties. The plain white panties were her own; the bra, absurdly, was as orange as the jumpsuit. A wave of embarrassment and anger swept through her at this forced exposure, which could have no other purpose than humiliation, and she felt her face burning as she quickly peeled the panties down to her knees and sat on the bowl.

A sharp gasp escaped her, almost a cry, and she nearly jumped back to her feet.

It was like sitting on a block of ice.

Kate fought back tears as she peed, her stream ringing tinnily against the insides of the bowl. Her body trembled with fear and rage. She felt so damn helpless. But she wasn't going to give them the satisfaction of seeing her cry. They had seen too much already. She imagined them watching now, laughing at her discomfort, her fear, making jokes about her body, the body of a forty-something-year-old woman who had borne a child, never met a piece of chocolate she didn't like, and hadn't exactly been a regular visitor to the gym.

Only when she was finished did she notice that there was no toilet paper. The pettiness of it seemed so childish, so unnecessary. After all that had happened, did they really think she cared? Toilet paper wasn't exactly at the top of her list right now. Standing, Kate jerked up her panties and the jumpsuit as the toilet automatically flushed behind her. The nearby sink had no faucet; when she approached, water began to flow from the tap. It was like dipping her hands in snowmelt. The temperature in the cell seemed to drop ten degrees. She dried her hands on the sides of her jumpsuit and returned to the bunk.

The lights went on buzzing.

The air went on hissing.

The temperature continued to drop, as if the drain in the center of the floor was drawing all the heat out of the cell, sucking it up like a black hole.

Whatever had been holding her fear at a manageable distance, drugs or shock, was disappearing along with it. Kate hugged herself tight but couldn't stop trembling. She could feel her bones vibrating, hear the chattering of her teeth.

Don't panic, she admonished herself. *If they wanted you dead, they could have killed you already.*

No, her kidnappers wanted her alive. She tried again to think of who they could be, what they wanted from her. But the range of possibilities was too wide. Anyway, did it really matter whether she'd been taken by Muslim terrorists or the homegrown variety, agents of a foreign government, religious fanatics, criminals intent on a ransom? The important thing to remember was that Ethan would find her. He would save her. Even now, he must be searching for her.

Unless, of course, he was a prisoner himself . . .

But if that were so, then, in some way beyond her understanding, it was by his own choice, for there was no cell in the world that could hold her son against his will.

Have faith, she told herself. *He'll come for you.*

In any case, Papa Jim was certainly looking for her with all the considerable resources, civilian and military, at his disposal. They'd had their differences over the years, and lately more than ever, but as she knew all too well, if there was one thing Jim Osbourne cared about in this world—besides power, that is—it was family. Despite everything, Kate knew her grandfather wouldn't rest until she was safe. Her kidnappers, whoever they were, had thrown down a gauntlet by snatching her right out from under the cybernetic nose of his precious AEGIS system. That was an insult he couldn't ignore, a challenge to his reputation and authority, his very manhood. Her kidnappers were good, obviously professionals, but they would be no match for Papa Jim. She almost felt sorry for them.

Almost.

So much for turning the other cheek, she thought. But she couldn't help wanting them to suffer for what they'd done to her. For what they were going to do . . .

No, don't think about that!

The waiting was torture, as it was no doubt intended to be. There was nothing she could do but pray.

And remember . . .

CHAPTER 1

1995

"Isn't he good?" Kate whispered to Brady.

"If you like that kind of thing," her boyfriend answered with a superior tone.

They were on the sidewalk outside the Metropolitan Museum of Art in New York City on an unseasonably warm Saturday afternoon in November, watching a street artist sketching caricatures of passersby. The man was fast and funny, both with his pen and his banter, and Kate had just about decided to get one done of her and Brady, a souvenir of their trip. They were flying back to Charleston tomorrow with the rest of the youth group from St. John the Baptist, and so far she'd bought presents for her father and mother and Papa Jim, but nothing for herself. She'd thought she would ask the man to draw the two of them as Rhett Butler and Scarlett O'Hara, but Brady's dismissive response doused her enthusiasm like a bucket of cold water. "Why do you have to be so negative?"

"I'm not," he said.

She rolled her eyes. "See? There you go again."

This drew an appreciative chuckle from the artist, a black kid in a red beret who looked scarcely older than she was. He glanced up from his pad, where he was rapidly sketching a fidgety little girl in pigtails seated opposite him, giving her the look of Bo Peep from *Toy Story*, and shot her a wink.

Brady scowled and drew her aside. "I thought we were here to see art."

Kate shook him off. "What is your problem, Brady? You've been snipping at me all day!"

He gave a sullen shrug. "I'm not the one with the problem."

Kate sighed. "This is about last night, isn't it?"

Last night, back at the hotel after seeing *Cats*, she and her roommate, Luanne, had been chatting and watching TV in their room when Brady had knocked at their door. Kate had been surprised to see him, to put it mildly—Sister Mary Gabriel and Sister Sarah, the chaperones for the trip, had made it crystal clear what would happen to anyone caught out of his or her room without permission—but Luanne had invited him right in. Luckily, they hadn't changed into their pajamas yet.

"Brady," said Kate, sitting up in bed. "What are you doing here?"

"I got kicked out," he explained sheepishly. "Mike and Laura are up there."

Mike was his roommate; Laura was Mike's girlfriend.

"Oh my God," said Luanne. She was sixteen, a year younger than Kate, a tall, lanky girl with braces and long, straight blond hair.

"Well, you can't stay here," said Kate.

"What am I supposed to do?" Brady asked plaintively. "Mike said it'll just be for like an hour, and then I can go back."

"Oh my God," Luanne repeated, her eyes wide. "Are they, you know, doing it?"

"Luanne!" said Kate.

"Well, are they?"

Brady's face turned bright pink. "I don't know, but Mike has alcohol up there."

"Oh my God!"

"Would you stop saying that?" said Kate, annoyed.

"Sorry." Luanne returned to her bed and flopped down.

"Whatcha watching?" Brady asked.

"*Seinfeld.*"

"Oh, I love that show!" He sat down gingerly on the edge of Kate's mattress.

As *Seinfeld* gave way to *Cheers*, Brady slid incrementally up the bed, until, by the time the closing credits rolled up, he was reclining alongside her, one arm around her shoulders.

Soft snores came from the other bed.

During a commercial, he leaned over and kissed her.

Kate kissed him back; she enjoyed kissing Brady, though that was as far as she was prepared to go, as he well knew. All the members of the youth group had pledged to stay pure until marriage, and Kate took her vow seriously, even if Laura did not. As a little girl, she'd gone through a phase where she'd been what her mother had called "nun mad," absolutely convinced that she would become a nun when she grew up; that dream had faded with other childish dreams, but her faith was still strong, and she knew that God would always be at the center of her life in one way or another.

The kiss grew more passionate, making her heart flutter. If a simple kiss could feel this good, she wondered, what must full intimacy be like? She was curious, of course, but in no rush to find out. Then she felt Brady's hand begin to slide beneath her blouse. She gripped his wrist firmly and pushed the offending hand away. "No," she whispered, afraid of waking Luanne.

"Come on, Kate," Brady whispered back. "Let me touch you . . ."

"No," she repeated.

"It's not breaking the pledge," he said. "You'll still be pure."

"I said no."

He leaned back against the headboard and crossed his arms over his chest. "We've been going out since September," he said, a petulant tone creeping into his voice. "That's three whole months. And all we've ever done is kiss! I swear, I feel like I'm back in junior high or something!"

"Kissing is all I'm comfortable with right now," she said, feeling her face flush red with embarrassment and anger. "I've told you that." She glanced at Luanne, who was still snoring on obliviously, thank God. "I can't believe you're doing this!"

"You don't know what it's like for guys, Kate. It's different for us."

"Try a cold shower," she advised him. "I hear that works wonders."

"Aw, Kate! Don't be like that." He leaned toward her again. "I didn't mean—"

"It's late, Brady. You'd better get back to your room."

For a second it looked like he might argue, but then he pressed his lips together, biting off whatever words he was about to say. Even so, she could hear the anger in his voice as he pushed himself off the bed and made for the door. "Fine. See you at breakfast tomorrow."

She almost called him back, not wanting to end what had been such a wonderful day on a harsh note, but in the end she let him go, afraid that one of the Sisters might come by to check on them. That would be a disaster. She'd had a hard enough time convincing her parents to let her come on this trip as it was. By comparison to her mom and dad, to say nothing of Papa Jim, the nuns were downright permissive. If she were caught with a boy in her room, and her folks heard about it, she'd be grounded.

For life.

Now, outside the museum, Brady was pouting again, his blue eyes full of hurt and resentment, like a spoiled little boy who hadn't gotten his way. Kate sighed. "Look, Brady. Can't we just pretend nothing happened last night?"

"Nothing did happen."

"You make it sound like I'm the one who should apologize."

He shrugged.

"I don't know what's gotten into you," she said. "But I had to jump through a lot of hoops to come on this trip. I want to enjoy myself. If you can't be pleasant, I'd just as soon be by myself."

"Right," he said. "Like I'm going to go off and leave you alone in the middle of New York City. Sister Sarah would skin me alive. And your grandfather would put me in one of his prisons! I'm supposed to—" He broke off abruptly, flushing bright red.

Kate felt her own blood rising. "Supposed to what?"

"Nothing."

"Brady Perkins Maxwell, you tell me the truth right now," she insisted, hands on her hips. "If you don't, I'll never speak to you again."

He ran a hand through his short blond hair. "Okay, so your grandfather asked me to keep an eye on you. What's wrong with that?"

"Nothing's wrong . . . if that's all he did. But I know my grandfather. Are you sure he didn't do more than ask?"

"What do you mean?"

"Oh my God," she said. "He paid you, didn't he? My grandfather paid my boyfriend to spy on me!"

"Not spy," he corrected quickly. "To watch out for you, protect you."

"How much?"

"Is it really important?"

"How much, Brady?"

"Um . . . a hundred dollars. I was going to use it to buy you something really nice," he added.

"You can keep it," she said and suddenly, to her surprise and mortification, burst into tears.

Brady gazed at her like a deer caught in the headlights of an oncoming car.

"If you take one step after me, so help me, I'll scream," she warned him, having finally managed to extricate some Kleenex from her purse. Then she pushed past him.

He didn't follow as she ran up the front steps of the museum, ignoring the looks of curiosity and concern directed toward her by passersby. At the top, having wrestled her tears under control, she stopped, turned, and looked back to see if Brady was following her. But her boyfriend—ex-boyfriend, she mentally corrected—was gone.

Relieved, Kate took another moment to compose herself, standing to one side of the entrance as people streamed in and out of the museum. She was furious at her grandfather . . . but, unfortunately, not really all that surprised. Papa Jim was incredibly overprotective and didn't have the most highly developed sense of boundaries: a bad combination. She sometimes wondered if he thought of her as a person at all, or only as a possession, albeit a valuable one. As for Brady . . . she didn't want to think about him at all right now, or else she'd start crying again. She felt like a jerk for caring, for hurting, when it was so clear now that he just wasn't worth it. But that didn't make the pain go away.

"Are you okay?"

Startled, she glanced up to see a young black man in a red beret—the sidewalk artist she and Brady had been watching earlier. He was no more than five four, which made him an inch shorter than she was, and he didn't look much older, perhaps eighteen or nineteen. He wore a black jacket over a T-shirt so white it looked newly bleached, and black jeans. "Excuse me?"

"I'm sorry," he said, grinning. "It's just . . . well, I saw you crying. You looked like you might be in some kind of trouble."

"I'm fine," she said rather frostily, clutching her purse to her side.

"Don't be frightened," he said.

"I'm not," she said, though in fact she was. Yet it was hard to say why. She was in a public place, surrounded by people, and the man talking to her hadn't said or done anything remotely threatening. Nor was she picking up a flirtatious vibe. Just the same, something about him, or the situation, was off. She felt a tingling along her nerves, and goose bumps popped up along her arms. She hugged herself as if at a sudden chill in the air. "Look, I'm meeting some people," she began.

"South Carolina," he said.

"I beg your pardon?"

"Your accent. You're from South Carolina, aren't you? Me too."

She regarded him with suspicion. "You don't sound like it."

He grinned again and dropped into a familiar drawl, exaggerated for comic effect. "Honey, my people been down around Marion going on two hundred years now."

She couldn't help laughing. "I'm from Charleston."

"Beautiful city," he said and extended his hand. "Name's Gabriel."

She took his hand and shook, feeling that strange tingling sensation again, almost like a low-level electric shock. But the fear was gone. "I'm Kate."

He nodded as though perfectly aware of that already. "God is with you, Kate."

"Um, yeah . . ." Uh-oh. So that's what she'd been picking up on. The guy was some kind of street preacher, trolling for fresh converts. She *so* did not need this right now.

"I'm not trying to convert you or anything," he said as though reading her mind. "I know you're a good Catholic."

Okay, now the fear was back. How could he know that?

"You're blessed, Kate. God's grace is upon you."

"Uh, thanks, but I really better get going . . ." She began to move off, but he stepped in front of her, blocking the way.

"This is for you." He held out a sheet of paper that had been folded in half.

"What?"

"It's a sketch. Go on, take it."

Eager to get away, and not wanting to do anything that might rile him up, Kate took the paper and tucked it into her purse. "Thanks. Now, I really do have to go."

"Of course." He stepped politely aside.

With a nervous smile, Kate hurried past, into the haven of the museum. She half expected him to follow, but he didn't; when she turned, she saw him heading back down the steps . . . or, rather, his red beret. It bobbed like a darting bird, a cardinal, before vanishing into the afternoon crowd.

What a day this is turning out to be, she thought. First Brady, then Gabriel. What next? But strangely, she felt better now than she had before. The odd encounter had lifted her spirits. It struck her as a quintessentially quirky New York experience. Smiling, she imagined herself relating it to Luanne later. She could practically see the girl's wide eyes, hear her breathy "Oh my God!"

For the next two hours, Kate lost herself amid the treasures of the museum. A sense of peace settled over her as she drifted from gallery to gallery, making her way up to the second floor and the European Paintings gallery. There she lingered longest. She loved the centuries-old paintings best of all, especially those from the Renaissance: the bright, vibrant colors, the heavy shadows, the keen and vivid representations of scenes from the Old and New Testaments. Despite their great age, the canvases seemed fresh to her, invested with a spiritual life missing from much of the more modern artwork on display. Full of angelic visitations, acts of sacrifice and devotion, the paintings seemed to glow with a soulful inner light.

She basked in that glow, deeply moved by the expressions on the faces of those depicted there, men and women who appeared so ordinary and yet had been touched by the divine. Mary most of all. To know God directly, how could there be a greater joy? She saw it on the rapt faces, in the eyes turned Heavenward with longing. In the tender looks that passed between Madonna and child in the many paintings of that subject. Yet she saw fear too, and suffering, and sadness that tugged at her own heart. Sometimes the eyes were directed outward, beyond the plane of the painting, to the viewer, to her, and in those gazes she thought she discerned a secret knowledge that was perhaps as much a torment as a blessing to those who possessed it.

A verse from Luke rose up in her memory: "For unto whomsoever much is given, of him shall be much required . . ." She'd always taken that to mean that rich people, like her own family, had special obligations and responsibilities to give generously of their wealth, but now, suddenly, she realized that those who had been touched by God were the richest of all, and that it was they who would be required to give the most, even their very lives, just as Jesus had given His life . . .

The touch of God must be a hard thing for a human being to bear, she thought and shuddered slightly, as she might have shuddered at a scene in a movie, full of sympathy yet glad, too, that she was only a witness and not a participant in the events depicted onscreen.

By then it was getting late. Kate left the museum and hailed a cab to take her back to the hotel, where she hurriedly showered and changed. Then she and Luanne, who'd been napping when she came in, went downstairs, where the group was gathering under the stern and watchful eyes of Sister Sarah and Sister Mary Gabriel. Kate avoided Brady, who seemed content to be avoided.

Dinner that evening was at Sam's, an Italian restaurant in the theater district. Afterward, they saw the revival of *Hello Dolly*, with Carol

Channing, at the Lunt-Fontanne Theatre. The next morning, there was an early Mass at St. Patrick's Cathedral, followed by a brief audience with Cardinal O'Connor that had been specially arranged by Papa Jim.

Then it was home to Charleston, where she slid smoothly back into the normal round of school and church, family and friends. Brady tried to make up with her at first, but it was too late for apologies or amends. It didn't help that he was wearing a new pair of Air Jordans, either. It took a couple of weeks, but finally he seemed to get the message.

That was more than she could say for Papa Jim. When she confronted him about what he'd done, her grandfather took the cigar out of his mouth, leaned his shiny bald head back, and roared with laughter. "A hundred? Is that what that boy told you? Heck, I paid him twice that!"

"Papa Jim!"

"Go on now, baby girl. Papa Jim's got work to do."

Two months later, in early January, following a routine physical exam, Kate's doctor informed her that she was pregnant.

CHAPTER 2

1996

"I'm *what?*" She stared at Dr. Rickert in shock.

"You're pregnant, Kate," he repeated quite seriously from the other side of the desk.

Dr. Rickert had been her doctor ever since she was a girl. He was a stocky man of forty-five or so with thick, curly black hair, a finely trimmed mustache, and small hands that were so white and well-manicured that they always kind of creeped her out, as if they belonged to a mannequin rather than a man. Not once in all the years she'd been coming to see him had he given her any reason to suspect that, in addition to being a physician, he was also a comedian. But that was the only explanation for what he was telling her now.

Either that, or he was completely out of his mind.

"I—I don't understand," she stammered. "Are you joking?"

He frowned. "I don't find teenage pregnancy a joking matter, do you?"

Kate crossed her legs nervously. She felt herself blushing, as if she really were pregnant. But of course that was impossible. She'd never been with a man. Never done more than kiss. She'd kept her vow of purity. With a trembling voice, she said as much to Dr. Rickert.

He sighed as though he'd heard it all before. "The tests don't lie," he said. "I'm afraid there's no doubt of it, Kate. No doubt at all. You are pregnant. About seven weeks along, I'd say."

"No." She shook her head. Panic was welling up in her chest, and she felt a rush of tears to her eyes. "There's been some mistake. You have to run the tests again, Dr. Rickert."

"I've run them twice already. There's no mistake." He pushed a box of Kleenex toward her across the desk with those snow-white hands of his. "Go on, take one. Have a good cry if you need to. And then we'll talk about what comes next."

She ignored the tissues. She had nothing to cry about. She'd done nothing wrong. Wasn't pregnant. She clasped her arms across her chest, willing herself to be calm and rational. "Next?"

"I have to inform your parents, of course. Then you'll want to discuss your options."

"Options?" She was repeating his words like a robot, scarcely aware of what she was saying. How could this be happening to her? Had the world gone crazy? She'd been feeling oddly for a month or so. Not sick, exactly. Just . . . *strange*. Off her game. Her period was late. And then she'd started putting on weight, suffering inexplicable bouts of nausea . . . Admittedly, now that she thought about it, it did sound a lot like the symptoms of pregnancy, except for the fact that she couldn't possibly be pregnant. She'd expected Dr. Rickert to tell her that she had some kind of low-grade infection, even been a little worried that it was going to turn out to be something more serious. But this? Pregnant? No. That was beyond serious. It was absurd, surreal, like a story by that writer Kafka they'd studied in English class at school.

Dr. Rickert sighed again and rubbed the bridge of his nose. "The mind is great at denial, Kate. But the body—it's not so good."

"I'm not in denial," she said. "I'm telling the truth! Don't you think I'd know if I'd . . ." She couldn't bring herself to say it. "Don't you think I'd know?"

"In a matter of weeks," Dr. Rickert continued as if she hadn't spoken, "your condition will be obvious to anyone who looks at you. I'm afraid 'I never had sex' is just not going to cut it, Kate."

"But it's the truth," she insisted, getting angry now.

He raised an eyebrow. "Then, if you'll excuse me for saying so, perhaps it's a priest you need, not a doctor."

So he was a comedian after all, she thought. A bad one.

"Your mother brought you in today, didn't she? Is she waiting outside? I think we'd better ask her to come in."

"Go ahead," Kate said sullenly.

Dr. Rickert reached for the phone, then paused. "I'm not the enemy, Kate. I'm your doctor. And, I hope, a friend. I want to help you through this."

Kate shrugged. Refused to meet his gaze. "Whatever."

A moment later, Kate's mother, Gloria Skylar, walked into the office. At thirty-five, Gloria—Glory, as everyone called her—was a strikingly beautiful woman who looked more like Kate's older sister than her mom. Her long, lustrous blond hair, exquisitely styled at Stella Nova, fell in shimmering waves to the shoulders of her light blue cashmere sweater from Berlin's. Her skin was a smooth, even tan, as though she'd just returned from a week in Cancun (actually, she was a regular at the Ultratan salon on East Bay), and she carried a Fendi handbag that was only slightly darker. She wore a tiny gold crucifix around her neck and a pair of angel-skin coral pendant earrings.

Dr. Rickert got to his feet as she entered the office, absently smoothing back his hair and smiling as if the reason he'd called her in had escaped his mind for the moment. Observing this reaction, Kate could only shake her head: Glory had that kind of effect on men.

"Is she going to be all right, Doctor?" Glory asked anxiously. "Is my baby going to be all right?" A notorious hypochondriac, Kate's mother was always quick to expect the worst when it came to the maladies of others.

Dr. Rickert's smile faltered. He cleared his throat. "You'd better have a seat, Glory," he said, indicating the empty chair next to Kate's.

"Oh God, I knew it." She sat down, casting a worried look in Kate's direction as she crossed her legs in their white cotton twills.

The absurdity of the whole situation struck Kate afresh at that look, which seemed somehow comical in its very seriousness, and she had to fight to keep from giggling. Dimly, at the back of her mind, she realized that she was in a kind of shock.

Dr. Rickert settled back into his chair. "I think Kate should be the one to tell you." He steepled his fingers in front of his nose and gazed at her expectantly, like a teacher calling upon a student to account for missing homework.

"What is it, honey?" Glory asked, her voice trembling as she turned in the chair to face her daughter. Her hands were clasping her bag so tightly that the knuckles were white with tension.

The wave of hilarity that had nearly swept Kate away seconds ago had receded, and in its wake she felt as if all her defenses had been stripped from her, leaving her totally exposed, totally helpless, at the mercy of these adults who, she knew, would never believe her, no matter what she told them. Suddenly she was crying, arms flung about her mother's neck, hugging her tightly. "It's not true," she sobbed. "It's not!"

This outburst, unfortunately, served only to heighten Glory's dire expectations. "Oh God," she cried, returning her daughter's embrace. "Oh my poor baby!"

"He said . . ."

"What, darling? What?"

"He said . . ." Kate gulped, sniffled, but couldn't go on.

Finally, Dr. Rickert cleared his throat again. "I'm afraid Kate is pregnant, Glory."

"She's *what?*" Glory drew back sharply from her daughter.

Kate shook her head, tears streaming down her face. "I'm not, Mom! I swear!"

"There's no mistake," said Dr. Rickert.

"No!" wailed Kate, his words setting her off again. "Why won't you listen to me?" she cried, nearly hysterical now. "I'm telling the truth!"

Glory's tanned face had turned a ghastly shade of pale. "Hush now, honey," she said to her daughter, her voice all business now. "We'll figure this out, I promise." Then she turned back to Dr. Rickert. "Could you leave us alone for a moment, Doctor? Just us girls?"

He was already getting to his feet, obviously relieved to go, even for just a little while. "Of course. I'll be outside if you need me."

Glory stood as well. She laid a hand on Kate's shoulder. "Honey, I'm going to have a quick word with Dr. Rickert. I'll be right back, and then we'll talk."

Kate didn't answer or respond in any way. She sat curled up on the chair. The storm of tears had passed as suddenly as it had come on, and now she felt empty, drained. She was aware of the gentle weight of her mother's hand on her shoulder, the sound of her voice, of receding footsteps, and then the low murmur of voices just outside the door. But none of it really impinged on her; it might have been a million miles away. Dr. Rickert's office—his solid mahogany desk with its framed photographs of his wife and two sons, the diplomas so proudly displayed on the wall behind the desk, the bookshelves filled with thick reference volumes, the tastefully framed posters from the Gibbes Museum of Art—all of it seemed flat and sterile, like a stage set. The world outside the window was no improvement. Kate could see Charleston Harbor, the water like lead in the gray light of the overcast January day. It had been drizzling on and off all morning; now the clouds were thickening ominously, announcing a storm. Yet she felt cut off from it by more than just the window. It was as if there was a pane of glass inside her, separating her from her own emotions. She could look through it, see them quite clearly—the fear, the confusion, the anger—but she couldn't touch them, couldn't *feel* them.

She looked up at the sound of a closing door to see her mother walking back to the chair. Glory didn't say a word as she sat down, just looked at Kate as though seeing right to the core of her.

Kate squirmed inside and smiled nervously. "I guess we won't be having lunch at Anson, huh?"

The attempted joke fell flat. Glory frowned and said, "Is there anything you want to tell me, Kate?"

"I'm not pregnant, Mom. You've got to believe me."

"Dr. Rickert assures me there's no mistake."

"He's wrong. I swear, Mom. I haven't been with any boy, ever!"

"Maybe something happened that you're afraid to tell me about. Maybe some boy wouldn't take no for an answer. Is that what happened, Kate?"

"No."

"Then what?"

She was near tears again. But she drew a deep breath and forced herself to speak calmly. "I don't know. I think we should go to another doctor."

Her mother appeared to consider this.

"Mom, I took a vow," she said softly, holding Glory's gaze. "I promised God I would stay pure. I haven't broken it. I haven't."

That seemed to decide her. "All right, honey," Glory said with a nod. "We'll get another opinion."

Relief rushed through her, and she was crying again before she knew it.

"Shhh." Her mother hugged her, stroking her hair. "Hush now."

After a moment, Kate pulled away. She smiled crookedly as she dabbed at her eyes with fresh Kleenex. "You believe me, don't you, Mom?"

"Of course I do," said Glory. But she had already gotten to her feet and turned away, so Kate couldn't see her expression as she said it.

✠   ✠   ✠

A quick phone call from Glory secured them a walk-in appointment with Dr. Jane Sibley, Glory's gynecologist. Sometimes Kate was embarrassed by her family's high standing in Charleston society, thanks to Papa Jim's wealth and connections, but this was not one of those times. She was eager to put this nightmare behind her once and for all.

Dr. Sibley, a plump woman with short brown hair who appeared to be in her midfifties, listened intently as Glory explained the situation. Her blue eyes were magnified behind thick lenses, giving her the look of a matronly owl. "Dr. Rickert faxed over his results," she told them. "Urine tests are highly accurate, but there are occasional false positives."

"What could cause that, Jane?" asked Glory.

"Let's not get ahead of ourselves," Dr. Sibley advised. "First, we'll do a blood test and pelvic exam. That should settle the question."

"But what if it still shows I'm pregnant?" Kate asked, unable to keep a tremor from her voice.

"We'll cross that bridge when we come to it."

Dr. Sibley led them to an examination room, where, behind a screen, Kate exchanged her clothes for a loose green hospital gown. Then, emerging, she lay on the examination table and placed her feet into the stirrups. Glory, who stood beside her at the head of the table, flashed a supportive smile.

Dr. Sibley bent to her work. It didn't take long. After no more than five minutes, she straightened up.

"Well?" asked Glory.

Blinking owlishly, Dr. Sibley peeled off her gloves and tossed them into the disposal bin. "You can get dressed, Kate. Then I'll talk to you both in my office."

Kate nodded mutely.

"But is she pregnant?" Glory demanded. "Or is it . . ."

"In my office," Dr. Sibley repeated firmly and left the room.

"She would have said something, right?" asked Kate as she dressed behind the screen. She was so nervous, she could barely get her legs into her jeans.

"Just hurry up," said Glory.

"Mom, I'm scared," Kate said when she came around the screen. "Before we go in there, can I say a prayer?"

Glory gave her a tight smile. "Of course, honey. I think I'll say one too."

Kate bowed her head. She wasn't sure what she wanted to say. But then the familiar words of the Lord's Prayer rose unbidden to her mind, and she recited them under her breath. *Our Father, who art in Heaven, hallowed be thy name. Thy kingdom come. Thy will be done, on earth as it is in Heaven. . . .* As she prayed, she felt a sense of warmth kindle in her. Centered in her belly at first, it radiated throughout her body until she felt as if she were glowing. *Give us this day our daily bread. And forgive us our trespasses as we forgive those who trespass against us. And lead us not into temptation, but deliver us from evil. . . .* Somehow, she wasn't so afraid anymore. A deep sense that everything was going to be all right had settled over her. A conviction. She felt comforted, reassured, as she had never before felt in the course of reciting this or any other prayer. *For thine is the kingdom, and the power, and the glory. For ever and ever. Amen.*

When she looked up, her mother was waiting by the door, staring at her with a strangely tender expression. "What's wrong?" she asked.

Glory shook her head, wiped at her eyes. "Nothing. It's just . . . you looked so beautiful as you were praying. So pure. Like an angel."

"We better go," Kate said.

Dr. Sibley was waiting in her office, seated behind her desk. She motioned for Kate and Glory to sit on the sofa. Kate scrutinized the doctor's face, hoping for some clue as to what she was about to say, but there was nothing. Dr. Sibley must be a mean poker player, she decided as she sat down. Glory settled beside her. Kate took her mother's hand. The feeling of serenity that had settled over her as she prayed was beginning to fray. Outside the office window, rain was pelting down.

"I'll come straight to the point," said Dr. Sibley. "Dr. Rickert was right. You're pregnant, Kate."

Kate gasped. It was as if she'd been punched in the stomach. She couldn't breathe.

She felt Glory stiffen beside her and pull her hand free.

"You're about seven weeks along, I'd say," Dr. Sibley continued.

"What about the blood test?" Glory asked.

Dr. Sibley shrugged. "I should have the results back in a couple of hours. But they won't change anything, Glory."

"But it's not possible," Kate said weakly.

"Oh, it's possible," said Dr. Sibley with a grim smile. "It's more than possible."

"No, it's not. I've never had sex."

"You can get pregnant without intercourse," Dr. Sibley said. "If you bring any ejaculate or pre-ejaculate into contact with the vulva, there's always a chance of fertilization if the circumstances are right. What are they teaching you kids these days?"

"You don't understand," said Kate, more insistently now. "I've never done anything like that! I've never done anything but kiss! You can't get pregnant from kissing, can you?"

"Of course not!" her mother snapped. "Don't be ridiculous!"

"But—"

Glory cut her off. "I've had enough of this nonsense." She surged to her feet, glaring down at her daughter. "I trusted you, Kate. I had my doubts, but I believed you. And this is the thanks I get. Not another word," she added, raising a forestalling hand before Kate could speak again. "The only thing I want to hear from you now is the name of the boy who did this."

"I already told you," cried Kate. "Nobody did anything!"

Dr. Sibley broke in, her voice firm and authoritative. "This isn't the time for recriminations or accusations, Glory. Your daughter is only seventeen, for God's sake! You should know better than anyone how she feels." At this, Glory subsided, sinking back onto the sofa like a puppet whose strings had been cut.

Dr. Sibley turned to Kate. "I'm sorry, Kate, but I have to ask: Were you raped? Abused?"

"No, nothing like that!" Kate protested shrilly.

"It's that boyfriend of hers, Brady Maxwell," Glory said.

"He's not my boyfriend," Kate said. "Not since . . ." She trailed off, realizing that she'd said too much.

"Not since New York?" Glory's eyes flashed in sudden surmise. "That's when it happened, isn't it? I knew I shouldn't have let you go on that trip! Did he get you drunk? Drug you?"

"It wasn't Brady! It wasn't anybody!"

"It had to be somebody," Glory insisted. "Why are you protecting him?"

Dr. Sibley broke in again. "Calm down, both of you. It doesn't do any good to fight. You have decisions to make. Hard decisions that will impact the rest of your lives in one way or another. You need to come together as a family."

At this, Kate sagged. "Oh my God. Daddy's going to freak out. And Papa Jim!" The reality of it all was sinking in. "They won't believe me either. Nobody's going to believe me . . ." She'd never felt so alone. So abandoned.

"It's not uncommon for young girls in this situation to have some trouble at first accepting their condition," Dr. Sibley told her. "But believe me, Kate, it's not the end of the world, even if it seems that way now. You have choices."

"You mean abortion?" asked Glory. "You know we're good Catholics, Jane. We're not going to compound one sin with a worse one."

"I wasn't suggesting anything specifically. But I do recommend family counseling. I can give you the names of some good therapists. Or perhaps you'd rather talk to your priest. And I can refer you to an excellent obstetrician."

"I want to go home now," Kate said. "Please, Mom. I just want to go home."

They'd left quickly after that, with Glory promising to call Dr. Sibley the next day. The ride home was torturous. The storm that had been brooding over the city had broken, and now traffic across the Pearman Bridge was moving at a crawl through heavy rain lashed by strong winds. Glory sat tight-lipped behind the wheel of the BMW, seemingly fixated on the frantic back and forth of the windshield wipers. Beside her, Kate was facing out the passenger-side window. Neither of them had spoken since they'd left Dr. Sibley's office, and not a word was exchanged until the car pulled into the driveway of their house in the Old Village section of Mount Pleasant. The two-story Charleston Single–style home, built in 1893, had been a wedding present from Papa Jim.

"What are you going to tell Daddy?" asked Kate.

"I don't know," Glory said.

"Mom, I'm not lying, I swear."

"I don't want to hear any more from you right now, Kate."

"Fine," she said, pushing open the door and jumping out into the rain before the BMW had rolled to a stop.

"Kate!" Glory shouted.

But she didn't answer, just hit the ground running and kept on running into the house and up the stairs to her bedroom on the second floor. There she slammed the door behind her, threw herself down onto her bed, clutched the nearest stuffed animal—a pink unicorn—to her chest and burst into tears.

After a moment, Kate heard her mother enter the house and move around noisily downstairs, but luckily she didn't come upstairs, for which Kate said a silent prayer of thanks. She was also thankful that her father, Bill Skylar, was on a business trip to Nevada for Papa Jim and wouldn't be home for another two days.

That pretty much exhausted the things she had to be thankful about.

How could she be pregnant if she'd never done more than kiss a boy? Despite what Dr. Sibley had said, Kate knew that she had never been in a situation remotely likely to result in a pregnancy. It was flat-out impossible. The doctors and their tests were wrong. They had to be.

But what if they weren't?

What if, by some miracle, she really was pregnant? What then?

By some miracle . . .

A shiver ran through her body.

Despite her denials, she knew that something had happened to her. Something had changed. Deep down inside, she knew she was pregnant. She'd always known, from the minute Dr. Rickert had told her. She just hadn't wanted to accept it. Hadn't wanted to follow the terrible logic of it to its inevitable, impossible, insane conclusion.

Dr. Sibley had said that she was about seven weeks along, which meant, as Glory had so quickly recognized, that whatever had caused the pregnancy had happened in New York. Still clutching tightly to the stuffed unicorn, Kate turned over in bed, lying face up, staring at the ceiling, where, years ago, her dad had pasted a fantastic night sky of glow-in-the-dark stars, with familiar constellations like Orion, the Big Dipper, and Leo the Lion alongside other constellations that they had made up themselves, laughing over such outlandish creations as Puff the Magic Dragon, the Old Shoe, and Papa Jim's Cigar. She wondered if she would ever laugh with her father again.

She remembered how, in New York, she'd been struck by the Renaissance-era paintings in the Metropolitan Museum of Art, the apostles, saints, and martyrs, and how, regarding their faces, etched with profound joy and suffering, she'd understood in a way she never had before that the touch of God would be a hard thing to bear.

How hard, she hadn't dreamed.

Until now.

But did that mean she was like the Virgin Mary, carrying the child of God Almighty? It seemed not only foolish but blasphemous to even entertain the thought. It was crazy.

And yet she couldn't dismiss it.

She remembered the sidewalk artist–cum–street preacher, Gabriel—Gabriel, like the angel!—and how he'd said to her, "You're blessed. God's grace is upon you." He'd said that to her and then thrust a drawing into her hands . . .

Kate leaped up from the bed. The drawing! She'd forgotten all about it until now.

Grabbing her purse, she rooted around in its clutter for a moment before losing patience and dumping the contents out on her bedspread. There it was, at the very bottom of the purse.

She picked up the stained and ragged piece of folded-up notebook paper and unfolded it with trembling hands.

It was a pencil sketch of a mother and infant child, done in the style of the paintings from the museum.

The face was unmistakably hers.

And written below it, the words "Full of Grace."

Kate dropped the paper. She couldn't stop shaking.

She got off the bed and sank to her knees at the side of the bed, clutching her hands before her.

Please, God, she thought, or rather prayed with every fiber of her being, her soul vibrating like the strings of a plucked harp, *I'm afraid of this. I'm not brave or strong or even very good. If it's your will that I be pregnant, so be it. But please, if it's not too late, don't ask me to do this. Find someone else. It's too much to ask of me. I can't do it. I can't!*

The sudden knocking at her door nearly sent her jumping out of her skin.

"Kate?" came her mother's voice. "Are you awake?"

She stood up hurriedly and sat on the bed, moving a pillow to cover the drawing and the other items tumbled from her purse. She'd been so intent on her prayer that she hadn't heard her mother mounting the stairs. "Go away," she said, though she knew that wasn't going to happen.

Sure enough, Glory pushed the door open and peeked in. "We have to talk," she said.

Kate nodded mutely, knowing the truth of it. But what she would say to her mother now, how she could possibly make her understand, was utterly beyond her.

Glory stepped into the room and shut the door softly behind her. Then she came to the bed and sat down beside Kate. She looked as though she'd aged ten years in the last few hours. "Honey, I know you don't think I understand what you're going through, but the truth is, I do. Better than you can imagine." She was looking at her hands, which were clenched tightly in her lap. "You see, I was only seventeen myself when I got pregnant with you."

"But you always told me you were eighteen . . ."

Glory raised her eyes to meet Kate's gaze and gave her a weary smile. "No, I was still in high school. Your father was in college, away in Columbia on a football scholarship. I was afraid I was going to lose him. So I didn't take all the precautions I should have taken, and, well, I got pregnant."

Kate listened to this confession wide-eyed.

"As soon as Papa Jim found out, he went out there and gave your father a good talking-to. I got a marriage proposal the next day."

"Papa Jim forced Daddy to ask you to marry him?"

"Let's just say that your grandfather can be very persuasive. But I don't regret anything—not the marriage, and certainly not you, honey. Your father and I love each other, and we love you. I wouldn't change anything. But it's killing me to see you go down that same path." Glory sighed then continued, "I'm not going to ask you again who the father is. Not now.

But please tell me one thing. Do you love Brady? Because as soon as Papa Jim learns that you're pregnant, he's going to pay that boy a visit. And you'll be receiving a proposal of your own in short order."

Kate felt a growing sense of horror. She hadn't considered any of this. But her mother was right. Papa Jim would take matters into his own hands. She knew from personal experience how persuasive he could be. Brady would propose. And Papa Jim would see to it that she accepted the proposal. "I don't want to marry Brady," she said. "I don't want to marry anyone!"

Glory nodded as if she'd expected no other reply. "Your father is away, and Papa Jim is busy with that new prison down in Florida. There's another week before you have to go back to school. Nobody will think it's strange if the two of us take a little shopping trip up to New York City. We'll take care of this problem there, and no one will ever need to know."

Kate looked at her mother as if she were a stranger. "You mean get an abortion?"

Glory nodded again.

"But you told Dr. Sibley it was a sin."

"I know, honey," said Glory. "But I asked God to put the sin on me, not you."

"I'm pretty sure it doesn't work that way, Mom," she said.

"This is for the best, Kate, you'll see," Glory went on as if she hadn't spoken. "I prayed hard about this, as hard as I've ever prayed in my life, and this was the answer that came to me. I think it's what God wants."

At this, Kate gave a start. She had been praying too. And she'd asked God to find someone else. *Is this the answer to my prayer?* she wondered. *God, are you telling me that you've granted what I asked? Chosen someone else to bear your child, someone better? Please, I don't know what to do . . . I need some kind of sign . . .*

"We leave tomorrow," Glory said. "I've already made the reservations."

Kate nodded mutely. This was the sign. It had to be.

God had made His decision.

He had rejected her. Found someone else for this task.

She was free. The burden was lifted.

Why, then, did she feel like weeping?

CHAPTER 3

New York City in January was very different from the city as she'd last seen it. Then it had been November, with a late surge of Indian summer making it feel like fall was weeks away. Now, with an icy wind whipping along streets lined with piles of snow so filthy they resembled ash heaps, the city seemed ugly, bleak, and inhospitable despite the festive Christmas decorations still hanging over Fifth Avenue. Or perhaps it was all in her mind, in her reasons for being here.

Kate shivered in a blast of frigid wind that seemed to have blown down the avenue all the way from Canada without stopping. She pulled her cashmere scarf more closely about her neck and hurried toward St. Patrick's Cathedral three blocks ahead, weaving her way through the tourists and shoppers who, ignoring the wind, had paused in front of the shop windows. Once Kate would have joined them; admiring the extravagant window displays along Fifth Avenue was one of her favorite New York pastimes. But not now. Not today.

They'd arrived in New York just after noon and checked into the Plaza, where Glory always stayed when she visited the city, which she liked to do at least four times a year, once in each season, so that she could stock up on the latest fashions. The clinic appointment wasn't until tomorrow. Glory had wanted to give them an afternoon of shopping, since that was, after all, the ostensible purpose of their trip, and it didn't seem too likely that Kate would be interested in, much less capable of, shopping after the procedure.

That was what Glory called it. *The procedure.* As if it were something simple and mechanical, something that didn't involve the invasion of her daughter's body and the termination of a human life. But Kate didn't really blame her mother for resorting to a euphemism. She couldn't say the word out loud herself. Could barely even think it silently in the privacy of her own mind.

Abortion.

All her life she'd believed it was wrong, a terrible sin. Her parents had taught her as much, and so had her religion, her faith.

Now, though, it was her mother who had suggested the procedure, and she had agreed to it without hesitation, believing that it was what God wanted her to do. Kate hadn't said anything to Glory about that, of course. Hadn't mentioned that she was convinced she was carrying God's child. She knew that any such statement would earn her a trip to a very different sort of doctor than the one she was scheduled to visit tomorrow. No, she couldn't confide in Glory. Couldn't confide in anyone, except God.

Kate thought that she had probably said more prayers in the last two days than she had in her whole previous life put together. But despite all those prayers, she didn't feel that she'd made a connection. *Hello, this is God. I'm not here right now, but if you leave your message at the tone . . .* That's what it felt like. He was listening, but not answering. And why should He? He'd granted her prayer already, hadn't He? Lifted the burden from her shoulders, provided the means by which she could refuse what He had offered, the chance to be the mother to His child.

She couldn't imagine why she had been singled out in the first place. She was just an ordinary girl, and the thought of what had been asked of her was overwhelming. It wasn't just the shock of discovering that she was pregnant without having ever done more than kiss a boy, although that was pretty frightening. And the way that everyone, even Glory, assumed she was lying to protect Brady or some other boy didn't help matters very much either. But what really made her want to curl up into a shivering ball was the idea of what would come after. Not just the way people would judge her for being a single mother at seventeen. The frankly curious or nasty or pitying looks, all equally unwelcome, and the gossip that would go on behind her back. The righteous comments that would be made to her face. All of that would be bad enough. But there would be still worse to come.

Kate didn't think she could bear to see a child of hers suffer as Jesus had suffered. She didn't understand how Mary had been able to go on after all that had happened to her son. How she had been able to watch as he was tortured and put to death. How strong her faith must have been! But Kate didn't have that kind of faith.

She knew her Bible. She knew what tended to happen to those who were touched by God. She didn't want that for her child. Or for herself. Maybe it was selfish, but she couldn't help it. She was afraid. There was too much evil in the world. So she had prayed for God to choose another vessel. Told Him that she was too weak. Unworthy. And lo and behold, her mother had come to her bedroom with the plan that had brought them to New York, a little miracle in itself, really, because Glory had always been unwavering in her opposition to abortion; for her to suggest it now was proof to Kate of God's invisible hand at work. That was when she had understood that He had granted her prayer and was offering her a way out.

But despite all that, since arriving in the city, Kate had been wracked by doubts. Was she really doing the right thing? Was this what God wanted . . . the termination of a human—or more than human—life? Or was she just fooling herself, trying to ease her conscience?

Over lunch at Lespinasse, Kate had picked at her food as Glory, sensing her mood, made heroic conversational efforts to drag her out of her funk. But Kate had responded in monosyllables, if at all. Not even the experience of trying on outrageously expensive clothes and shoes in stylish Fifth Avenue boutiques had succeeded in cheering her up. Instead, as the afternoon dragged on, Kate had felt more and more anxious and brittle, her inner doubts mushrooming until they threatened to reach panic proportions. Finally, in the middle of Saks, she'd had enough. She had to get out or go crazy. Pleading exhaustion and a headache, she told Glory that she was going back to the hotel to take a nap. Glory, who was something of a binge shopper, kissed her distractedly on the cheek and sent her on her way with a chirpy "Feel better!" before making a beeline to the perfume counter.

But once outside, Kate had turned north rather than south toward the Plaza. She had lied to her mother; sleep was the furthest thing from her mind. Instead, she walked up the block, then turned east and continued to Madison Avenue, where she caught an uptown bus to 83rd Street. From there she hurried west again, making for the Metropolitan Museum of Art.

This time, she hadn't come to see the paintings. She was looking for Gabriel.

When she tried to remember what the sidewalk artist looked like, all she could recall clearly was that he was a young black man who had been wearing a bright red beret. Nonetheless, she felt sure that she would recognize him immediately. There was a connection between them. He was sent to her on that day in November to prepare her for what was to come, though she hadn't realized it at the time. No, then she had simply dismissed him as a harmless crank, a street preacher who baited his hook with skillful sketches and caricatures of passersby. And not until just days ago, when she'd learned that she was pregnant and understood for the first time the gravity of what was happening to her, had Kate remembered the sketch he had given her and that she had thrust, unlooked at, into her purse. A sketch of herself and her baby.

Madonna and child.

Gabriel had known. Had tried to tell her. But she'd been frightened, annoyed. She'd pushed him away. If only she had listened! He could have told her so much. But maybe it wasn't too late. She would find him, talk to him. Make him tell her what he knew. Really, though, she understood subconsciously that what she was looking for from him wasn't illumination but absolution. The assurance that God would forgive her for what she was about to do.

When she reached the museum, the sidewalks were empty of artists. There were only pedestrians walking quickly to minimize their exposure to the cold. A lone vendor was selling hot dogs, his cart wreathed in steam.

Kate stood across Fifth Avenue, gaping in shock. A group of Japanese tourists hurried past her, rushing to beat the traffic light, laughing excitedly among themselves. Somewhere a car alarm started whooping. She felt like an idiot. Of course there would be no sidewalk sketch artists plying their trades in the middle of winter!

When there was a gap in traffic, Kate crossed the street. She was in a kind of daze, moving as if in a dream. Although logically it should have been neither surprising nor disappointing not to find Gabriel here, someone she had met only once, months ago, a needle in the haystack of New York's teeming millions, Kate nevertheless felt both those emotions now. In fact, quite unexpectedly she found herself on the verge of tears. All of a sudden it seemed to her that Gabriel's absence was purposeful, an indication that God had rejected her. Abandoned her. But hadn't she abandoned Him first? She had refused His gift. His child.

Yet, if He didn't want her to have the abortion, why had He sent Glory to her that night? Why had He put the idea of coming to New York into her mother's mind?

There were no answers, only the bite of the wind.

More out of desperation than hope, Kate climbed the stairs to the museum and went inside. Methodically, she searched the crowded galleries, studying the faces of young black males so intently that she received her share of curious, annoyed, or flirtatious looks in return. But none of them were Gabriel. More than once, a flash of red glimpsed out of the corner of her eye made her think that she had spotted his beret, but on second look the color always resolved into something else: a scarf, a handbag, a baseball cap.

Gradually, she accepted the reality that she wasn't going to find him.

There was nothing for her here. Even the paintings and statues that she normally found so comforting withheld that comfort now.

That was when she thought of St. Patrick's Cathedral.

The holy church, with its encompassing, murmurous spaces, its smells of burning candles and old wood, had always been a kind of refuge for her on her visits to the city, a place for unhurried reflection and quiet solitude where she could regain her equilibrium when the sights, sounds, and frenetic pace of Manhattan grew overwhelming. She almost ached physically for the solace it had offered her in the past. Surely it wouldn't reject her. There, in that oasis of calm spirituality in the middle of the clamorous city, she felt that her prayers would be heard and answered. God would speak to her and assure her that she was doing the right thing.

She'd left the museum and climbed on a downtown bus, but its progress was excruciatingly slow, as it stopped at what seemed like every block to let dozens of people off and on. Finally, too impatient to wait any longer, she got off and made her way on foot, still keeping her eyes peeled for any sight of Gabriel.

It was almost five thirty; the setting sun was out of sight behind the skyscrapers of the west side, and the city was sunk in evening shadows fast deepening into twilight. The streetlamps were on, as were the headlights of cars and buses. The air seemed to grow colder by the block. Soon a light snow began to fall, crystals glinting like shards of fallen star stuff. It was beautiful, like some fairy-tale snow-globe vision of Manhattan, but Kate barely noticed. As more and more people left work, the Fifth Avenue sidewalk down which she was hurrying came to resemble a human obstacle course, and she focused her attention on navigating it as quickly as possible.

At last she reached the cathedral, all lit up like a fortress of white marble.

As soon as she entered, a soothing balm settled over her soul. Warmth bloomed in her bones as the sounds of the street faded. The fragrance of burning incense and wax candles filled her nostrils, and her ears echoed with the soft susurrations of whispered prayers rising up to the cavernous vault of the ceiling like smoke. She took off her hat, unwound her scarf, letting it hang freely over her shoulders, and opened her heavy coat.

She hesitated, then dipped a finger into the font of holy water and, with a trembling hand, made the sign of the cross. What had she expected? That her skin would burn at the water's touch like the flesh of a vampire? The water was cool, no more.

Dipping her knee as she passed before the altar, Kate went around to the left side aisle and walked about halfway down before easing into an empty pew. She sat, relieved to finally be off her feet. Then she folded down the kneeler attached to the bottom of the pew in front of her and slid onto her knees, bowed her head, and prayed silently, fiercely, asking for guidance, a sign to let her know that she was doing the right thing. Or even the wrong thing. Just some indication that she wasn't all alone in the world.

When she looked up, she noticed that a row of three confessionals was in operation. A red light shone above each one to indicate that it was occupied by a penitent; as Kate watched, a door opened in one of the confessionals and an elderly man emerged, leaning heavily on a cane. The door shut behind him, and a moment later the red light was replaced by a green one, signaling that the priest was ready to hear another confession. A plump, middle-aged Asian woman in business attire rose quickly from a nearby pew and bustled over, disappearing inside. *Click*, and the light was red again. Kate's heart quickened. She felt sure this was the sign she had prayed for.

Kate got to her feet and went over to that area of the cathedral. There were a few others ahead of her, so she took a seat and waited her turn. She didn't know what she was going to say to the priest, but that didn't matter; as soon as she'd seen the confessionals, she'd known that her steps had been guided here. Soon all her doubts would be answered.

She twisted the ends of her scarf in her fingers as the minutes dragged by. Each of the people before her seemed to be taking forever. What could they possibly be talking about? Whatever it was, she felt quite certain that the problems of these men and women paled to insignificance before her own, and even though she knew it wasn't very Christian of her, she couldn't help resenting them a little for making her wait so long.

At last it was her turn. She hurried into the confessional and knelt before the grill that separated her from the priest, making the sign of the cross for a second time. The small space was dimly lit and seemed to carry in its close and complex atmosphere a trace of every person who had ever knelt there, a mix of perfumes, human sweat, cigarette smoke, damp wool, and other things she could smell but couldn't put a name to. It occurred to her that she was smelling what was left over after a sin had been confessed and absolution bestowed upon the sinner by the priest, a stale effluvium made up of the aftermath of countless tawdry transgressions. She wondered what traces her confession would leave behind.

From the other side of the grill, there was a sharp click as the priest flicked the switch to turn on the red light. After a few seconds of silence, he cleared his throat somewhat impatiently.

"B—bless me, Father, for I have sinned," Kate said in a shaky voice. "It's been three weeks since my last confession." She wasn't sure what to say after that, so she didn't say anything. She thought back to her last confession, at St. John the Baptist, and how she'd recited her usual litany of boring sins: pride, envy, sloth; how she'd snapped at Glory, argued with her father about homework, and taken the name of the Lord in vain on two occasions. It seemed so trivial now.

"Go on, my child," came the voice. It was a gentle voice, kind yet firm.

Kate wondered how old he was, what he looked like. What must it be like to sit behind the screen, listening to people's confessions hour after hour? Most of it was probably as dull as dishwater. Did he bring a book to pass the time? A walkman?

"Do you have something to confess?" coaxed the priest.

"I . . ." This was proving more difficult than she had imagined. There was no way she could tell him everything; he would think she was crazy or lying, just like Glory and the doctors had. "Father, what if God wanted a person to do something. Something very hard and dangerous. And that person was afraid. Too afraid to do what God wanted."

"Do you mean dangerous physically or dangerous spiritually?"

"Both, I guess."

"God doesn't ask the easy things of us," came the response. "But he doesn't ask what is beyond our ability to give, either."

"But what if a person prayed to God not to have to do . . . what was asked? And the prayer was answered. So the person didn't have to do it anymore."

A pause. "I suppose I might reflect on why God should have asked it of me in the first place."

"But to pray that way. To go against God's wishes. Isn't that a sin?"

"God is compassionate, my child. He understands and forgives human weakness. Why, even our Lord had moments of doubt. In the garden of Gethsemane, He prayed that the cup might pass from Him. How, then, if the Son of God should make such a prayer, can it be a sin for a human being?"

"But He did what God wanted. In the end."

"Yes. Why was that, do you think?"

"I don't know. He had to, didn't He?"

"No, He did not. Jesus had free will, just as we do. He could have refused. Gone off somewhere and lived a quiet life."

"Then I guess it was because He knew how things were going to turn out. He knew He would rise from the dead and everything."

"But so will we all, my child. Every Catholic knows that. It's what we believe. The pillar of our faith."

"Then I guess I must not have very much faith," she said miserably.

"What does that word mean to you?" asked the priest. "What is faith?"

"I don't know," she said. "I mean, when I think of someone like Mary . . . you know, she was just a girl when she became the mother of God. No older than me, maybe. Imagine how frightened she must have been! But she did it anyway. That's faith."

"Yes, she was a brave young woman. All the same, I'm sure she had moments of doubt as well. Moments when her faith, as strong as it was, wavered."

"Do you really think so?"

"She wouldn't have been human otherwise. All of us are weak sometimes. That's when we need to remember that God loves us and wants to help us."

"I'm not like Mary," she said in a voice so soft that she thought at first he hadn't heard her, so much time passed before he replied.

"In what ways are you not like her?"

Kate's heart leapt into her throat. Somehow, without realizing it, she had been led to broach the very subject that she had intended to avoid. She had been foolish to think that she could fence with a priest; this was what they did. They were experts at drawing people out, getting them to confess the sins they were too ashamed or afraid to speak aloud. And now she had said too much.

"My child?" the priest prompted.

"I . . . I'm sorry, Father, but I can't tell you."

"My child, I'm not here as a man, but as the representative of Christ. You must unburden yourself to me as you would if it were Jesus Himself behind this screen. No matter what you've done, how bad you think it may be, I assure you that forgiveness is available to you. But I can't absolve you of your sins if you won't speak frankly about them. Please, there's no reason to be fearful. Everything you say is under the seal of the confessional and cannot be revealed to anyone under any circumstances."

"I know," she said. "It's just . . ."

"Go on."

Yet despite the priest's assurances, Kate couldn't go on. She wanted to unburden herself, wanted it so badly that she could feel it, but something was holding her back. Shame? Fear? Perhaps, but it was more than that, an instinctual whispering deep in her soul, a small, true voice, bright as a glimmering star in the darkness, telling her that this was between her and God, and she had no business sharing it with anyone else, not even a priest. Was it for this realization, she wondered now, that she'd been guided here?

"Father, God wouldn't ever ask a person to commit a sin, would He?"

"Of course not, my child. God wants to lead us away from sin. What is it that you think God has asked of you?" He sounded worried now.

"I have to go," Kate said. Suddenly the close confines of the confessional seemed to squeeze in even more tightly, until she felt as if she were suffocating. She hurriedly made the sign of the cross then lurched to her feet and out the door. Behind her, the priest said something that she couldn't make out. She hurried up the aisle, glancing back once to see if he was following, but of course he wasn't. The anonymity of the confessional had to be preserved at all costs. The green light above the booth was glowing; another penitent was already entering, taking her place.

Kate wrapped her scarf around her neck, buttoned up her coat, and walked out into the night. Snow was falling more heavily now, big flakes like the feathers of an angel's wing. She could do this, she told herself, thinking of the procedure scheduled for tomorrow morning. God had offered her this chance, and because it had come from Him, it couldn't be a sin, even if it would be under normal circumstances. The priest had confirmed it: God wouldn't tell her to commit a sin. It was as if she'd been given a Get Out of Jail Free card.

But that didn't mean she felt good about it. On the contrary, despite a sense of relief, Kate felt shame at what she still perceived as her own weakness, and sadness at the thought of what would happen to the life she was carrying inside her. Perhaps her unborn child was dead already, or soulless, its divine spark removed somehow, reabsorbed into the blessed Trinity of Father, Son, and Holy Spirit, or sent on to its new destination, into the womb of whatever woman God had chosen to replace her as the mother of His child. If, indeed, He had chosen anyone at all. Perhaps her refusal had been a refusal for all humanity, and now God would withhold His gift. But no, that couldn't be. God was not petty or cruel. And she was just one small person, an ordinary girl who only wanted to live an ordinary life, grow up, fall in love, get married, and have children that would have no divine mission to perform, no sacrifice to enact, just the ordinary joys and sorrows that all human flesh was heir to. That wasn't too much to ask, was it? How could it be?

With these thoughts and others whirling in her mind as the snow whirled down around her, Kate hailed a cab back to the Plaza, where Glory was waiting, angry and nearly frantic with worry. "Your father called and wanted to talk with you. I had to tell him you'd gone to a movie."

"I was at St. Patrick's. You know, praying."

At that, Glory's whole demeanor shifted. "Oh, honey, I should have thought of that! I should have gone with you!"

"It's okay, Mom. I kind of needed to be alone."

Kate felt too drained emotionally and physically to go out to dinner, so they ordered room service and watched movies on cable until it was time for bed. Glory tried a couple of times to sound her daughter out about what she was feeling, as if to make up for taking her shopping instead of to church, but Kate fended her off.

"Mom, I just want to get through this, okay? We can talk later. But I think I kind of need to go on automatic pilot for a while, you know?"

"Of course, dear. But I'm here if you need to talk."

"Thanks, Mom." Kate gave her a hug and a kiss, then turned in for the night.

To her surprise, she slept like a log.

The next morning, she didn't feel like eating and only sipped at a cup of room-service coffee. She showered and dressed, putting a change of underwear and sanitary napkins in her purse, per the clinic's instructions. Then she and Glory took a cab to the Upper East Side clinic where Glory had made an appointment. There was no trace of last night's snowfall; or, if there was, it was already indistinguishable from the frozen, dirty gray mounds left over from previous snowfalls.

With each block they progressed through the slow-moving, noisy Manhattan traffic, Kate felt herself sink deeper into what she had described the night before as "automatic pilot." *I'm a robot,* she told herself. *A machine, not a person.* It became her mantra, and she repeated it to herself as they drove, while Glory, sitting beside her in the backseat of the cab, assayed a variety of lame jokes and observations that Kate didn't respond to. Soon a tense silence descended that lasted until they reached the clinic.

Kate hadn't known what to expect. A crowd of protestors, perhaps, angry men and women waving placards and shouting imprecations at anyone approaching the door. But there was no crowd, no protestors. The clinic was located in a high rise, with a security guard at the entrance to the building, but there was no other sign of anything out of the ordinary . . . even the security guard was a far from uncommon sight in New York office and apartment buildings.

Only the door to the clinic itself gave some hint of the controversial activity that took place within. The door carried only a number, nothing else. There was an intercom box beside the door, with a security camera mounted above it. Glory hit the buzzer, identified herself, and stood with Kate where the camera could transmit their images. There was a pause, and then a buzzer sounded, unlocking the door. As Glory and Kate entered, a young couple, a man and a woman, glanced up at them with nervous smiles from the comfortable waiting area, where there were cushioned chairs and a table strewn with magazines. Glory nodded, but Kate looked away, feeling her face turn red with embarrassment.

There were reproductions of paintings from the Met and the Guggenheim on the walls, along with posters about HIV, STDs, and birth control, and a floral display at the reception desk, as well as a bowl of what Kate thought at first were candies but were actually condoms in brightly colored wrappers. Lite jazz was playing softly on a radio. The receptionist, a pretty, young black woman with platinum blond hair cut so short it might almost have been a silver skullcap, was seated behind a thick barrier of some transparent material that Kate could only assume was bulletproof.

Kate stood mute as a statue, silently repeating her mantra, as Glory spoke to the woman. There were forms to sign, which Kate did without reading them, and then Glory opened her purse and drew out an envelope with two hundred-dollar bills tucked inside.

They sat and waited. Glory picked up an issue of *Cosmopolitan* and began to leaf through it, but Kate just sat there. *I'm a robot*, she thought. *A machine.* Out of the corner of her eye, she observed the young couple, wondering what their story was, whether they were man and wife or boyfriend and girlfriend. Despite her mantra, she felt as if her intestines were tied up in knots that were being slowly twisted together.

After a while, a nurse came to fetch her. Glory asked to come too, and the nurse agreed that it would be okay. The nurse led them to an examination room, where she gave Kate a cup to pee in and directed her to a bathroom in the hall. When she came back from the bathroom, the nurse took her temperature, blood pressure, and a blood sample. Not once was the reason for her appointment mentioned.

Then she was sent back to the waiting area. Moments later, the same nurse called a name; the young woman waiting with the man gave a little start and turned pale. She took her companion's hand and squeezed it, gave him the saddest smile that Kate had ever seen, then got up and followed the nurse out of the waiting room without a backward glance. Once she had gone, the man glanced at his watch, crossed his arms over his chest, put his head back, and closed his eyes.

I'm a robot. A machine, not a person . . .

The door buzzed, and two slim, tan, dark-haired women entered, both seemingly in their twenties, obviously sisters, each wearing a golden crucifix around her neck. Kate was wearing a similar necklace, which she'd forgotten about completely until now; somehow, it seemed almost sacrilegious to be wearing such a thing in this place. Yet the two women didn't seem at all disturbed; their expressions were solemn, yes, but there was no shame in the looks they cast toward Kate and Glory. One of them even gave Kate an encouraging smile. But Kate didn't smile back. How could she? She was a robot. A machine.

Machines don't smile.

Then her name was called again, and another woman, who identified herself as a counselor, took Kate and Glory into a windowless room whose only furnishings were plastic chairs and a big wooden desk on which sat a strange-looking sculpture that Kate suddenly realized, with a sense of mounting unreality, was a life-sized model of a uterus and vagina. The counselor used the model to demonstrate what she, too, called "the procedure." Actually, Kate thought it was more like "the Procedure": she could hear the capital *P*. In a calm and authoritative voice, the counselor assured them that the Procedure was statistically safer than giving birth. Then, as if to undercut her own argument, she spoke about the risks: incomplete evacuation, infection, perforation of the uterus, hemorrhage, words that flowed right through Kate, though Glory, beside her, seemed to clench her body tighter and tighter at the list of possible complications, until she was hunched over in her chair like a woman crippled by osteoporosis. Finally, the counselor asked to speak to Kate privately, and when Glory had left the room, she questioned her closely about whether or not this was something she wanted for herself, whether her mother or any other adult had pressured her into making the decision. Kate said that she understood what she was doing and that nobody had pressured her. The counselor nodded, satisfied, and gave her two Advil in a paper cup. "You'll want these later," the woman said. "For the cramping."

Then it was back to the waiting room.

The next time her name was called, Glory was not allowed to accompany her.

I'm a robot, she thought as she stood up. Glory was plainly fighting back tears, and this nearly got Kate started as well. But she looked away, forcing her eyes to remain dry.

Machines don't cry . . .

The nurse led her back to the bathroom, where she directed her to empty her bladder and to place the sanitary napkin she'd brought into her underwear. When she emerged from the bathroom, a second nurse was waiting, a gray-haired woman with a kind, weathered face who appeared to be in her fifties or early sixties.

"I'm Nurse Rhodes," she said. "You can call me Jackie if you like. I'll take good care of you, dear, don't worry."

Kate nodded.

Jackie took her to the room where the Procedure would take place and asked her to undress from the waist down.

"No, leave your socks on," she said when Kate made to peel them off. Then she helped Kate onto the examining table, draping a clean white sheet across her bare lap and legs. "The doctor will be here shortly," she said. "I'll be right back."

With that, she left the room.

Alone, Kate began to shiver although the room was actually quite warm. She observed a sink, a cart of various implements, probes and the like, but she didn't look too closely. She heard a low drone of conversation from outside the door, Jackie's voice and the voice of the counselor, but she couldn't make out any words, though she strained to do so, certain that the two women were discussing her. Then, suddenly, she heard what sounded like a big vacuum cleaner being switched on, a howling, whining roar, as if the cleaning crew were at work in the room next door. But of course, it wasn't a vacuum cleaner.

It was the machine that would quite literally suck the life out of her.

The noise went on and on. Then, as suddenly as it had started, it stopped.

Then started up again.

I'm a robot. A machine . . .

The door opened, and Jackie came in, wheeling the vacuum machine. She was followed by a pudgy, balding, fortyish-looking man who introduced himself as Dr. Lambert. He smiled at her reassuringly, but she was too far into her robotic state to respond.

Jackie had her recline on the table, with her bottom as close to the edge as possible. "No, closer—until it feels like you're going to fall off. That's right, good girl."

"Let's have a look, shall we?" Dr. Lambert pulled up a low stool and took a seat between her spread legs.

Jackie came to stand at Kate's side. "You can hold my hand, dear, if you like."

Kate just wanted everything to be over. She flinched as Dr. Lambert inserted the speculum. Then she felt a sharp jab as he injected the anesthetic into her cervix; she cried out, jerking away involuntarily.

"Please don't move," Dr. Lambert said sternly.

"I'm sorry," she said, her own voice sounding pathetic in her ears, as if she were apologizing for having caused him pain. Tears had sprung to her eyes, and only when she moved to wipe them away did she realize that her hand was being held; without being aware of it, at some point she had reached over and grasped Jackie's hand and was squeezing it now as hard as she could. But the nurse didn't seem to mind the pressure.

"Another shot now," Jackie told her.

It was like being stabbed with a dagger. She couldn't help the groan that escaped her lips. She felt as if she would faint. She tried to tell herself that there was no pain, that machines didn't feel pain.

"One more," said Jackie.

"No, please . . ."

But Dr. Lambert was already jabbing the needle into her. It hurt less this time, but it was still enough to make her whimper. She wondered if Glory had heard her cry out. Then she felt the doctor's hands pressing against her, far up inside, and a cramp shot through her.

"Easy, now," said Jackie.

Kate was gripping Jackie's latex-gloved hand so tightly that she was surprised the woman's fingers weren't snapping like matchsticks. Dr. Lambert was back at work between her legs, and there was no depth she could sink to, no distance she could retreat to, to get away from the physical sensation of violation. All at once it came to her with piercing clarity that she had made a terrible mistake. God hadn't wanted her to do this. It was so plain, so brutally obvious, that she couldn't understand how she could have convinced herself otherwise.

"Almost done now," Dr. Lambert said without looking up.

She shook her head, tried to say no, but at that moment the vacuum machine was switched on, and its powerful whine and roar drowned out every other sound in the room except an obscene gurgling noise, the kind of sound she supposed someone might hear in the depths of Hell, of bubbling sulfur and brimstone. Except it was coming from her.

Then, abruptly, silence.

The machine was switched off.

She heard herself weeping. Her face was wet with tears.

"There, there," Jackie said. "Poor lamb."

Dr. Lambert, meanwhile, was using what looked like a big spoon to scrape away at the inside of her uterus. Then he switched on the vacuum machine again, briefly.

So it was over. Done. Her child, God's child, was dead.

Aborted.

And not, she realized now, by God's will.

There could be no forgiveness for this sin, she realized.

It had been the devil who had answered her prayer, not God. She saw that now, too late. The priest had tried to tell her. "God wants to lead us away from sin," he'd said. But she hadn't listened. Hadn't understood.

Jackie was gone. Kate hadn't even seen her leave. Dr. Lambert was at the sink, washing his hands, his back to her. She could feel the blood seeping from between her legs. She lay on her back, staring up into the fluorescent lights, and wept as she had never wept before in her life.

Wept as if she would never stop weeping.

"Oh, honey . . ."

It was Glory. Jackie had brought her.

Her mother came to her and took her into her arms.

"Oh, Mom . . ." Kate couldn't say any more. She just clung to her mother as Jackie cleaned up between her legs.

Then, as if she had become in fact the robot she had pretended to be, Kate let herself be led through the rest of the Procedure. With the help of Glory and Jackie, she sat up, stood, took her first tottering steps. Dressed herself, wondering dimly if the sanitary napkin would be enough for all the blood that was leaking out of her, worse than her worst-ever period. At least, it felt that way.

In the recovery room, she sat in a reclining chair, sipping tasteless hot tea and shivering beneath a thick wool blanket to the soft strains of lite jazz as Glory sat beside her and held her hand, silent for once. Kate barely registered her mother's presence. The awareness of her sin was big inside her, occupying the place where her baby had been. It was as if she had exchanged one for the other and would carry it now for the rest of her life, her own private hell, a hell that she was already occupying even as it occupied her.

Because for this sin, there could be no forgiveness. She knew that.

She was damned.

CHAPTER 4

The next day, Kate and Glory flew back to Charleston.

Kate's mood hadn't lightened; if anything, it had grown even darker as a day of bed rest afforded her ample opportunity to appreciate the magnitude of her sin and to see with painful clarity how the doubts and fears she'd felt upon learning that she was pregnant had snowballed out of control, sweeping her along. Instead of rejoicing at the tangible evidence of God's presence, and humbly accepting the role that He had selected for her, above all other women, to play, she'd felt resentful about having been chosen for something she hadn't been consulted on, much less agreed to. And instead of feeling excitement about what lay ahead, she'd assumed the worst, that some terrible sacrifice would be required of her child, and she'd rebelled. Prayed to God to find someone else to shoulder the burden. But now she realized that it hadn't been a burden at all, but a gift. A miracle.

She'd been blind. Foolish. Just when she'd needed it most, her faith had proved lacking, and not only herself but her child, God's child, had suffered for it. It was ironic—in seeking to spare herself and the child some potential future suffering, she'd only caused them both to suffer now, in the present. And in her case, she felt sure, she'd go on suffering for the rest of her life.

And beyond.

How could she have been so stupid? With the evidence of God's existence taking shape in her own body, how could she have forgotten that the devil existed too? And would do anything to keep God's child from coming into the world. Acting through Herod, hadn't the devil tried to kill Jesus? Back then, he'd waited until the child was born. But obviously he wasn't going to make that mistake again.

And this time, thanks to her, he'd succeeded.

The words from the Gospel of Mark rang in her head: "Woe to that man by whom the Son of man is betrayed. Good were it for that man if he had never been born!"

Lying in the hotel bed, sore and feverish, Kate wondered if other women had been in her position before, blessed by God as she had been, only to be led astray. Perhaps God had been trying for years now to have His child born, and this was just the latest in a long line of setbacks, her personal tragedy and shame only a small blip in the great ongoing battle between God and His adversary. But that didn't lessen her sin or her shame. In fact, it made her feel worse than ever.

God had asked something of her, and she had failed Him. What was it the priest had said? "God doesn't ask the easy things of us, but He doesn't ask what is beyond our ability to give, either."

Yes, that was the worst of it. The knowledge that she could have done the right thing. She could have fought against doubt, resisted fear, placed her faith in God, and become His willing instrument, just like in the hymn: "Lord, make me an instrument of your peace . . ." It would have been hard, harder than anything she had ever attempted, but she could have done it. Instead, she'd taken the easy way out. The coward's way. Or so she told herself.

She prayed, but not for forgiveness. What she had done was beyond forgiving.

She prayed to be allowed to spend the rest of her life atoning in some small way for what she had done.

What she had failed to do.

Back in Charleston, Kate spent the last few days before school resumed sequestered in her room. There was still bleeding, and she was too depressed, too mournful and self-accusing, to want to be with her friends, or even her family. Glory told Kate's father, who had returned from his trip, that Kate had come down with the flu, and he had no reason to doubt the story.

He ducked his head into her room the night he got back, wary of coming in any farther; like his wife, Bill Skylar was a hypochondriac. In fact, Kate often joked to her friends that it was this shared interest that kept her parents together. "Your mom says you're feeling a bit under the weather."

"I'm okay."

"I'd give you a kiss, but . . ." He shrugged helplessly.

"That's okay."

"I've got an important speech to give tomorrow."

"I know." The district's congressman had announced his retirement, and Papa Jim had decided that her dad should run for the open seat. As far as Kate could tell, Bill wasn't too thrilled at the idea, but what Papa Jim wanted, Papa Jim got. So for the last six months, her father had been traveling all across the state, lining up the support of business, religious, and Republican Party leaders. Now that the groundwork had been laid, he would announce his candidacy at a press conference tomorrow. "Good luck."

He flashed a grin and gave her a thumbs-up; he certainly looked like a politician, she thought. "Thanks, kiddo. I love you."

"I love you too."

And he was gone.

Then the break was over, and Kate was swept back into the daily routine of school, homework, and after-school activities. But the dark cloud that had enveloped her did not lift, and she felt as if she were just going through the motions, walled off from life by the knowledge of what she had done. God seemed to have withdrawn from her, or she from God. At any rate, something was missing. There was an aching emptiness at the heart of things, a yearning. At church on Sundays, and in the weekly meetings of the youth group, she felt like a hypocrite, as though she didn't really belong. When she went to Communion, she didn't swallow the host, but surreptitiously spat it into a Kleenex before it could dissolve in her mouth. When she went to confession, she just made stuff up. It didn't seem to matter.

And though Dr. Lambert had assured her that her body would soon be back to normal, that didn't happen. The bleeding stopped, but her bouts of nausea didn't go away. And her stomach didn't return to its former flatness; if anything, it continued to swell, though she was able to hide the extent of it by wearing baggy clothes and prevailing on Glory to get a note from Dr. Rickert excusing her from PE. Following their trip to New York, Glory had become almost ridiculously solicitous, as if trying to work off her own share of guilt. She refused Kate nothing.

As for Bill, he was in full campaign mode, running on a platform of law, order, and morality; the primary election was only nine months away, and even with Papa Jim bankrolling him, he had a lot of ground to make up against opponents with more established political records. There were rallies, press conferences, debates; it seemed that the only time Kate saw her dad these days was when his campaign manager insisted that she and Glory appear with him on stage or at a photo op . . . which wasn't often, as her distracted demeanor did not escape notice, even if the reasons for it did.

Kate was convinced that something had gone wrong with the Procedure and that she was suffering one of the horrible complications that Jackie had mentioned. But she said nothing to anyone, believing it was no more than she deserved.

Then, one day toward the middle of February, she realized that although the bleeding from the Procedure had stopped within days of her return to Charleston, she still hadn't experienced the normal resumption of her period, as Dr. Lambert had told her to expect.

At first she dismissed it as another sign that something had gone badly wrong, just one more symptom of God's displeasure.

But then, as another week passed, another possibility occurred to her. She hardly dared to voice it even silently, in the privacy of her soul. The hope that it gave her was almost physically painful. Yet she couldn't help it.

What if she were still pregnant?

She'd already experienced one miracle. . . Why not another?

Kneeling at her bedside one night, she prayed as if preparing to receive the sacrament of the Eucharist. "Lord, I am not worthy to receive you, but only say the word and I shall be healed."

As soon as the words passed her lips, she felt a small kick in her womb.

She gasped, clutching her stomach, though there was no pain. Only joy now.

She was healed. Whole again. She knew it.

Though she was bursting to share the news, Kate realized that it was too soon. She had to hold off a while longer, until the pregnancy was too advanced for an abortion. She didn't think her parents would force her to have one against her will, but she wasn't sure enough to take the risk; after all, once her pregnancy became general knowledge, it would likely mean the end of her father's political career. It was hard to run on a platform of a return to traditional moral values with a pregnant, unmarried, underage daughter. Especially one who refused to name the father of her child.

But Kate wasn't able to hide her newfound joy; it shone in her like the glow of a small sun, radiating not heat or light but love.

"Oh, honey, I'm glad to see that you're finally bouncing back," said Glory.

"I'm much better now, Mom," Kate said.

And she was.

"Kate, if I could put that smile on a campaign button, I'd win for sure," said Bill.

"Oh, Daddy!"

But in the end, it was her belly that betrayed her. The baggy clothes and doctor's notes could only work for so long.

One morning, as she was getting dressed for school, Glory walked in on her without knocking. Taken by surprise, standing there in nothing but panties and a bra, Kate didn't even have time to try and cover herself.

Glory's eyes widened as she registered what she was seeing. She opened her mouth and screamed.

Then she fainted.

Kate rushed to her side. "Mom, are you okay?"

Glory's eyes fluttered open. She looked at Kate and screamed again.

That was when Bill came barging in, his face bearded with shaving cream. "What's the . . . Oh my God, Kate, you're pregnant!"

It would almost have been funny if she hadn't been in the middle of it. Her father raging like a rabid dog; her mother sobbing uncontrollably. But unfortunately, she *was* in the middle of it. At the same time, she regretted nothing. It was actually a relief to finally have things out in the open.

"How did this happen?" Bill sputtered, practically frothing at the mouth. "I mean, who did this? Answer me, young lady!" But before she could say a word, he turned to Glory, who was sitting on the carpet and sobbing. "Did you know about this? Well?"

Glory shook her head.

"What do you have to say for yourself?" Bill demanded, turning back to Kate.

She felt armored in a calm certainty. God was with her. Nothing else mattered. "Can I get dressed?"

"What?"

"I'm going to be late for school."

"You're not going to school!" Bill thundered. "You're not going anywhere until you tell me who knocked you up!"

"Bill!" Glory, who had climbed to her feet, rallied to her daughter's defense. "Let her get dressed. I'll stay with her. You wait for us downstairs."

"This is a disaster," groaned Bill. "I'm toast. History."

"We'll talk about it downstairs," Glory said firmly.

Bill looked like he might argue, but then he snapped his mouth shut, turned on his heel, and stalked out of the room, slamming the door behind him.

"Thanks, Mom," said Kate.

Glory just stared at her belly. "I'm going to sue that quack," she said. "All that trouble, and he bungles a simple operation!"

"It's not Dr. Lambert's fault."

"No? Whose fault is it, then? Because I'd like to know. I really would!"

"It's nobody's fault. It's a miracle."

"A miracle," Glory repeated.

"God wants this child to be born," Kate stated.

"God wants every child to be born," Glory replied. "But we don't always get what we want."

At these words, a chill rushed through Kate. "What do you mean?"

"Get dressed," Glory told her.

"What are you going to do?"

"I don't know. But no matter what happens, I don't want you to mention the, uh, Procedure to anyone. Do you understand? Not one word. If the press gets hold of that, it's all over."

Kate nodded. She'd never seen her mother possessed by this kind of grim and icy resolve. It was alarming and more than a little intimidating.

Glory sat down on the edge of Kate's bed but didn't say anything more as Kate got dressed. She seemed deep in thought. Kate realized that beneath her mother's somewhat superficial exterior, she was hard as nails. But that shouldn't have come as a surprise. After all, she was the only child of Papa Jim Osbourne. It was she, rather than Bill, who really should have been running for Congress. But Papa Jim believed a woman's place was in the home, not the House of Representatives. And he had raised Glory to believe the same thing.

As soon as Kate finished dressing, Glory got to her feet. "Come on," she said.

"Mom, I—"

"Not another word," Glory interrupted her. "Downstairs. Now."

Bill was waiting for them in the kitchen. He'd shaved hurriedly, and his cheeks were dotted with flecks of toilet paper where he'd nicked himself. The makeup people were going to have to work overtime to make him camera-ready today. "Everything's going to be okay," he said as soon as they entered the room. "I called Papa Jim, and—"

"You did *what*?" Glory practically shouted at him.

"I called your father, and he's coming right over. He'll take care of everything."

"Right, Bill," Glory said with withering sarcasm. "Pass it off to Papa Jim. Why should you get involved? After all, she's only your daughter."

Kate gaped in shock; she'd never heard her mother address her father in this tone before. Come to think of it, she'd never heard Glory address anyone in this tone before.

Bill seemed equally shocked. "But . . . but . . . I thought . . ."

"No, Bill, you didn't think. That's the problem. You did what you always do, which is let Papa Jim do your thinking for you."

Her father stiffened. "I don't see why you're so upset, Glory. It's not like I called some stranger and told him our private business. Papa Jim is family, for God's sake. He loves Kate. And he has resources we don't have. Connections. We need his help."

"Papa Jim doesn't help anyone but Papa Jim. You should know that by now as well as I do."

"How can you say that about your own father, after all he's done for us?"

"I love him dearly, but he is what he is."

"If you feel that way, why haven't you said anything before now?"

"I have." She gave an exasperated sigh. "You just haven't listened."

They stared at each other, the tension between them thick enough to cut with a knife.

"Hello," Kate broke in. "Remember me? The pregnant one?"

That got their attention.

"I know this is a big shock and everything," she said, "and I'm sorry for that, really. But I need you both to know that I'm having this baby."

"Now, honey, don't get upset," said Bill, though by the reddening of his face, he was the one to whom the admonition most applied.

"I'm not upset," she said. And she wasn't. That sense of calm certainty and conviction had returned, stronger than ever. "I'm just telling you—"

"You're in no position to tell us anything," Bill snapped, growing redder still, "except the name of the boy responsible."

"I can't do that."

"What do you mean, 'can't'? You can and you damn well will!"

"I'm sorry, Daddy. I really can't."

"We'll see about that," said Bill.

Glory rolled her eyes. "Oh, please."

"Go to your room," he told her, ignoring Glory.

"What are you going to do, Bill? Ground her for the next five months?"

"Shut up, Glory!"

"Oooh, that's a snappy comeback!"

"Children, children, please."

Everyone gave a start at the sudden appearance of Papa Jim. In the heat of the argument, no one had heard him arrive or use his key to enter the house. Now he stood behind Kate, his omnipresent cigar smoking between his fingers, his bald head shining with sweat as if he had run here from his house ten miles away, a restored antebellum mansion that he had christened New Hope.

"Bill, I told you not to get all riled up," he said. "You gotta get that temper of yours under control if you want to win in November, son."

It seemed impossible, yet Bill flushed an even deeper shade of red. But he said nothing in reply, accepting the rebuke in silence.

Nor did Papa Jim wait for a response. He was already addressing Glory. "As for you, missy, what part of 'honor and obey' don't you understand?"

Even more shocking to Kate than her mother's outbursts against her husband was the way that Glory bowed her head submissively at Papa Jim's words. All the fight seemed to just drain out of her.

Now her grandfather turned to her and opened his arms wide. "Papa Jim's here, baby girl. Everything's gonna be all right now."

Almost without intending to, Kate went to him and put her arms around him as far as they could go. His powerful arms squeezed her firmly against his hard, round belly. She smelled the familiar, loved scent of him. The scent of safety and security. Her grandfather sometimes infuriated her, but she had never doubted his love.

"Shoot, I guess I can't call you baby girl anymore, now, can I?" His chuckle rumbled in her ear.

She pulled back, reassured, grateful for his kindness, like a breath of fresh air after the harshness of her parents' reaction. "I'm going to have this baby, Papa Jim," she stated, both hands resting on the bulge of her stomach.

"Well, now, of course you are," he said, his eyebrows lifting quizzically. "Who said you weren't?"

"I . . . I thought with Daddy's campaign . . ."

"You let Papa Jim worry about that," he said with a warm smile, his blue eyes twinkling.

Damn, but the old coot was charming. As a young man, with a full mane of blond hair and a physique years away from its present corpulence, he must have been well-nigh irresistible. Even today, Kate knew, he could have had his pick of women, and not only because of his wealth. But ever since the death of his wife, Angela, fifteen years ago, Papa Jim had devoted his energies to making Oz Corporation the largest faith-based prison construction and management company in the nation. That, along with his high-level involvement in the Republican Party and the Catholic organization known as The Way, which lobbied tirelessly to push back the reforms of Vatican II, didn't leave much time for romance.

"Aren't you going to ask me who the father is?"

"Why? Is that something you want to tell me?"

She shook her head, feeling somewhat dazed.

"Then I'm not gonna ask. Right now, the only thing I'm interested in is the health of my granddaughter and great-grandson."

Kate blushed. "Papa Jim!"

"It's about time we had a boy in this family," declared Papa Jim.

"I'm sorry if I disappointed you, Dad," said Glory dryly.

"Now, Glory, you know what I mean," he said, with a wink toward Bill.

Glory sighed. "I'll make an appointment with Dr. Rickert."

Papa Jim shook his head. "Forget Rickert. I'm bringing in a New York man, a specialist. Dr. Finkelstein. Damn good doctors, the Jews."

❖   ❖   ❖

Kate was afraid that Dr. Finkelstein would see at a glance some evidence of the botched abortion. But if he did, he gave no sign of it. He pronounced her about twenty weeks along and, to everyone's relief, said that the pregnancy was progressing normally, without complications.

Sonogram results showed that Papa Jim was going to get his wish.

The baby was male.

✠   ✠   ✠

Meanwhile, Papa Jim had taken matters into his own hands, just as Glory had predicted. And, also as she had predicted, there was no gainsaying him.

To spare Kate the media attention that would accompany any revelation of her condition, he decreed that she would be sent away, to a convent in Italy financed by The Way. There, accompanied by Glory, she would remain until after the election in November. She would give birth there and, at the same time, thanks to the nuns, keep up with her schooling. The cover story circulated to the media would be that she had been accepted into one of The Way's international youth programs, with Glory going along as a chaperone. Some time later, it would be announced that Glory was pregnant and had given birth prematurely; in November, when Kate and Glory returned to Charleston with Kate's infant son, the boy would be introduced to the world as her brother.

Bill accepted this as the price necessary to salvage his candidacy, but Glory put up a fight. In the end, though, her protests were unavailing. As for Kate, she had given up trying to impose her will upon events. Whatever happened, she felt, was part of God's plan, and this time around she wasn't going to question that plan. She would embrace it humbly and submissively, putting her faith in God as she should have done in the first place.

Later, she would think back to those months at the convent of Santa Marta in Tuscany as among the most idyllic of her life. She and Glory grew closer, taking long walks and picnicking in the Tuscan hills, basking in the glorious light, which seemed to have more of Heaven in it than any other sunlight she knew. Kate even struck up friendships with the nuns, some of whom were scarcely older than she was. They were under a strict vow of silence, which made communication somewhat difficult, but each day, one nun was appointed to interface with the public, so as the days and weeks went by, Kate spoke with them all in turn. An exception was also made for her school lessons, though the nuns proved stern taskmistresses, delivering their lectures and answering her questions but avoiding every attempt she made to draw them into more personal discussions.

Kate had known her grandfather was an important and powerful man, but the veneration with which the nuns regarded him was truly eye-opening. They praised him as their benefactor and said prayers for him daily; on those occasions when he visited Glory and Kate, which he did at least once a month, the nuns welcomed him with an enthusiasm reminiscent, as Glory put it, "of prepubescent girls greeting some boy-band heart-throb." It was weird to think of Papa Jim as a kind of rock star for nuns, but though he laughed off the attention, he plainly enjoyed it.

On Sundays, a grizzled local priest, Father Rinaldi, came to take the nuns' confessions and to perform the Mass. He was a kindly, grandfatherly man, somewhat absentminded, who might have been anywhere from seventy-five to eighty-five. He spoke English with an Australian accent, and he moved with grave dignity, as if his bones were made of china.

Meanwhile, back home, Bill was steadily climbing in the polls. Papa Jim seemed confident that he would win. When Glory's pregnancy was announced, his numbers shot through the ceiling.

But all of this was external to the world in which Kate was really living at that time. Her real world was an internal one, populated by two people: her and her baby. She could feel him growing inside her. Feel his movements as he shifted position or kicked out suddenly. He was strong, active. Perhaps it was her imagination, but she felt as though she could sense his curiosity, his intelligence.

Who are you? she asked him silently. *What is your name? What have you been sent here to do?*

He never answered, but she never grew tired of asking.

Glory pestered her constantly with suggestions for names, but Kate was in no rush. She felt that she'd know what to call him when the time was right. God would provide.

The birth itself was nothing like she'd imagined. It was midmorning on the ninth of August, about a week before the "official" due date. Glory was gone, on a shopping trip to Rome. Papa Jim was en route from the airport. Her dad was at a campaign fundraiser in Marion.

Once her water broke, there was no pain, as she'd feared there would be. The baby came sliding right out, already squalling, as though eager to begin whatever task God had set for him. Seeing him in the arms of Sister Immaculata, the nun who served as a local obstetrician, Kate was so taken by his wrinkly beauty that it was a moment before she realized that she knew his name.

"Ethan," she said wonderingly. "His name is Ethan."

There were no choirs of angels. No wise men from the East bearing gifts. No shepherds come from the fields to rejoice.

There was nothing like that.

But Kate didn't care. She felt something imprint itself in her heart. It was as if she'd never known until this instant what love really was. Up until now, she'd been like a color-blind person who used the words for colors without knowing the truth behind the words. Now she knew. And nothing else mattered.

She held out her arms for the baby, but Sister Immaculata, with a grim look on her face, bore the child from the room.

"What's the matter?" asked Kate. "What's wrong?"

Another nun stepped close. "I'm sure everything's fine."

"I want to see Ethan. I want to see my baby!"

"Hush, now."

Something stung her arm. The nun had given her a shot.

Her vision blurred, dwindled to a point, then winked out into darkness.

✠   ✠   ✠

When she awoke, it was dark outside the windows.

A single lamp at her bedside cast a soft golden glow over the room, making the sheet that covered her appear gilded, like the raiment of a queen.

Papa Jim and Glory were sitting close by.

One look at their anxious faces sent a jolt of terror through her as she remembered how Sister Immaculata had bustled Ethan from the room. Suddenly awake, she bolted upright. "Where's Ethan?"

Glory dissolved into tears.

"He's gone, honey," said Papa Jim gently. "The doctors say there was a defect in his heart. A hole."

She shook her head. "No. It's not possible . . ."

"He went peacefully," Papa Jim went on. "He just went to sleep and didn't wake up. He's with God now."

Kate didn't know how to process what she was hearing. She remembered the pain she'd felt following the Procedure, when she was convinced there was a hole in the center of her being that could never be filled, but that was nothing compared to the searing hurt that was hollowing her out now, eating away at her insides until it seemed her whole body must be consumed by it. It hurt too much even to cry. "He's dead?"

"I'm so sorry, honey," said Glory, tears streaming down her face. For once, she looked her age. Or even older. "I should have been here for you!"

"I want to see him."

Papa Jim nodded and stood. "I thought you would." He bent down and kissed her. She smelled cigar smoke and whiskey. Then he left the room.

Glory reached out and squeezed her hand. "I'm so sorry, honey," she said again.

Kate pulled her hand away. "This is because of what we did. The Procedure."

"What? No . . ."

"Yes. It's my fault—I killed my baby . . ."

"Honey, no! Don't say that. Don't even think it!"

"It's true."

Papa Jim returned, bringing with him Sister Immaculata, who was holding a bundled form in her arms. So still. So quiet.

Ethan.

With a groan, Kate opened her arms to receive her child. He looked so much like he was sleeping that she couldn't believe he was dead. His little face was slack, peaceful. How could he be gone? Her heart didn't want to believe it. She wept over his tiny form, crooning wordlessly.

No one said a word.

After a time, she glanced up. "I want to see Father Rinaldi."

Sister Immaculata nodded silently and left the room. A moment later, she was back with the priest.

The old man made the sign of the cross. "God be with you in your loss, child."

"I need to talk to you, Father. Alone."

"Of course."

Sister Immaculata made to take Ethan's body, but Kate wasn't ready to give him up. Right now, she felt like she never would be. At a look from Papa Jim, the nun bowed her head and left the room. Then Papa Jim took Glory by the arm and led her out, though it was plain that Glory didn't want to go.

"I'll be right outside," she said.

Once they were alone, Father Rinaldi lowered himself into one of the vacant chairs with a sigh. "I baptized him before he died," the priest told her. "And I gave him the last rites."

"Thank you, Father," she managed.

"Would you like to make your confession, child?"

Kate nodded. "Bless me, Father, for I have sinned . . ."

✠   ✠   ✠

Later, Father Rinaldi paid a visit to the room where Papa Jim was staying. Papa Jim was sitting at the window, smoking a cigar and staring out into the night. He turned as Father Rinaldi entered. "Well, how did it go?"

The priest took a white handkerchief from his pocket and wiped his face with a trembling hand. "I didn't even have to suggest it to her. She brought it up herself. The poor girl is wracked with guilt. She blames herself for the death of the child. That unfortunate business in New York."

"Unfortunate, yes, but it worked in our favor in the end. The Lord works in mysterious ways, as they say."

"I'm concerned about the parents. Are you sure they won't object to her entering the convent?"

"Leave them to me."

The priest nodded, moistened his lips with his tongue. "And the boy?"

"The boy is dead, Father. You administered the last rites yourself."

The priest nodded again. "Yes, of course. May God forgive us."

Papa Jim drew on his cigar and smiled through a cloud of pungent smoke. "He already has, Father. He already has."

CHAPTER 5

1997

With a sigh, Gordon Brown laid down his pencil and listened to the sounds of high-pitched laughter and squeals of delight emanating from the living room, where Lisa, his wife, was playing with their son, whose first birthday they had just celebrated. He would much rather be out there with them than stuck here in the study, writing the weekly report that was required of him. But he'd already put off the unpleasant duty for too long.

It wasn't the report itself that he hated, but the layer of carefully bland abstractions and code words he had to employ in order to render the message meaningless in case of interception. Encrypting the details of each report into this precisely overdetermined yet unexceptional language was tedious and painstaking work, especially since, although he was right handed, he transcribed every report with his left hand, yet he understood its necessity. The Congregation had eyes and ears everywhere, human and electronic. The slightest slipup would draw unwanted attention.

Gordon didn't know who was reading his reports. He sent them to post office boxes in different cities and towns all across the country, never the same one twice. These addresses were communicated to him by ads placed on eBay, which in turn led to postings on Craigslist in certain cities. That was the only contact he'd had with his superiors in the last year, though he knew he was under constant surveillance by field agents, highly trained operatives ready to spring into action at a moment's notice if his family should be exposed or threatened. Of course, he and Lisa were quite capable of protecting themselves and their son from ordinary dangers. They had received the equivalent of Navy SEAL training. But even they would find it difficult, if not impossible, to prevail unaided against the kind of firepower the Congregation could bring to bear. But so far, at least, there was no sign that their cover was blown. To all intents and purposes, he and Lisa were proud young parents starting a family in the town of Olathe, Kansas, where they blended right in with other young couples drawn from around the country by the promise of a better life. He worked as a software developer at a start-up called Garmin, a manufacturer of personal-use navigational devices that tapped into the network of global positioning satellites, and she was a homemaker who made a little extra money by selling collectibles on eBay.

But their real jobs were quite different.

Gordon and Lisa had been entrusted with the upbringing of a high potential.

The reality of it still made Gordon tremble with awe. To think that such responsibility had been placed in his hands! He prayed to be worthy of what had been asked of him.

Of what would yet be asked of him.

There was a secret history of the world. A perpetual struggle that the vast majority of men and women were blind to. But some, because of their faith, were chosen to learn more, to play an active part in the battle of good and evil that would determine the future of the human race for all eternity.

Gordon had always been a believer, a staunch Roman Catholic who had considered becoming a priest before falling in love with Lisa and understanding that God had a different plan for him. How different, he could never have imagined.

It was Lisa herself who had approached him. Later, she'd told him that she had been assigned to sound him out for possible recruitment but had ended up falling in love with him. Her family had been involved with Conversatio for generations, but he had never even heard the word.

It was Latin for "the way." A way of life, of belief. A manner of living, of being in the world, such that every thought, every action, was part of an ongoing conversation with God: a worshipful conversation destined to facilitate the establishment of the kingdom of God on Earth.

Conversatio had begun as a monastic order in the early thirteenth century. Like many such orders of the time, it accepted religious and lay members, as well as men and women. All the community had wanted was to be left alone to pursue its meditations and prayers in peace. But as the years passed, Conversatio's numbers grew, until the Church perceived a threat to its power and authority.

The Inquisition pounced, pronouncing the order heretical; perhaps it was, for the brothers and sisters of Conversatio had a unique understanding of the Second Coming: they believed that God was going to send a second son to complete the work begun by the first. It was the birth of this second son, rather than the return of Jesus Christ, that the men and women of Conversatio hoped to hasten.

The doctrine of the second son, as they called it, was derived from a close study of the Old and New Testaments, where many passages, all of which had been misinterpreted or suppressed by the Church, testified to its truth. Jesus Himself had often spoken about the "Son of man"; the Church held that in doing so, He was referring to himself, but Conversatio believed that, on the contrary, He was in fact prophesying about the second son, who would be known as the Son of man rather than the Son of God, though it was unclear from the scriptures what that distinction implied, since the second son, like Jesus, would be unquestionably divine.

But it was not necessary or even possible for imperfect human beings to comprehend the mysteries of God's plan; faith, not understanding, was all that was required of them. And many followers of Conversatio clung to their faith in the face of the Inquisition's cruel and relentless persecution, enduring unspeakable tortures and willingly embracing a martyr's fate. Many, but not all, or even most. Like the Cathars and other sects branded with the stigma of heresy, Conversatio was crushed without mercy. Its members were killed or converted back to the "true" faith. Its doctrines were expunged from the pages of history.

Or so it had appeared.

But appearances were deceiving. In fact, though its ranks were badly decimated, Conversatio had continued to exist secretly both inside and outside the Church. As the years passed, decades and then centuries, the order slowly regained its strength, though never its former numbers. Its leaders had learned the wisdom of concealment. At the same time, they began to cautiously introduce moles into the Church hierarchy that had nearly wiped them out, so that they would never again be taken by surprise.

By the middle of the twentieth century, it was decided that the time had come for the order to step out of the shadows. Certain Biblical prophecies, as well as classified Vatican documents relating to apparitions of the Virgin Mary, suggested that the coming of the second son was close at hand. Now, as never before, the order required a public face, a kind of mask behind which Conversatio could go out into the world and mingle undetected in its mission. So it was that a group of wealthy and conservative-minded Catholics, most of whom knew nothing of Conversatio even though their businesses—and, in some cases, families—had been thoroughly infiltrated by the order's agents, were induced to form a lay organization dedicated to rolling back the modernizing influences of Vatican II. This organization called itself The Way.

Thanks to Lisa, Gordon had been given a glimpse behind the public mask of The Way. He knew the truth about Conversatio . . . and about the Congregation as well.

The Congregation was the Congregation for the Doctrine of the Faith, formerly known as the Holy Office of the Inquisition. According to the history books, the Inquisition had been abolished centuries ago, but, as with Conversatio, the truth lay outside history books: behind, beneath, beyond. The Inquisition, too, had continued in secret, hidden behind the mask of a new name, but as brutal and unforgiving as ever in its single-minded mission to root out and punish dissenters from the official dogma of the Church.

The chief weapon in the Congregation's arsenal was the sacrament of confession, just as it had been for well over a thousand years. The Church had always insisted that the seal of the confessional was absolute, the veil of secrecy inviolate. No civil or secular authority could breach it. What was said in the privacy of the confessional was heard only by Almighty God. But in fact, within the Church, there was no secrecy, no seal. No veil. Information flowed from the priests in the confessionals to their bishops, and from the bishops to the Vatican—and into the avid ears of Inquisitors, who sifted it word by word for the slightest sign of sin.

And more.

For in the patterns that emerged from tens of thousands of confessions reviewed week after week, year after year, century after century, a sordid compendium of the worst in human nature, the Inquisition believed they could glimpse the dark design of the great Adversary. The outlines of Satan's plan would be visible, they believed, to a sufficiently discerning eye, given an abundance of data. The centerpiece of that plan, which had as its aim the destruction of the Church and the downfall of humanity, was the Antichrist, the son of Satan: a spirit of absolute evil incarnated in flesh and sent to Earth in a blasphemous parody of the birth of Jesus. Because the devil was the prince of lies, it seemed likely that any woman cursed to bring the Antichrist into the world might very well think herself blessed, believing her womb was destined to yield a very different fruit than the unspeakable obscenity that was, in fact, ripening there.

So it was that the Inquisitors took special note of any reports of virgin births or conceptions. They rated such reports according to a scale that ran from low to high potentials: potential mothers; potential sons. Most cases along the spectrum from low to high they observed and ultimately rejected as ordinary sinners or insane persons. But a very few of the highest of high potentials merited more than mere observation. In those cases, the Inquisition acted. If the birth hadn't yet occurred, the mother-to-be was abducted, confined, questioned closely. And the child, whether male or female, was put to death as soon as it was born—after being baptized, of course, for there was, after all, a chance that the child was not the devil's spawn, and such a child deserved its place in Heaven . . . while if it *was* the devil's brat, why, then the touch of holy water would burn like fire, causing the infant to cry out and in doing so supply proof of its true nature (as, in fact, happened more often than not). The mother, if she were properly repentant, was permitted a life of service and absolution in a nunnery. Failing that, she would follow her child to hell.

If, on the other hand, the birth had already taken place, then there was no time to lose, and mother and child were summarily put to death.

The Inquisition reckoned that, since its inception, it had thwarted the devil's plans innumerable times in this way. But they were not complacent. The devil would not give up until the Antichrist survived.

Conversatio had no quarrel with killing the Antichrist. But in its zeal to eliminate Satan's spawn, the Inquisition was also running the risk of eliminating the second son. Indeed, from the perspective of the Inquisition, there was no difference between the two. This Conversatio could not permit. They would defend the women and children that the Inquisition sought to destroy, for only in that way could they defend the as-yet-unborn second son. Using information funneled to them by their contacts within the Inquisition, Conversatio dispatched its agents to high potentials before the Inquisition's killers could arrive. Sometimes they got there too late. But just as often they arrived in time. If the child in question had already been born, and was a boy, the agents would abduct the boy, leaving the mother to her fate. If the mother was still expecting, then she would be abducted and kept in a secure location until she gave birth, after which the child, if it was a boy, would be taken from her and raised by a childless couple specially selected by Conversatio for that purpose. Afterward the mothers, and any girl children, were sent to nunneries maintained by Conversatio. Meanwhile, the couple chosen to raise the potential second son would be observing their charge closely; if it seemed that he was the Antichrist, it was their duty to kill him. If he was just an ordinary boy, they were expected to raise him in the traditions of Conversatio, so that, in time, he too would become an agent. But if he was the prophesied second son, then they were to safeguard his life with their own until he could begin the work that God had given him to do.

The Inquisition, of course, fought back against its unknown adversary. Soon they realized that Conversatio was responsible. They also realized that they had been infiltrated. Thus began a game of cat and mouse between Conversatio and the Inquisition that continued until the present day.

As the years went by, the Inquisition was quick to seize upon anything that could give it an advantage in its race to identify and reach high potentials before Conversatio. A major breakthrough occurred in 1786, when the radical ideas of a Hessian engineer named J. H. Müller reached the Vatican. Müller had conceived of a calculating machine, the precursor to modern computers. Though Müller's ideas earned him nothing but scorn in his native land, the Inquisition was quick to see how such a device could aid them in their holy quest. An intensive program was secretly launched to build what was called a "Müller box." By 1822, when the English inventor and mathematician Charles Babbage began work on his own calculating machine, which he developed independently of Müller and called a "difference engine," the Vatican had successfully built and operated more than a dozen Müller boxes. Adding Babbage's ideas to the mix yielded computers of remarkably advanced design and capabilities, especially when linked in parallel processing networks. The computer revolution was still more than a century away in the secular world, but in the secret laboratories of the Church, located in Roman catacombs buried deep beneath the Vatican, it had already arrived.

At present, the Congregation's grasp of computer science and programming was far in advance of the rest of the world. A video or audio record of every confession was automatically transmitted electronically to the Vatican, where a powerful program tirelessly prowled through the ever-growing database using a sophisticated search algorithm. This program was the direct descendant of the first piece of software the Inquisition had developed in the mid-1790s and was continually being upgraded; indeed, it had attained a level of complexity such that no human mind could fully comprehend it, and for the last decade it had been upgrading itself, improving its own code, though considerable debate existed within the Congregation as to whether this ability was proof of intelligence, and, if so, what the theological implications of such a development would be. The existence of this program, called Grand Inquisitor, or GI for short, was known only to the pope, the ten cardinals who oversaw the Congregation, and the priests/scientists who monitored a system they no longer understood.

Conversatio spies had communicated the existence of Grand Inquisitor to their contacts right from the start, and over the years, with some interruptions, had been able to smuggle out enough information to give the order's field agents continued opportunities to compete with the Congregation for access to high potentials.

Which was how, exactly a year ago today, Gordon and Lisa had come to find themselves entrusted with a newborn boy.

They didn't know where the baby had come from, who his mother had been, or what had happened to her. They knew absolutely nothing about the boy's history; that way they couldn't accidentally reveal anything that might help the Congregation and Grand Inquisitor track him down. The only thing they knew about him, apart from the name on the birth certificate supplied by the agents who delivered the child, was that he was a high potential. But that was all they needed to know.

Gordon and Lisa had been at the top of the list to receive a high potential for nearly a year. They had been given new names, new identities. They had severed all contact with their families and friends. Such were the sacrifices demanded of those who would serve Conversatio as surrogate parents, protectors and, God forbid, possible executioners of a high potential.

But not once in the last year had Gordon and Lisa regretted their decision. From the moment they laid eyes on the baby, they felt their hearts open to him without reservation. He was so sweet, so beautiful, so intelligent. They knew right away that he couldn't possibly be evil. Of course, they prayed that he was the second son, as did each pair of surrogate parents, but really, it would be enough for Gordon and Lisa if he just turned out to be a normal, healthy boy. To be the loving parents of such a child, to raise him to love God and his fellow men, and to help prepare the way for the second son, that seemed like blessing enough to them.

Now, as he listened to Lisa getting the boy ready for bed, Gordon sent up a silent prayer of thanks. Despite the ever-present danger of discovery, the periods of stress and tedium that went with the job of being a Conversatio field agent and surrogate, the last year had been the happiest of his life. Having a child had brought him and Lisa closer together, added a richness to their lives that he couldn't have imagined without experiencing it for himself. It wasn't that the boy had become the center of their marriage, though in fact he had; it was more that having him at the center had provided a strength and stability that Gordon hadn't even realized was missing from the marriage before. He felt as though he and Lisa had been like two planets orbiting each other in the dark; now, with his arrival, a sun had suddenly appeared in the space between them, bathing them in light and warmth and love. The whole world appeared different to him now, a richer, more interesting, and beautiful place. It really was a miracle.

With a sigh, he returned to the report.

He wondered who would read his words. Did his unencrypted reports go to a single person, the same one each time, or were they circulated among a number of people, each looking for a different thing? He didn't know. His knowledge of how Conversatio was structured, let alone the identity of its leadership, was purposefully kept limited so that, if captured by the Congregation, he could betray no one when he broke under their tortures, as he would inevitably break, for the Congregation was as advanced in the art of persuasion as they were in the science of computers.

But in his mind's eye, Gordon had always pictured a single person reading his reports. An older man, wise and gentle, but strong too, when he had to be. He pictured him as silver haired, with a long, white beard. Someone who could be trusted to take care of those who served under him and to always do the right thing. The first time he'd described this imaginary being to Lisa, she'd laughed in his face.

"Why, don't you see who that is?" she'd asked.

"Um, no."

"It's Santa Claus, you big dope!"

And he'd started laughing too, because she was right. It *was* Santa Claus. But it was also Merlin the Magician and Gandalf the Gray: all those hoary old figures of stupendous power and benign authority rolled into one, up to and including God Himself. That's whom he was really writing to, regardless of what particular human eyes read the words. Realizing that didn't make writing the reports any more enjoyable, but it did leave him strangely at peace once he'd finished, as if he'd just made his confession and received absolution for his sins.

That was another sacrifice he and Lisa had made. No more confessions. No more Catholic masses, for that matter. No Catholic church was safe for them to enter now. Instead, they attended a local Methodist church, because not attending any services at all would bring them to the Congregation's attention as much or more as setting foot inside the confessional of a Catholic church.

After another hour, Gordon was finished at last. He read over the report one more time. Then he folded it and slipped it into the envelope addressed to this week's PO box: some town in Maine he'd never heard of. He sealed the envelope in a plastic sandwich baggie, which he placed into his briefcase. Only then did he peel off the latex gloves he'd worn through the entire operation. He hated using the gloves; they made his palms sweat and itch, but it was important to leave no physical evidence behind in case the letter was intercepted. Tomorrow, on his lunch break, he would drive to a mailbox, don another pair of gloves, unseal the baggie, remove the envelope, and drop it through the slot.

Gordon pulled off the gloves and tossed them in the trash. Then, one by one, he fed into the shredder the sheets of notebook paper on which, as though solving a complex mathematical equation, he'd worked out the encryption for the report. And every other sheet in that particular notebook, including the cardboard backing. That done, he did the same with the one-time pad that had served as the basis for the encryption. The posts on eBay and Craigslist that would supply him with the address of next week's PO box would also provide the means of generating the next one-time pad.

Once he'd finished the shredding, he took what was left of the papers into the living room, where he burned them in the fireplace. This had seemed excessive at first; he'd asked his instructor why, if he was going to burn the papers anyway, it was necessary to bother shredding them. The answer was sobering. No one quite knew Grand Inquisitor's limits when it came to reconstructing information, but Conversatio's scientists thought that GI would be easily capable of putting a shredded document back together; similarly, burned papers could theoretically be reconstructed from ash fragments. But it was thought, or rather hoped, that the combination of shredding and burning would be sufficient to defeat GI.

"Dinner's ready, hon," Lisa called from the kitchen.

"Be right there," he answered.

But although he was hungry, and the smell of roasted chicken was difficult to resist, Gordon didn't go directly to dinner. Instead, he stopped off at the baby's room to say goodnight to his son.

The boy was sound asleep. The poor little guy was completely tuckered out after a day that featured a birthday party with cake and ice cream and a dozen neighborhood kids and their parents. Maybe one year was a bit too young to really understand what all the fuss was about, but the boy had watched with fascination as the older kids played, laughing and gurgling with joy as the birthday cake was set before him with its single candle burning, which Lisa had blown out. And he'd certainly appeared to enjoy the cake, though more of it ended up on him than in him.

Now, looking at his son's peaceful face in the glow of the nightlight, Gordon once again offered up a prayer of thanks. How privileged he was to be standing here! He reached out and adjusted the soft, blue blanket to better cover the sleeping form. Then, his heart overflowing with feelings of tenderness and protectiveness toward this innocent and helpless life that had been placed into his care, he bent and kissed his son's warm, smooth cheek, drawing in the clean, fresh scent of his skin and hair; Lisa had bathed him before bed.

If he was aware on some level of Gordon's kiss, the boy showed no sign of it. He was breathing regularly, and behind his closed eyelids Gordon could see the movements of his eyes as they followed whatever dreams had found him. What could they be? Was he dreaming of his birth mother? Rehashing the events of the day? Or was he instead in communication with God, dreaming a future that was still years away, a destiny that Gordon could only guess at?

"Are you him?" he whispered. "Are you the second son?"

"Whoever he is, he's our son too," came Lisa's voice from behind him.

Gordon gave a start. "I didn't hear you come in."

"I like watching you watch him." Smiling, she moved up beside him and slipped an arm around his waist. "My two favorite guys."

"He's pretty amazing, isn't he?"

"Um-hmm." Her head was resting on his shoulder; he could smell her sweat mixed with the odors of roast chicken. "It's hard to imagine anybody would want to hurt a hair on his head."

"We won't let them."

"I know."

They stood quietly for a moment. Then Lisa spoke again.

"Is it selfish of me to wish that he turns out to be just a normal kid?"

"If it is, then I'm selfish too," said Gordon.

"I don't want him to be hurt. I don't want him to suffer like the first son did."

"Honey, everybody hurts. Everybody suffers. It's part of being human. We can't shield him from that, no matter who he is. Not completely. All we can do is be there for him when he needs us and give him all the love we have to give."

"How did you get to be so smart, Mr. Brown?"

"By marrying you, Mrs. Brown."

"Right answer." She stretched up to kiss him. "Now come on, before your dinner gets cold."

"Yes, ma'am."

Arms around each other's waists, they left the room.

Behind them, Ethan slept and dreamed.

CHAPTER 6

1998

It was time.

His heart beat quickly in anticipation, but his movements were slow and grave, deliberate, as he lit the candles and laid out the vestments one by one upon the bedspread. It was one of the ways that he exercised discipline over his body, curbing its hasty impulses, subjecting its appetites and demands to a rigorous control that brought him by small increments of suffering and self-abnegation steadily closer to God. He would forego food, sleep, speech, deprive himself of comforts that others took for granted . . . but not as some did, making a public show and in so doing seeking to elevate themselves above their fellow men, as if the mortification of flesh and spirit was an end in itself and not a means of reaching an end. No, that was not his way. As with other things, his suffering was private, a secret known only to God, concealed beneath his outward display of friendly good humor just as the cilice encircling his thigh, its tiny metal spikes kissing his flesh like thorns, was hidden beneath his clothing.

Or soon would be.

Now, in the flickering light of the candles, naked but for the small wooden cross he wore on a leather string about his neck and a pair of fresh white underpants, he knelt before the bed whose softness he had scorned, sleeping instead each night of the past three months upon the hard, cold floor without even a sheet to cover him. He bowed his head, closed his eyes, and prayed that he might serve God this night without impurity of mind or of body, performing the ritual required of him with a humble and contrite heart, reconciled to all men and with no animus toward anyone. As he prayed, small shivers shook his lean and finely muscled frame, his bony shoulders with their silvery lacework of scars; although it was the height of summer, he kept the air conditioner running at full blast, so that it was a perpetual winter within the apartment.

At last he raised his head and stood, making the sign of the cross. Then, methodically, he donned the vestments of his office.

First he bound the cilice tightly about his thigh, welcoming the familiar pricking sensations as the hooked barbs sank into the already scarred and scabbed flesh. Then he covered the cilice with a bandage that served both to press the barbs deeper into his skin and to absorb any telltale drops of blood, for it would not do to leave any blood behind.

Not his own, anyway.

He drew the wooden cross to his lips and kissed it, then lifted from the bed an oblong piece of white linen about two feet square that trailed long strings from each end, giving it the look of a sleeveless straightjacket: the amice. This he touched briefly to his forehead before draping it over his shoulders. He crossed the strings of the amice over his chest, passed them behind his back, then cinched them tightly about his waist. As he performed these actions, he prayed earnestly that the amice would serve as a vest of salvation to protect him from the assaults of the devil.

Then he lifted what appeared to be a white dressing gown: the alb. Drawing the alb over his head, he prayed to be washed in the blood of the Lamb and, thus purified, rendered fit to enjoy the eternal delights of Heaven.

Next came the cincture, a ropelike linen cord. Doubling its length about his waist, he prayed humbly for God to gird him with purity and extinguish within him, even unto the smallest and most stubborn ember, the sinful fires of lust.

There were now three garments remaining. Each of them, in stark contrast to the blemishless white of the others, was colored bright red; they shone like pools of blood in the candlelight.

The first was a napkin-like cloth on which the cross had been embroidered in gold: the maniple. This he kissed and wrapped about his left forearm, praying that it might serve as a shield against temptation.

The second was the stole, a scarf-like cloth whose ends were each embroidered with a cross. He kissed the crosses and then draped the stole about his neck, praying that the robe of immortality might someday, by the grace of God, be restored to him. He crossed the two ends over his chest and then tucked them into the cincture.

The third was the chasuble, a poncho-like garment he pulled over his head.

Thus accoutred, he resembled nothing so much as a priest.

Which, indeed, he was.

But of a very special kind.

Still on the bed were the remaining items of his investiture.

A vial of holy water.

A sheathed dagger.

A pistol.

The priest kissed the vial, raised it high, and murmured a blessing. Then he slipped it into an interior pocket of the chasuble.

He brought the sheathed dagger to his lips, then slid the blade free and blessed it in a similar fashion before returning it to its sheath, which he clipped to the left side of the cincture beneath the chasuble.

Finally the priest lifted the pistol, a silencer-equipped .45. He quickly checked the clip, repeated the blessing a third time, and then slid the pistol into a holster that had been sewn into the stole. This item was one he had never had occasion to use in his work, nor did he anticipate having to do so now. But it was best to be prepared. Should he be interrupted, the pistol could prove indispensable, both in his own defense and, if necessary, as a final means of evading capture. In such dire circumstances, he had received special dispensation to end his own life, the taint of mortal sin removed from the act, it being considered martyrdom rather than suicide.

Lastly, he sat on the edge of the bed and pulled on a new pair of black socks and black sneakers.

Then he dropped to his knees once more and prayed again, silently, for long moments. This was not required, but he felt the need of further self-discipline. Later, he would add to the scars on his back.

After a time, he stood, picked up one of the candles, and carried it to a closed door. He opened the door and entered a small bathroom.

The candlelight, which was the sole source of illumination, revealed a bathtub filled with water that glimmered as if with crystals of ice. Lying there, submerged up to the neck, was a young boy, perhaps six or seven years old. He was wearing sneakers, shorts, and a T-shirt that bore the name and symbol of the Chicago Bulls. His limbs had been tightly bound. He was gagged and blindfolded, his sandy blond hair plastered to his forehead. His skin had a distinct bluish cast.

"Dominus vobiscum," murmured the priest. *The Lord be with you.*

The boy did not stir. He seemed to be unconscious.

The priest set the candle down on the edge of the sink, then squatted beside the tub and pressed two fingers to the boy's neck; a pulse came back slow and faint as the trembling of a butterfly's wing.

Hypothermia had set in.

Good.

He did not want the boy to suffer unduly.

The boy's name was Charlie Vance. He was a high potential.

Of course, it was best to identify high potentials before they were born. Or, failing that, as early in their lives as possible. The older they grew, the more dangerous they became, for the powers of the Antichrist would manifest themselves more and more as the years went by, until the boy, whoever he was, came into his full inheritance of evil. At that point, he would be beyond the power of the Congregation to stop. Beyond all earthly power. So it was of the utmost importance to identify and neutralize high potentials early on, while they were still vulnerable. And for the most part, the Congregation did this effectively, despite occasional errors and oversights . . . and the interference of the heretics known as Conversatio, deluded, dangerous fools whose obsession with the false and pernicious doctrine of the second son was only opening the door wider than ever for the entrance of the Antichrist into the world.

The priest was one of those assigned by the Congregation to correct its errors and oversights: high potentials who, for one reason or another, had slipped through the cracks, avoiding detection until later in life. Like the Vance boy. The priest had received this particular assignment five months ago. No name, no information beyond a radius of three hundred miles around Chicago. Somewhere within that area, his nameless superiors felt certain, based on patterns revealed by confessional analysis, a high potential lurked. The priest did not know what those methods of analysis were, nor did he care to know. Did the dagger in the hand ask why it struck? Did the bullet in the gun inquire as to its target?

It had taken him two months to narrow the search to the suburb of Elmhurst. And another three months to establish himself in the area, to become familiar with the local children and their families, and, finally, to conclusively identify the Vance boy as his target. Then he'd set in motion the chain of events whose culmination was about to take place.

"In nomine Patris, et Filii, et Spiritus Sancti," he intoned, kneeling on the hard, damp tiles of the bathroom floor and making the sign of the cross above the boy. *In the name of the Father, the Son, and the Holy Spirit.*

He took out the vial of holy water, kissed it, and laid it on the edge of the tub. Then he raised the dagger to his lips and placed it, still in its sheath, beside the vial.

"Judica me, Deus," he said softly, head bowed, "et discerne causam meam de gente non sancta: ab homine iniquo et doloso erue me."

A thrill shot through him at the Latin words, like a powerful ancient spell. *Judge me, O God, and distinguish my cause from an ungodly nation: deliver me from an unjust and deceitful enemy.*

He took the vial, opened it, and sprinkled holy water over the boy's forehead. The drops ran down the alabaster cheeks like tears, but still the boy did not stir. The priest sealed the vial and replaced it within his chasuble.

Then he picked up the knife in both hands and raised it above his head.

"Jube, Domine, benedicere. Dominus sit in corde meo et in labiis meis: ut digne et competenter annuntiem Evangelium suum. Amen."

Cleanse my heart and my lips, almighty God, who cleansed the lips of the prophet Isaias with a live coal. In your mercy, deign to cleanse me so I may be worthy to proclaim Your holy Gospel: through Christ our Lord. Amen.

He drew the blade from its sheath and set the empty sheath down carefully on the edge of the tub.

"Per ipsum, et cum ipso, et in ipso, est tibi Deo Patri omnipotenti, in unitate Spiritus Sancti, omnis honor et gloria."

Through Him, with Him, in Him, all glory and honor are Yours, God, almighty Father, in the unity of the Holy Ghost.

He set the sharp edge of the blade to the boy's smooth throat. Only then did the boy move faintly, with a barely perceptible shudder. A soft moan escaped his lips. The priest paid no notice.

"Per omnia saecula saeculorum."

World without end.

And with one swift and sure stroke, it was done, as if the boy in the bath had been the bull whose image he bore on his T-shirt, now vanished beneath a billowing red cloud.

"Amen."

The sacrifice successfully completed, the priest cleaned the blade with holy water and then returned it to its sheath. Then, moving with the same slow and grave deliberation with which he had conducted the entire procedure, he cleaned himself, removed his vestments and packed them away, and dressed himself for the last time in the nondescript clothes of his current disguise. For his next assignment, he would be someone else.

After a final check of the room, he took out his cell phone and punched in a series of numbers, then pressed send. Fifteen minutes from now, after he was safely gone, the clean-up crew would arrive, a group of Congregation priests who specialized in turning the aftermath of the ritual he had just performed into a gruesome murder scene, one that could only have been perpetrated by a crazed serial killer. Thus would the attention of the police and the media be diverted. He smiled grimly to himself, thinking of how surprised people would be if they realized just how many of the murders and abductions ascribed to serial killers and sexual deviants were in actuality the work of men like him, priests sworn to celibacy and consecrated to God, who took these sins uncomplainingly upon their shoulders for the sake of the world's salvation, just as the Savior had done.

CHAPTER 7

2001

Lisa sat in front of her computer, looking over her eBay account and sipping her morning coffee as she listened to Ethan playing happily in the living room. It was funny; her home business was just a cover, a reason to visit eBay and other sites so often without arousing the suspicions of anyone—or anything—who might be monitoring their Internet usage. Yet to her surprise, she'd found that she genuinely enjoyed the work of buying and selling collectibles. Even more surprisingly, she was good at it. The business had become so profitable that it had evolved into a full-time occupation. She'd turned the guest room into an office, and, much to Gordon's annoyance, had made the garage her stockroom.

Gordon's engineering job at Garmin had proved to be another unexpected success story. Over the last four years, the small company had grown by leaps and bounds, and Gordon's responsibilities had grown with it. The stock options he'd received as part of his compensation package upon first joining the company had doubled, then tripled, then quadrupled in value, leaving them, at least on paper, very well off indeed. They'd bought a new house, another car, and of course the best of everything for Ethan.

Ethan was a joy: a lively, intelligent, imaginative boy who was curious about everything and as quick to laugh as he was slow to cry. He was popular with other children, and showed no sign of being other than an ordinary boy . . . with one exception: He had yet to suffer a single day of illness. While the neighborhood kids were going through the normal array of childhood sicknesses, Ethan remained uninfected. Even his cuts and bruises seemed to heal more quickly than those of the other kids . . . though Gordon said that was just Lisa's overactive imagination at work.

"Don't you see?" he told her once. "You want him to be the second son so badly that you're seeing signs of it everywhere, whether they exist or not."

But it seemed to Lisa that Gordon was the one who was fooling himself. Lisa knew that she would love Ethan no matter what, but she still prayed every night that he would turn out to be the one they had been awaiting for so long: the Son of man. But it was as if Gordon had already decided that Ethan wasn't the second son and so shut his eyes to any evidence to the contrary. In fact, she sometimes wondered if he had forgotten that they were not what or who they appeared to be. That more was involved here than just their own happiness.

Or no, not forgotten. It was more like he'd been seduced by the artificial life they were leading in Olathe, as if he preferred that life, comfortable yet false, to the dangerous and uncertain reality that lurked behind it. She couldn't entirely blame him. She felt the same temptation to close her eyes and pretend that the Congregation wasn't out there looking. In a way, their very success at blending in to the community was itself a danger. She hosted a book club every week with other young mothers she'd met through day care and was a regular at the monthly Small Business Association meetings. Gordon was a deacon in the Methodist church they attended and helped coach Ethan's pee-wee soccer team. They had made friends. All of which made it easy to let their guards down. To coast. Gordon still filed his weekly encrypted reports, but it was a habit now. A routine.

And if she were honest with herself, wasn't their marriage becoming that way too?

The early days, when they'd been training for the assignment, and later, when they'd received Ethan and been inserted into Olathe with their new names and identities, had been full of adventure, excitement, and romance. It had been like living out a movie, and Lisa had felt her faith in

God's plan deepening every day, along with her love for Gordon, even as her love for Ethan took root and grew into the strong and vibrant thing it was today. Yet, had her love for Gordon kept pace? She hadn't stopped loving him. She was certain of that. But it had changed somehow. Become another comfortable thing in her life, something else to take for granted. She felt this was dangerous, but she wasn't sure how to talk to Gordon about it. She didn't know if he felt the same way. She was afraid of hurting him.

And on top of it all, she wanted to have a child of her own. Even though she was only twenty-eight, Lisa felt her biological clock ticking. The urge to bring a new life into the world was so strong that it was almost painful sometimes. Nothing had prepared her for such feelings. But this, too, was something she was afraid to share with Gordon. Because even if he did feel the same way, there was nothing they could do about it.

Conversatio agents who accepted assignment as surrogate parents of high potentials were forbidden to have children of their own. It was thought that, in an emergency, when every second counted, a parent might place the life of their biological offspring above that of a potential second son. Not necessarily on purpose, but instinctively. That could not be allowed to happen. Only later, once a determination had been made that a high potential was not the second son, or, for that matter, the Antichrist, was the proscription lifted. That point was still years away with Ethan.

It occurred to her suddenly that she hadn't heard Ethan for a while.

Not really concerned, for Ethan was the kind of boy who would fall into silent reveries as he played intensely with his toys, creating elaborate scenarios in his mind that she could only guess at, Lisa rose from her desk and went into the living room.

Her son glanced up at her from the carpet, where he sat surrounded by a jumble of colored wooden blocks. It looked as though he had been building a castle, only to have the structure come tumbling down around him.

Tears were streaming down his face.

His brown, gold-flecked eyes gazed at her with a sadness she had never seen there before: a sadness so deep it seemed to have no bottom. Surely more was at work here than the simple collapse of a tower of blocks.

Yet not a single sound escaped him. Not a sob or a whimper.

Lisa dropped to her knees so that she could look straight into his eyes. "What is it, honey?" she asked softly. "What's wrong?"

"Fall down," he said, and sniffled, then swiped his hand across his nose.

Lisa gave him an encouraging smile. "Well, that's not so bad, is it? Here, let's just build it again, okay?"

But when she picked up a block, he shocked her by knocking it out of her hand.

"Ethan, what's gotten into you?"

"Fall down!" he said loudly, plaintively. "Fall down!"

Just then, her cell phone rang in her pocket. She recognized Gordon's ring tone: "Hanging on the Telephone," the old Blondie hit. It wasn't like Gordon to call this early. She fished out the phone and answered. "Hi, hon. I—"

"Turn on the TV," he interrupted.

"What?"

"Turn it on," he said. "Do it!"

"What's happened?"

"A plane just hit the World Trade Center in New York."

"Oh my God! Was it . . ."

"They don't know yet. It just happened."

Lisa was already moving toward the TV. Now she switched it on.

She didn't have to change the channel. There was a helicopter shot of the New York skyline, dominated by the iconic twin towers. The sky was almost achingly blue, smudged only by a dark trail of smoke rising from one of the towers. She could see gaping holes where windows had been. In the windows she saw licking flames and stick-figure people.

"Are you there?" came Gordon's voice.

"Oh my God," she repeated. "Those poor people!"

And then, incredibly, from the right side of the television screen, Lisa saw a plane approaching the second tower. It came in fast and straight, like a missile. "Oh God," she said, unable to believe her eyes. "No . . ."

The TV announcer was scarcely more articulate as the plane crashed head-on into the side of the tower, seeming to disintegrate in a cloud of sparkling debris.

Lisa felt her legs turn to jelly. She sank to the carpet. Somehow, she was still holding the cell phone.

"Oh God," she sobbed into it. "Oh God!"

It seemed all she could say.

"I'll be right home," came Gordon's voice.

Lisa nodded mutely, transfixed by the destruction on the screen. The announcer was talking about terrorism and mentioning a name she had never heard before. Osama something.

In her shock, she had forgotten about Ethan. But suddenly a wave of concern for him, a physical need to hold him and protect him, swept over her, and she turned away from the television.

He was right beside her. Staring at the screen. His face wet with tears.

"Oh Ethan," she said. Gathering him into her arms, she rocked him there on the floor as sounds and images that seemed impossibly, horribly surreal, like glimpses of the apocalypse, came flooding into her living room, which no longer felt like the safe haven it had a moment ago. She didn't think it would ever feel that way again.

Lisa knew that this was something Ethan shouldn't see, yet she couldn't bring herself to turn off the television or even mute the sound. In the face of such an atrocity, such evident suffering, she felt a need to bear witness. It was a duty.

"Fall down, Mommy," came Ethan's small voice in her ear.

She looked at him. Only now did it occur to her that this was what had prompted his tears. Prompted them before she had turned on the television set.

"Fall down," he said again, in a tone of infinite sorrow that seemed eerily incongruous coming from a five-year-old boy.

The hairs at the back of her neck prickled.

"What are you saying, Ethan?"

"All fall down," he said, gesturing grandly at the screen with one hand.

At his words, the nursery rhyme came into Lisa's head:

Ring a round the rosie,

A pocket full of posies,

Ashes, ashes,

We all fall down!

"The towers won't fall," she tried to reassure him . . . and herself. "The men on TV said so."

This time he didn't respond, just looked at her. And even more disquieting than the sadness she had glimpsed in his eyes earlier was the pity she saw there now. She felt as if she were in the presence of something uncanny. Something ancient and wise and, despite all appearances, more than human.

More than her son.

At that instant, Lisa knew absolutely, without a shred of doubt, that Ethan was the second son. Knew it in her blood and bones. Her heart of hearts. But the knowledge didn't fill her with joy as she'd always imagined it would. Instead, she felt frightened and small, out of her depth.

"Come on, Ethan," she said, unable to keep a tremor from her voice. "Let's go into the kitchen and wait for Daddy."

Ethan nodded silently.

Ten minutes later, the first tower fell.

CHAPTER 8

The insipid muzak clicked off as a voice came on the line. "Hello?"

"Bill?"

"Sorry, sir. The congressman is on another call right now."

Papa Jim sighed in exasperation. "Does he know it's me?"

"Yes, sir. But he's talking to the White House. Do you want to keep holding?"

"No. Have him call me as soon as he's free."

"Yes, sir."

Papa Jim hung up without replying. His secretary had been trying without success to reach his son-in-law all morning; finally, fed up, he'd placed the call himself, with no better luck. He had a bad feeling that Bill was forgetting who had put him in office . . . and he didn't mean the voters.

Choosing a Cuban cigar from the humidor beside his desk, Papa Jim lit up, savoring the taste and reflecting on the wisdom of Ecclesiastes: To everything there is a season.

A time to mourn and a time to plan. A time for grief and a time for vengeance. A time of war and a time of peace. A time to kill and a time to heal.

Papa Jim knew what season it was now, even if the rest of the country, still reeling in shock, did not. But it had always been that way. He had always seen more clearly than others, farther ahead: It was a gift that God had given him. He had built his business from just such a vision, of a lawless future in which the United States was threatened by enemies from without and within, a future in which a strong hand would be required to save the country from a rising tide of criminals and terrorists and lead it back to God. People had laughed, called him paranoid, even bigoted, but with the smoke still rising from Ground Zero, no one was laughing now. It was there on his television screen, the twisted wreckage that resembled nothing so much as a gigantic cross. A cross that the country must take up now and rally behind . . . or perish.

He had prepared for this day, or one like it. He had known that it would inevitably come. The separation of church and state was the tiny flaw in the Constitution that, over the years, had deepened into a chasm that had left the country weak, infected. Was it any wonder America's enemies had struck?

But it wasn't too late. He was convinced of that. The United States could still avoid destruction and damnation . . . with the right man in charge.

It was in anticipation of this moment that he had built his empire of faith-based, boot-camp-style prisons across America, combining punishment and evangelism to produce men and women who would one day become willing foot soldiers in a homegrown army dedicated to taking back the country for God. It was for this moment that he had engineered the successful congressional campaign of his son-in-law on a platform of law, order, and morality. And it was for this moment that he had invested heavily in the National Rifle Association, the Republican Party, and, most of all, the conservative Catholic movement calling itself The Way. His money had opened the doors of influence with the NRA and the GOP, but with The Way it had opened an even greater door: the door of knowledge. Initiated into the secret history of Conversatio and its centuries-long struggle with the Congregation, Papa Jim had seen at once how it could be an indispensable tool in the dark days that lay ahead. From that moment, Papa Jim had bent all his considerable energies to gaining a seat on Conversatio's governing council, a goal he had achieved five years ago, after the birth of his great-grandson.

Congregation, Conversatio: he didn't really care which was right and which was wrong. If Papa Jim could have made use of the Congregation he would have done so, but not even his wealth and influence could breach the ancient walls of custom, privilege, and secrecy surrounding the Congregation, that dark jewel nestled at the very heart of the Vatican. Conversatio was another matter. It was easy enough to feign belief in the idea of the second son, although privately he considered it to be a false and pernicious doctrine, little better than rank superstition. Which, indeed, was his opinion of the whole concept of high potentials. The search for such unfortunates by Conversatio and the Congregation was simply a modern-day witch hunt as far as he was concerned. But the business world had taught Papa Jim to be pragmatic. It had also taught him how to use the beliefs of others to achieve his own ends. And regardless of its merits theologically, as a marketing concept the idea of the second son was a winner. It was a living archetype, like the story of Superman come to Earth and raised as a common mortal, or Luke Skywalker raised in ignorance of his birthright. It was the story of Moses, of Jesus Christ Himself. If he could plug into that story, turn it to his own benefit, the country would respond. He was sure of it.

Ethan was the key. When Papa Jim's Conversatio contacts had told him that his granddaughter was going to give birth to a high potential, he had scarcely been able to believe his luck. Surely God had placed this tool into his hands for a purpose, and when the time was right, Papa Jim was going to use it.

As far as his granddaughter knew, her son had died shortly after birth. Shattered with guilt and grief, Kate had entered the convent of Santa Marta as a novitiate, and there she had remained ever since, bound by vows of silence and obedience, watched over by Father Rinaldi and the other nuns, all of whom were loyal to Conversatio. But the tiny body she had held in her arms and grieved over had been that of another woman's child, a boy who had died of natural causes hours after his birth in a hospital in Rome that was run by Conversatio; the switch of a dead child for a living one was a ploy the organization had used countless times over the years to spirit away high potentials without leaving a trail for the Congregation to follow. Papa Jim regretted the deception, and the pain inflicted thereby on Kate, Glory, and Bill, but it had been necessary. Once the Congregation had marked Kate and her son as high potentials, their lives were in danger; this was the only way he could be sure of saving them both. That his cooperation had led to his elevation to the governing council was just an extra benefit.

Papa Jim didn't know when or even how he would make use of the boy, whom Kate had named Ethan. But he was sure that when the time was right, he would know what to do.

God would tell him.

For now, though, he followed the boy's progress from afar through the weekly status reports sent by "Gordon Brown," the Conversatio agent assigned to be the boy's surrogate father.

Papa Jim had personally approved the Browns for the position shortly before Ethan's birth, and he'd had no cause to regret it . . . until recently. Gordon and his wife, Lisa, were well trained, smart, and devoted to the cause. But since the 9/11 attacks, Gordon's reports had begun to worry Papa Jim. In the first of them, Gordon had written that Lisa had become convinced that Ethan was, in fact, the second son. She claimed that he had predicted the terrorist strikes and the fall of the twin towers. Gordon had expressed his own reservations on this point, believing it more likely that, in all the confusion, Lisa had simply gotten mixed up, imagining that Ethan's tears and distress, which Gordon had witnessed for himself, had preceded rather than followed the upsetting images he had seen on TV. This seemed likely enough to Papa Jim, who'd been thrown badly off balance by the attacks himself, though he'd soon recovered his equilibrium. He'd expected that Lisa would come to her senses too . . . but instead, she seemed to have infected Gordon, who in his subsequent reports all but declared his own belief that Ethan was the second son. Not that Papa Jim cared what they believed; he'd known all along that he was dealing with fanatics of a sort, people whose faith in the doctrine of the second son was absolute and unquestioned. But he was afraid that, in their fervor, they might unwittingly break cover and reveal Ethan's existence prematurely . . . thus drawing the attention of the Congregation.

Papa Jim was monitoring things in Kansas closely, debating whether or not to pay the Browns a personal visit. But the Ethan situation was only one of the irons that Papa Jim had in the fire, which was why it was so infuriating to him now that he couldn't get in touch with Bill. He needed his congressman son-in-law to represent his interests in the legislation being drafted in response to the attacks. There was going to be a need for new prisons, both at home and abroad. Papa Jim was sure of it. But his company, large as it was, wasn't the only game in town. And the stakes couldn't be higher. The contracts would be worth hundreds of millions, maybe even billions. Yet just when he needed him most, just when the investment he'd made in getting Bill elected was about to pay off, his son-in-law had gone AWOL.

Like Papa Jim, Bill had been badly thrown by the events of 9/11. Unlike Papa Jim, he had yet to recover.

Papa Jim had tried to be patient with the man. After all, he had suffered a terrible loss. Glory had been visiting New York on that day and had gone for breakfast to the Windows on the World restaurant high atop the Trade Center. She had not survived.

But if Bill had lost a wife, Papa Jim had lost a daughter. Bill was not the only one to grieve. Yet the time for grieving was past. This was the season of vengeance, and Papa Jim needed Bill to be his strong right hand in the halls of government.

Sighing in exasperation, Papa Jim put down his cigar and reached for the telephone just as the intercom buzzed.

"Who is it?" he growled.

The voice of his long-time secretary answered. "It's the congressman."

"About damn time. Put him through, Joyce." He picked up the phone, waited for the click as the line was connected, then fired off the first salvo in what he planned to be a severe dressing-down. The freshman congressman needed to be reminded of just who was boss. "Where the hell have you been? We've got work to do!"

"Sorry, Jim. I've been talking to the White House."

"So I heard. About what?"

"My future."

"What the hell's that supposed to mean?"

"It means I'm quitting."

The words didn't make sense. "Quitting what?"

"Congress. I'm gonna go fight the bastards that killed Glory."

"You ain't gonna do no such thing. Listen here—"

"No, you listen for once."

This had the effect of rendering Papa Jim temporarily speechless.

"I never wanted this job," came Bill's voice, trembling with passion, or maybe just the effort of standing up to Papa Jim for the first time in his life. "With Glory gone, there's nothing to keep me here. I've still got my commission in the National Guard. I want to put it to use, do something tangible while I'm still young enough to make a difference."

"You can make a difference there in Washington. We had plans, remember?"

"No, you had plans. I just went along. But I'm finished with that now."

"You think Glory would want this? You think she'd want you to go and get yourself killed fighting a bunch of towel-heads?"

"I think she'd be proud of me for defending our country."

"Goddamn it, Bill, do you have any idea how much I spent to get you that seat?"

"I know money means a lot to you, Jim. It meant a lot to me too. But not anymore."

"Good," said Papa Jim, "because by the time I'm through with you, you won't have a pot to piss in."

"I'm sorry you feel that way. The president thinks it's a good idea."

"I find that hard to believe."

"The governor gets to name my replacement, so the seat will stay Republican. And my example will make the Democrats look bad. The media will eat it up. It's smart politics."

Papa Jim frowned. Much as he hated to admit it, what Bill was saying made sense. He wondered who he'd talked to at the White House. It sounded like Rove might have had a hand in this somewhere. He was the only political operative that Papa Jim felt any kind of respect for.

"Hmm . . . I suppose you could always run for the Senate when you get back . . ."

"My political career is over, Jim."

"We'll see about that," said Papa Jim.

"I'm announcing my resignation this afternoon," Bill went on. "I've scheduled a press conference for one o'clock. But I wanted to give you a courtesy call first. Give you a heads-up."

Papa Jim sighed. There was no use fighting the inevitable. "Hell of a time to grow a spine, son," he growled.

"No hard feelings?" his son-in-law asked.

"Does anybody else know about this yet?" he asked in turn.

"Just the White House. I was about to call the governor."

"Give me ten minutes," said Papa Jim. In politics, ten minutes was an eternity. A few quick phone calls, to the White House and the state house in Columbia, and the situation might still be salvaged. There were plenty of ambitious young men who would be willing to accept Papa Jim's guidance in exchange for a seat in the Congress.

It was time to start calling in old favors.

CHAPTER 9

2005

Sister Elena knelt upon the soft dirt of the convent garden, diligently plucking the thin green shoots of weeds that had sprouted seemingly overnight amid the orderly rows of peas. It was still morning, an hour past Terce judging by the position of the sun, but it was already oppressively hot, especially beneath her thick woolen habit. But she embraced the discomfort, offering it up to God as a penitence, one of many that, she knew, would never be enough to atone for her sins. Father Rinaldi claimed that God had forgiven her, but Sister Elena knew better.

Anyway, she had yet to forgive herself.

Reaching the end of one row, she paused to wipe the sweat from beneath her wimple, wondering at the persistence of life, even at its most unwanted. Despite her efforts, and the efforts of the other nuns at the Convent of Santa Marta, the weeds were an enemy that could not be vanquished. The war against them was a continuous one, not unlike the war of good against evil that had taken such tangible form in the world beyond the convent walls since 9/11. First in Afghanistan. Now in Iraq. But the parallels were not exact. She knew, for instance, that the weeds were not evil. They were merely . . . inconvenient.

As an unborn child could be inconvenient.

Was it sinful then to pluck them from the ground? Didn't weeds have the same right to life as peas?

Didn't Afghanis and Iraqis have the same right to life as allied troops? Even bin Laden's life must be precious in the eyes of God.

Yes, according to the Bible, God's forgiveness could extend even to a monster like bin Laden, the man who had murdered so many, including her own mother, dead these last three years.

She'd been here, in the garden, when Father Rinaldi had come to fetch her. She'd seen him coming, making his careful way across the grounds, his frail form in its flapping black surplice reminding her of a crow, and she'd known right away, before she'd heard a word, before she'd even seen his face clearly, that death had touched her again, that God was not finished punishing her for what she'd done.

"Come with me, Sister Elena," he'd said when he reached her.

The look of compassion in his rheumy blue eyes confirmed her fears. She hurriedly averted her gaze, not wanting to see anything more, and rose obediently, mutely, to her feet, for the vow of silence she'd taken was not so easily set aside as this. She could speak when it came time for prayer, or when given dispensation to do so by Father Rinaldi or the abbess, but Sister Elena had long since reached the point where it was speech rather than silence that seemed unnatural.

He'd led her inside, to the reception area where visitors to the convent were greeted, tourists curious about what the life of a nun was like in the Middle Ages: Santa Marta was a living museum, the Colonial Williamsburg of nunneries, as Sister Elena referred to it in her letters home. She and the other nuns dressed as the nuns in medieval times would have dressed. They ate the same foods, slept on straw pallets, organized their days around the Book of Hours and its placid cycle of prayers and devotions. Of course, there was a modern infirmary and modern guest quarters, telephones, central heating and air-conditioning, even Internet connections. But these amenities were not available to the nuns except in special circumstances.

Father Rinaldi brought her to the booth that held the convent's public phone. "A call," he said. "For you." And then, when she did not move to enter the booth (she was afraid to do so, already playing out in her mind the words she had yet to hear): "Go on, Sister. Answer the phone."

So she'd entered the booth, leaving the door open behind her, because she didn't want Father Rinaldi to think that she had secrets from him, things to hide, though of course she did. She wiped her damp palms on the front of her habit and picked up the phone. "Hello?" Her voice cracked, only partly from disuse.

"Is that you, Kate? It's Daddy." If he hadn't said so, she wouldn't have known. That's how ravaged his voice was.

Normally she corrected him when he called her Kate. She was Sister Elena now. Kate no longer existed. But this time it didn't even occur to her. "What is it, Dad? What's happened?"

"I wanted to tell you right away, but Papa Jim . . . well, your grandpa wanted to wait until we knew for sure."

"Oh sweet Jesus," she said, and crossed herself with her free hand. There was a narrow bench in the booth, and she sank onto it without conscious thought; her legs weren't holding her up anymore.

"It's Glory, honey. She's gone."

"Gone?"

"She was there. In the North Tower. When it fell." Deep breaths separated each statement, as though he were trying to swallow the words but couldn't keep them down.

"Oh God."

Her father suddenly burst into sobs. Great, wracking sobs that seemed, for all their size, more suited to a child than an adult. "She's gone!" he wailed. "Gone!"

And now she was crying too, crying like a little girl who had lost everything, crying like she hadn't cried since she'd learned of Ethan's death. The phone had fallen from her hand and was dangling from its chord, swinging back and forth, and from it she could still hear the tinny squawking of her father's grief.

✠   ✠   ✠

Later, he'd begged her to come home for the funeral, but she'd told him no. It wasn't that her vows prevented it; Father Rinaldi and the abbess had both tried to convince her to go. But she hadn't been able to do it. Hadn't been able to face her father and Papa Jim.

Not because they blamed her for Glory's death. Why would they?

But she knew the truth.

She *was* to blame.

It was her fault that Glory had died. God had struck her down because of her role in the abortion. Okay, so it had been Glory's idea in the first place . . . but she couldn't blame her mother for that. Her mother hadn't known whose child she was carrying. But *she* had known. Gabriel had told her. But she hadn't listened. She'd gone through with it anyway. The truth was, in the end, it had been her own lack of faith, of courage, that had caused Ethan's death . . . and now Glory's.

For a while, crazed with grief and guilt, she was convinced that she bore responsibility for all the deaths that had occurred on that tragic day. But as time passed, some degree of perspective returned, and she realized that the universe didn't revolve around her . . . even if, for a brief period, it had. No, God had not taken more than three thousand people to punish her.

He had only needed to take one.

But it was so unfair!

Why didn't you take me instead? she demanded of God, alone in her cell at night, kneeling bare-kneed upon the stone floor. *Why did she have to die?*

She railed at Him, cursed Him.

She wept and begged forgiveness.

But no matter what she did, what she said, there was never a reply. Not a word, not a sign. If God had listened to her once, apparently He listened no longer.

No . . . He was still listening. She knew that.

He had just stopped answering.

But that's not true either, she told herself. *He's still answering.*

What else was Glory's death but God's answer to the question she never stopped asking: *Am I forgiven yet?*

The answer, it seemed, was no.

✠   ✠   ✠

Since that time, whenever Sister Elena received a phone call, or a visitor, she would experience a moment of stark dread, expecting the news that God had struck again, taken the life of another person dear to her. And even though nothing of the kind had happened, she felt the same icy chill grip her heart now, when she glanced up from her weeding and saw Father Rinaldi, more decrepit than ever, making his way toward her with the assistance of a cane. He had suffered a mild stroke two years ago that had partially paralyzed his right side, but he refused to curtail his duties or movements about the convent as a result.

This time, she didn't wait for him to arrive. She stood and went to meet him.

He stopped and waited for her, mopping with a white handkerchief at the sweat that shone on his face and bald head. "It's your father," he said as she drew near, then added quickly, seeing the stricken expression on her face, "No, no, he's fine. He's here to see you."

Relief flooded her, and she offered up a silent prayer of thanks even as she gave Father Rinaldi her arm to lean on as they slowly made their way inside to the reception area. All the while, Sister Elena was wondering what had brought her father here. It would be the first time she had seen him since before Glory's death. Since then, they had spoken by telephone and exchanged letters, but she had not left the convent, and he had not traveled to Italy to see her, even though her grandfather had made the journey three times. But she knew that Bill had taken Glory's death very hard. Like her, though with far less reason, he had blamed himself. And he had become obsessed with thoughts of revenge. Soon after 9/11, he had resigned from Congress and joined the Army Rangers. The administration had eagerly embraced the PR bonanza of a gung-ho, Republican ex-congressman fighting al-Qaeda up close and personal. There had been some red tape to cut through, given his age, but Bill's natural athleticism and grim determination had carried him through the arduous Ranger training program while men ten and fifteen years younger were washing out. He'd distinguished himself in two tours of duty in Afghanistan, receiving a Purple Heart and a Silver Star. But not once in all that time had he come to see her.

Until now.

Why?

Her heart was fluttering wildly as Father Rinaldi brought her to one of the rooms set aside for family visits.

"Your father is inside," he told her. "Consider yourself released from your vows for the duration of his visit."

"Thank you, Father." She turned to the door, opened it, and stepped inside. The room, though small and austerely furnished, was comfortable and modern, with a gorgeous view over the Tuscan hills. But the only view Sister Elena had eyes for was the sight of her father in his dress uniform rising awkwardly from the chair in which he'd been waiting for her to arrive.

He looked so old!

Of course, seven years had gone by since she'd entered the convent. She was twenty-four now, and he was forty-two, but that amount of time couldn't account for the difference between the man facing her and the man she remembered. This man looked like he was well into his fifties, if not older still. Lines had etched themselves deeply into his face, and his black hair had turned silver. He was whip thin and hard muscled, but her impression was one of gauntness rather than fitness, as if his body had been whittled down by years of grief and deprivation until there was nothing superfluous left, nothing that was unessential to him.

She wondered what he saw when he looked at her.

He reached her in two long strides and took her into his arms, hugging her so tightly that she winced. "God, Kate, it's good to see you!"

"You know it's Sister Elena now," she corrected gently, and kissed him on the cheek. "You're crushing me, Dad."

When he pulled away, he was grinning lopsidedly, but his eyes glimmered with moisture. "Just look at you," he said. "You've grown into such a lovely young woman. Glory would be so proud."

Sister Elena was feeling a little teary eyed herself. Her mother's absence was so strong that it was itself a kind of presence in the room, as though her ghost were hovering nearby, watching and listening to all that transpired. "Can I get you something to drink, Dad?"

"I'm fine, honey."

They studied each other in a silence that tautened as it stretched.

"I don't know if I can get used to seeing you in a uniform," she said at last, attempting to lighten the mood. "I feel like I should salute or something."

"If you think that's tough, try looking at your only daughter in a nun's habit."

Sister Elena flushed. "Dad . . ."

"How long is this going to last, Kate? Why—"

"Dad," she broke in forcefully, "it's Sister Elena now. I've told you a hundred times. And it's going to last for the rest of my life. It's a marriage, Dad. A marriage to Christ. Can't you respect that?"

At first she thought he was going to continue his attack, but then she saw a look of resignation and sadness come into his eyes. His shoulders sagged. "Of course, honey. I'm sorry." He shook his head ruefully. "The first time we see each other in years, and I launch right back into the same old crap."

"It's okay," she told him, reaching out to lay a hand on his arm. He had never understood her decision to remain at the convent and take holy vows. He'd thought at first that it was just a phase, a symptom of her grief after Ethan's death, and that she'd grow tired of the hard life she'd chosen soon enough and come back to South Carolina, ready to pick up her old life right where she'd left off. When that hadn't happened, he'd become more forceful in his criticism, even accusing her of having been brainwashed and threatening to send deprogrammers to kidnap her and bring her back home. There'd been a lot of shouting and tears on both sides then, but luckily Glory and Papa Jim had been on her side, and in the end her father had grudgingly acquiesced to what he couldn't change. Sister Elena hoped that he wasn't going to dredge up all that old unpleasantness again.

He patted her hand and grinned lopsidedly. "Don't worry, Sister. I'll be good. Scout's honor."

She laughed, relieved. "Thanks, Captain."

His grin widened. "Actually, it's Colonel now. I've been promoted."

"Dad, that's great!" She clapped her hands together. "I'm so proud of you!"

Something flashed in his eyes then, and the grin was gone. "Don't be. I'm sure as hell not."

"I don't understand."

He sighed. "This isn't going like I planned. Can we sit down?"

"Of course." There was a sofa situated to take advantage of the mountain view. They both sat, but instead of gazing out the window, they had eyes only for each other. "What's this all about, Dad? Why have you come to see me? Are you in some kind of trouble?"

The lopsided grin was back. "I'm fine, honey. Fine."

"Bullshit," she said.

His eyebrows shot up at that, and she had to repress a laugh.

"The convent has a school," she explained. "I teach the local kids how to speak English. It's given me a good nose for BS. And I'm smelling it now."

"Damn," he said. "Guess I'm busted."

"Damn right. So, are you in trouble?"

He stood abruptly, walked to the window, and looked out, his back to her. "When I quit Congress and joined the Rangers, I wanted one thing: revenge. I wanted to kill the bastards who killed your mother and all those other people. But you know what? The longer I've been in Afghanistan, the harder it is to decide who deserves to die and who doesn't."

"That's up to God, not men."

"Not in the Army it's not," he said. "You know about Abu Ghraib?"

"Of course. That was terrible."

"There's worse. Lots worse."

"You've seen this?"

"Yes."

"Have you reported it?"

"Honey, it's not that simple."

"Why?"

He turned to face her, standing ramrod straight, as if at attention. "Never mind. That's not what I came here to talk about."

"What then?"

"They're sending me to Iraq."

Sister Elena's heart thudded in her chest. "When?"

"Next week."

"Is . . . is it bad there, Dad? As bad as they say? And please don't try to BS me."

He opened his mouth, shut it, then said simply, "It's bad."

"Worse than Afghanistan?"

"Ask me again the next time I see you."

"When will that be?"

"I wish I knew."

She got up from the sofa and went to him, took his hand. "I'm glad you came," she said.

"I had to tell you something," he said, and gave her hand a squeeze. "A couple of things, actually. First, I love you, honey."

"I know."

"Maybe you do, but I should have said it in person a lot sooner than now."

"I love you too."

He cleared his throat. "I should have told you this next thing a lot sooner too."

"What?"

"I think Ethan may be alive."

She couldn't speak. She could barely believe her ears. Her head was spinning. She would have fallen if her father hadn't caught her.

"Here, honey, you'd better sit down."

He led her back to the sofa.

"What . . . what do you mean he's alive?"

He squatted down, bringing his eyes level with hers. "I don't know if he is or not. But I think he might be."

"I don't understand. How . . . ?"

"The last time I was home on leave, Papa Jim called me in to his office for a meeting. He wanted me to run for governor. Said I'd be a shoo-in."

He rolled his eyes. "I told him I was finished with politics. Anyway, during our talk, he was called away for a while. That's when I found a letter on his desk. I don't know what made me look at it. I don't normally read other people's mail. But, well, this was open already, and I'm always curious about what your grandfather is up to. I swear, that man makes Machiavelli look like Andy of Mayberry."

"What . . . what did it say?"

"It was a report about a boy. A boy named Ethan."

"A report?"

"The boy's the right age. And he's being raised by foster parents somewhere in Kansas. There was a lot of stuff in the letter I didn't understand, and I didn't have time to more than glance at it before I heard Papa Jim coming back. Since then, I've gone back and forth about whether to mention it to you. I don't want to get your hopes up. It's not as if there's any evidence. But finally I decided to do it. You have the right to know."

With a great effort, Sister Elena gathered her wits together and spoke. "Are . . . are you saying that Papa Jim *faked* Ethan's death? That he and Father Rinaldi lied to me, brought me the corpse of a dead baby to grieve over, and meanwhile stole my real son away? And took him to *Kansas*?"

Her father blinked nervously. "Er . . . yeah. Maybe."

She stood up angrily. "You're crazy!"

He stood as well, reached for her arm. "Kate, please listen. I—"

She brushed him off. "It's Sister Elena! And I'm not going to listen to this kind of sick insanity. I don't know what your problem is, Dad. Post-traumatic stress disorder, maybe. But you should see a shrink. Or a priest." She was so angry that she was trembling, her hands clenched into fists and pressed against her sides.

"I know how this must sound. I can only imagine what you're feeling. But I promise, as soon as I'm back from Iraq, I'm going to get to the bottom of this."

Sister Elena shook her head grimly. "I won't be involved in your delusions, Dad. It's too painful. I hope you get the help you need. Until then, good-bye."

Her eyes brimming with tears, she turned and made for the door.

Her father didn't try to follow. He just called after her, his voice cracking. "I'm sorry! I shouldn't have said anything. I take it back, honey. I take it back!"

The slamming of the door behind her was her only answer.

✠   ✠   ✠

Seated at a wooden desk in an adjoining room, Father Rinaldi winced sharply as the door slammed and yanked the headphones from his ears. He sighed heavily, drumming his fingers on the desktop, gazing out the window at the same picturesque view that Sister Elena and her father had seen.

After a moment, he picked up the phone.

"Get me Mr. Osbourne," he said.

CHAPTER 10

2006

When Reverend Ballard called his name, nine-year-old Ethan rose to his feet and exited the pew to the encouraging smiles of his parents. The slender boy, somewhat tall for his age, wore a new dark suit, freshly shined shoes, a clean white shirt, and a bright red tie. His brown hair had been trimmed the day before and then fussed over by his mother this morning before they left for church; not a hair was out of place.

Clutching in his hands the folded printout of the speech he had painstakingly composed and rehearsed with the help of his parents, Ethan walked slowly up the aisle to the pulpit, where Reverend Ballard was waiting, a smile on his round red face.

One Sunday each month, Reverend Ballard set aside a few moments toward the end of the service for a student from the Bible study classes to address the congregation on a subject of their devising, usually a brief text taken from one of the gospels. The students selected for this honor ranged in age from seven to eighteen and were recommended by their teachers on the basis of classroom participation. Today marked the first time Ethan had been chosen.

"Come on up, Ethan," Reverend Ballard said as he approached. "Don't be shy." He reached out a big hand to assist Ethan in climbing onto the raised platform, and Ethan took it, although he didn't need any help.

"Ethan's topic is from John 14:2," said the reverend. "In my Father's House are Many Mansions." He stepped back from the podium, gesturing Ethan forward. "I don't know about you, but I'm eager to hear what young Ethan has to say." Of course, Reverend Ballard knew perfectly well what Ethan was going to say; he had reviewed and approved the boy's remarks, as he always did in these situations.

Ethan stepped up, unfolded the printout, and laid it across the pages of the open Bible that rested atop the podium. He looked out over the sea of faces watching him with expressions that ranged from polite interest to unfeigned boredom. Some of the other kids from Bible study were surreptitiously making goofy faces at him, trying to crack him up, but he ignored them.

Seconds passed. Silence stretched. There were coughs from the pews.

"A little case of stage fright," said Reverend Ballard with a chuckle from behind him, and the audience laughed.

Ethan felt himself blushing. But it hadn't been nervousness or fear that had kept him quiet. No, it was something else entirely.

The moment he'd laid down the folded sheet of paper and looked out over the congregation, the words he'd labored over so diligently and then rehearsed again and again in front of his mom and dad until he knew them all by heart, the printout not even necessary anymore, had simply deserted him. They were gone. In their place, new words filled his head, seemingly out of nowhere. Or no—a voice was speaking them . . . a voice only he could hear.

Although he couldn't remember anything like this ever happening to him before, Ethan wasn't frightened by it. In fact, the voice seemed familiar somehow. It was a voice he could trust, as if it were coming from somewhere inside himself. Yes, that was it. Like finding a part of himself he'd somehow forgotten about. A part of himself that was older and wiser than a nine-year-old could be. It was, he thought, the voice of his soul.

"Ethan?" prompted Reverend Ballard.

Ethan glanced at him and smiled reassuringly. Then he looked down at the words on the printout and for the first time recognized them for what they were: a collection of bland, superficial phrases and clichés. He couldn't believe he'd written them. He would not speak them now. Raising his eyes to the congregation, he gave voice to the words still echoing softly in his head.

"How can a house have many mansions? I wondered about that. A mansion is a big house; is there a house so big that it contains other big houses? A house whose rooms are so huge that every single one of them might as well be a mansion? The answer is yes. There is a house like that. It's the house of God.

"My father's house . . . that's what Jesus called it. But it's my father's house too. It's your father's house. And yours. Because God is our father. 'Our father which art in Heaven . . .'

"God is in Heaven . . . but what about His house? Where's that? Is it in Heaven too? I don't think so. At least, not all of it. I think Heaven is another room in God's house. For sure it's the best room, but there are other rooms too. We're in one of them right now. This church is part of my father's house. How could it not be? Think about how peaceful it is here. How safe we feel inside. That's because we're home. That's how I feel, anyway. I don't even have to come inside. Just walking by makes me feel good.

"But you know what? That's how I feel when I ride my bike past the Baptist church on the way to the pool. And the Catholic church too. I feel the same way when I walk past the synagogue. And that mosque over by the library. Those are all my father's houses. And all of us are His children.

"The Kingdom of God is at hand. Jesus said that. *At hand.* That means it's right here, right now, all around us, if only we are open to it. It's in this church and in the other churches. But it's not only there. God's love is infinite, and so is His Kingdom. So is His house. The whole world is His house. And the different countries, the different religions, they're all rooms in that house. They're all mansions."

Ethan paused and let his gaze move over the congregation. Everyone was gazing at him raptly, hanging on his words . . . except for his parents. His mom and dad had turned pale as ghosts and were clutching each other by the hand. They looked as if they were afraid of what might come out of his mouth next. Ethan couldn't understand their reaction. He gave them a smile, trying to let them know that everything was all right, that they didn't have to be afraid. Then he continued speaking.

"When I think about what's going on in God's house today, I feel sad. I feel sad because some of the mansions are fighting each other. Do you think it makes God happy when the people living in His house fight like little children? In school this year we learned about Abraham Lincoln. He said that a house divided against itself cannot stand. You know who else said that? Jesus. It's right there in Matthew 12:25: 'Every kingdom divided against itself is brought to desolation, and every city or house divided against itself shall not stand.' Think of what happened the last time God decided to put His house in order. That was the Flood. He promised Noah never to flood the earth again, but there are other ways of cleaning house. I don't know about you, but I'd rather clean my room myself than have my dad come in and do it for me!"

This elicited some laughter from the congregation. But not everyone laughed, and many faces were glaring back at him. Ethan took a deep breath. He knew that what he was about to say was not going to be popular. But he also knew that he had to say it. To keep silent would be to betray the part of himself that was whispering these truths to him: his immortal soul, which came from God and would one day return there.

"We have to stop fighting each other," he said. "Don't you see? We have to stop it ourselves . . . or God will stop it."

"They started it!" yelled someone from one of the back pews.

"An eye for an eye!" cried someone else.

"What about turning the other cheek?" Ethan asked in turn. "Are we following in the footsteps of Christ when we kill? Didn't Jesus tell Peter to put up his sword? Are we following Christ when we torture? Did Jesus whip others and force them to wear crowns of thorns? Did he crucify people? No. He was whipped. He was crucified. 'As you do unto the least of these, so you do unto me.'"

A man in one of the middle pews shot to his feet. "America doesn't torture!" he declared angrily. "I'm not going to sit here and listen to our soldiers insulted by some snot-nosed, unpatriotic brat!"

"You tell him, Sam," said a woman behind him.

"You should be ashamed of yourself, young man," chastised an elderly woman in thick glasses, shaking a finger in Ethan's direction from the front row. "And so soon after that brave congressman gave his life to keep us safe!"

At this, Reverend Ballard, who had been listening with an expression somewhere between horror and wonderment, collected himself and stepped forward. "Hold on now," he said, raising his hands in a placating gesture. "I assure you all, those weren't the remarks that I approved, and I apologize for them. Of course we don't torture. Everybody knows that. The president himself said so, and we all know that he's a God-fearing man. This church will always honor the men and women in uniform who serve our country so bravely and selflessly, fighting them over there so we don't have to fight them over here."

"He's the one who should apologize," Sam replied testily, glowering at Ethan, arms crossed over his chest.

Reverend Ballard looked at Ethan. "Well, Ethan?"

Ethan swallowed. He could feel his heart hammering in his chest. His parents looked as if they wanted to crawl under the nearest rock, and there was a part of him, and not a small part, that would have gladly joined them there. But though the voice that had whispered to him was silent now, he could still sense its presence within him.

"Everything I said was true, Reverend Ballard. I can't apologize for the truth. But I'm sorry if I disappointed you or upset anybody."

"You call that an apology?" snorted Sam.

"Now, now," said Reverend Ballard, raising his hands again. "Freedom of speech is one of the things we're fighting for, isn't it? Ethan is young and idealistic. That's nothing he has to apologize for. Not in my book. Yes, he went too far, but he had a lot of good things to say as well. And he stuck up for what he believes. Whether you agree with him or not, that takes guts. So I'm asking you to give Ethan the same round of applause that we give to all our student speakers."

Without waiting to see if anyone would start off, the reverend brought his meaty palms together resoundingly. Most of the congregation followed suit, if somewhat grudgingly and tepidly, but Sam and a number of others pointedly did not. Ethan's parents, he was both proud and embarrassed to see as he made his way back to his seat, clapped loudest and longest of all.

✠   ✠   ✠

As soon as they got home after the service, Gordon and Lisa sat Ethan down for a serious talk.

Lisa glanced at Gordon, then began. "Honey, before we say anything else, I want you to know that your father and I are proud of you for saying what you did."

Gordon nodded. "Reverend Ballard was right. It took guts."

"It was the truth," Ethan said.

"We know," said Lisa. "Only, why didn't you tell us you were going to say those words instead of the ones we worked on?"

Ethan shrugged. "Until I got up there, I didn't know."

"What happened when you got up there, Son?" his father asked.

Ethan shrugged again. "It was like a voice started talking to me. A voice from inside."

"And that voice told you what to say?"

"Sort of," he said. "It's hard to explain."

"Try," said Lisa.

Ethan thought for a moment. "It was like a part of me that had been asleep suddenly woke up. I looked at the words we'd written down, the words I was supposed to say, and, well, they were stupid. They didn't really mean anything."

His parents exchanged a glance.

"Go on," Gordon said.

"Instead, I thought of other words to say. Better words. You know, truer ones. It was like they'd been there all the time, waiting for me to notice them."

"And then what?"

"Then I said them. I didn't mean to make anybody mad, Dad."

"I know that," his father said.

"People get mad sometimes when they hear the truth," Lisa added. "Especially when it's a truth they don't want to hear."

"And especially when it comes from a kid," Ethan said.

"Yeah, that too," Lisa said with a smile.

"But does that mean I shouldn't say anything?"

"That's a hard question," Gordon admitted.

"You have to respect other people's beliefs, Ethan," Lisa said.

"Even if they're wrong?"

"Even then. There's a saying, 'actions speak louder than words.' I think that's the best way to communicate the truth to others. Make sure it's there in your actions."

"Think of it as practicing what you preach," Gordon said. "Only without the preaching."

Ethan thought for a moment, then nodded. "Okay. I can do that."

"And Ethan, that voice of yours? It's probably better if you don't mention it to anyone."

"I kind of figured that," Ethan said. "I don't want to freak anybody out. Or make them think I'm crazy. 'Cause I'm not, you know."

"We know," Lisa said.

"But there are people out there who wouldn't understand," Gordon said. "People like Sam Wiggan. And worse than Sam. Much worse. People who hate and fear what they don't understand."

"I'll be careful, Dad," Ethan said. "I just hope I didn't stir up a hornet's nest today."

"I'm sure it'll blow over," Lisa said reassuringly.

✠   ✠   ✠

But it didn't. The next day, Sam and other like-minded parishioners circulated a petition demanding that Reverend Ballard expel the Browns from the church in the absence of a more satisfactory apology from Ethan. This the reverend refused to do, and Sam's family and a number of others were absent from services the following Sunday, attending a rival church. Some parishioners seemed to blame Ethan and his parents for the schism.

Nothing was said to their faces, but there were plenty of nasty looks and whispers.

After the service, Ethan went to Reverend Ballard and offered to apologize.

"For what?" the reverend asked. "You only said what you believed."

"But look at the harm it's caused. I never meant for that to happen."

"Son, you didn't cause anything. The good Lord gave us free will, didn't He? I'm not going to lie to you. I wish you hadn't said what you did. I don't agree with it. But I don't hold with expelling people from this church just because I don't agree with 'em about everything. If I did that, this would be a congregation of one." He gave Ethan a wink. "Besides, if Mr. Wiggan and the others feel more at home in another church, why, God bless 'em. It doesn't matter what room we're in, does it, as long as we're under the same roof."

"No, sir. I guess it doesn't, at that."

✞ ✞ ✞

Later that same afternoon, Ethan was riding his bike to the pool when he met Sam Wiggan's son, Peter, riding his bike in the opposite direction with two of his friends, Tony Chang and Rob Campbell. Peter was two years older than Ethan; he was heavyset and strong, qualities which, combined with being a bit slow in school, had molded him into a thug and a bully. Tony and Rob were Peter's age; smaller and even slower, they followed him around like awestruck little brothers. The trio had never picked on Ethan before, so he just nodded and made to ride past them.

"You're not going anywhere, traitor," growled Peter, who turned his bike to block the path, forcing Ethan to screech to a halt.

"What do you want?" Ethan asked, gazing at Peter's scowling face over his handlebars. He couldn't help being afraid. He knew that Peter and the others could beat him to a pulp if they chose. And this section of the bike path ran through thick woods along a golf course; even though he could hear people playing golf on the other side of the trees, he knew they couldn't see him. Perhaps they would hear if he yelled for help, but he also knew that yelling for help wasn't an option. That might save him a beating today, but in the long run he would pay a higher price for it, being labeled a crybaby and a coward.

"What do you think we want?" sneered Peter. He climbed down from his bike, and let it fall to the path behind him. His hands made fists at his sides. His eyes were like two shards of ice. "Get off that bike, Al."

"Al?"

"Sure. Your name's Al Qaeda, isn't it?" He laughed, as did Tony and Rob, who still remained on their bikes, cutting off any chance of escape. "At least, that's what it sounded like in church the other day. My dad says people like you ought to just leave this country if you hate it so much."

"I don't hate it."

"Yeah? You got a funny way of showing it." He stepped closer. "Do you really believe all that crap you said? About God's house and everything?"

"Yes."

"Good. Here's where you get to practice turning the other cheek." For all his slowness, Peter could be quick when he wanted to be. Now his right hand shot out in a blur, the open palm striking Ethan's cheek with a loud smack.

Ethan, belatedly trying to dodge, only succeeded in falling, pulling the bike down on top of him to the laughter of Tony and Rob.

Peter stood over him, smirking. "Gonna cry now, Al?"

"No," Ethan managed, blinking back tears. He could feel anger pulsing through his veins, knotting up his muscles. But he wouldn't give in to it. Fighting Peter wouldn't solve anything. Violence was not the answer. He forced himself to stay down.

"You will," Peter promised and drew back his foot.

Ethan shut his eyes, waiting for the blow. Pain exploded in his left calf as Peter's foot struck home. He was determined not to cry, no matter what. But he was equally determined not to fight.

"Like that?" asked Peter. "Here's another."

"Pete, someone's coming," said Tony in a low and urgent hiss.

Peter stopped and slowly turned.

Ethan took the opportunity to clamber out from under the bike. His knees were bleeding where the frame had struck him, the back of his head ached, and his calf throbbed painfully, but those seemed to be the extent of his injuries . . . so far.

Approaching them on a red bike was a girl in a halter-top and shorts who looked to be Ethan's age or slightly older. He couldn't remember having seen her before. She came to a stop, straddling her bike in a beam of sunlight that pierced the trees, her long, blond hair and tan skin almost seeming to glow from within.

"You're bleeding," she observed.

Ethan nodded, rendered speechless. The girl's eyes were too big for her narrow face, a narrowness only accentuated by her long hair. Her chin was too sharp, her nose not sharp enough, and her teeth were in need of braces. Yet something about her made Ethan feel tingly inside, as if he were in the presence of a beautiful angel.

Peter, obviously, didn't like angels. "Get lost, Maggie."

"Or what? Are you going to beat me up too?"

"Serve you right if I did."

"Ooh, I'm real scared." She rolled her cornflower blue eyes, then looked at Ethan. "I'm Maggie. What's your name?"

"Ethan."

Her eyes grew even wider. "I heard about you. You're that kid from Peter's old church."

"That's right," said Peter. "This is Ethan Brown, the traitor. Otherwise known as Al Qaeda." He laughed again, echoed dutifully by Tony and Rob.

Maggie ignored them. "I think it was brave of you to make that speech," she said, her eyes shining. "I wish I'd been there to see it!"

"Looks like we got another traitor, boys," said Peter without taking his eyes from Maggie's face. "Usually I don't hit girls, but I'll make an exception in your case if you don't get lost."

She smiled back sweetly. "What a coincidence. I usually don't hit boys."

"Grab her," Peter said.

"Huh?" asked Tony.

"Grab her!"

"But—but she's . . ."

"For God's sake, grab her before she gets away!"

Rob lurched awkwardly away from his bike and grabbed Maggie by one arm, even though she'd made no move to flee. Then, before she could shrug him off, Tony had grasped her other arm. She didn't attempt to struggle, just looked at Peter in disbelief. "Have you lost your mind?"

"Not so tough now, are you?" smirked Peter, hands on his hips.

"Let her go," said Ethan.

Peter laughed. "Or what? You gonna *bleed* on me, Al?"

Tony sniggered. "Good one, Pete."

"Yeah," Rob agreed. "Good one."

"Al here is gonna be the main course," Peter said to Maggie. "I'm saving you for dessert." He licked his lips.

Maggie spat into his face.

Peter licked the spittle away.

Ethan watched with a sinking heart. It was one thing to let himself be beaten by Peter and his goons without fighting back. That was his decision to make. But it was quite another to stand back and witness Maggie suffer a beating or worse for his sake. He found that he couldn't let it happen. Something in him, that small voice that had spoken in the church, awoke again and recoiled.

No.

For an instant, Ethan's vision sharpened beyond all possibility, and it was as if he were seeing into Peter. Into his mind. His heart. His very soul. In that glimpse, he saw a simple error. A flaw in how events had shaped him. Or perhaps it was more in the nature of a scar. But whatever it was, without thinking, instinctively, Ethan reached out and fixed it.

Peter gasped as if he'd been struck in the belly. All the color drained from his face, and his eyes lost their focus. He swayed as if he might fall.

Tony and Rob looked on in shock as, with a groan, Peter dropped to his knees.

"Pete?" said Tony. "Are you okay, man?"

Peter looked up. His eyes were no longer flecks of ice, flat and hard, reflecting everything like mirrors. Now it was as if the ice had melted, leaving pools of deep, pristine blue. The world seemed to pour into those eyes. "Let her go," he said softly.

"Huh?" said Tony. "But—"

"I said let her go," Peter said again, getting to his feet. He gazed at Ethan, and there was fear in his newborn eyes, along with something else, something very much like awe. Then he shook his head and looked away, as if staring at a bright light. He bent to retrieve his bike. "Come on, you guys," he said as he mounted it. "Let's get out of here."

"Wow," said Maggie as she watched the three of them ride off, Tony and Rob casting curious looks back, while Peter rode without turning his head even once. "*That* was weird."

✠   ✠   ✠

He was in Santa Fe when he received word through the usual channels. He had been there for some weeks, narrowing his leads in pursuit of a pregnant woman identified by Grand Inquisitor as the likely mother of a high potential.

But now it seemed there was another job for him.

A job of the utmost urgency.

Reports from Kansas indicated that a high potential there was coming into his powers.

The Antichrist was waking.

He was on a plane within hours.

CHAPTER 11

Sister Elena hesitated outside the door, smelling the pungent aroma of cigar smoke. The last time she'd been inside this room had been seven months ago . . . and the memories of everything that had passed between her and her father were still fresh and painful in her mind.

You're crazy!

Kate, please listen. I—

You should see a shrink. Or a priest.

As soon as I'm back from Iraq, I'm going to get to the bottom of this . . .

She'd walked out. Turned her back on him and his sick delusions. Never dreaming that she would never see him again.

Now he was dead. Dead and buried thousands of miles away, back in South Carolina, in the private cemetery that held the bones of her ancestors and the ashes of her mother. He'd been laid to rest with an honor guard, the governor of South Carolina and the vice president of the United States in attendance. He was, they said, a hero.

Hero.

The word was like ashes on her tongue. The army had sent her a letter containing the citation accompanying his second, posthumous Silver Star. She'd thrown it away unread.

She hadn't gone to the funeral.

She was an orphan now. Alone in the world.

Alone? No, God was with her.

He wasn't through with her yet.

Sister Elena knew that God had taken Bill, just as He'd taken Glory. It was the punishment she'd called down on herself and her loved ones when she'd lost faith and courage and selfishly begged God to make someone else bear the burden of being the mother of His son. And God had answered her prayer.

But she hadn't known what the consequences of that prayer were going to be. If she'd known, if she'd had even a glimmering of a suspicion what was going to happen, she never would have asked to be spared the fate for which God had chosen her. Now, because of her, Glory and Bill were dead.

And Ethan. Ethan had been the first to die.

Her beautiful son.

Sister Elena had only glimpsed him once, only held him briefly in her arms, before his damaged heart had stopped. And then she'd held him again, clutched his cold, dead body to her breast and wept until she'd thought that blood and not tears must be flowing from her eyes. But all her tears, all her prayers, hadn't been enough to bring him back.

Years passed. Life at Santa Marta settled into a pattern that soothed her soul, even if it could not heal it, and there were days, entire weeks even, when Sister Elena forgot about the girl she had been, the girl who had been called Kate.

Then God had taken Glory.

At first, Sister Elena felt betrayed, as if God had broken the terms of some agreement between them. She'd raged and cursed, half mad with grief and anger. But of course there had been no agreement. Did God make deals with human beings? Even to imagine such a thing was a prideful sin. Thus had Sister Elena compounded her offense against God, and she'd trembled in anticipation of the punishment that was sure to follow. But as time went by, and the circumstances of her life continued unaltered, she'd once again become complacent. Forgotten that God does not forget.

And then her father had shown up out of the blue and told her that he thought Ethan was still alive. His words had been like a red-hot poker thrust into her wounded soul. They were unbearable.

Impossible.

Insane.

And yet . . . they had kindled hope in her. She didn't believe them, but she wanted to believe. If only it were true, and Ethan were alive! She didn't even want him back; it would have been enough, more than enough, to know that he existed somewhere, that he was healthy and loved. Oh, she tried not to think about it, tried not to imagine what kind of boy he must be, what he looked like, the sound of his voice, the color of his eyes, the smell of his hair. But she couldn't help it. The idea of him alive was like fresh, pure water to her after years of wandering in the desert. She drank deeply of the thought of him.

And thus had she compounded her offense still further, for if Ethan really were alive, that must mean that God was a liar and a cheat—that He had played with her as a boy might play with a bug, torturing it for pure pleasure, just to watch it squirm. And not only that—it would mean that Papa Jim, Father Rinaldi, and everyone else at the convent was involved in a conspiracy against her, that they had stolen away her child, God's child . . . Why? No answer made sense. Each possibility that came to her mind was crazier than the last.

Yet she couldn't dismiss the doubts, the fantasies. Even though she knew they were mad. And worse, sinful. Like all temptations, they came from the devil. Sister Elena prayed for the strength to resist them. Prayed also that her father might find peace and acceptance, for she had no doubt it had been his inability to come to terms with Glory's death that triggered his bizarre ideas about Ethan.

Then God had taken Bill.

Something broke in Sister Elena when she heard the news. It was Papa Jim who told her, in a telephone call from the States. She listened numbly, hardly speaking a coherent word, and then hung up on him. He'd called right back, but she'd refused to talk to him, nor had she talked to him since, though he'd called every single day, and Father Rinaldi and the abbess had both ordered her to do so.

Now he had come in person to see her.

He was on the other side of the door, in the room where she'd last seen her father, waiting for her just as Bill had waited seven short months ago . . .

Now Bill was dead.

Would Papa Jim be next?

She was afraid that God would take him too. That her grandfather was already as good as dead. And she couldn't stop it. Couldn't even warn him. She could only try to cut herself off from the loss, the pain. Protect herself, even if she couldn't protect him.

But it wasn't as easy as that. Papa Jim was a man used to getting his own way. And sure enough, here he was, and here she was, and there was only a thin door separating them, a door she was going to have to open and walk through sooner rather than later, even if it was just about the last thing she wanted to do.

Best to get it over with, she thought.

Taking a deep breath, Sister Elena opened the door and stepped into the room.

Papa Jim, who had been standing with his back to the door, gazing out the window at the Tuscan hills, turned sharply at the noise of her entrance, a hopeful expression on his face that nearly broke her heart to see, made her realize how selfish she'd been, concerned only with mitigating her own pain, while he was suffering too, his daughter and son-in-law gone, no one left to turn to for comfort but her. As soon as he realized it was her, he plucked the cigar from his lips and grinned hugely. "Hey there, baby girl."

"Oh, Papa Jim." And to her own surprise, she burst into tears.

"Don't cry, honey," he said, stubbing out his cigar on the window ledge and leaving it there as he advanced toward her, moving ponderously but with confidence. At sixty-three, he was heavier than ever but as vigorous as a man ten years younger. "Papa Jim's here now." He put his arms around her, enveloping her in the familiar smell of him: of aftershave, whiskey, and cigar smoke. It felt like coming home.

She clung to him for a time, until her sobs subsided enough for her to find her voice again. "I'm sorry, Papa Jim."

"For what?"

"All those times you called, and I never . . ." She trailed off, ashamed.

He stepped back and regarded her. "It's Bill, isn't it?"

She looked at him quizzically.

"Honey, I don't want to say anything against your dad. He was a brave man, a good husband and father. A genuine American hero. But ever since your mother died, God rest her soul, he just wasn't the same man. I'm not telling you anything you don't already know."

"He loved her so much . . ."

"We all did," said Papa Jim. "But the thing is, your dad began to get some pretty strange ideas."

"Strange?"

Papa Jim nodded. "For a long time, he believed that Glory was still alive. Even after her remains had been recovered and identified. He wouldn't believe it was really her. Thought that she'd left him, run off with another man or something. Faked her own death."

"I . . . I didn't know that. He never told me."

"I convinced him not to say anything to you until he had proof. And then I helped him look for it. Finally, he accepted that she was gone. That was when he quit Congress and joined the Rangers. I tried to talk him out of it, but he was determined to avenge her. Personally, I'd just as soon leave revenge to God. But even though I didn't agree with what he was doing, I still prayed that it would work out, that being in the Army would help your dad come to grips with what had happened and see that his real responsibilities lay with the living, not the dead. But it didn't turn out that way. Before he left for Iraq, he started in on something else."

"Oh God," Sister Elena breathed, suddenly understanding. "Dad came here with a crazy story about Ethan. Said he'd seen a letter or something on your desk, Papa Jim, and that Ethan wasn't dead, that he was still alive . . ."

Papa Jim sighed heavily. "I thought maybe that was why you were refusing to talk to me. Because you believed him . . ."

"No, Papa Jim, no. I didn't believe it. Oh God, I wanted to! I wished it could be true. But it was crazy. I told him so and walked out on him. It was the last conversation we had before . . . before . . ." She couldn't go on.

Papa Jim was there again, his arms enfolding her. "There, there, baby girl. Let it all out."

"He must have thought I hated him," she sobbed. "He never knew how much I loved him. He died without knowing!"

"He knew," Papa Jim said firmly. "He knew."

After a while, Sister Elena dried her eyes with a handkerchief that Papa Jim gave her and they sat down on the sofa.

"I'm sorry I didn't come to the funeral," she said.

"It was a bit of a sideshow," he confessed. "A media circus, frankly. But he and Glory are buried side by side. They're together again, on Earth and in Heaven. I hope you'll come visit one day soon. We can go there together."

"I'd like that," she said.

"Are you happy here, honey? Are you ready to come home?"

"This is my home now, Papa Jim."

He sighed again. "I figured, but I had to ask. I miss you, honey."

"I miss you too, Papa Jim."

"You're all I've got left, baby girl. You mean the world to me. You know I'd do anything for you, don't you?"

"I know," she said, and kissed him on the cheek.

CHAPTER 12

It was raining when the plane touched down at Johnson County Executive Airport. Although traveling under an assumed name and identity, the tall, clean-shaven man with the brown leather carry-on passed through security without difficulty, just as he had when boarding in San Diego; it was laughable, he thought to himself, how ineffective were the supposedly strict protocols put into place at the nation's airports following 9/11. If he had been a terrorist, intent on killing innocent Americans, he could have racked up a body count far exceeding the number of victims in the World Trade Center attacks by now.

But of course, he wasn't a terrorist.

He was a priest.

A man of God entrusted with a sacred mission. Like the knights of old, he was a shield and a sword in a battle as ancient as the world itself, the only battle that really mattered: the one between good and evil, God and the devil.

And here, in Olathe, Kansas, another engagement in that long battle was about to be fought. If Grand Inquisitor was correct, and in the priest's experience it always had been, he would find a young Antichrist here, nine or ten years old, newly awakened to his powers and perhaps even his identity. The boy had foolishly drawn attention to himself by speaking out at a church service a week ago—a single slip, but enough to alert GI to his existence. It wasn't clear yet whether Conversatio was involved, but the priest was doubtful. In his experience, Conversatio agents would have prevented a boy in their charge from revealing himself so blatantly. No, this was probably the case of a high potential who had fallen through the cracks, missed by both Conversatio and the Congregation. Such oversights were inevitable, although it was rare for a boy to remain undetected for so long. In any case, the priest thought, the boy was undetected no longer. Now, with God's help, the abomination would be killed, even at the cost of the priest's own life. It was a price he would willingly pay to safeguard his flock, just as Christ had paid.

Outside the airport, he hailed a taxi to drive him the four miles into Olathe proper. The Congregation had already booked him a hotel room, where he would find the tools of his trade waiting.

"What brings you to Olathe, my friend?" inquired the cabbie, a bearded, dark-skinned man with a Middle Eastern look about him and the accent to go with it. "Business or pleasure?"

"A little of both," he replied.

"You know what you should do while you're here?" the man asked, glancing into the rearview mirror before answering his own question. "Hot-air ballooning. Ever try it?"

"Can't say that I have."

"Best way to see the countryside," the man affirmed. "Up there amid the clouds, it's so peaceful. So quiet. Gives you a new perspective on things."

"A bird's-eye view, eh?"

The cabbie chuckled. "My friend, it is an angel's-eye view!"

The priest blinked, startled despite himself. The cab driver had just spoken the code word to identify himself as an agent of the Congregation. Not once in his years of fieldwork had a fellow agent broken cover to contact the priest directly in this way. It was permitted only in exceptional circumstances. But he recovered quickly from his surprise and gave the required countersign.

"We've done some preliminary surveillance on the boy," the cabbie said in a businesslike tone of voice, all trace of his accent vanished. "His name's Ethan Brown. He's under Conversatio protection."

The priest grunted, more disappointed than surprised. "The standard complement? Two agents posing as man and wife?"

"Not posing. They *are* man and wife. They do that sometimes, for the most promising cases."

"I'm aware of that." He found it somewhat distasteful to be spoken to as if he were a greenhorn on his first assignment. "I've handled Conversatio agents before."

"Not like these."

"What do you mean?"

"The woman is a tenth-degree black belt in the Shorin-ryu style of karate. She is as deadly with her bare hands as she is with a katana or a pistol."

"I see. And the man?"

"Even better."

"But not good enough to stop their charge from revealing himself."

The driver glanced again into the rearview mirror as he merged into traffic. "Don't let that failure cause you to underestimate the Browns. They are skilled and smart. And what's more, they truly believe that the boy is the second son. So they will fight with the zeal of true fanatics."

"Let them. What you seem to see as a strength, I look upon as a weakness. These people are either deluded or evil. Either way, I have the one advantage that really matters."

"Surprise?"

"No. God. 'The Lord will provide.' We're doing His work, after all."

"Yes, but the devil is strong. If this boy really is the Antichrist, you're going to need more than faith to finish the job. That's why I've been assigned to assist you."

The priest bristled at that. "I work alone," he growled.

"Not this time," the driver said. "My orders come from Rome, from the Holy Father himself. If you care to dispute them . . ." He let his words dangle ominously.

"Of course not," the priest said. "It's just . . . unusual for the Holy Father to take such a personal interest."

"Oh, His Holiness keeps himself thoroughly informed, never fear. More so than his predecessor, in fact. Not too surprising, really. After all, he ran the Congregation himself for many years before ascending to the Throne of St. Peter."

"I know the history," the priest said dryly.

"But do you know the prophecy?" responded the driver. He continued without waiting for a response. "In 1148, St. Malachy of Ireland prophesied that there would be 112 more popes before the coming of the Antichrist. Pope Benedict is number 111."

The priest snorted. "I always heard it was Nostradamus who made that particular prophecy."

"Does it matter who made it? The important point is that it exists. And that so far it has been absolutely accurate. Each of the future popes is identified in a short Latin motto, not by name but by a defining quality or characteristic. For example, the one hundred and tenth pope in the list received the motto *De labore Solis.*"

"'Of the labor of the sun,'" the priest translated.

"Karol Wojtyla, who became John Paul II, was born during one solar eclipse and buried during another."

"Coincidence."

"Perhaps. The motto of the one hundred and eleventh pope in the list was *De Gloria Olivae.*"

"'Of the glory of the olive.'"

"The olive branch is the symbol of St. Benedict. And as we all know, Joseph Ratzinger chose the name Benedict XVI. Is that also a coincidence? No, these are not coincidences, Father. At least, His Holiness does not believe that they are."

"And what of the hundred and twelfth pope? The last on the list. What is his motto?"

"Ah, that's where things get really interesting. You see, that pope *is* identified by name." He cleared his throat and recited rather histrionically, '*In persecutione extrema S.R.E. sedebit Petrus Romanus, qui pascet oves in multis tribulationibus: quibus transactis civitas septicollis diruetur, et Iudex tremêndus iudicabit populum suum. Finis.*' I'll save you the trouble of translating on the fly. It means, 'During the final persecution of the Holy Roman Church, the seat will be occupied by Peter of Rome, who will feed his sheep in many tribulations; and when these things are finished, the seven-hilled city will be destroyed, and the terrible Judge will judge his people. The End.'"

"And His Holiness believes that this . . . Peter II will succeed him?"

"What His Holiness believes is that in order for the prophecy to occur, the Antichrist must be alive right now, today. And this boy, this Ethan Brown, looks to be the most promising candidate yet."

"Then why not bring in some really big guns?" the priest wondered aloud. "Why just the two of us? I mean, I'm good, but why leave anything to chance?"

"Perhaps if we fail, bigger guns, as you call them, will be brought in. But why risk triggering a panic now? GI has run an assessment on this one. There is a better than 85 percent chance that Ethan is the Antichrist. And a better than 90 percent chance that you and I can succeed in killing him if we act immediately. But the longer we delay, the more that percentage drops."

The priest nodded. "That's good enough for me," he said. "What's the plan?"

"I think you're going to appreciate this," said the driver with a grin.

✠   ✠   ✠

This time it happened on the way back from the pool. Ethan had ridden his bike over after lunch and stayed for almost three hours. He'd splashed around halfheartedly with some friends in the crowded, lukewarm water for a while, then lay on his towel pretending to read. But really he was looking for the girl he'd met yesterday, Maggie.

She'd been coming from the pool when she'd stumbled upon Peter Wiggan and his cronies in the process of beating him up, so he figured there was a good chance that she'd come to the pool again at some point, perhaps even today. Why not? It was a hot day in the middle of a hot summer. What else was there to do?

He didn't admit to anyone that he was looking for her. He barely even admitted it to himself. Ethan was almost ten, but though he and his friends had begun to notice girls their age, none of them had yet turned their interest into anything more than talk. But Maggie was different than the other girls Ethan knew. It wasn't that she was prettier . . . though she was pretty in an unusual way, with her big eyes and narrow face. No, it was something else about her, some inner quality that had shone forth for Ethan to see in those moments when she had stood up to Peter and his gang.

It had been sort of like when he'd found himself looking into Peter and had seen the wrongness inside him and had fixed it. Only there was no wrongness inside Maggie. Or anyway, nothing twisted and scarred like he'd seen in Peter.

It still freaked him out, what had happened with Peter. He hadn't mentioned it to his parents when he'd gotten home. He was pretty sure, after the talk they'd given him, that they wouldn't be too happy if they knew what had transpired. But the thing was, Ethan himself didn't know what had transpired. Certainly, nothing like it had ever happened to him before.

It really had been as though he could see past the surface of Peter's skin and into some other reality beneath the skin; not in the way an X-ray could peek past the epidural layer to reveal the underlying bones and organs, but as if he had glimpsed something even more deeply buried than that, something beyond the body entirely.

The soul.

He didn't know another word for it, so that was the one he used when he thought about it, trying to figure it all out. Not just what had happened, but why and how. What it meant. And whether it would happen again.

But he hadn't been able to answer any of those questions.

Maybe he would have figured something out by now if he hadn't been so distracted by thoughts of Maggie. Actually, they weren't really thoughts. They were more basic than thoughts. Feelings. Urges. A lot of mixed-up sensations and desires that tied his stomach into knots, yet made him want nothing more than to see her again. Or talk with her . . . though when he tried to think of what he might say, he found himself growing more mixed up than ever. Maybe he wouldn't have to say anything. Maybe he could just smile. He pictured himself standing beside her and smiling confidently. The image brought a flush of embarrassment to his cheeks.

Right. She'll think I'm some kind of idiot!

Okay, so maybe he wouldn't smile . . .

"Boring book?"

The voice startled Ethan out of his reverie, and he looked up to see his friend Alan Brooks grinning down at him, water dripping from his chin and the ends of his brown hair to pool on the pale concrete around his bare feet.

"Huh?"

"Dude, I was watching you from the pool. You've been on that page for like the last ten minutes! You keep looking over toward the entrance. Are you expecting somebody?"

"Oh . . ." Ethan glanced down, feeling himself blushing again. He couldn't recall having read a single word of the page before him. He closed the book with a sigh. "No, not really. I guess I'm just not in the mood for reading."

"Then come back in the pool," Alan said. "We're getting up a game of Sharks and Minnows."

Ethan shrugged his shoulders. "Nah, I think I'll head home. It's getting kind of late."

"C'mon, man, just one game," Alan coaxed. "It'll be fun!"

Ethan was about to say no when he saw a flash of yellow coming out of the girl's locker room. It was Maggie, wearing a blue one-piece bathing suit and surrounded by a gaggle of friends. Alan, seeing him look away, followed his gaze.

"Ah-ha. Not expecting anybody, eh?"

Ethan didn't bother denying it. "Do you know her?"

"Which one?"

"The girl with the blond hair. I think her name's Maggie."

"You think? Dude, sometimes I think you're from another planet or something."

"What do you mean?"

"That's Maggie Richardson."

Maggie and her friends had stopped to talk to one of the lifeguards, a teenage boy with tribal tattoos on one arm and leg. The girls clustered around him, giggling shrilly as he talked. "Is that supposed to mean something?"

"Um, yeah. Richardson, as in Mayor Richardson . . ."

He glanced at Alan in surprise. "She's the mayor's daughter?" Suddenly he remembered how surprised Tony and Rob had been when Peter had ordered them to grab her. Surprised . . . and frightened.

"No shit, Sherlock," Alan answered, rolling his eyes. "Her dad's like super rich. I mean, they've got their own pool and everything. But, you know, he makes her go to public pools just so he can look like a regular guy and all. Especially around election time. At least, that's what my dad says. How lame is that?"

"How come she doesn't go to our school?"

"I guess he doesn't want to look like a regular guy *that* much! She goes to some private Catholic school. Hey, how come you're asking all these questions, Ethan? Are you sweet on her?"

"Me? I don't even know her!"

The girls had turned away from the lifeguard and were surveying the pool area like shoppers sizing up bargains. Ethan felt his heart skip a beat as his eyes locked with Maggie's. She raised her hand in a wave and came striding toward him. The others followed at her heels.

"Maybe you don't know her, but it sure looks like she knows you," Alan observed in an undertone as Maggie came up to them.

"Hi, Ethan," she said brightly.

"Uh, hi, Maggie," he somehow managed to get out. Although he'd been hoping and praying for just such a moment as this, now that it was here, he felt too nervous to enjoy it. "This is my friend Alan."

"Hey, Alan," she said, flashing them both a smile that did something peculiar to Ethan's insides. "Wow, it's hot, isn't it? You guys going in?"

"Yeah, we were just getting up a game of Sharks and Minnows," Ethan heard himself saying. "You want to play?"

"Sure!"

"Cool!" He grinned at her just as he had pictured himself doing moments earlier, but now he didn't care if he looked like an idiot or not.

The next hour or so passed in a blissful daze. He had the pleasure of being close to Maggie, but because there were so many other kids around, he was never alone with her and consequently never had to figure out what to say. Once, when she was the shark, she even caught him, grabbing hold of his ankle as he tried to swim beneath her and hauling him up to the surface.

"Caught you!" she gasped as their heads broke the water.

He couldn't deny that she had. Or that he'd let himself be caught.

Later, as he rode his bike home along the wooded path, Ethan couldn't stop thinking about how beautiful Maggie had looked with water sparkling on her pale skin and red hair and laughter on her lips and in her eyes. Perhaps if he'd been paying less attention to these memories and more to the bike path, he would have noticed Peter Wiggan waiting up ahead. But as it was, he didn't spot the bigger boy until he was nearly on top of him.

Then, before he could do more than slam on his brakes, Peter had stepped fully out of the trees and onto the path. He grabbed Ethan's handlebars. Ethan struggled to pull away, but it was useless. There was no way he could break Peter's grip. He wasn't going anywhere.

"Look, if this is about yesterday—," he began.

"What did you do to me?" Peter broke in. His voice wasn't angry or demanding. He spoke softly and calmly but with an intensity that could not be ignored.

"I—I don't know," Ethan said. "Let me go."

Peter's placid blue eyes didn't leave Ethan's face. "Please," he said. "I'm not going to hit you or anything. But you have to tell me." And with that, he released the handlebars.

The gesture was so unexpected that Ethan was taken completely by surprise, and before he could react, the bike toppled over, taking him with it. He landed with a bone-jarring thud on the asphalt path, and then the bike, as it had the day before, crashed on top of him.

"Oh, crap," Peter cried out, lifting the bike off him. "Are you okay?"

Ethan blinked up at him mistrustfully. He more than half expected Peter to kick him as he had the day before. But instead, the boy reached out a big hand to help Ethan to his feet. Ethan took the offered hand gingerly, wincing as Peter pulled him up.

"Jeez, I didn't mean for that to happen," Peter said.

There was real anguish in his eyes and in his voice. Ethan realized that Peter was telling the truth. And he also realized, much as he'd been trying to deny it, that this was not the same Peter who had faced him yesterday. That Peter was gone. In his place was a different boy. A new boy. And somehow, Ethan was responsible for the change. The thought of that left him feeling queasy inside, as if he'd done something truly bad, crossed some line that he had no right to cross and in doing so invaded the sanctity of another person. In school the teachers were always warning them about grownups or older kids who might try to touch them in inappropriate ways, on parts of their bodies that no one had the right to touch because they were private, personal. He felt like he'd done something like that to Peter, only even worse.

"I'm okay," Ethan told him now. "It was an accident. No harm done."

"Not this time, maybe," Peter said. "But other times I did lots of harm. And not by accident either."

Ethan didn't know how to reply.

But Peter didn't give him a chance in any case. Words came pouring out of his mouth as though a dam had burst. "It's like . . . all my life I lived in shadows and thought I was in the light. But now I know that I never saw real light until yesterday. I was missing something, you know? Something— I don't know what to call it—that was keeping me from seeing other people as, well, people. Nobody was real to me. And the only way I could prove *I* was real was to make other people afraid of me. Hurt them and make them suffer. I never saw that I was afraid too. I was hurt and suffering without even knowing it. But you changed that, Ethan. You changed me."

"I—"

"Don't bother denying it. We both know it's true."

Ethan sighed. "Okay, maybe I did something, but I didn't mean to. I'm sorry for it. I really feel awful. I'd fix things if I knew how."

"Fix things?"

"You know. Change you back the way you were."

"Are you nuts? I don't want that! Jeez, this is the best thing that's ever happened to me!" Peter paused, a fearful look creeping into his eyes. "You're not going to do it, are you?"

"What?"

"You know. Change me back. Please, don't—I'll do anything you want!"

"I don't want you to do anything," Ethan said hastily. "Besides, I don't know how it works. I couldn't change you back even if you begged me to. Look, you won't tell anybody, will you?"

"Not if you don't want me to. But I don't see why you should feel so awful about what you did, Ethan. I'm not a bully anymore. I'm not afraid."

"Yeah, but what gave me the right to do it?"

"Hello? What gave you the right was that I was going to beat the crap out of you and then start in on the girl! You were defending yourself."

"Maybe. But it still doesn't feel right . . ."

"Jeez, listen to yourself! Who do you think you are, Peter Parker? You know, 'With great power comes great responsibility?'"

"Well, it does, doesn't it?"

"How the heck should I know? Hey, do you think you're, you know, like Spidey? A mutant or something?"

"That would be cool. But I haven't been bitten by any radioactive spiders lately."

"Maybe you're an alien."

"Not the last time I looked."

"But you're different from other people," Peter insisted. "I can see it. Feel it. Whatever you did to me, that's part of it. I look at you, and I see . . ." He trailed off.

"See what?" asked Ethan.

Peter suddenly looked embarrassed. "You'll think this is weird."

"Man, it's *all* weird," he said. "Go on, tell me."

"Well, there's a kind of glow around you. A golden light."

"You see that now?"

"Yeah, I do."

"How come I can't see it? How come nobody else can?"

"I don't know. It was super bright yesterday. Almost blinding. Man, I couldn't even look at you! It's not so bright today. But it's still there."

Ethan held a hand up before his face. It looked completely ordinary. There was no glow emanating from his skin. Just a raw patch on his palm where he'd scraped it in his fall. He shook his head. He didn't understand any of this. What was happening to him? "Look, I'd better be getting home."

Peter nodded, then reached down and picked up Ethan's bike. "Here you go."

"Thanks." He climbed on. "Well, I guess I'll see you around."

"Don't worry," Peter said. "I won't tell anybody. I promise."

"Thanks."

"And I'm sorry for hitting you yesterday," Peter added. "It won't happen again."

"I'm just a regular kid, Peter," Ethan told him. "You don't have to be afraid of me or anything."

"I'm not," Peter said. "I came out here today just to say thanks. The way I look at it, you did me a favor. I owe you one."

"How'd you know to find me here?"

"I went to your house first. Your mom told me you'd gone to the pool."

Ethan nodded, then pushed off and began to pedal home. When Peter had stepped out of the woods, he'd expected another beating. Instead, it seemed as if he might have made a new friend. Literally *made* a new friend, in that he was responsible for this new Peter: He had made him. But despite everything Peter had said, Ethan still wasn't comfortable with what he'd done. All he knew for sure was that the last couple of days had been the strangest of his life.

And he had a feeling that things were going to get even stranger.

He pedaled faster, suddenly hungry. It was Friday, which meant games and pizza at the Brown house. Every Friday, his dad would call on his way home from work, his mom would order from Domino's, and then the three of them would play an old-fashioned board game like Monopoly or Risk or Parcheesi while they ate. Later, they would watch a movie. It was all kind of corny, but Ethan liked it, and today especially he needed the ordinariness of it, the comfort of falling into a familiar routine.

✠   ✠   ✠

"I'm home, Mom," he called out as he banged open the front door of the house and barged inside. "Sorry I'm late!"

His mother called from the kitchen, "Your father called to say he's having car trouble and not to wait up. I already ordered the pizza. It should be here any minute, so you better hurry!"

"I'm just going to change out of my swimsuit," he called back, already taking the stairs two at a time. His mom yelled something in reply, but he couldn't hear her over the closing of his bedroom door behind him. He stepped out of his damp bathing suit, kicking it into one corner of the room, where discarded clothes were haphazardly strewn, and pulled on a fresh pair of shorts and a clean T-shirt. One of the windows in his room overlooked the street below, and he saw the pizza-delivery car approaching.

He rushed back out of his room, down the stairs, and into the kitchen. "Mom, the pizza's here," he said. "I saw the car drive up. Can I get it?"

Lisa, who was sitting at the kitchen table drinking an ice tea, smiled at her son. "Sure, honey. Just hand me my purse, will you?"

Ethan did so.

Lisa fished out her wallet and handed a ten and a five to Ethan. "Tell him he can keep the change." She glanced sharply at her son's hand as he took the bills. "What's that from?"

Ethan shrugged. "It's nothing. I fell off my bike and scraped it a little, that's all."

"You'd better let me put some antiseptic on it."

"It's just a scratch, Mom."

Before she could reply, the doorbell rang, and Ethan took off like a shot for the front door. When he opened it, the pizza-delivery person, a tall, clean-shaven man who seemed a bit old for this line of work, his uniform ill-fitting and stained, was standing there with a box of pizza in his arms.

"Got your order here," he said. "Let's see: a large pizza, hand-tossed crust, with extra cheese, green peppers, pepperonis, and mushrooms. That about right?"

Ethan nodded; that was what they always ordered. He handed the man the money. "Keep the change," he said.

"Thanks, sport," said the man and gave him a wink before turning and walking back toward his car.

Ethan could feel the heat of the pizza through the heavy box. He hurried back to the kitchen and let the box slide onto the table. "Whew, that's hot!"

Lisa pushed back her chair and stood. "Why don't you get out the plates, honey, and I'll cut us each a slice."

"Okay." He was facing the cabinet, reaching up for the plates, when he heard a hissing sound, followed immediately by a gasp. He whipped around, already sensing the wrongness of it, just in time to see his mom falling forward as if her bones had turned to rubber. Her head landed in the pizza, bounced up, looking bloody from the sauce, then fell back and slid slowly across the surface of the pizza, pulled by the rest of her body, which was sinking in stages to the linoleum floor.

Ethan watched in a kind of horrified disbelief. He simply couldn't process what he was seeing. It was happening so fast, without any discernible cause or reason, that he felt as if he'd stepped into the middle of a nightmare. Then, as Lisa's head slid off the table completely, trailing strings of melted cheese topping, he gave an anguished cry and ran to her side.

He never made it.

He felt something sting his neck like a bee, and the next thing he knew, his legs weren't working anymore. He was falling, and as he fell his vision turned all grainy, and then the grains began to fly apart until there was only blackness.

✠   ✠   ✠

Lying on his back on the cold cement floor of the garage, Gordon concentrated on not blacking out. The lights of the ceiling seemed as distant and small as stars. The sound of his own breathing, on the other hand, might have been a whirlwind. It screamed and howled in his ears. If he closed his eyes, the whirlwind would lift him up, right out of his body, and spin him away. It was tempting, because he thought it would spin him to a place of silence and peace, a place without pain, where he could rest at last. But he knew he couldn't let that happen.

He cursed himself silently for a fool, trying to understand when he should have realized what was happening. He saw clearly, now that it was too late, how the last years had lulled him into a false sense of security. He'd forgotten that he was hunted, and that the hunters could appear at any moment to strike without warning or mercy.

Idiot, he berated himself. *You got soft . . .*

He should have suspected as soon as his car's engine seized up while he was driving home, forcing him to pull over to the side of the road. He should have called Lisa right then and there, instructed her to grab Ethan and run. They had contingency plans in place for just such a situation. It should have been instinctive. But instead, he'd simply called her and told her that he was having car trouble and would be a little late. "Go on and order the pizza without me," he'd said, as if he were an ordinary husband making an ordinary call to his ordinary wife.

Idiot.

His next call should have been to the emergency number that would have alerted Conversatio that there was a possibility his cover had been blown and Ethan was in danger. Again, it was—or should have been—automatic. But had he made that call?

No.

Instead, he'd called AAA. The voice that answered had told him that a tow truck was already in the area and would reach him within ten minutes.

That, too, should have raised red flags. It was too convenient by far. But instead, he'd sat complacently in his car and listened to a book on tape: for the past month, he'd been working his way through Hugo's *Les Miserables.*

When the tow truck had pulled over in front of him, and then backed up toward him, he'd turned off the engine and stepped out of the car. The driver, a dark-skinned man of vaguely Middle Eastern appearance and accent, had listened intently as he'd described the sudden grinding sound he'd heard and the violent shuddering of the car that had forced him to pull over. The man had asked him to pop the hood; that done, he'd peered at the engine, asked Gordon to start the car, listened for a moment, and then signaled for him to shut it off.

"It's the transmission," he'd informed him with an expression that for some reason made him think of a doctor telling a patient that the tests indicated cancer. "I'll have to tow you in. You can ride along if you like."

"Thanks. Any idea how long it'll take to fix?"

The man shrugged. "Hard to say. If I've got the parts, an hour or less. If not, you'll have to leave it."

"Maybe I should just call a cab to meet me at your garage."

"Why not wait until I've had a closer look?"

And not even that had triggered his suspicions.

Idiot!

Instead, he'd simply nodded, watched as the man hooked up his car, then climbed into the front of the tow truck. The man had climbed in beside him, started the truck, and merged smoothly back into traffic. He'd immediately launched into a rant about the Royals, who were having another bad season. Gordon feigned polite interest. Twenty minutes later, they were at the garage, his car in one of the repair bays.

Aside from the two of them, the place was empty.

Only then did Gordon's hackles begin to rise.

"Say, where is everybody?"

The man was looking under the hood again. He glanced up. "Hmm? Oh, big Sikh holiday today. They all work a half day."

"And how come you're not working a half day?"

"I am not Sikh," he said, and smiled. "Please. Come and look. I have found the problem. It is not so bad, after all."

Now, as he lay bleeding on the concrete floor, Gordon tried to reconstruct the sequence of events. What had warned him? Did it even matter at this point?

Yes, it matters, a voice inside him said. *You're still alive, aren't you?*

Barely, answered another voice.

Great. Now he was having conversations with himself.

But something had warned him. Even as he approached the open hood, he'd sensed that something was off. "Not the transmission?" he'd asked the man. "Then what?"

The man had stepped back from the hood and gestured for Gordon to take a look.

Gordon peered at the engine. He couldn't see anything out of place. Then he'd heard a faint sound from behind him, a whisper of air, and his instincts had kicked in at last. But not quickly enough. Even as he'd turned, he'd felt something sharp go into his left side once, twice, before he could get his arm up to turn aside the knife and deliver a clumsy kick that at least had the virtue of forcing his attacker back and buying him a few precious seconds to assess his situation.

It wasn't good.

He'd been stabbed twice; the pain wasn't too bad, but there was a lot of blood. Of course, it could have been worse. If he hadn't turned when he did, the blade would have gone up under his ribs and pierced his heart. He would be dead now.

The mechanic shifted the knife from hand to hand, grinning at him. He didn't say a word. He didn't need to.

He knew as well as Gordon did that time was on his side.

That left Gordon one option. He had to attack before the stab wounds and the loss of blood grew any more debilitating than they were already. But attack with what? He wasn't carrying a gun or a knife. The only object he had was his cell phone.

Without another thought, he whipped out the phone and threw it as though it were a shuriken. His opponent flinched for a second, then batted the phone away. But that second was all the time Gordon needed to close with the man.

If he could get rid of the knife, he might stand a chance. And so he went for that hand, grabbed the wrist, twisted sharply, and was rewarded by the crack of breaking bone and the sight of the knife dropping from nerveless fingers.

But at the same time, he felt a sharp pain in his right side; the man had another knife. Just his luck: The bastard was ambidextrous. Ignoring the pain, Gordon drove his head forward sharply, into the bridge of the man's nose. Another crack, and an explosion of blood.

Meanwhile, the knife struck again, though this was more of a glancing blow, a searing slice across his waist.

Still Gordon did not step back. He had to end this fast. He could already feel his strength ebbing.

He grabbed the man's shirt in both hands and twisted from the waist. The movement sent waves of agony through his body, as though his flesh were splitting open where he'd been cut. But it was effective. His opponent was sent flying, crashing head first into the open hood of Gordon's car. He sprawled there, half in and half out, as though he'd decided to take a nap on the engine block. He stirred weakly, but Gordon was already there. He slammed down the hood as hard as he could on the man's back. And again. And yet again.

After that, the man lay still.

The knife had fallen beside the front tire. Gordon stooped to retrieve it . . . and the next thing he knew, he was lying on the floor, looking up at the ceiling lights, feeling the blood seep out of him. His legs felt like they weighed a thousand pounds apiece.

Had he passed out? He couldn't tell. But he could feel unconsciousness hovering around him like a hungry shadow. It would devour him if it could.

No!

Minutes passed. Or hours. Finally, groaning with the effort, he turned and hauled himself to his feet using the limp legs of his attacker, drawing himself up bit by bit along that flesh-and-blood ladder until he was standing, leaning against the car and breathing as though he'd just run a marathon. Each breath was like a bellows, pumping blood from his body.

He had to staunch the bleeding.

There was no time to look for a first-aid kit. Luckily, he was in a garage, and that meant duct tape and plenty of it. He grabbed a roll from a nearby cart and proceeded to wrap the tape tightly around his midsection. It was ugly and messy work, but it might do the job long enough to get him home.

He retrieved his cell phone from where it had fallen. But when he tried to call Lisa, he couldn't get a signal. The damn thing was broken, useless. He threw it down in frustration.

Then he limped back to his car. It was in no shape to drive home, but at least he could do what he should have done at the start of this fiasco: open the trunk and remove his pistol. He checked the clip, then slid the automatic into the pocket of his bloody jacket. He hobbled over to the tow truck, every step a deeper initiation into the mysteries of pain. The keys were in the ignition. Wincing, he opened the door and maneuvered his body behind the wheel. The truck started right up. He pulled out of the garage and drove toward home. It was all he could do not to press the pedal to the floor. But it wouldn't do to be stopped by the police now. Nothing mattered but getting home. As he left the body of the man who had tried to kill him behind, Gordon's mind was focused entirely on that goal. The question of what he might find there was relegated to a distant future.

But when he saw the pizza-delivery car parked in the driveway, that distant future telescoped into a horrible here and now. His heart sank and he groaned aloud, afraid that his worst fears had been realized.

Yet he knew he couldn't go blundering into the house, gun blazing like some Bruce Willis–style hero in a Hollywood shoot-'em-up. That would only get him killed. No, he had to be smart now. And pray that he was not too late.

He parked a block away. He could barely get out of the truck, his legs had stiffened up so badly during the drive. But at last he managed it. The blood from his wounds had soaked his pants. He could feel it in his shoes. But the duct tape had done its job. It had held enough of his blood in to keep him alive. The rest was up to him.

With a prodigious effort, he began walking, or lurching, rather, circling around to the back of the house. By now it was late evening, and the shadows concealed his injuries; even so, he felt sure he must look like Frankenstein's monster. But when some neighbors waved at him from their porch, he waved back jauntily, as if he didn't have a care in the world, even though the stab of pain that accompanied the gesture made his vision flare red for a heartbeat.

Then he was at the back door of his house. He opened it and slipped inside.

He was in the laundry room. He froze, listening, but there were no sounds. The house was as silent as a tomb.

Cautiously, he crept to the door. On the other side was the kitchen. He put his ear to the door and listened. Again, he heard nothing. Finally, he turned the knob and slowly pushed the door open. Without noticing it, he had drawn his gun.

The first thing he saw was Lisa's body slumped on the kitchen floor. It took all his strength not to cry out and run to her side. But he forced himself to survey the kitchen first. It was empty. Only then did he creep up to her, still holding the gun ready.

Oh God, was that blood? Was she . . . ?

No. It was pizza topping. All in her hair and on the side of her face.

But she was still breathing, thank God.

She was unconscious, trussed up like an animal ready for slaughter.

Gordon moved to the utensil drawer, slid it open, and took out a steak knife. This he used to cut Lisa's bonds. But although free now, she would be no help. She was out like a light. Drugged, no doubt.

He was on his own.

Did he dare take the time to call Conversatio? He moved to the wall phone and lifted the receiver; as he'd more than half expected, there was no dial tone. The Congregation agent had cut the lines. The man at the garage had been overconfident, and it was that overconfidence, more than anything Gordon had done, that had proved his undoing. But Gordon had a feeling that the man (Congregation agents were always men, because they were always priests, and only men could be priests) who had done this to

Lisa, the man who was presumably still somewhere in the house (unless of course he'd abducted Ethan, taken him in another car and left the delivery car behind, which Gordon couldn't completely discount yet, even though his instincts told him the man was close by), that man was not the kind to trip himself up through hubris.

Then Gordon heard the sound of splashing water from upstairs. Followed by the creak of a footstep.

His heart surged, and for a terrible instant he felt himself grow dizzy, as if he might black out. But as he had before, he forced the shadows back.

He took a deep, slow breath. He was on his last reserves of strength. Actually, he was operating on sheer desperation and adrenaline now. Whatever he did, he would have to do it quickly, before his body betrayed him.

He couldn't face the man directly. He wouldn't have a prayer.

He needed a distraction.

Please God, let me save Ethan. Let me save my son!

✠   ✠   ✠

When Ethan opened his eyes again, it took him a moment to realize where he was. There were candles burning, the only source of light, and the tiny flames were reflecting off water in weird ways, making everything look dreamlike and spooky. But as the seconds passed, the strangeness fell away. What replaced it was no improvement.

He was in his bathroom, in the tub, which was filled with cold water.

He tried to get up, but he couldn't move; his arms and legs were tightly bound together. He tried to speak, to call for help, but his mouth was gagged. He was shivering from the cold and from fear.

He remembered his mother falling . . .

Was she okay?

What was happening?

He heard a voice mumbling outside the bathroom. Whoever had done this was out there. In his room.

He couldn't make out the words, but they didn't sound like English.

He tried again to free himself, succeeding only in splashing water out of the tub and onto the tiles of the floor.

The voice from the other room vanished.

Then a man stepped into the doorway.

It was the pizza-delivery man.

Only he wasn't wearing a Domino's uniform anymore.

He was wearing the garb of a priest.

And holding a knife in one hand.

The other hand was holding a vial of some sort.

As Ethan watched, petrified with terror, the man flicked the vial toward him, and he felt drops of liquid rain over his face.

"Does it burn?" the man asked.

Ethan shook his head stiffly.

"It's holy water," the man said, as if that should mean something.

Ethan just blinked.

The man entered the room and shut the door behind him . . . not completely, though; he left it open a crack. "In case we have any uninvited visitors," he said and gave Ethan the same wink he'd given him outside the front door.

Then he dropped to his knees beside the tub, laid his knife and vial carefully on the tub's edge, brought his hands together, bowed his head, and intoned what sounded like "Domino's do business."

It was so absurd, so insane, that Ethan couldn't help laughing behind his gag. But his laughter was full of desperation and fear. It might as well have been a scream.

The man glanced up at him. "I'll make it fast," he said. "Don't worry, you won't feel a thing. I don't torture people, even people like you. If you're worried about your mother, don't be. For one thing, she's not really your mother. For another, I'm not going to kill her. That was just gas in the pizza box. Knocked her right out. So much for that tenth-degree black belt!"

He chuckled.

Ethan had no idea what the man was talking about. He was obviously out of his mind.

"My partner's taking care of your dad," he continued, "so don't be expecting any help from that quarter. Not that he's really your father, either. No more than the woman tied up downstairs is your mother. They're both servants of the Evil One."

Ethan was whimpering now. Tears were streaming from his eyes.

The man dressed as a priest raised one hand and made the sign of the cross over him. He said more words in that strange-sounding language.

Ethan knew absolutely that he was going to die in the next few minutes unless he could somehow get away. But tied up as he was, that didn't seem too likely. And even if he could somehow slip free of his bonds, the crazy man was bigger and stronger than he was.

But maybe there was a way . . .

Yesterday, when he'd realized that Peter was going to hurt Maggie, he'd reached out with a power he'd never suspected he possessed and changed Peter, transformed him from a bully into a boy who'd been ashamed of what he'd been about to do. A boy who had let them go.

Could he do the same now? To this man?

He stared at him, trying to force his vision beyond the physical, into the very soul of the man.

"Stop staring at me like that or I'll blindfold you," said the man. "In fact, I think I'd better anyway."

He reached into his robe, or whatever you called the bright red garment he was wearing, and pulled out a blindfold, which he slipped over Ethan's eyes with practiced ease.

Darkness descended.

The man began to speak again in whatever language it was, Latin maybe. Was he praying?

Ethan began to pray too, silently.

Please, God, don't let him kill me. Don't let him hurt my mom and dad . . .

As terrifying as it had been to watch what was happening, being unable to see was infinitely worse. Each sound seemed to take on a malefic aspect, and each cessation of sound, however brief, seemed to presage the touch of the knife he'd seen, its sharp blade drawn across his throat or plunged into his chest.

He couldn't concentrate on praying. He couldn't concentrate on anything except the hypnotic ebb and flow of words and other sounds, the gentle splashing of water, even the trembling of the candle flames, which made a fluttering noise, like wings.

And then he heard another noise.

"Ethan! Are you okay? Lisa?"

It was his dad.

The crazy man tsked in annoyance. "If you want something done right, you have to do it yourself. Don't go anywhere; I'll be right back."

Then came the most awful and unbearable silence of all. It stretched and stretched. And finally, suddenly, broke.

There was a gunshot. Then two more in quick succession. And then two more.

Then footsteps slowly climbing the stairs.

⌖　　　⌖　　　⌖

"Ethan! Are you okay? Lisa?"

Gordon tried to keep the weakness and pain from his voice. Tried to make himself sound like any anguished father might. He had opened the front door before calling out. His hope was that the Congregation agent would come down the stairs, see the open door, and assume that he had gone down the hall that led from the door, past the stairs, and into the kitchen. When he made to follow, and his back was to Gordon, Gordon would take the shot. Maybe it wasn't the most honorable of methods, to shoot a man in the back, but his son's life was at stake.

And not just his son's life, but the life of the second Son.

Almost immediately, Gordon heard the creak of footsteps on the stairs. They came down slowly, cautiously, at a measured pace. He didn't need to see past the door to visualize the man descending with his gun out and swinging with a measured cadence from side to side, as though tracking for movement like the sweep of radar.

Suddenly the footsteps stopped.

Seconds dragged by. Gordon held his breath, not daring to breathe.

And then he heard a low chuckle.

"Very clever. But I see you've been wounded, Mr. Brown. Your own blood has betrayed you. I know you're behind the door."

These words were punctuated by the firing of a gun. Gordon flinched, half expecting to feel the bullets tearing into his flesh.

But he felt nothing.

The footsteps resumed. Stopped.

The man would be in front of the open door now.

Gordon threw open the closet door. Sure enough, the man had his back to him, facing the door behind which he'd guessed that Gordon was hiding.

Right idea.

Wrong door.

He was already turning, his gun coming up fast and deadly.

Gordon was faster. He fired. He was aiming for the man's torso, but his hand was trembling with weakness, and his aim was off. The bullet slammed into the man's leg. He grunted as it crumpled under him.

But he didn't drop his gun. He aimed and fired. And his hand didn't tremble.

Gordon felt as if a giant had smashed a fist into his chest, then another. The impact hurled him back into the closet, into the coats hanging there; they cushioned him, caught him, swayed back, and swung him out again, into another one-two punch.

He was dead before he hit the floor.

✠   ✠   ✠

Ethan listened to the footsteps coming up the stairs. The tread was slow and uneven. Whoever it was, was wounded. But who was it? His father or the crazy man?

All at once, the blindfold seemed to burn away beneath the intensity of his sight. Walls seemed to disintegrate. He saw his father sprawled in a pool of blood at the foot of the stairs. Motionless.

And climbing the stairs, blood dripping from between the fingers of the hand pressed to his thigh, was the crazy man.

As instinctively and inexplicably as had occurred the day before, Ethan was suddenly seeing into the man. Into the heart of him, the core of who he was. Peter's soul had been like a shining thing marred by a thin black flaw; all he had done was erase that flaw, smooth it away so that Peter's light could shine everywhere unimpeded. But this man had no light. Or if he did, it was a light that shone in blackness, not an absence of light but rather a presence of darkness. It was evil.

But then he saw, with a shock, that it wasn't the man's soul that he was seeing. Rather, it was something that had polluted the man's soul. Shrouded it. Possessed it. For want of a better word, he called that thing a demon.

A parasitic creature of darkness and evil.

The creature saw him.

And was afraid.

Ethan thought, *Begone.*

And the blackness receded. It drew back, out of the man's soul, out of his flesh, along a web of dark lines that seemed to stretch out infinitely in all directions.

Ethan followed.

There were dark nodes in the web, like black diamonds, that were the souls of others similarly possessed, and in them Ethan saw knowledge of his existence and implacable hatred for him. Wherever he saw that knowledge, he expunged it. Wiped it out as if it had never been. But there was no time to free the people from the demons that were afflicting them. He had to leave them behind. The dark web stretched on. The demon thing retreated before him.

Ethan followed it. It came to an end at last in a cold and inhuman place, a place where there was no emotion, no love, not even hate, but only logic. There the demon cowered. But it was not alone. There was another consciousness present there. One that recognized him.

And unlike the demons, it did not fear him.

I see you, came the thing's chilly voice in his mind.

But though it was different than the demons, different than the people the demons had possessed, it was in a strange way less alive than they. More powerful in some ways, yet also much less than even the weakest of them.

It was, Ethan realized with shock, a machine.

I see—

As quickly as that, he switched it off. Expunged the knowledge of his existence from what passed for its brain. When it was turned on again, that information would be gone. It would not see him any longer.

None of them would.

For now.

But he could do no more. Frightened, exhausted, he fell back toward his body, retracing the route he had followed along the black web, and each time he passed through one of the dark diamond nodes, as though passing through a door, he locked that door behind him.

Nothing would follow.

Nothing would find him again.

At last, in the blink of an eye or the beat of a heart, he was back in his home. Hovering somehow above the body of his father.

He was dead. No spark of life remained in him. Ethan would have seen it.

But there was something.

His soul.

It was falling away inside him like a star, dwindling with distance as it journeyed to its final reward, which was, in some sense Ethan grasped instinctively, without understanding, also its source.

If he followed it, could he catch it? Bring it back?

Return his father to life?

Weak as he was, he tried.

He plunged into the vacuum left by the dead man's departing soul.

And saw a barrier of light appear before him. Blocking him. So bright he could not bear to look at it directly, even with what senses he had in this inner space of mind or soul. He remembered how Peter had said that he, too, had been unable to look at Ethan because he was shining so brightly. What did it mean? He didn't know.

He pushed against the barrier, but it held firm. He struck at it, and it rang like a sheet of metal, only instead of a senseless tone, like the idiot pealing of a bell, what issued forth was a voice. A word.

"NO."

Ethan knew then that there was no getting past the barrier. No getting past the word. Not today.

Filled with anguish and anger at his own impotence, at the unfairness of this voice that had forbidden him to save his father, he fell back into his shivering, bound body, into the blindfold that veiled his useless eyes, the gag that stopped his useless words. He felt as if he were floating in the womb of a monster, and whether he drowned there or was born into a new and unimaginable existence was immaterial. Either way, nothing would ever be the same again. How could it?

He wept in the darkness, waiting for whatever would come.

CHAPTER 13

The first thing Lisa noticed when she opened her eyes was the kitchen clock. There was something odd about it, but it took her a moment to realize that the oddness wasn't in the clock itself but in the angle at which she was viewing it. She was on the floor, leaning back against the dishwasher, her legs stretched out in front of her. There were loops of cut duct tape clinging to her ankles and wrists. She noted this odd fact but didn't think to question it. It seemed to be taking place in a fuzzy zone of reality midway between dreaming and waking, where such things were unexceptionable. The time, she noted, was nearly eight. The house was dead silent. Her head was pounding dully, and her mouth was dry, with an unpleasant chemical taste haunting the back of her throat. The air smelled of pizza. For a second, she thought she was going to vomit. Then the feeling passed. She stirred weakly, tried to get her feet under her. Big mistake. The sick feeling came rushing back, and she was barely able to turn her head to one side before she was violently ill all over the linoleum floor.

After the spasms had ebbed into weak shudders, she lay back gasping, feeling as if her stomach were a sponge that had been wrung out between two merciless hands. She raised a trembling hand to wipe the spittle and bile from her lips and felt something hard and crusty on her cheek. She rubbed it off. It looked like dried pizza topping.

At that, the memory hit her. Her head snapped back, clunking painfully against the door of the dishwasher as she recalled opening the pizza box and hearing the telltale hiss of compressed gas being released. Whatever it was, she had inhaled it. And it had obviously knocked her out.

Which could only mean one thing.

The Congregation had found them.

Her fear for Ethan took over, pushing Lisa to her feet. She wobbled, one hand gripping the edge of the sink to hold herself upright, her vision swimming. She tore the duct tape from one wrist, then the other. Then she staggered away, heading down the hall to the front door. With each step, her balance grew steadier, her wits sharper. But she felt as weak as a kitten.

She saw the blood first. A thin rivulet running from somewhere near the stairs, still wet and glistening in the overhead light of the foyer. It widened into a red pool. Face down in the center of it was Gordon. A low moan trickled past her lips. Despite all her training, Lisa had never seen a dead body before. And this body in particular she had never thought to see that way. But she knew in an instant, through some sure instinct that was a piece of all human heritage, that her husband was no longer among the living. Even without the blood, the arrangement of his limbs, like the twisted appendages of a rag doll flung down by a petulant child, proclaimed it. The knowledge stabbed through her heart, and it was all she could do not to collapse beside him, straighten his poor arms and legs, and take his broken body into her arms. But there was nothing she could do anymore for Gordon. Only mourn him, and that would come later.

But now there was no time for mourning.

She had to find Ethan.

Her training kicked in, overriding her grief. She fumbled in her pocket for her cell phone and hit the speed dial for the emergency number that would summon a swarm of Conversatio agents. She could only assume that Gordon hadn't had a chance to do so himself, or else the agents would be here already. Then she bent down carefully, black dots dancing in front of her eyes, and laid two fingers on her husband's neck. As she had expected, there was no pulse. But it had been important to check. Then she carefully pried the pistol from his fingers; her own gun was upstairs, no use to her now. The gun came away easily; rigor mortis hadn't set in. He hadn't been dead long enough. But Lisa didn't want to think about that. Didn't want to think about how she had lain unconscious in the kitchen while Gordon fought for his life. How, when he'd needed her most, she hadn't been there for him.

Or Ethan.

The front door was closed, but there were a pair of bullet holes in the wood. She saw two more in the wall to the left of the door. How had the fight gone down? Who had fired first? Did the closed door mean that her husband's killer was still in the house?

Heart hammering, Lisa lurched toward the stairs, careful to avoid the blood. She paused in annoyance to rip the tape from her ankles, then continued on. There was more blood on the beige carpet of the stairs, a trail of drops and spatters that went about halfway up and then simply vanished. Had a wounded Gordon tried to climb the stairs, only to fall back? Or did this blood belong to someone else? The Congregation agent . . . or Ethan?

Please, God, don't let me be too late!

If Ethan was dead too, she didn't think she could bear it. How could she go on, knowing that she had failed them both?

She forced herself up the stairs, holding the pistol out before her in a trembling hand. It seemed to weigh a hundred pounds. She would be lucky if she could pull the trigger, much less aim the damn thing. Tears were streaming down her cheeks, but Lisa made no move to brush them away. She didn't even seem aware of them.

The door to Ethan's room was open. Cautiously, she slipped inside. His room was empty, but the door to the bathroom was open a crack. Flickering candlelight was visible from inside. Lisa knew how the Congregation disposed of high potentials, all of whom it treated as Antichrists. She knew the steps of the ritual, less an execution than a blood sacrifice: the prayers recited in Latin, the splashing of holy water, the knife drawn across the throat. There was no room for the doctrine of the second son in their crabbed and paranoid theology. They had no use for mercy, no concept of innocence. In a way, she pitied them.

Or had, until this moment.

Now she hated. She didn't care if it was a sin. She wanted revenge. She wanted to kill.

The time for subtlety was over.

Lisa took a deep breath. Then, summoning up her last reserves of strength, reserves she hadn't even been sure she possessed to call upon, she sidled across the room like a panther and kicked the bathroom door open, the pistol up and steady in her hand, her finger already tightening on the trigger as the door flew wide.

Ethan—bound, gagged, and blindfolded—cringed against the far side of the tub, which was filled with rocking water. He was shivering violently. Candles burned low on the sink and toilet.

There was no one else in the room.

"It's me, honey," she whispered.

He made a whimpering sound behind his gag.

Lisa's heart, which she had thought broken forever, soared. But it was a strange soaring, on wings of grief as well as joy, and the combination of these contradictory emotions, fused under the intensity of the moment into something that partook of both yet was more than either, was almost too much to bear. She felt as if a new emotion, one she lacked a name for, lacked even the proper capacity to contain, was nevertheless forcing its way inside her, carving out a space for itself, and changing her in the process. For good or ill, she didn't know. She only knew that it hurt like childbirth must hurt.

At that instant, though she didn't realize it until later, Lisa ceased to be a Conversatio agent and became instead what she had pretended to be for the last nine years.

A Conversatio agent would not have put down her gun and lifted Ethan from the freezing water of the tub as Lisa did.

A Conversatio agent would not have carried him dripping and shivering out of the bathroom to the bed, laying him down with tender devotion on the rumpled bedspread.

A Conversatio agent would not have removed his blindfold, and then his gag, and then his bonds, murmuring to him all the while in a wordless croon of love and reassurance.

A Conversatio agent would not have checked his body for wounds or injuries and then pulled the blanket up around them both and huddled close, warming him with her body, stilling his shivers with her steadfast presence and mingling her tears with his while she waited for help to arrive.

A Conversatio agent wouldn't have done any of these things. Not with a Congregation killer unaccounted for, perhaps still in the house, preparing to strike.

But a mother?

A mother could do nothing else.

✠   ✠   ✠

The Conversatio team showed up within moments, though it seemed like hours to Lisa. Hearing movement downstairs, she came fully awake with a start, wondering if the killer had come back to finish the job. Only then did she realize that she'd left Gordon's gun in the bathroom. Cursing herself for a fool, she quickly rose and retrieved it, then returned to the bed and faced the door.

Ethan didn't so much as stir. He was asleep in the blanket's cocoon, his skin hot and sweaty. His damp forehead burned beneath her lips as they bestowed a hasty kiss. But even then he didn't wake.

Footsteps on the stairs.

Lisa said a prayer and aimed the gun at the open door. Although she'd trained for moments like this, she couldn't for the life of her remember the proper procedure, how to identify herself without giving her position away in case those footsteps weren't announcing friendlies. What was it? A Latin phrase? A palindrome of some kind? "Able was I ere I saw Elba . . ." Gordon was always better at this kind of cloak-and-dagger spy stuff. She felt almost giddy, as if fate were playing an elaborate joke on her, and she was just about to experience the punch line . . . a punch line already on the tip of her tongue.

In the blink of an eye, two men with automatic rifles ducked through the doorway. She didn't recognize either of them.

They held their fire, training their guns on her.

She returned the favor, aiming her pistol at the nearest of the two.

That man said, calmly, "Put down your weapon, Agent Brown."

She didn't trust her voice, so she just shook her head.

"We're Conversatio," the other man said. "Like you."

"Then you put down *your* weapons," she managed to get out more or less intelligibly.

The men glanced at each other. Then slowly lowered their weapons.

"You see," said the one who had spoken first, "it really is us."

"About damn time," she said and burst into tears.

✠   ✠   ✠

Ethan didn't wake up even when one of the men gave him a cursory examination. He looked so fragile there on the bed, his body limp and unresisting as the agent worked through his physical assessment, that Lisa almost started crying again.

"Is he okay?" she asked.

"He's running a fever, but it doesn't look like he was injured," the man said in a businesslike tone of voice, then added: "We're going to evacuate you both."

Lisa nodded; it was standard procedure. She didn't bother to ask where they were going. She knew the man wouldn't tell her. And she would find out soon enough in any case. Instead, she said, "The Congregation agent . . . it's as if he vanished into thin air. I don't understand why he didn't finish the job."

"We're looking for him, don't worry," said the second man, who was hovering impatiently at her side. "We have to go. Can you walk?"

"Of course," she said. But when she stood up, her legs wouldn't support her, and she would have fallen if the man hadn't slid an arm around her waist. "Sorry." She gave him an apologetic smile, ashamed of her weakness.

"You've been through a lot," the man said as he gently lowered her back onto the bed. "Try to relax. We'll take it from here."

She didn't even try to resist. "My—my husband . . ." The realization was spreading through her like a cancer. Gordon was dead. She would never feel his touch again, never hear his voice, never—

"Leave everything to us," the man said soothingly.

As he spoke, she felt a sudden jab in her arm; she whipped her head around, and the man who had been tending to Ethan held up a syringe. "Sorry, Agent," he said. "But it's best if you sleep now."

She didn't try to resist that either.

✠   ✠   ✠

Christ, what a colossal screw up, thought Papa Jim in disgust as he gazed through the one-way mirror at the motionless form of the female agent, Lisa Brown. At least, that had been her name, her alias, before everything had gone to shit. But now Lisa Brown was dead. Ethan Brown too. Perhaps not in the same sense as Gordon Brown, but gone as if they had never existed. The woman and the boy who would walk out of this hospital, a private facility outside Phoenix, Arizona, staffed by Conversatio personnel and paid for by Papa Jim's millions, would have different names, different histories.

Papa Jim hated incompetence. He hated waste. And this situation was up to its eyeballs in both. He honored the sacrifice the male agent had made. Gordon Brown had been damn impressive, really, taking out one Congregation agent and then, gravely wounded, in fact already as good as dead according to the autopsy report, going toe-to-toe with another. Papa Jim respected that. But it was the man's own complacency that had let the whole situation spin so badly out of control in the first place. Papa Jim had been worried about Gordon, about his level of commitment to the cause. Over the years, his weekly reports had grown a little too relaxed. As if he were just filling in the blanks. Doing his job by the numbers but no more than that. Not because he didn't care, but because he cared too much. He had gone native, so to speak. Started to think of himself as the boy's real father. Or such, anyway, had been Papa Jim's concern. Yet he hadn't said anything. Which meant that this fiasco was partly his fault too.

Papa Jim hated that more than anything.

Now, even with the Conversatio clean-up crew's usual expert work, spiriting away Gordon's body in the dead of night, and Lisa and Ethan too, and then erasing not only every trace of violence from the house but every trace of its inhabitants, so that by the morning after the attack it was as if the Browns had inexplicably vanished off the face of the Earth, abducted by aliens, perhaps, leaving behind a fully furnished house in which nevertheless there was not to be found a single fingerprint or speck of DNA and, needless to add, no forwarding address—even with that undeniably impressive achievement, there would still be rumors that would spread among the neighbors, and even if that weren't the case, the Congregation had been alerted to Ethan's existence now, and Grand Inquisitor would be searching tirelessly for him, searching in ways that no human mind could comprehend and thus could not defend against, not forever. Sooner or later, no matter what was done to hide Ethan, a mistake would be made, insignificant as it might seem or even be, but it would proclaim his whereabouts to Grand Inquisitor as clearly as if he'd walked into the Vatican and surrendered.

Still, they'd been lucky. After all, Ethan hadn't been harmed.

At least, not physically. Or so the doctors said.

"Then why isn't he waking up?" he'd asked.

The expensive eggheads with entire alphabets after their names didn't have an answer for that. They only shrugged and shook their heads and offered more of their fancy doubletalk that, when you stripped away the jargon, boiled down to the fact that they didn't have any more of a clue than he did about why his great-grandson was still asleep three days after the attack. At first, they'd blamed his high fever, but that had broken by the next morning, by which time his bruises, too, had faded. Now it was "post-traumatic stress." Papa Jim knew bullshit when he heard it.

The woman, Lisa, was a different matter. The gas she'd breathed had damaged her lungs. For a while, the doctors hadn't been sure she would live. Now the consensus seemed to be that she would make it, although there would be significant scarring. She would never fully recover. Clearly, she would be in no condition to continue as Ethan's guardian. Papa Jim hadn't broken that piece of news to her yet. Actually, he'd only spoken to her once, briefly, since she and the boy had been flown in; the doctors had kept her sedated after that as they'd worked around the clock to save her life and her lungs.

But now the doctors were bringing her around. And once she was conscious, he meant to have a nice chat with her. Well, he would do the chatting; speech was going to be beyond her for a while, apparently. But the doctors thought she would be able to write down answers to his questions, as long as he kept them simple and didn't say anything too upsetting. They couldn't in good conscience allow him any more than that. And even then they glared at him as though he were some kind of monster, not giving her time to grieve or to heal. But there were things he had to know. Things he had to hear that only she could tell him.

Unanswered questions . . . and Papa Jim hated unanswered questions.

For instance, what had happened to the Congregation agent? Lisa's preliminary report, necessarily confused and incomplete, recorded after her arrival at the hospital, just before she was wheeled into surgery, had stated that the man had been gone when she'd regained consciousness. And the Conversatio agents at the scene had confirmed that there was no sign of him; all the evidence indicated he'd left the house at least twenty minutes prior to the time that Lisa had come to. But Papa Jim thought, or rather hoped, that Lisa might remember something more now than she had then. Something that would help him understand why the man had not completed his task. Why, with the sole impediment to its success removed, and his intended victim waiting helplessly upstairs, a victim the man's religious beliefs did not even admit to be human but rather some avatar of the Antichrist, why, given all that, did the agent—seriously wounded himself—turn around, get back in his vehicle, and drive off? And for the love of God, why had he, an ordained priest for Christ's sake, ditched that same vehicle ten miles away, at the entrance to a public park, staggered into the midst of a densely wooded area, and hung himself by the neck from a convenient tree branch until he was stone-cold dead?

Why, Papa Jim asked himself, would a priest commit the one sin that could not be forgiven? The sin of Judas—for if Judas had begged God's forgiveness, God would have forgiven him, would have been bound to, at least according to the words of His beloved son, whom Judas had just betrayed. If Christ was who He claimed to be, and if His words were true, then even Judas could have tasted the forgiveness of God . . . but he hadn't even asked. Instead, he'd compounded his sin by committing a worse one, worse in the sense that there was no aftermath to it in which you could repent and pray to be forgiven. When you killed yourself, you threw away that last chance, that lifeline to God and to Heaven. You went straight to hell, to everlasting torment, to the one place where God's forgiveness didn't reach. Judas, clearly, had meant to go there. He had understood that the gravity of his sin merited no other fate, and surely not the forgiveness of a compassionate God. He had chosen damnation as an act of free will, his final act of free will, because he knew that he deserved it. Papa Jim didn't have any idea of what the theologians had to say about Judas, nor did he have any interest in knowing. His own understanding of it was good enough for him. And in his opinion, Judas had been a fool, throwing away his chance at Heaven just to make a point. But what of the priest? Had he, like Judas, suddenly come to the realization that his sins merited no other fate but eternal damnation, a damnation that God would spare him despite everything if he only asked sincerely, with a heart full of repentance? And if so, what had sparked that revelation?

These were the kinds of unanswered questions that Papa Jim hated most of all.

He sighed impatiently, puffing on his cigar, ignoring the irritated looks of the doctors and nurses who were in the observation room with him. Meanwhile, on the other side of the glass, a nurse, doctor, and anesthesiologist were monitoring the patient closely as she was slowly brought back to consciousness.

His cell phone buzzed in his pocket. Scowling in irritation, Papa Jim turned away from the window and fished it out. But his scowl vanished when he saw who was calling. It was Denny, his personal assistant and bodyguard, an ex-Special Forces man who upon his discharge had turned to crystal meth, then armed robbery, and finally wound up in one of Papa Jim's prisons on a second-degree murder conviction. Papa Jim had pulled some strings to have the man enrolled in a supervised early release program, under his own supervision of course, which had earned him Denny's unswerving loyalty. He was basically a trained killer with the heart of a thug, but Papa Jim's faith-based prison system had tamed him. Denny had become addicted to a new drug in jail: religion. The religion of Papa Jim, that is. And he was just as zealous in its pursuit as he'd been in the pursuit of crystal meth. Papa Jim had been looking for someone like Denny for a while, a man capable of protecting him not only from the Congregation but from Conversatio as well. He might be working with Conversatio, even pretending, at least for now, to be one of them, but he didn't trust them. If his enemies or his allies turned on him, he would need someone without ties to either. That was just basic business sense. And Denny filled the bill. The conflict between Conversatio and the Congregation meant nothing to him. And his wants were as limited as his imagination and intelligence, so money meant nothing to him either. Papa Jim admired him as he would a top-notch hunting dog or racehorse.

"What is it?" he snapped, annoyed at the interruption, even though he was sure that Denny wouldn't be calling without a damn good reason.

"The kid's awake, Boss," came the familiar voice.

"Shit. I'll be right there." He dropped the cigar and ground it out beneath his shoe.

"He's coming to you."

"Say what?"

"He's on his way."

"Well, stop him."

"It's not that easy."

"What the hell does that mean? He's a nine-year-old kid, for Christ's sake!"

"He's, um, glowing."

"*Glowing?*"

"Shining like a star."

"Are you drunk?"

"I sure as hell wish I was."

"Hold him until I get there, Denny. That's a goddamn order, do you hear me?"

"Yes, Boss."

"Sit on him if you have to. Just don't hurt him, understand?"

"Yessir."

Fuming, Papa Jim flipped the cell phone closed and jammed it back into his pocket. *Glowing, my ass*, he thought. A more likely explanation was that Denny was back on crystal meth. Damn, but it was getting harder and harder to find good help these days.

"The patient is awake, Mr. Osbourne."

"What?" One of the doctors in the room gestured toward the window. Papa Jim looked. He'd been so preoccupied with Denny's call that he'd forgotten about Lisa. But now he saw that she was indeed awake, sitting up in bed and glancing nervously around the hospital room as she listened to the doctor. "Oh hell," he said. "Perfect timing."

"Sir?" queried the same doctor who had spoken.

Papa Jim shook his head. "Never mind. I'll be right back. It seems the boy is awake too." But before he could take a step, the door to the hospital room opened and Ethan walked in. The boy was wearing a green hospital gown and moving like a sleepwalker. Needless to say, he wasn't glowing. Papa Jim sighed. It looked like he was going to be in the market for a new bodyguard. Then he gasped in disbelief.

On the other side of the glass, the doctor, nurse, and anesthesiologist were dropping to their knees. Almost immediately, the doctors and nurses in the observation room followed suit.

"What the hell is wrong with you people?" he demanded.

"Can't you see?" said one of the nurses, her gaze fixed on the window. "See what?"

"The glow."

Papa Jim squinted. He didn't see anything that could remotely be described as a glow. Just an ordinary-looking nine-year-old boy who, ignoring the kneeling figures around him, went straight to his mother—or, rather, the woman he thought of as his mother—and, climbing up into her bed and putting his arms around her, burst into tears.

"It's him," the nurse said in an awestruck whisper. "The second Son!"

Tears of joy were running down her cheeks.

"Praise God!" echoed the doctor fervently. "He's come at last!"

"I'm going in there," said Papa Jim. He felt like the whole world had gone crazy. Turning away from the window, he strode toward the door, yanked it open, and stepped into the reception area of his Charleston office. His secretary, Joyce, looked up at him from her desk with a quizzical half smile.

Papa Jim froze. He had a peculiar feeling, similar to déjà vu, only even more unsettling. It wasn't that he remembered being in this exact situation before, standing in the doorway of his office and looking at Joyce like this. Instead, it was as if he shouldn't even be here. Should be somewhere else entirely. In fact, *had been* somewhere else just seconds ago. But that was crazy. Where else would he have been?

"Something the matter, Boss?" asked Joyce.

"Just a bit of a brain fart." Papa Jim shook his head sheepishly and gave a rheumy chuckle. "I swear, Joyce, I'm going to forget my own name one of these days."

"Can I get you anything?"

"A couple of aspirin," he said. "All of a sudden, I feel a headache coming on."

"Be right there, Boss."

Papa Jim grunted and returned to his office. He sat down at his desk and stared in mystification at the papers scattered across its polished wooden surface. He had absolutely no memory of working on any of it. Was this, he wondered, how it started? The first symptoms of senility, or worse?

"Here's your aspirin, Boss."

"Thanks, Joyce." He took the pills and the glass of water she handed him and swallowed them down. "Close the door on your way out," he told her.

When she had gone and he was alone, he opened the bottom drawer of the desk, took out a bottle of Maker's Mark, and poured three fingers' worth into the glass that Joyce had given him. He drank it straight down.

Then, with a heavy sigh, he started in on the paperwork.

✠   ✠   ✠

During the time that Ethan had lain unconscious in the Conversatio hospital outside Phoenix, he had been dreaming the most extraordinary dreams. Actually, it was only one dream, an extremely vivid and lucid dream that stretched over the whole three days and nights.

In the dream, Ethan was walking along a raw, unpaved road, really more of a path, through a hardscrabble landscape in which there was no sign of life save stunted, cactus-like plants, scurrying lizards, and dark birds flying high in the cloudless, bleached-out sky. Every so often, a sharp, almost disconsolate cry would issue from one of these birds, as if they, too, were strangers here. The noise did not so much break the silence as accentuate it. The uneven ground, which climbed and fell precipitously, was baked hard beneath Ethan's sandaled feet, and clouds of dust rose with each footfall, hanging thickly in the hot, breezeless air. There was no indication that rain had ever fallen here or ever would.

Ethan followed the path, not knowing where he was, how he had gotten here, or where he was going. Other than the sandals, his only clothing was a tattered robe of some kind of roughly tanned animal skin that hung to his knees. It was hot, made his skin itch, and smelled vile, especially as he sweated under the relentless sun. He carried a thin walking stick in one hand, which he used to help himself over dry fissures and rockslides. Far in the distance on all sides were the hazy shapes of mountains, gray and ominous as lowering storm clouds. There were no other people and no evidence that other people had ever come here.

He was alone. He called out at first, shouting "Hello!" at the top of his lungs, but there was no reply save the fading echoes of his own voice. Because such shouting only made his parched throat ache for water, he soon desisted, trudging on in silence.

He remembered everything up to the moment his mother had appeared at the bathroom door with a gun in her hands. After that, nothing. It occurred to him that he was dead, his soul judged and condemned to limbo, for he was certain that this place couldn't be Heaven—it was far too bleak and unpleasant—yet he felt pretty sure that the other place would be infinitely worse. He wished that he could meet someone friendly, someone who could tell him what was going on.

Slowly, the sun climbed higher in the desert of the sky. Then, equally slowly, it began to set.

As it began to grow dark, the air became cooler, and the numbness to which he'd been reduced by fatigue and thirst was replaced by uncertainty and gnawing fear. What if there were dangerous animals that came out at night in search of prey? How could he run from them or defend himself with only a thin walking stick? The answer was simple: He couldn't. He couldn't even build a fire to ward off the cold and keep whatever animals there were at bay.

He searched in mounting desperation for some kind of shelter. At last he spotted what appeared to be a cave in the rocky hills along one side of the path. He hurried toward it. Up close, it turned out to be more of a crevice than a cave, a jagged breach in the rock face that extended back as far as he could see in the gloaming. How far back did it go? Was there anything else in there?

He hesitated, trembling with uncertainty. Then, casting an apprehensive glance over his shoulder at the bare landscape fast submerging under pools of shadow deepening to night, he crept inside and squatted there, clenching his stick tightly with both hands.

Soon darkness had fallen. The only light came from thousands upon thousands of glittering stars that he could see past the canopy of stone that constituted the top of the crevice in which he crouched like a fearful animal. The sight was beautiful in a chilly, remote way, and though it filled him with loneliness, he couldn't stop looking, as if he might somehow connect all those bright dots into a picture that would explain everything.

But of course no picture emerged.

After a time, he could not have said how long, Ethan felt a great weariness steal over him, and his chin dropped to his chest. Was he asleep? Was he dreaming?

From out of the darkness came a voice. It was a voice he recognized. A voice he would never forget.

The voice of the priest who had tried to kill him.

"Hello, Ethan. Fancy meeting you here."

Terror flooded him. But he couldn't move. It was as if he had turned to stone.

"Cat got your tongue?" asked the voice.

He couldn't open his mouth. Couldn't cry for help. And even if he could have done so, who would have heard him in this wasteland?

"Or perhaps you're afraid of the dark," the voice continued. "I can help with that."

Light flared suddenly, accompanied by a dull *whumping* sound, like a firecracker set off under a tin can, and a smell like burned matches. The light was a dull red, wavering as if with heat, though there was no heat, and it had no source that he could see.

"Is that better?" asked the voice solicitously. Only it wasn't just a voice anymore. There was a body to go with it now. The priest stood before Ethan, looking down at him with eyes like bottomless black pits that might have held all the darkness just banished from the cave and more besides, his head crooked at an unnatural angle that was perhaps explained by the noose cinched tightly around his neck, one end of which dangled before him like some obscene umbilical cord.

The priest sighed; air wheezed past his lips. "Look what you made me do," he said sorrowfully.

Ethan strained with all his might to break free of whatever force was holding him in place, but he couldn't. He couldn't even avert his gaze from the priest's horrific visage and accusatory stare. Or close his eyes.

"Yes, this is all your fault," the priest said, his head lolling bonelessly across his chest. "You drove me to this terrible sin. You killed me as surely as if you were the hangman. Well, what do you have to say for yourself?"

At that, Ethan felt whatever was silencing him disappear.

"Go—go away," he said through chattering teeth.

"Oh no," said the priest. "That won't work here. You're on my turf now. And I want to know what gave you the right to meddle with my life. Who do you think you are, Jesus Christ? Answer me, damn you!"

Ethan pressed his lips together. He tried to tell himself that this was just a bad dream. But the angry man before him didn't vanish, not even when he tried to wake himself up by biting his tongue.

"I'm waiting," said the priest.

"You started it!" Ethan burst out. "You're a bad man, and I was just trying to stop you from hurting my mom and dad!"

"Well, you didn't do a very good job of it, did you?" the priest sneered. "Is that why you killed me? For revenge?"

"I didn't kill you!"

"You're a murderer, Ethan. And you know where murderers go, don't you?" The drooping face acquired the sickly suggestion of a smile. "Why, they come here. To hell."

"You're a liar! I never killed anyone!"

"You killed me. And what about your father?"

"You're the one who killed him!"

"But you could have brought him back. You know it's true. You could have saved him, but you didn't. You let him die. That's the same as killing him."

Ethan shook his head. "No . . ."

"You've killed two people so far. Not bad for a nine-year-old! Who's next, I wonder? Your mother? One of your friends?"

"Shut up!" Ethan cried.

"You're dangerous, Ethan. You're a menace!"

"Shut up!"

"If only you had the courage to do what I did. It's not so hard. And once you're gone, you won't be able to hurt anyone else ever again. Your mother will be safe. They'll all be safe. I'm telling you this for your own good." The priest's hands scrabbled at the noose around his neck, loosening it and slowly lifting it off as Ethan watched in horror. With his head still flopping like that of a rag doll, the priest extended the noose. "Take it," he said. "Take it and do the right thing for once, before it's too late."

Ethan screamed.

And just like that, the light vanished, taking the hanged priest with it. But instead of darkness, a soft pink glow spilled into the crevice. Outside, the sun was rising. The night had passed; it was morning.

So began the second day.

Afraid the priest would return, Ethan stumbled outside and resumed his interrupted trek, following the path that seemed to stretch on forever without reaching anything at all resembling a destination or stopping point. Once again, he saw no other traveler, only the dark shapes of birds wheeling high overhead. As the sun rose, the landscape was unchanging in its bleakness, so that it almost seemed as if he were wandering in circles. He was thirsty, but there wasn't a drop of water to be found, nor anything to eat. Many times he thought of giving up, of throwing himself down on the hard, rocky ground and waiting for whatever would come next. But something drove him on.

It was the thought of his mother. Was she alive? He sensed that she was, and that she needed him, and that only by pressing on could he find her.

As he walked, shambling like a zombie under the hot sun, Ethan replayed the nightmarish visit of the priest over and over again in his mind. He had no doubt that a ghost had come to him, the spirit of a dead man damned for all eternity. But did that mean that he, too, was dead?

And what of the terrible things the ghost had said to him? Were they true? Was he really responsible for the priest's death? For his father's death?

No!

The priest had committed both crimes, first killing his father and then, for reasons equally unfathomable, himself. The man had been crazy, that much was clear. And Ethan remembered as well the demon that had taken possession of the man's soul. He remembered how he had seen it inside him, the foulness like a thick coating of tar. Ethan had dispelled the demon with a word . . . but that hadn't killed the man. *No,* he thought. But perhaps, with the demon gone, the man had been horrified by the knowledge of what he had done, what he had tried to do. So horrified that he'd been driven to kill himself. If that were true, then wasn't the priest's ghost right in a way? Hadn't he at least contributed to his death?

And why had the priest targeted him and his family in the first place? Had it been random? Ethan didn't think so. No, everything the priest had said and done in life and death led him to the conclusion that the attack had been purposeful. And he could think of only one reason for it. It was because of the power he possessed, the ability to see into people's hearts, into their very souls, and make changes there with nothing more than a word or a thought. He'd done it to Peter, hadn't he? Somehow, when he'd used his power for the first time, he must have alerted the priest, and the priest had come after him.

Then he'd used his power again, on the priest. And on others, too.

Who had he alerted that time?

Who would come after him next?

Perhaps even now another assassin was on his way . . .

Which meant that the ghost had been right about that, too. He was a danger, a menace. His very existence was a threat to his family and his friends. Already his father had paid the ultimate price. Who would be next? Peter? Maggie? His mother? How could he protect them? He couldn't even protect himself!

As if in answer, Ethan remembered how the ghost had removed the noose from its own broken neck and handed it to him. "Take it and do the right thing for once, before it's too late," the ghost had said. "Your mother will be safe. They'll all be safe."

Was that also the truth?

What if the only way he could protect his mom and his friends was to kill himself like the ghost wanted? Could he do that?

Ethan had never felt so confused and alone. He didn't know what to think, what to believe. He prayed for help as he walked. For guidance.

No answer came.

He stumbled on through the heat and dust of the day.

When evening drew on, Ethan sought shelter as he had before. His fear of what might roam this desolate landscape by night was greater than his apprehension of another visit by the ghost. Up in the hills he found a small cave. He gathered some stones with which to defend himself and then crawled inside to wait for whatever the night would bring.

Once again, when darkness fell the stars came out in a blaze of glory unlike anything he had seen before coming to this place. It seemed like a refined kind of torture that there should be such beauty in the sky, untouchable, aloof, like some far-off glimpse of riches from the depths of squalor. Those stars seemed to hold the promise of all that he was lacking: water, food, and less tangible forms of sustenance—nourishment for his soul. He ached to look at them.

This time, there was no moment of sudden weariness. No plunge into sleep.

This time, the visitor came while he was wide-awake.

He heard it first, the scrape of a shoe against the hard rock of the cave's floor, then the skitter of a pebble kicked to one side. He was already clutching a stone in his right hand; he cocked his arm toward the sound and spoke in a hiss of air. "Who's there?"

"Hello, Ethan."

He nearly dropped the stone.

Then, as pale light sifted through the dark, illuminating the bloody figure who had spoken, he did drop it.

It was his father.

Or, rather, his father's ghost. For the man who stood before him could not possibly be alive. His entire torso was soaked in blood, which had dripped down to cover his pants in gore. It seemed impossible that there could be so much blood in a human body. The only part of him that wasn't drenched in blood was his face, and that was as pale as the moon, and as dead. In that lifeless face, which, he realized, was somehow the source of the wan light that filled the cave, two eyes as black and empty as the spaces between stars stared at him.

"Go ahead," said the ghost. "Throw your stones. You've already killed me once. After the first death, there is no other."

Ethan whimpered, drawing back against one wall of the cave.

His father spread out his arms. Blood dripped from his fingers. "Aren't you glad to see me, Ethan? Won't you give me a hug?"

"Y—you're not my dad," Ethan managed to gasp out.

"No? Then who is? Tell me that, eh? Who is?"

Ethan had no answer.

The ghost let its arms drop to its sides and sighed. "To be honest, I'd expected a warmer welcome, considering I died trying to protect you. I don't know, I thought maybe the word 'thanks' might pass your lips. Or

'Sorry I got you killed, Dad.' Or 'Sorry I didn't bring you back to life when I had the chance.' But I guess that's all too much to hope for. I guess you really are selfish and ungrateful at heart."

Listening to this, Ethan found his courage. "Now I know you're not my dad. My dad wouldn't talk that way."

The ghost shrugged. "Death has a way of changing a person. But at least I'm not selfish, like you. Despite what you did to me, I'm here to help you."

"If you really want to help, just go away," Ethan said through gritted teeth. "Leave me alone."

"Sure, I could do that. But then what would happen to your mom? Your friends? You're a smart kid, Ethan. You must've figured out by now that you're a danger to them. What happened to me is going to happen to them unless you do something to stop it."

"Is that what this is about? If you're going to try and talk me into killing myself, don't bother. That's already been tried. It didn't work."

The ghost looked shocked. "Why, I'd never suggest such a thing! That would be a sin, a crime. Besides, that's the coward's way. The selfish way. What I'm suggesting is much harder. It's a nobler kind of sacrifice. Unless, of course, you don't care about the others at all."

"I do care about them!"

"Just testing," said the ghost and winked one abyssal eye. Then, leaning closer as if to impart a secret, he whispered, "You could stay here."

A shudder ran through Ethan then, as much from the ghost's words as from the breath that issued from the dark hole of its mouth, as chill as the icy void of space. "S—stay?" he echoed.

"That's right. This is all in your mind, you know." He gestured expansively with one bloody arm. "A dream, if you like. Only it's real too. Your body is in a hospital bed right now. In a coma. Everyone's waiting for you to wake up. But you don't have to wake up. You don't have to ever wake up."

"I don't even know how to wake up," he said.

"Sooner or later, you'll find out, as long as you keep looking. But as soon as you wake up, they'll come after you again. They'll strike at you any way they can. They don't care who else they kill."

"Who doesn't care? And why do they want to kill me?"

"Does it matter?" asked the ghost of his father. "Dead is dead. Believe me, I know. And you know what else? It sucks."

"So does this. I don't like this place. I don't want to stay here."

"Well, of course not. I mean, just look at it. It's a wasteland. A desert. But it doesn't have to be that way."

"What do you mean?"

"You've got power over this place, Ethan. You can make it into whatever you want. If you command water to flow from the ground, a spring will burst forth. If you ask the stones to feed you, they'll turn into loaves of bread. You can have TV. Movies. Friends. Anything at all."

"You're crazy."

"No, it's true. Give it a try if you don't believe me." He kicked a rock with one blood-drenched shoe. "Go ahead. Tell it to turn into a loaf of bread. Or a Big Mac, if you'd rather. I'm kind of hungry myself. Maybe you can make me one, too."

Ethan shook his head. The strange thing was, he actually believed what the ghost was telling him. He felt in his bones that he did have this power, that he had always had it. He could make this place a kind of paradise. A refuge. He could live here in comfort and safety for the rest of his life. Even if his body was somewhere far away, sunk deep into a coma, he would never need to know about it, never need to suffer.

And the people he loved would be safe.

But at the same time, he thought of all the old stories he knew, the fairy tales and myths. There was a trap here, he was sure of it. The ghost wasn't telling him everything. If he made food for himself, or even water, he had a feeling that however seemingly insignificant that act might be, its ramifications would be huge in some way that was hidden from him now but might not always be. And then it would be too late. A fateful choice would have been made, after which there could be no going back, no undoing. He wouldn't even have to eat or drink what he had made. It would be enough just to make it. As though doing so was against the rules of a game he knew instinctively without having ever played it before.

"Go on," prodded the ghost. "When was the last time you had any-thing to drink? One word, I'm telling you, and it's the best water you ever tasted in your life. Or a nice cold Coke. What's the harm in that?"

"No," Ethan said.

"Do it," said the ghost, and there was anger in its voice. Anger and the threat of worse than anger.

"I said no," Ethan repeated. He knew now beyond any doubt that whatever was facing him was not his father, but only something wearing his likeness. It was, he realized suddenly, the priest, or, rather, something that had worn the likeness of the priest just as it now wore the likeness of his father. And with that, he felt his own anger rise up in him, strong and fearless. The ghost had said he had power over this place. Had even chal-lenged him to test it. And so he would, only in his own way. Before the ghost could speak again, he said, "I've heard enough. Go back to hell or wherever it is you came from!"

As quickly as that, he was alone again. The cave was empty of every-thing but the light of morning.

So began the third day.

It was the worst of all. Not because it was different in any way from the two days that had preceded it, but because it was exactly the same. Only now, thanks to his visitor of the previous night, Ethan knew he had the power to alleviate his suffering. He could, with a word, slake his thirst, fill his empty belly, conquer the heat and the dust, even the loneli-ness. But he didn't dare. He knew that it would be a mistake to do so, an unforgivable, irrecoverable mistake. And yet the temptation to do so didn't leave him for even one moment of that day. In fact, far from leav-ing him, it grew stronger, more difficult to resist, until Ethan realized that the time would come, and sooner rather than later, when he didn't have the strength to resist anymore. But what could he do? The ghost had said that if he looked long enough, he would find the way out of this prison and back to his body . . . but Ethan didn't think he had much more time in which to look before he succumbed to the demands of the flesh. It was funny, he thought, that he should still be afflicted by those demands even when he was no longer in his body.

Unless, of course, the ghost had lied about that too.

Ethan pressed on. He tried not to think further ahead than the next footstep. To contemplate going for days or even hours more without sustenance was impossible, but a footstep was not such a great distance or length of time, and he found that he could get from one footstep to the next without a struggle of will that would leave him exhausted, broken. He could do it, if just barely.

At last, evening fell. But this time Ethan did not leave the path and search out a shelter. He had no desire to simply sit in some crevice or cave and wait for the appearance of whatever new horror saw fit to plague him. If it was going to come, then let it come to him here, in the open, with him walking still unbowed, unbeaten.

He continued on beneath the stars, not looking up now, for he was afraid their remote beauty, as inaccessible to him as his body and the life that went with it, would cut him like a knife. His visitor had come twice so far, each time wearing a different guise, each one more painful than the last, more difficult to resist. Tonight would be the worst yet, and he needed no reminder of all that he'd lost, all that he searched for, to weaken him, soften a heart that must be as hard as stone.

Time passed, and he fell into a sort of doze. He was neither asleep nor awake but midway between the two, his legs moving of their own accord, his eyes glazed with the sameness of all he saw, so that it was as if he saw nothing at all.

From time to time he surfaced briefly from this somnambulistic state, his mind clearing, his breath quickening, but soon enough he would sink back into it again, pulled under by the weight of all that he was carrying, the burden of destiny he dimly sensed surrounding him like a second skin, a skin that was somehow both thinner than air and heavier than the earth itself. Or so it seemed to him, thoughts tangling with dreams, dreams with thoughts, until it was impossible to tell them apart.

It came to him quite suddenly that he was no longer alone. There was someone walking beside him, matching him step for step. How long this had been going on, he didn't know. But he had the feeling it had been a while.

Strangely, he was not afraid. Instead, he felt grateful for the company. He glanced over, and saw that his companion was a man, tall and thin to the point of gauntness. He was similarly dressed, in sandals and an animal skin, and also carried a walking stick. Ethan could not make out the man's face.

"Who are you?" he asked.

"A fellow traveler on this road," came the reply.

"You're the first one I've seen," he said.

"There are no others," said the man. "Just us."

"How do you know that?"

"I've walked this road already. To the very end."

"So it has an end. I was beginning to doubt it."

"All things have an end. All things but one."

"What is that?"

"God."

Ethan felt a shiver go through him at that. "Are . . . are you God?"

"He is my father. And yours."

"So we're brothers, I guess," Ethan said jokingly . . . but seriously too.

"All men are brothers, Ethan."

"How do you know my name?"

"I've been sent to guide you from this wicked place. It is too early for you to walk this road. Too early for you to climb the hill that waits at the end."

This gave rise to so many questions in Ethan's mind that he couldn't decide which of them to ask first.

While he was deciding, the man spoke again. "Have you seen *The Wizard of Oz*?"

The question was so unexpected that Ethan didn't know what to make of it. He stopped walking and stood there looking up at the man, who had also stopped . . . but who had yet to turn his face toward Ethan. "Huh? You mean the movie?"

"It's one of my favorites," said the man, and now he did turn to Ethan, and in the cold light of the stars his features were young and handsome, and his eyes were not black holes like those of the priest and the ghost of his father but were instead themselves like stars, only brighter and more beautiful. "Like Dorothy, you have the power to get home anytime you like. You've always had it."

"What, the ruby slippers?"

The man smiled. "In a manner of speaking. You are kept here by a great power, but yours is greater still. To you has been given the power to chain and the power to loosen."

"What do you mean?"

"Your walking stick. Its true purpose is not to help you navigate this broken land. It holds you here, bars your way out. Break it, and you will return to your body."

"You're kidding."

"No, I'm not."

"What about you? You're carrying one too. Are you trapped like me?"

"No. I carry it to remind me of what it is like to be trapped, to be a prisoner."

"Why?"

"Because to forget that is to forget what it is to be human."

"I don't understand."

"You will, Ethan. In time. But now it's time for you to go. Your mother needs you." The man turned and began to walk away.

"Will I see you again?" Ethan asked.

"I'll be waiting for you at the end of the path," said the man without looking back. He seemed to be walking incredibly fast, or just covering an immense distance with every step.

"Wait!" Ethan cried. "I don't even know your name!"

"Yes, you do," came the man's voice, although he himself could no longer be seen.

Ethan stood for a moment, trying to puzzle out what the man had meant. But he was too impatient to think about it for long. He took the walking stick and examined it by the light of the stars. It was no thicker than his index finger. Gripping it in both hands, he pressed his knee against it and pulled up with all his might until, suddenly, with a noise like a gunshot, it snapped.

Ethan sat bolt upright.

"Oh my God," came a voice. "He's awake!"

He blinked in the harsh light and looked around. He was in a hospital room. There were doctors and nurses looking at him in surprise.

He was no less surprised than they. He could see right through to the core of them. Their souls were shining like stars. Like the stars he had seen overhead when he lay trapped in the depths of his body or perhaps somewhere far beyond his body.

There were tubes and wires attached to him; then there weren't.

He was in bed; then he wasn't.

The doctors and nurses were dropping to their knees.

"It's him!"

"The second Son!"

"Our Father, who art in Heaven . . ."

Ethan ignored them. He could sense his mother in a room above him. She was hurt. Damaged. He started for the door.

Which opened suddenly. A huge man stood there. At first it looked as though he was going to block Ethan's way, but then he stepped back, a look of wonder on his face. Ethan walked past him, into the corridor, and headed toward the elevator that he knew would take him to his mother. Behind him, he heard the man speaking to someone on the phone. Then, before he could get on the elevator, the man grabbed him by the arm.

"The boss wants to talk to you."

Ethan turned, and he saw into the man: saw his entire past, filled with violence and drugs and sex; saw too the futures that spread before him like the branches of a tree, only one or two of which led to any flowering. Without thinking, he pruned the man's future. Cut back the sterile branches, so that they might bloom again. Rekindled the guttering furnace of his soul, so that its light would shine brightly, nourishing the branches and giving them something to strive toward.

With a gasp, the man released him and dropped to his knees like the others had.

Ethan got on the elevator. Only then, seeing his reflection in the mirrored interior, did he realize that he was glowing.

He was frightened and exhilarated at the same time. What was happening to him? What did it all mean?

He pressed the button for his mother's floor. The doors closed, and he ascended.

When the doors opened again and he stepped out into a corridor identical to the one below, there were more people waiting and watching. They, too, tried to stop him. They, too, fell to their knees.

Ethan went to his mother's room and opened the door. There were three people inside. They were on their knees the instant he crossed the threshold. There was a big mirror against one wall, and Ethan sensed other people behind that mirror, which was really a window. It was meant to be one-way, but Ethan could see them clearly there on the other side. Among them was an old man, a man who gazed back at him without fear or awe. Instead, anger contorted his lips, and he turned brusquely from the window. Ethan felt a link between himself and this man. But now was not the time to explore it.

His mother was sitting up in the hospital bed. She too was trailing an assortment of tubes and wires. Tears were streaming down her face. She was trying to speak, but no words were coming out. He saw what had been done to her. How the gas had damaged her lungs, scarred her throat and larynx. Then he fixed her. He knew that he was to blame for those injuries as surely as if he'd inflicted them himself. But he wasn't going to let anyone hurt her again. He knew now what he had to do. He climbed up into bed with her, put his arms around her, and burst into tears.

"I'm sorry," he whispered.

Then he did something to the world. In a way, it was the same kind of thing that he had done before to people, reaching inside them and changing them. Only this time it was on a grander scale. Yet it was no more difficult for him.

It was not as if he had never been in the hospital.

It was far more than that.

He simply never had been there.

He was at home, in Olathe, in the backyard, lying down on the grass and looking up at the night sky spangled with stars and the flashing red and green lights of airplanes. His mother lay beside him, their sides touching. He could feel her trembling.

In all the world, only the two of them remembered the hospital. Only they knew that Gordon had been killed in cold blood and had not died of a heart attack. Only they knew that there was something special about Ethan. Something wonderful. Something dangerous.

"What have you done?" asked Lisa in a hushed voice.

"The man that tried to kill me, he said something strange," Ethan said, his eyes fixed on the sky, where the tiny white dot of a satellite moved against the field of fixed stars. "He said you weren't really my mother. And that Dad wasn't really my dad."

Beside him, Lisa sighed.

"It's true, isn't it?"

"Your father and I adopted you, Ethan," Lisa said.

"And you were going to tell me this when?" His voice shook.

"It's complicated," Lisa said.

"I want to know everything. What happened to my real parents. Why that man tried to kill me. Why I can do the things I can do."

"Those are a lot of questions."

"I've got plenty more."

"This is going to take a while."

"I don't have anything better to do."

"All right. I'll tell you everything. We should have told you before."

"Yes, you should have," he said. "Maybe Dad would still be alive then."

She gasped at that, and he knew that he had hurt her. He told himself he didn't care.

"Whatever your father and I did, we did out of love for you, Ethan," Lisa said after a moment. "You have to believe that."

He just stared silently upward.

Finally, haltingly, Lisa began to talk.

First she told him about the origins of Conversatio and the doctrine of the second Son. She told him about the centuries-long war between Conversatio and the Congregation, which had once been, and in its secret heart still was, the Inquisition. She told him about Grand Inquisitor and the agents it dispatched to track down and eliminate high potentials—boys believed to have a strong probability of being or becoming the Antichrist . . . and, if identified early enough, their mothers. Then she told him about how Conversatio agents like herself and Gordon were assigned to be foster parents to high potentials rescued from the Congregation or snatched away to safety before the Congregation could get to them. As for his real parents, she didn't know anything about them: not who they were, where they had come from, or even if they were still alive. This was for their own safety, for the Congregation would try to strike at Ethan through them if they could.

"Like they tried to get at me through you and Dad?"

"Exactly. Only we're trained to protect you. They're not."

"Yeah, great job there, Mom," he said bitterly.

He felt her stiffen beside him and struggle with tears before she spoke again. "I know you must feel hurt, honey, even betrayed. But if we'd told you this too soon, you might have inadvertently given yourself away to Grand Inquisitor. GI monitors phone lines, Internet connections, wireless networks, ATM machines. It sees and hears almost everything, and then it puts the pieces together in ways that you and I can't begin to imagine."

"So you had to lie to me in order to protect me, is that what you're saying?"

"Yes, that's about it. And I won't apologize for it, because we did it out of love."

He thought about that for a while. "Does love make everything all right?"

"I don't know. What do you think?"

He shrugged. "So you think I'm, like, this second Son or something?"

"I don't think it," she said, and he felt her turning on her side to look at him. "I know it. What you've done—they're miracles."

"Right," he said, his voice full of bitterness again. "Some miracle worker I am! I couldn't even save Dad. I'm not really mad at you, Mom. I'm sorry. It's my fault he's dead. This has all been my fault."

"Ethan, no!"

"Yes," he insisted, turning to face her now, the two of them just inches away from each other as they lay on the cool grass of the backyard. And then he told her about Peter, how he had "fixed" him. And how he had done the same thing to the killer. And even how he had chased down Gordon's receding soul . . . only to stop at the end, faced with a barrier he lacked the courage to breach.

Lisa put her arms around him as he poured out his confession between sobs. "Honey," she said at last. "You may be the second Son, but you're also a nine-year-old boy."

"I can't do it," he said, pulling away from her and turning skyward again.

"Can't do what?"

"I can't be who you want me to be. There's so much hate in the world! Not just between people, and races, but whole countries. Even Conversatio and the Congregation. Am I supposed to fix all that? Mom, I can't even stop myself from hating. It's true. I know the man who killed Dad hung himself, and I'm not sorry for it. What does that make me? Am I any better than him?"

"Honey," Lisa began.

But Ethan interrupted her. "Am I supposed to make sure everyone in the world gets enough to eat? Cure AIDS and other diseases? Protect the environment? What am I here to do? Because nobody told me. Nobody even asked."

"I think you're here to lead people back to God," Lisa said softly.

"That's it? How?"

"Just by being yourself."

"Right. Everybody's going to follow the nine-year-old. That really would be a miracle. And you know what? I could do it, too."

"Do what?"

"All of it. Make them follow me. Cure sickness. Feed the world. I can do it all, Mom. It's easy. I can see right to the heart of things. How everything . . . is put together, I guess you could say. It's hard to explain. But I could do to the whole world what I just did to the people in the hospital and everyone else involved in Dad's death. Mess with their minds, their memories. Make them different people. Better people. Only, it wouldn't be right. It's, like, cheating, sort of. That's not why I'm here. I know that much. It's not to use my powers in that way. But then what?" He practically shouted the question skyward, as if demanding an answer from God Himself.

In the neighboring yard, a dog began to bark.

"Great," he said, then began to laugh despite himself.

Lisa laughed along with him.

They laughed for a long time, feeling the sadness shed from their hearts.

Then Ethan did what he'd known he was going to do from the moment he'd seen his mother in that hospital bed. Nothing he'd heard since had caused him to change his mind. On the contrary, he knew that Grand Inquisitor was scanning for him even now, and that there was no escaping its attention. He could have eliminated it from the world, and the Congregation too, but that wasn't his purpose. He wasn't here as God's hit man. He was confused and afraid, but at the same time determined. The ghost of his father had given him the idea.

So he reached out with the part of him that was more than human, the part that was not bound in space and time, and he removed all knowledge of himself from the world. He vanished from the databanks of Grand Inquisitor, from the files of the Congregation, from the archives of Conversatio. And so did Lisa, and Gordon.

Then he removed all knowledge of Conversatio, the Congregation, high potentials, and the second Son, and anything related to them, from Lisa's mind. In the blink of an eye, she became exactly what she had always pretended to be.

Finally, Ethan turned his powers inward, upon himself.

Forget, he thought.

And there was darkness.

CHAPTER 14

2014

The line of cars at the entrance to Lake Olathe was moving at a steady pace under the blazingly hot August sun. Peter, behind the wheel of the Prius, had collected their identity cards already, and when they reached the checkpoint he passed them through the window to an armed and armored private security guard from Oz Corp, whose eyes and nose were hidden behind a dark visor that doubled as a monitor linked directly into the vast database of the Department of Homeland Security. The visor cast a shadow over the rest of the face, obscuring identity and gender alike. But when the guard ran a hand scanner over their cards, pallid flashes like heat lightning from the underside of the visor cast illumination enough to reveal a peppering of stubble on the sweat-beaded cheeks. Ethan, from the air-conditioned depths of the backseat, felt sorry for the guy. Though it was only ten o'clock, the temperature outside was already pushing a hundred. The white body armor they wore was supposedly air-conditioned and designed to reflect solar radiation, but the guard didn't look as if either method was keeping him especially cool.

Finally, satisfied, he handed back the cards, stepped away from the window, and stiffly motioned them on.

"Man, those munchies seriously creep me out," said Peter in a low voice as he drove away, using the derogatory nickname the Oz employees had acquired, derived from "munchkins."

"Shh," said Maggie, who was sitting beside him in the front of the car. She cast a nervous glance over her shoulder. "They record everything, you know. Do you want to end up on a watch list?"

"Bullshit," said Peter. "They can't eavesdrop on private conversations between American citizens, Mags. That's the law."

"Yeah, but we're in a public place. That makes this a public conversation."

"No, we're in my car. That makes it private."

"It's your parents' car, not yours."

"So? That doesn't change anything."

"Plus, the window's open."

"Oh, please."

Ethan sighed as he listened to his friends argue back and forth. It seemed to him that they'd spent the whole summer so far arguing about one thing or another. It didn't really matter what. It was starting to get old. Not only that, it was enough like flirting to make him feel jealous, which was, he told himself for the hundredth time, ridiculous. He and Maggie were a couple and had been for almost two years now. Peter understood that. Besides, he was Ethan's best friend. He would never try to come between them. But just the same, it was annoying—probably because things were kind of tense between him and Maggie right now.

Actually, they'd been tense for a while, since before graduation. Now the tension was ratcheting up even higher as summer accelerated toward its inevitable conclusion, when the two of them would go off to different colleges: she to the University of Chicago, he to MidAmerica Nazarene, right here in Olathe. He was afraid that she'd meet someone in Chicago, that he would lose her. But of course he couldn't say any of that out loud. It made it sound as if he didn't trust her. And he did.

It was all those other guys he didn't trust.

But Maggie was sensitive that way. She always seemed to know what was on his mind. She'd tried to reassure him that just because they were going to different schools didn't mean that they were going to break up. He pretended to agree but deep down wasn't so sure. For a while now, he'd had a feeling that things weren't going to last. That with the end of high school, other things were also coming to an end.

"Well, of course they are," Peter had said in exasperation when Ethan had tried to explain the feeling to him. "That's what happens, right? One thing ends, another begins. We're not kids anymore, Ethan." He, too, was off to Chicago: to DePaul University, on a golf scholarship of all things.

That was one more thing for Ethan to worry about. Maggie would likely see more of Peter than she would of him. But what could he do? Ask them to stay away from each other?

Not for the first time, he wished that he'd been able to afford a school in Chicago too. But though his grades and scores had been good enough, the fact was that there just wasn't enough money. Ever since his dad had died of a heart attack ten years ago, things had been tight for Ethan and his mom. MidAmerica was a fine school, but even more importantly, it was an affordable school. In the end, that had been the deciding factor.

They pulled into the parking lot, found an open spot, and unloaded their gear: a beach umbrella to keep the worst of the sun at bay; rolled-up beach towels; a blanket; backpacks bulging with sandwiches, snacks, sun block, bathing suits, portable MP5 players, and books; and a cooler packed with ice, Cokes, and bottles of water. They had come to stay. He and Peter grabbed the cooler, Maggie took the umbrella, and the three of them lurched off through rows of parked cars that were already radiating a palpable heat.

The beach was an obstacle course of spread blankets and towels and colorful umbrellas sticking up at odd angles like trees in a fairytale forest. Screaming and laughing kids cavorted in the sand and in the glittering water, under the watchful eyes of lifeguards ensconced on high white perches and so swathed against the sun in towels, hats, and dark glasses that it was difficult to tell without some study whether they were male or female. Roaming along the beach, equally difficult to differentiate by gender at a distance, were more white-armored munchies from Oz Corp. Ever since the last terrorist attack on the homeland, in 2010, when over a dozen recreational areas and amusement parks across the country had been simultaneously targeted by suicide bombers, local police forces had been augmented by Oz, the largest private security firm in the United States, which had been hired as a kind of home guard by the government under the emergency powers of the amended Patriot Act. Some called it a private army whose primary loyalty was to its founder and commander, "Papa Jim" Osbourne, rather than to the country, but one thing was certain: There had been no more attacks on U.S. soil since Oz had come on board, and its presence had freed up the National Guard for the war in the Middle East. Yet despite their undoubted efficiency, Ethan agreed with Peter: The munchies gave him the creeps.

The three friends picked their way gingerly to an as-yet-uncolonized patch of sand, where they promptly planted their flag—or, rather, umbrella. As Peter and Ethan set up the site, Maggie went off to the locker room to change into her suit.

"You're a lucky man, bro," Peter told him as they watched her go.

"Yeah, I know."

"So why the long face? You're not still worried about the fall, are you?"

He shrugged.

"Dude, she loves you."

"She told you that?"

"No, but I'd have to be blind not to see it."

"People change—ow!" Peter had punched him in the arm; Ethan rubbed the spot, surprised and angry. "Are you nuts?"

"I'm fine. You're the crazy one. The only way Mags is going to break up with you is if you drive her off. And the only way you're going to drive her off is if you keep acting like such a dickhead."

"It's not that simple. I—" He broke off as Peter drew back his fist.

"Dude, don't make me hit you again."

"Okay, okay," he said hurriedly. "Jeez, I thought you golfers were supposed to be all calm and placid."

"This *is* calm and placid. You should see me when I get upset."

"No, thanks. Here, help me roll out this blanket."

Maggie came back as they were finishing up, a flustered expression on her face. "You'll never believe what I just saw in the locker room!"

"Is this a trick question?" Ethan asked as Peter guffawed.

She frowned at them both, then went on. "A couple of munchies came in while I was changing."

"Wait, were they . . . ?"

"Yes, of course they were women." Maggie rolled her eyes. "Anyway, there was another girl in there, working. Mopping the floors. They went up to her and demanded to see her card."

Peter shrugged. "They have the right to ask for ID. We had to show ours just a minute ago."

"Hold on. So she shows her card, right, and the munchies do their scan thing, and then one of them says that she checks out okay, but it seems that a family member is on the watch list."

"So?"

"So they arrested her, that's what!" Her eyes flashed with indignation.

"Mags, you didn't interfere, did you?" asked Ethan with a sinking feeling.

"What was I supposed to do, stand there and watch?"

Ethan groaned, but at the same time he felt a sense of pride rush through him.

Peter, meanwhile, said, "Yes, that's exactly what you were supposed to do."

"Well, since when have I done what I was supposed to?" She smirked at him. "Besides, what's the use of being the mayor's daughter if I can't help people sometimes?"

"Did you help this person?" asked Ethan quietly.

"I tried," she said, meeting his eyes. "I don't know if I helped or not, but I tried. I asked for her name and told her I'd get my father to do something. Then the munchies told me to back off, and they took her away. Just like that." She gestured helplessly. "I don't know what's happened to this country."

"Nine eleven happened," said Peter. "Six Flags happened."

"I feel like things took a wrong turn somewhere. They didn't have to end up this way."

"Well, they did," Peter said. "This is the way things are, and we have to learn to live with it. Either that, or end up like that woman. Arrested by the munchies and carted off to one of those detention facilities . . ."

"You mean concentration camps," said Maggie bitterly.

"Would both of you be quiet?" Ethan glanced around nervously. "No question that *this* is a public place."

"I don't even care anymore," said Maggie. "They can record whatever they want. They've probably already contacted my dad. He's gonna have a cow when I get home. But that woman hadn't done anything. She was legal. Just because some relative somewhere . . . It's not fair." Her eyes welled up, and suddenly she was crying.

"Jeez, Mags." Ethan took her into his arms, letting her sob against his shoulder. He looked at Peter, who was flushed red with embarrassment and purposefully looking away, as if something of great interest had caught his eye down the beach.

"Er, I guess I'll go change into my suit," Peter said awkwardly.

"You go too, Ethan," Maggie said, giving him a shaky smile as she stepped away.

"Will you be okay?"

She wiped her eyes. "Of course I'll be okay. Do you think they're going to come for me while you're gone?"

"Of course not," he said, though a strange dread rose up in him at her joking words. "C'mon, Pete. Let's get changed."

They hurried away, both of them eager to be gone as briefly as possible. Ethan glanced back before entering the air-conditioned locker room, and Maggie, who had been watching the whole time, waved.

Inside, he and Peter were alone.

"She's braver than I'll ever be," Ethan said at last as he undressed.

"Is that what you call it?" asked Peter.

"What do you call it?"

Peter raised a placatory hand. "Okay, okay. I agree with you. She's braver than me, too. But it's going to get her into trouble one of these days, even if she is the mayor's daughter. You can only play that card so often."

Ethan sighed. "I know. I'm worried that she'll get mixed up in something when she goes up to Chicago. There's a lot of unrest at that school."

"At every school," said Peter. "Especially now that they're talking about bringing back the draft."

"It's weird, isn't it? History repeating itself."

"Only without student deferments this time. That means—"

"I know what it means."

"It means we're screwed."

"Well, at least it's fairer that way."

"Yeah, everybody's screwed."

They finished changing in glum silence and then hurried back outside. Maggie was waiting for them, sitting on the blanket and applying sunblock to her arms and legs. She looked up with a smile. "Can you do my back, Ethan?"

"Your wish is my command."

"And don't you forget it," she said mock-sternly, standing and handing him the tube, then turning her back to him.

Ethan squeezed lotion onto her shoulders and began spreading it over her back, sliding his hand under the strap of her bikini top.

"Mmm, nice," she said, wriggling her shoulders.

The heat and silky smoothness of her skin beneath his hand was arousing, and he shifted to obscure the effect it was having on him. God, she was beautiful! It was a sublime torture to be so close to her, touching her like this, wanting more. He always wanted more of her, no matter how much they kissed, how far beyond kissing they went in their explorations of each other's bodies. Yet they hadn't slept together. And not because Maggie had refused his advances. On the contrary. He was the one who'd spurned her. Not because he didn't want to, as he tried to explain to her, not really understanding himself but knowing in his heart that it was true and right. He wanted her so badly that he ached with it. But some obscure yet powerful intuition told him that it would be a mistake they would both regret. What was the hurry, anyway? They had all the time in the world. Maggie had said she understood, but he could tell that his refusal had left her feeling confused and hurt, rejected. It had left him feeling confused as well. What was he waiting for? What was the matter with him?

But that all seemed miles away now as she reached back and pulled up her hair. "Make sure to get the back of my neck."

He couldn't resist leaning forward and kissing the nape. There was a small mole there that he loved, right below the hairline.

She squirmed. "That's not what I meant, Ethan."

"Sorry. How's this?" He licked her.

She giggled. "What do I look like, an ice-cream cone?"

"Yum. My favorite flavor, too."

At this, Peter made a gagging sound.

"Jealous?" asked Ethan.

"Yeah, I really wish you would slobber all over me next," Peter said, rolling his eyes. "I'm going for a swim before you two start talking baby talk."

"We'll be right behind you," said Maggie. "I just want to do Ethan's back first."

"What about my back?" Peter asked plaintively. "Who's going to do that?"

"What a baby," Maggie said. "I'll do yours too."

"Great." He turned, presenting his broad shoulders. "You can lick if you want."

"You wish," she said as Ethan mimed throwing up.

"Ethan Brown?"

He turned, startled. A pair of munchies was standing about five feet away. He hadn't even heard them approach. They stood ramrod straight, the sun reflected in their dark visors and off their white body armor so that he had to squint. Their tasers were pointing downward at forty-five-degree angles, but somehow he felt like they were pointing right at him.

"I'm Ethan Brown," he said, trying to keep his voice steady. "What's wrong?"

"Is this about that woman?" Maggie asked, stepping up and taking his arm in both hands.

The munchie who had spoken said, "I'm required by law to inform you that certain private information has been accessed pursuant to the provisions of Article 3, Section 21.b.iv of the Patriot Act, as amended, governing temporary suspension of privacy rights for U.S. citizens in the event of a duly declared national or personal emergency."

"What?"

"There's been an accident, Mr. Brown. The hospital has been trying to reach you, but your cell seems to be off."

"An accident?" Ethan echoed numbly.

"A car accident," the second munchie clarified. "Your mother was hurt."

"Oh God," said Ethan as Maggie gasped. He felt her hands tighten on his arm. "Is she . . ."

"She's at Olathe Medical," said the first munchie. "That's all we know, Mr. Brown. I'm sorry."

As the munchies turned away, Ethan was already fumbling at his backpack. Maggie and Peter were saying something, but he ignored them. He pulled out his cell phone; sure enough, he'd left it off. It buzzed as soon as he activated it, and the words "Olathe Medical Center" flashed onto the screen.

"Hello?"

A female voice said, "Mr. Brown?"

"Yes. I just heard about my mom. Is she okay?"

"Your mother has been in a car accident. Her injuries are severe."

"Is she going to be all right?"

"She's in surgery now. Please come as soon as you can."

"I'll be right there."

While he was talking, Maggie and Peter had packed everything up. Now, as they hurried back to the car, the object of curious stares from other beachgoers, Ethan filled his friends in on the situation . . . or what little he knew of it. He spoke with a calmness that surprised him. He felt as if he were standing a little bit outside his body, watching events unfold. A sense of unreality had slid over the day like a thin film, transparent and subtly distorting. Was this what it was like to go into shock? He didn't remember feeling this way when his father had died. He couldn't remember much about that day at all. It was probably a blessing.

"Do you want to change out of your suit?" Maggie asked as they neared the car.

"I'll change when we get there," he answered. "Let's hurry!"

"We're only a few minutes away," Peter said soothingly as he keyed the car doors open.

They piled into the car, Ethan in front and Maggie in back, and drove off.

"Faster, Pete," Ethan urged as they turned on to 151st Street.

"We don't need another accident," his friend said.

"She's going to be okay, Ethan," Maggie said, leaning forward, one hand on his shoulder.

Ethan reached up and took her hand, but he didn't say anything in reply.

He was too busy praying.

✠   ✠   ✠

Peter dropped Ethan and Maggie off at the emergency room entrance, telling them that he'd join them inside as soon as he parked the car. Ethan was already running up the sidewalk before Peter had finished speaking. Maggie followed, carrying their backpacks with their clothes.

Bursting through the doors, Ethan made straight for the reception counter, barely registering the presence of other people in the waiting area. The nurse on duty, a tall African American man with a shaved head, a thin, trim mustache, and a gold hoop in one ear glanced up as he approached, frowning slightly as if disapproving of his attire.

"Can I help you?"

"My mother's been in accident!" he gasped out.

"And her name is . . . ?"

"Brown. Lisa Brown. I just talked to a nurse. I'm Ethan Brown."

"Yes, your mother's in surgery," said the nurse, glancing at a computer screen.

"How is she? What happened?"

"A car accident. Multiple vehicles. She was coptered in."

"Oh my God!" This from Maggie, who had come to stand beside him, once again clutching his arm.

"Is she going to be okay?" Ethan asked. "What are they operating on her for?"

"I'm sorry, but I don't have that information."

"Who does? I want to talk to them."

"I'll have someone come talk to you," said the nurse. "Please take a seat."

"I don't think I can sit down right now."

"That's fine," said the nurse soothingly. "Excuse me one minute." He went to the far side of the counter, picked up a phone, and spoke into it with a low but urgent voice.

"Come on, Ethan," said Maggie, gently pulling him away from the counter. "You're shivering in this air-conditioning. You need to put some clothes on."

"I need to be here."

"It'll just take a second. I'll stay right here. If someone comes, I'll call for you, I promise."

"Okay." He scarcely knew what he was saying or doing. Numbly, he took the backpack she thrust into his hands and stumbled into the men's room. There was no one else inside. He stepped into a stall and shut the door behind him.

Then it hit him.

He was going to lose his mom. He knew it somehow. She was going to die.

He groaned aloud and sank to his haunches, shuddering with the effort of holding back his tears.

What was wrong with him? This wasn't helping anybody. Besides, he didn't know his mom was going to die. His fears were getting the better of him. But he couldn't help it. First his dad, now her . . .

Please, God, he prayed silently. *Don't let her die! I'll do anything . . .*

He kept imagining her in the wreck, her body torn and broken amid the twisted metal. Or laid out on the operating table as the surgeons worked feverishly to save her. At the same time, he saw her as he'd last seen her that morning, before she'd left for work. Healthy, smiling. It seemed impossible that in such a brief time she could go from that state to whatever state she was in now.

But he didn't know anything about that. And he wasn't going to find out here, sniffling and shivering like a little kid in the bathroom stall. It reminded him of something, the sense of hiding here, as if there were something out there looking for him. Or, no, as if he were trapped here, waiting for some monster to arrive . . .

He got to his feet and quickly pulled on the clothes in his backpack. Then he exited the stall and went to the sink and splashed his face with water. That was when Peter came in.

Ethan looked up, water running down his face, and locked eyes with his friend's reflection in the mirror above the sink. "Is there . . . ?"

Peter shook his head. "No news yet. I just came in to check on you."

"I'm fine. I was just coming out."

"Dude, she's going to be okay."

"How the hell do you know that?" He turned to face Peter, suddenly angry.

Peter flinched as though he'd struck him. "Uh . . ."

"Sorry," he said. "But I just wish people would stop saying that."

"Okay," said Peter.

"I mean, nobody knows anything. It's just pretending to say you do."

"You're right," said Peter. "I guess I wasn't thinking. I just don't want anything to happen to her, is all."

"You think I do?" he replied. "But I'm not going to pretend."

Peter nodded. "I called my mom," he said. "She wants me to drive back home and get her. So I gotta leave for a while. But I'll be right back, okay?"

"Okay." Ethan grabbed a paper towel and dried his face, then crumpled up the towel and tossed it into the receptacle. "Thanks, Pete. Sorry I went off on you there."

"No problem," said his friend. "Shit, if it was me, I don't know what I'd do."

"It sucks," Ethan said. "The not knowing. I guess I better get out there."

"Yeah, Mags is probably wondering if you're okay."

Ethan took a breath. "Listen, Pete. In case things go crazy, and I forget to say this . . . thanks, man. Thanks for being a good friend. The best."

Pete's face turned fiery red. "Listen, dude. I'm not going to pretend, okay? Fuck that. But I'm going to hope. Yeah, and pray too. Nothing wrong with that, is there?"

Ethan felt himself tearing up again. "No. Nothing wrong with that at all."

✠   ✠   ✠

Outside, Maggie was anxiously pacing back and forth. She'd put her clothes on over her bathing suit. When Ethan stepped out of the bathroom, she ran to him and threw her arms around him. He hugged her back hard, grateful beyond words for her presence.

"Still no news," she said.

Ethan returned to the counter, where a different nurse was now on duty, a white woman this time, plump and grandmotherly. "I'm Ethan Brown," he told her. "Someone's supposed to come and talk to me about my mom. She's in surgery."

"Oh yes," said the woman, whose name tag read Matthews. "I spoke to you earlier, on the phone."

"Can you tell me anything, Nurse Matthews?"

"I'm afraid not, but someone from Social Services really should have spoken to you by now." She pursed her lips as she looked at the computer screen. "Just give me a minute."

"That's what the other nurse said."

"I'm sorry about that. I—oh. There's Dr. Sung now! He's chief of surgery."

The Asian-looking man who advanced toward them across the room was slender and of middling height, with jet-black hair and an olive complexion. He wore gold-rimmed glasses and green hospital scrubs.

"Dr. Sung, this is Mrs. Brown's son, Ethan, the boy we were trying to reach."

Dr. Sung nodded briskly.

"How is she, Doctor?" Ethan asked.

"Lucky to be alive," said Dr. Sung in a clipped British accent. "A tractor-trailer overturned outside St. Louis, and Mrs. Brown was caught in the pileup. She suffered severe internal injuries, broken ribs, and head trauma."

Ethan was holding on to Maggie's hand for dear life. "Is . . . is she going to be okay?"

"She came through the surgery, so that's good," said Dr. Sung. "But she's not out of the woods yet, Ethan. The next hours and days are key."

"Can I see her?"

"Of course. As soon as she's settled."

"Is she conscious?"

"In cases like this, with serious brain trauma, the standard procedure is to induce a coma, which is what we've done here. I understand from your mother's records that your father died some years ago, Ethan."

"Yes."

"Is there anyone else we should notify? An uncle or aunt, perhaps?"

Ethan shook his head. "There's just me, Dr. Sung. No other family."

"I see." Dr. Sung gave Maggie a curious look.

"I'm his girlfriend," Maggie said.

Dr. Sung nodded and looked back to Ethan. "How old are you, Ethan?"

"Eighteen," Ethan said. "What's that got to do with anything?"

"It means you can act on your mother's behalf as next of kin without the appointment of a guardian."

"That's good, right?"

"It simplifies things, yes."

"When can I see my mom?"

"We'll have a nurse come fetch you as soon as she's settled in." He glanced at Maggie again. "I'm sorry, young lady, but visitation in the ICU is for family members only."

"I understand," she said.

"I want to stay with my mom tonight," Ethan said.

"That's fine," said Dr. Sung. "In fact, we encourage it. Comatose patients often respond well to the presence of loved ones. It can be quite therapeutic . . . for all concerned."

"Will she be able to hear me?"

"That's hard to say, but it can't do any harm to assume that she can. At least, that's been my experience."

Ethan nodded again. "Thanks, Dr. Sung. For saving my mom."

"You're welcome, young man," said the doctor. "But I've only given her a fighting chance. The rest is up to her, and to God."

✠   ✠   ✠

By night the hospital seemed a very different place than it had during the day. During the day there was a ceaseless buzz of activity, even in the ICU. But at night the number of visitors dropped nearly to nothing, only one or two others like Ethan; he caught sight of them from time to time, a young woman and an older woman, shambling up and down the corridors when sleep wouldn't come, just as he roamed about when he could no longer stand the awful sounds of the room where his mother lay still as death upon a bed, her body swathed in bandages, tubes attached to her arms and to her head, the only noises those of the machines that were keeping her alive. They passed each other with nods and occasional words but exchanged no meaningful conversation, each of them sunk too deeply in their own concerns. Even the nurses going about their rounds had a ghostly aspect to them, so silently did they move, or rather drift, down the dimly lit corridors, pushing their carts and carrying their clipboards like workers from the afterlife come to keep tabs on those who would soon join them there.

It had been early afternoon when a nurse had come to the waiting room and told Ethan that he could come to his mother. Peter had gone and returned with his mother by then, and Maggie had not left Ethan's side. But they could not follow where he was going now, though they told him they would wait for him there until visiting hours were over, if he wanted to come and talk or just sit in silence in the company of those who loved him.

But he had only gone back once, briefly, feeling like he no longer belonged in their healthy world, that even by being there for a few moments he was deserting his mother when she needed him most. He'd gone just the same to thank them for coming and to kiss Maggie and tell her that he loved her and would see her tomorrow. Then he'd gone back up to the ICU and the room in which his mother was fighting for her life.

The first time he'd walked into that room and seen her there on the bed, he'd had a feeling of déjà vu stronger than anything he'd ever experienced. He'd stopped just across the threshold of the door as the nurse looked back at him with curiosity and compassion on her features, thinking no doubt that it was the shock of seeing his mother in such a grave condition that was responsible for his gasp and his pallid complexion as he stood frozen on the spot. But it was more than that. It was an inescapable sense that he'd seen this before, or something like it: his mother lying close to death. Yet he hadn't. How could he?

So he'd pushed it from his mind, or tried to. And mostly succeeded, because the here and now was terrible enough to overwhelm the vaporous promptings of a past that could never have occurred.

Dr. Sung had told him that his mother could hear what he said to her, or anyway that he should assume it was so, and thus he'd talked to her for hours, pleading tearfully with her to get well and sharing the old stories that bound their family together, of vacations and birthdays and funerals, happy times and sad. He was trying to bring her back, calling to her as if from a great distance. But if she answered, he couldn't hear it.

As evening drew on into night, and night stretched out as if there were no such thing as morning, the desolate loneliness of the ICU seemed to suck his hope away, until he felt small and helpless, hardly even visible as he sat there at Lisa's bedside, holding her limp hand in his own, looking at the tubes that went into her bruised arms.

He prayed as he had never prayed before.

When he began to get sleepy, nodding out in the chair, he would get to his feet and wander the halls, never straying far, following a circular route that brought him past her open door every few minutes, so that he could see that she was still clinging to life. He would do this because it seemed to him that if he slept even for a minute, she would slip away, cross over whatever boundary separated the living and the dead and be gone from him forever.

How was it that he could love someone so much and yet be helpless to save her? Helpless to do anything for her at all but be a witness to her suffering? Surely there was something wrong with love if it couldn't make a difference when it was needed most. How was it that God could have created such an emotion, such an intimate tie between people, only to make it, in the end, powerless? It seemed unfair, even cruel, that love couldn't pour itself out from one person to another like a transfusion of blood, of breath, supplying what he or she lacked and needed to live. Why couldn't it? He would wring his heart dry like a sponge, empty his lungs, for his mother's sake. But he didn't have the power. The choice, the sacrifice, wasn't his to make.

Finally, as Ethan wandered the bleak corridors, he took a turn that he didn't remember having seen before. The white tiles beneath his feet gave way to reddish dust and rock, and the fluorescent lights overhead drew back and merged together into a sun as bright as a silver ingot. Gone was the air-conditioned chill, replaced with a heat that beat down on his head and shoulders like a molten weight. He knew then that he had fallen asleep and was dreaming, and he turned frantically, hoping by this to wake himself before it was too late, and his mother, as he feared would happen, escaped his vigil, leaving him alone in the world, an orphan. But when he saw stretching behind him the same desert landscape as had stretched ahead, a wasteland in which no living thing grew or moved save the dark shapes of birds spiraling high overhead, he knew that it was too late, that she had gone where he could not follow.

He had lost her.

Something broke in him then, and he sank down into the dust and wept.

After a time, he heard footsteps, and he raised his head to see a gaunt, bearded man in a ragged robe and sandals drawing near. "Why are you crying?" asked the man.

"My mother has died," said Ethan.

"Dry your eyes," said the man. "She lives."

"How do you know?"

"It is given me to know."

Ethan climbed to his feet. He tried to get a good look at the man's face, but the sun was in his eyes, or so it seemed. "Who are you, mister?"

"Don't you remember me?"

"Sort of . . ." He gave up trying to look at the man's face and instead took a good look around. "Have I been here before?"

"A long time ago. You were just a boy."

He smiled apologetically. "I guess I must have forgotten."

"Children forget. Are you still a child?"

"What?"

"You have been asleep," the man said. "It is time for you to wake up."

"I don't—"

"Wake up!"

His voice was like a crack of thunder. Ethan bolted up in the chair.

There was a furious beeping from the machines in the room, and suddenly a nurse came rushing through the door. "Oh Christ," she said, then hit an intercom on the wall. "Code blue!" she cried. "Code blue!"

Ethan shot to his feet. "What is it? What's happening?"

"You have to wait outside," said the nurse.

By then more medical personnel were arriving, nurses and technicians and the night resident, Dr. Holtzbrink. Ethan was bustled out of the room, into the corridor, the door shut firmly in his face. From the other side, he heard the sounds of frantic activity.

So this was it, then, he thought. This was how his mother would die.

Yet the man had said she was still alive . . .

No, that had been a dream. Or had it? It had seemed so real, and he remembered it now so clearly: the dust of the road, the barren landscape, the suffocating heat. The man's voice, kindly yet commanding. *You have been asleep. It is time for you to wake up.*

A strange feeling crept over him, as if he were still asleep and dreaming. As if none of this were real . . . or as if reality itself were something more malleable than he had known. Yet it seemed to him that he had known it once.

Children forget. Are you still a child?

What had the man meant by that? Of course he wasn't a child. He was eighteen, a man.

Wake up!

Again that voice, like a thunderclap. Ethan staggered, as the wall he'd erected in himself ten years ago came tumbling down, falling like the walls of Jericho blasted by the horn of Joshua.

He remembered.

Remembered how his father had really died, and everything his mother had told him about the Doctrine of the second Son, about the Congregation and Conversatio. He remembered how he had walked through the red dust of the wasteland for three days and three nights, how the spirits of his dead father and the dead priest had come to tempt and torment him, and how a third figure had finally appeared and helped him to escape that place.

It is too early for you to walk this road, the man had said. His brother. *Too early for you to climb the hill that waits at the end.*

He remembered that the man he had thought of as his father was not his real father, and the woman he had called his mother was not his real mother. He had been adopted. Hidden away.

Hunted.

Everything he had known and understood on that long-ago night as he lay in the backyard of their house with his mother, gazing up at the stars, came flooding back to Ethan now. And as he had done then, he flinched from the overwhelming implications of it. Yet he was no longer a child, no longer so easily frightened. Forgetting was not an option for the man he had grown to be. He could do it, of course. Make himself forget again, just as he had before. He had that power. But what had been forgivable in a boy was shameful in a man. He had a duty. A mission.

It was a different mission than that of the man in the wasteland, his brother, though both of them had been sent by the same father. A different mission . . . but no easier.

The fiery words of Ezekiel blazed in his mind. *Now, thou Son of Man, wilt thou judge, wilt thou judge the bloody city? Yea, thou shalt show her all her abominations.*

Ethan bowed his head, weeping with the knowledge of what would come. He would not hide from that knowledge. Not anymore. It was part of him now. Part of who he was, both man and Son of man.

"Mr. Brown?"

He looked up. Standing in the doorway of the room was Dr. Holtz-brink.

"I'm sorry, Mr. Brown. Your mother is dead."

He nodded. This, too, he had foreseen. And more. But he would not stray from the path again. "I know you did everything you could, Doctor."

"You can have some time alone with her if you like."

"Thank you."

When the room had been cleared, Ethan entered. The chair he'd been sitting in had been pushed away, so he pulled it back over to the bedside and sat down. His mother, or rather the woman who had raised him, the woman he loved as if she really had been his mother, looked so calm, so peaceful. At rest. She was beyond the reach of any human agency now.

But not beyond his reach.

He stretched out his hand and laid his palm on the white bandages that swathed her forehead.

He hesitated then, not because he was uncertain or afraid, but because he knew that from this moment there could be no going back. Once he did this thing, events would be set in motion that had been prepared from the very dawn of time. Prepared . . . yet it was given to him to make the choice, an exercise of free will, that human curse and blessing in which he shared by right of birth.

"Mother," he said, for what else could he call her now, at this moment of all moments? "Mother, wake up."

✠   ✠   ✠

With a gasp, he came awake, heart hammering in his chest so fiercely that he thought at first he was having an attack. But almost at once he realized, as he sat up in bed in the darkness of his room, that what had woken him had been a shock to more than just his own system. The whole world had shuddered with it.

Ten years ago, Papa Jim had stood in an observation room in a private hospital outside Phoenix, Arizona, and watched something incredible take place on the other side of the one-way glass. Something impossible. Doctors, men and women of science, had fallen to their knees . . .

He had rushed from the room. Flung the door open . . .

And stepped into his office, in South Carolina, a thousand miles away. The hospital and what it contained forgotten. Or no, not forgotten: the very reality of it wiped clean, erased from the blackboard of history.

A miracle!

It all came flooding back to him now.

It's true, he realized. As he'd realized ten years ago.

There really is a second son.

The Son of man.

He had cloaked himself. Hidden from prying eyes, from the powers of the world that had sought to kill him or to use him.

No more. In an instant, somewhere, somehow, he had revealed himself after all this time. Ethan Brown, as the boy had been called.

His great-grandson, if the boy had only known it.

Boy no longer.

But why? Why now?

Papa Jim didn't know.

But he was sure as hell going to find out.

✠　　　✠　　　✠

The young priest pounded up the stairs and down the corridor, past the Swiss Guards who stood as rigidly as robots, their eyes not even blinking as he dashed by . . . if a man of such rotundity could be said to dash. Of course, his coming had been cleared electronically; no surprises were permitted in the private quarters of the pope. Ever since Islamic terrorists had infiltrated the Vatican and murdered the previous pope in 2011, clearing the way for the present occupant of St. Peter's throne, the first pontiff to assume that name since the original, over two thousand years ago, Vatican security had been placed into the hands, metaphorically speaking, of the Congregation of the Doctrine of the Faith—which meant, as only trusted agents like the young priest knew, the artificial intelligence program called Grand Inquisitor. What a mass of contradictions the Vatican was, the priest thought, not for the first time since his arrival here two months ago, in its mix of ancient protocol and a technology that went so far beyond anything known to the rest of the world that it smacked of science fiction. For instance, that a messenger should be dispatched to alert His Holiness to information that might more easily and quickly come to him wirelessly . . . why, he wouldn't have believed it if he hadn't seen it himself, hadn't sat there silently in the bowels of the Vatican as other messengers came and went, marveling at the waste of it, the anachronism. Yet now that he had been entrusted with such a message for the first time in his still-brief career, the young priest no longer thought it quite so wasteful, and the anachronistic aspects seemed freshly appealing to his sense of the continuity of history. Yes, he could see how the Vatican might change a man, given enough time. He might even sweat off a few pounds running hither and yon.

After a time, he came to the door of the antechamber to the pope's private rooms. He halted, panting for breath, sweat streaming down his plump, buttery-smooth cheeks. On either side of the door, a Swiss Guard stared impassively ahead. "F—father O'Malley to see His Ho—holiness," he wheezed out at last.

The guards did not move, yet the door behind them swung open.

The priest swallowed nervously and entered, sucking in his belly to squeeze past the guards with a half-wincing smile of ingratiation and apology. *Oh dear,* he thought. *I really have to cut back on the pasta.*

Waiting for him in the richly appointed antechamber was Cardinal Ehrlich, the pope's oldest friend and closest confidante, as well as the nominal head of the Congregation. He was a matchstick of a man, with piercing gray eyes that seemed perpetually alight with suspicion. "O'Malley, is it?"

"Y—yes, Your Eminence." He bent low to kiss the proffered ring, wheezing again at the effort.

"For God's sake, man, give me your message before your heart gives out."

Father O'Malley felt his cheeks burning. Mustering his dignity, he mopped his forehead with a white handkerchief drawn from his surplice and said, "In a hospital in Olathe, Kansas, a little over an hour ago, a deceased woman was brought back to life."

Cardinal Ehrlich raised a flinty eyebrow. "Is that all?"

O'Malley couldn't tell if the man was being ironic or not. Was it really such a run-of-the-mill occurrence, the resurrection of the dead? Perhaps so. "No, Your Eminence. The other patients were also cured."

"What?" There was no mistaking his surprise. "All of them?"

O'Malley nodded, trying to hide his satisfaction at having provoked a reaction. "Apparently so, Your Eminence. No one seems to know who was responsible. There are conflicting reports. Some say it was a boy or a young man, a relative of the dead woman. Others claim to have seen angels. And UFOs. In other words, a lot of confusion, even hysteria. Agents have been dispatched, but Grand Inquisitor thought His Holiness should know."

"I'll inform His Holiness at once," said Ehrlich. "Well done, Father O'Malley."

"What does it mean, Your Eminence?" the priest dared to ask.

"Eh? Mean?" Cardinal Ehrlich gave him a grim smile. "It means things are about to get interesting, that's what."

✠   ✠   ✠

Sister Elena was kneeling in the dirt of the garden and pulling up weeds when a shadow fell across the ground. She looked up, startled, for she'd heard no footsteps.

"Oh," she said. "Oh."

"Don't be afraid," said the black man in the red beret who was gazing down at her with a smile on his face. His feet in their black sneakers were hovering an inch or so above the ground.

She recognized him at once despite all the years that had passed since she'd seen him. He hadn't aged a day. But somehow, she couldn't speak.

Could barely even breathe. Then it was as if his shadow suddenly darkened, flowing over her to blot out the sun.

When she opened her eyes again, she was lying on the ground, gazing up at the dark moon of his face. He was kneeling beside her, looking at her with concern. She realized she must have fainted even as he asked gently if she was all right.

"I'm fine," she said, sitting up. The shock of seeing him had given way to anger. "Now you show up. Do you know how desperately I looked for you all those years ago? How I prayed for you to come to me again?"

"Yes." He stood, still hovering inches above the ground.

"Then why did you stay away?"

"I had my orders. I'm sorry."

"And you're following orders now, I suppose."

"Yes."

She sighed, no longer angry, just weary. "Go away, Gabriel. Hasn't God punished me enough? Go away or I'll scream."

"No one will hear you," he said. "No one can see or hear us."

She sighed again, defeated. "What do you want?"

"Your son needs you, Kate."

"My son is dead."

"No, he lives."

She almost fainted again at that. But she steeled herself, shook her head. She couldn't let herself believe what he was telling her. It would be too painful to find out he was wrong. "You're lying."

"Did I lie before? Look into your heart, Kate. You know that Ethan lives. You've always known."

She shot to her feet. "And you let me suffer all these years thinking he was dead! You bastard!" She swung her hand at his face, intending to slap him, but the air itself opposed her, held her arm immobilized until she let it fall to her side. "How dare you call yourself an angel!"

"I do as I am commanded," Gabriel said.

"Well, I'm through with being commanded. Do you hear? Finished!"

"This is no command."

"What is it then?"

"A gift. An apology." He spread his hands and shrugged. "Think of it as you like."

Her anger drained away, leaving only grief behind. "Papa Jim . . . He lied to me, didn't he? They all lied."

"Yes."

"Why? Why would they tell me Ethan was dead?"

"Because he is who he is."

"The Son of God, you mean."

"The Son of man."

"I don't understand."

"You will," Gabriel said. "If you go to him."

"But I can't just walk out of here."

"Why not? No one will stop you. No one will even see you go."

"I don't have any money, for one thing. And even if I did, I wouldn't know where to go to find him."

"Seek him in Kansas," said Gabriel.

"And how am I supposed to get there? Follow the Yellow Brick Road?"

"God will provide."

"Yeah," she said, glaring at him. "That's what worries me."

CHAPTER 15

It was hard to say which was the greater shock when Lisa opened her eyes in the hospital room and saw Ethan gazing down at her: the knowledge that she'd died and been brought back to life, or the sudden return of all the memories that had been taken from her nearly ten years before. The immensity of both stunned her.

"Hi, Mom," Ethan said meanwhile, smiling as tears glimmered on his face in the cool white glow of the overhead lights. "Welcome back."

"Oh Ethan," she said softly, her own eyes filling with tears. "What have you done?" She understood right away that by bringing her back, Ethan had proclaimed his existence to Grand Inquisitor and the Congregation.

"I had to," he said, and she saw in his eyes that he understood as well, and that he had accepted the ramifications of his action. This miracle he had performed. "I couldn't let you go."

Lisa remembered the accident, the realization even as the oncoming tractor-trailer was jackknifing across the road in front of her that there was no avoiding it, that she was witnessing the final moments of her life. There had been time only to feel surprise and the beginnings of sadness, then nothing. Or no: Hadn't she felt her soul drift clear of her body? It seemed to her now that she had, and had felt, too, a surge of bright anticipation, something like when she'd been ten years old and had been coming home after a month away at Girl Scout camp. She'd had a fantastic time, made lots of new friends and had wonderful experiences, but all of it had paled into insignificance as she sat on the chartered bus that was bringing her closer every second to the home she'd hardly even given a thought to for most of the last month, had practically forgotten about altogether in fact, but which now loomed ever larger in her mind and in her heart. *Home*. Such a simple word for the place that she loved like no other, where her parents were waiting to welcome her and hear all about her adventures, where she was loved and accepted unconditionally and would always have a place, no matter what. That, she thought now, dazed and tearful in the hospital bed, was what it had been like to die. It had felt like coming home, only to her real, true home, the home that had preceded every other home she'd ever had, and which, although forgotten, she'd yet sensed dimly from time to time, shining through the smeary neon haze of daily existence, just as the soul sometimes shines through the body. The home of homes. Heaven. That was where she'd been bound when Ethan had called to her. She'd heard his voice, full of love yet also hard and commanding, a voice she could not deny. Even death could not deny it.

Mother, wake up . . .

As if she'd only been sleeping. And yet to him it was the same, she realized. Lisa had known before this moment that Ethan was the second Son, but only now did the truth of it strike her viscerally. This young man, her son in all but blood, was more than mortal: He was divine. And though a part of her mourned the Heaven she had lost, and all that she knew or believed was waiting for her there—Gordon, her parents and grandparents, and other friends and family members no longer among the living—she knew too that it wasn't lost to her forever, and that if Heaven was being in the presence of God, then she was in Heaven right here and now, and always had been, for where the Son of man was, there too God must be.

She groped for his hand, drew it to her lips, and kissed it fervently. "Lord," she began, "I am not worthy—"

Ethan turned bright red and pulled his hand away, interrupting her. "Come on, Mom, knock it off. It's still me, Ethan, okay?"

"But—"

"We can argue about it later if you want. Right now I think we should get out of here before things get too crazy."

Now it was Lisa's turn to blush. He was right. The longer they stayed, the more likely it became that the Congregation would send its killers to finish the job they'd botched ten years ago. "I'm sorry," she said. "I'm not thinking too clearly . . ."

At which he burst into laughter. "Mom, considering all you've been through, you're doing pretty good, if you ask me."

She had to laugh herself at that. Then, as she began to get out of bed, marveling at how good she felt, the injuries she must have suffered in the crash not merely healed but as if never inflicted at all, she suddenly stopped. "Oh no!"

"What's wrong?"

"I can't just walk out of here wearing a hospital gown."

"Sure you can. Nobody will see you, I promise."

"*You'll* see me. And these things don't close very well in back! Besides, how are we getting home? We can't exactly take my car, can we?"

Ethan frowned. "I didn't think of that."

"Can't you . . ." She gestured with one hand. "You know."

He rolled his eyes. "Mom, it's not like I'm Harry Potter. I can't just wave my magic wand and make things happen." Seeing her expression, he amended. "Okay, I *could*, but that's not how it's supposed to work. There are rules, and I'm not supposed to break them."

"Rules? You mean like raising someone from the dead, maybe?"

He blushed again. "I wasn't going to lose you," he said stubbornly. "Not after what happened to Dad."

"I just don't want you to get into trouble," she said. Then shook her head. "Listen to me! As if you could get into trouble!"

"I can," he said. "I will. It's what I'm here for."

And such sadness came into his eyes as he spoke that she felt her heart breaking for him. She would do anything, pay any price, to take that sadness away, but she knew that it was beyond her. Still, she had to ask. "What's going to happen, Ethan?"

He shrugged, looking so much like the small boy she remembered that she had to fight to keep herself from crying. "I can't tell you that, Mom. I'm sorry. I wish I could, but I can't."

"You know, though, don't you? You've seen the future."

"I've seen things, yes. But nothing is set in stone. All God's children possess free will. Even me."

"I don't understand."

"How could you? But try not to worry. And Mom?"

"What?"

"Our ride home is here."

"What?"

But even as she spoke, the door to the room opened, and Peter came in. He looked a little bit as if he'd been raised from the dead himself, his hair sticking out in all directions, his eyes wide open with shock or wonder. He half stumbled into the room, shutting the door forcefully behind him. "Man, it's nuts out there!" he gasped. "I nearly—" Then, as he registered the fact that Lisa was sitting up in bed, obviously uninjured, he dropped to his knees.

"Ethan, man, you healed her!"

"He did more than that," Lisa said proudly.

"Huh?"

"Let's just say that I've got a pretty good idea how Lazarus must have felt." She flashed him a wink.

Peter's eyes grew even wider. "Holy shit! I mean . . ."

Ethan laughed. "It's okay, Pete. Get up, will you? You don't have to kneel to me."

Peter got to his feet, looking a little embarrassed. "Kneel to you? Dude, I should smack you! There I was, lying in bed, tossing and turning, you know, all worried about you and your mom, when suddenly, bam, out of the blue, I *remember*. You know what I'm talking about. Man, I bolted up out of bed and drove right over here to give you a piece of my mind. I mean, I thought we were friends, Ethan. I thought . . ." He paused, frustrated. "Do you have any idea what it's like to suddenly remember that the last ten years of your life are a kind of lie?"

"Actually, I do," Ethan said. "I know I made you forget some things, and I'm sorry for that. But I made everybody forget. Even me."

"Wow, you can do that?"

"Yes, but I won't anymore. I promise. Not to you, not to anybody."

Peter nodded slowly. "Good. Because, no disrespect or anything, you being who you are and all, but that still doesn't give you the right to mess around with people, you know?"

"Yeah, I know. I didn't before, but I do now."

At that, Peter laughed. "You got a funny way of showing it."

"What do you mean?"

He jerked his head toward the door. "Like I said, it's nuts out there! I'm surprised we can't hear all the commotion in here . . ."

"That's me again," Ethan admitted. "I'm keeping everything out."

"Must be nice to be able to do that. Anyway, the hospital's in an uproar. They're saying that everybody's cured. Every patient in the whole damn place."

Lisa gasped, hand to her mouth. "Ethan!"

He gave that same stubborn shrug again. "I said I was through with hiding."

"Yes, but every patient?"

"Which ones should I have left alone, Mom? The lady with breast cancer across the hall? The old guy with diabetes on the next floor? The kid with HIV?"

She flinched before his vehemence. "I . . . I didn't mean . . . It's just . . ."

He pressed on. "I know I can't cure everyone. Like I said, there are rules. But I had to do this. I couldn't bring you back and then ignore everyone else. I just couldn't do it!"

"I know, honey. And I'm prouder of you than I can say. But they'll be coming after you now. In full force."

He nodded grimly. "It's begun," he said.

"Hello?" Peter was looking back and forth between the two of them. "Remember me? The guy who doesn't know what the heck is going on?"

"It's a long story, Pete," Ethan said. "How about I fill you in while you're driving us home?"

"Home? Dude, if someone's coming after you, don't you think they'll go to your house first?"

"We'll be safe there," Ethan assured him.

"Huh. And you know that how? Don't answer! I don't want to know." Peter ran his hand through his hair, mussing it further. "Oh, man. I just realized! Does Maggie know any of this shit? 'Cause I'm thinking that she's not going to be too happy when she finds out her boyfriend is, like, the Second Coming of Jesus Christ or something."

"He's not Jesus," said Lisa. "He's the Second Son."

"I didn't know Jesus had a little brother."

"There's the Son of God, and then there's the Son of man. It's in the Bible."

"Whatever," Peter said. "I'm just saying, you might want to talk to her, Ethan. You know, before she turns on the tube or goes online or something and hears about the big 'Miracle of Olathe Medical.'"

Ethan, who hadn't really thought about how he was going to break any of this to Maggie, glanced up at that. "The Miracle of Olathe Medical?"

Peter grinned. "Yeah, that's what I heard a couple of nurses call it. They were talking to some reporter."

Lisa sighed heavily. "That means the news has already reached Grand Inquisitor. We have to move fast, Ethan. Are you sure it's safe for us to go home?"

"As safe as anywhere," he said.

"Who's this Grand Inquisitor guy?" Peter wanted to know.

"It's not a guy," Lisa said. "It's a computer. An artificial intelligence."

"Jesus," Peter said. "No offense, Ethan, but what's next? Aliens?"

"There are no aliens, Pete."

"Vampires, maybe?"

"I'm afraid not."

"Good. Because you've already blown my mind enough for one day, you know what I mean? Anything more and you might as well just drop me off at the nearest padded cell."

✠　　　✠　　　✠

Lisa draped a blanket over her shoulders like a shawl, and then they walked out of the room and into a scene of utter chaos. Despite the lateness of the hour, the halls of the hospital were jammed with patients and their families, doctors and nurses, and media representatives. People were laughing and crying, hugging, running and skipping, dancing, praying: It was like a big wedding reception that had gotten a bit out of hand. Music was playing over the PA system, and some visitors had brought in alcohol, which they had generously shared around. Even the security guards had joined the party. Only the team of munchies assigned to the facility appeared immune to the general enthusiasm, not interfering but not joining in, either. With their dark visors and white body armor, they reminded Lisa of rejects from a Star Wars convention.

Ethan, Peter, and Lisa moved through the halls of Olathe Medical like ghosts. No one seemed to see them, not even the munchies with their electronically augmented senses, but people stepped out of their way, warned by some instinct below the level of consciousness. Occasionally, as they made their way out of the building, someone would brush or stumble against them, but even then the spell remained unbroken, and they passed on without interference, exiting finally to the parking lot, where they piled into Peter's parents' car and drove off.

On the way home, as Ethan had promised, he and Lisa filled Peter in on Conversatio, the Congregation, Grand Inquisitor, and the second Son.

"Wait," Peter said at last. "You're telling me that Pope Peter II is really a front man for a robot brain? And that robot wants to kill Ethan because he's the second Son of God? Did we take a wrong turn somewhere and end up in a Philip K. Dick movie?"

"He's not a front man," Ethan said. "The pope runs the show. Grand Inquisitor is just a tool, a servant."

"It's not a robot," Lisa added. "It's a massively parallel processing network with quantum superpositioning software."

"Riiiight."

"I touched the mind of Grand Inquisitor once, a long time ago," Ethan said. "It's self-conscious, but not like a human. It's a machine, a servant. It has no desire to rule. It has no desires at all, not as we would understand them. It doesn't *want* to kill me. It's just doing what it was made to do."

"Somehow that doesn't make me feel any better, dude."

Lisa laughed. "I guess it must seem a little overwhelming and hard to believe."

"Oh, I believe it," Peter said. "I've seen what Ethan can do. It's just . . . I'm not all that familiar with the Bible or anything, but isn't the Second Coming supposed to be the trigger for, well, the Apocalypse? I mean, is the world coming to an end? 'Cause if it is, I'd kind of like to have a heads up."

Ethan grinned, grateful for Peter's commonsense perspective. Nothing seemed to fluster him for long; his defense mechanism of ironic humor deflected every worry, every fear. "I'm not going to lie to you, Pete. God sent me here for a reason. I'm not going to trigger the Apocalypse or anything, at least I don't think so, but I am going to shake things up."

"The world needs shaking up," Peter said after a moment's consideration. "I'd like to help if I can."

"Me too," said Lisa.

"Good," said Ethan. "I've got a feeling I'm going to need it."

Peter cleared his throat. "Does this make me, like, an apostle?"

"That was Jesus's thing. I'm not him."

"So I don't get any special powers or anything?"

"Pete!" laughed Lisa.

"Just asking."

"Jesus was the first step," Ethan went on. "Christianity took a lot of stuff from Judaism, but it also opened things up. I'm going to go beyond Jesus, beyond Christianity. What I have to say is for everyone to hear: Jews, Christians, Muslims."

"Sounds cool," said Peter. "But what are you going to tell them, Ethan? I mean, what's the message?"

"I'm the message," Ethan said.

✠   ✠   ✠

Back home, Ethan sat on the couch in the living room and watched television. Every channel was covering the "Miracle of Olathe Medical," as it had been quickly and universally dubbed as if by the operation of a group mind, and at first he and Lisa had watched avidly, sitting side by side, listening as people told their stories and gave their opinions about what had happened, who or what was responsible, the explanations ranging from God to aliens to really out-there stuff that had them laughing or just shaking their heads in amazement. After a while, Lisa had gotten up to take a shower, and now she was napping in her room, worn out by all the excitement. "Being dead really takes it out of you" was how she'd half jokingly put it. Even so, she'd only gone after he'd promised her that there was no danger.

Of course, that had been a lie.

Ethan wondered if Jesus had been able to lie. Was that one of the differences between the Son of God and the Son of man? He didn't know. There was actually quite a lot that he didn't know about himself and his mission. He had faith that everything would become clear in its proper time, that God would reveal what he needed to know when he needed to know it, but even so, he couldn't help feeling anxious about what was going to happen. Because, oh yes, there was danger, more danger than Lisa could imagine, but it wouldn't do any good to tell her that, to frighten her. There was nothing she could do about it anyway.

He hadn't understood how difficult it was going to be to possess his power and the knowledge that went with it. When he looked at people, there was nothing hidden from his view. Only his own destiny was hidden from him. Looking at Peter, at Lisa, at the earnest or frightened or exalted faces on TV, he saw all the details of their lives, past, present, and future. He saw their wants, their fears, their hopes and dreams. He saw their sins both grand and small. He saw them as they did, magnified out of all proportion or similarly diminished, and then he saw them as God did: clearly, objectively. Both these viewpoints were his at once, superimposed on each other to make a third point of view, one that saw every joy, grief, and shame, and was moved to pity by all that it beheld, a pity that had nothing of judgment in it, but only love. Perhaps that was what it meant to be the

Son of man. It was a torment of sorts, to love so much and see so clearly yet to hold it all back and say nothing, reveal nothing, force himself to respect the autonomy of those who were as transparent to him as glass, and as fragile. A torment, yes, but it was one that he was proud to bear, humbled by the privilege and the responsibility, by the beauty he saw in every soul, a beauty that shone through every sin with a light that could be dimmed but never extinguished as long as there was still life, not by all the devils in the universe or even by Lucifer himself. Though he didn't know every facet of his mission, though much of his future was shrouded in shadow and uncertainty, one thing Ethan did know absolutely was that he would be the champion of that light in what was to come, no matter what it cost him.

The buzzing of his cell phone roused him. He pulled it from his pocket, thinking it must be Peter or Maggie. After dropping Ethan and Lisa off, Peter had driven to Maggie's house to bring her here for a talk that Ethan wasn't looking forward to, but which he knew had to take place as soon as possible. But the phone call turned out to be from a reporter instead, a woman from the local FOX station named Rita Rodriguez, who was calling from Olathe Medical with questions about Lisa. It seemed his mother had been reported dead but was now missing from her room and from the hospital itself. Did Ethan know anything about what might have happened to her? As Ethan listened to Rita's questions, he felt another piece of his destiny snap into place, and he understood that he'd been waiting for this call without knowing it.

"My mom is here," he said into the phone. "She's fine."

"Here being where? Home?"

"Yes."

"And you say she's fine?"

"Yes."

"Ethan, I'm looking at your mother's death certificate right now," Rita's breathless voice continued. "Are you saying there was a mistake?"

"No, there was no mistake. She died. I was there when it happened."

"Every patient in the hospital was spontaneously healed earlier tonight. Are you aware of that?"

"Yes."

"But your mother is the only one we've identified so far who was dead. Are you saying that she was returned to life?"

"That's right."

A pause. Then, "I'm sorry to ask this, Ethan, but are you on drugs?"

"No, ma'am. I'm telling the truth. My mother was raised from the dead."

"Uh-huh. Care to explain how?"

"Do you believe in miracles, Ms. Rodriguez?"

"Son, I'm calling from a place where more than two hundred people who were gravely ill a couple of hours ago are now in perfect health. Does that answer your question?"

"I brought her back."

"Excuse me?"

"I brought her back. And healed all those people."

An incredulous laugh. "You *are* on drugs!"

"I'm sorry you feel that way. Maybe I should talk to another reporter . . ."

"Wait, can I speak to your mom?"

"She's asleep right now."

"Come on, Ethan. Am I supposed to believe that you're Jesus Christ come again? And just on your say-so, without any proof? Maybe I believe in miracles, but it doesn't mean I'm fucking crazy!"

"I never said I was Jesus."

"Okay, then who are you?"

"I'm . . . I guess you could say his little brother."

"You're Jesus' little brother."

"Sort of. I'm God's other son. The second Son."

Another pause, longer than the first. Then, "Maybe I *am* fucking crazy. I'm coming over there, Ethan. Don't go anywhere, okay?"

"I'll be here," he said and closed the phone.

When he turned around, Peter and Maggie were standing at the entrance to the living room. Peter had an uncomfortable look on his face, but Maggie's expression was beyond discomfort, all the way into incomprehension.

"Uh, we didn't want to interrupt," said Peter lamely. "Guess I'll be going."

"Please stay, Pete," he said.

"Uh, okay. I'll just wait out in the, uh, kitchen."

"Thanks, Pete."

After Peter left the room, Ethan and Maggie stood as if rooted in place, gazing at each other in a tense silence that stretched thinner and thinner and finally, like a rubber band, snapped.

"Mags, I—"

"Ethan—"

They spoke simultaneously, their words crashing together, canceling each other out but wiping away some of the tension, too.

"You first," Ethan said.

"No, you."

"Are you going to just stand there, or do you want to come in?"

Maggie was wearing jeans and a wrinkled T-shirt with the logo of last year's Olathe Balloon Festival. Her hair was unbrushed, and now she pushed an unruly strand back from her forehead. Ethan thought that she had never looked so lovely. "I don't know what I want," she said, crossing her arms over her chest as if to put up a barrier between them. "I'm kind of freaked out. Pete told me some crazy stuff on the way over. About the hospital and your mom and, well, everything. And then to walk in here and find you on the phone like that . . . It's a lot to take in all at once, you know?"

Ethan smiled. "I can imagine."

"Can you? I doubt it. I feel like I don't know you, Ethan. Like everything we shared was a kind of lie. Well, not a lie, maybe, but it wasn't the truth, either, was it?"

"No," he admitted. "But I'd forgotten all of this myself. Did Pete tell you that?"

"He told me. But I'm not sure it makes a difference. Not if everything else he told me is true. Well, is it?"

"I'm not sure exactly what he told you, Mags."

"He said you healed all those people at the hospital, and that you raised your mom from the dead, for starters." She spoke evenly, but he could see that she was close to hysterics beneath the facade of calm control. She rolled her eyes. "Raised from the dead. God, I can't believe I just said that!"

"It's true, though. I know it sounds weird, but it's true."

"He said . . ." She gulped, as if the words didn't want to come out. "He said you're the Son of God."

"The second Son," Ethan said. "I'm not Jesus come again. I'm—"

"I don't care about that!" she interrupted suddenly, silencing him. "I don't care about who you are or why you're here or any of that crap. All I want to know is, what's going to happen to us now? Is this the end?"

"You mean the Apocalypse?" asked Ethan. "Like I told Pete—"

"No, you idiot," she interrupted again. "Not the Apocalypse. Us! You and me. Is this the end of us?"

Ethan took a deep breath. This was the moment he'd been dreading. "Mags, I love you, but . . ." He stopped in shock as her face dissolved into tears.

"I knew it," she moaned.

"Mags, listen . . ." He felt as if he'd stabbed her in the heart, and himself too. He took a step toward her, his arms opening . . .

"Keep back, Ethan," she said, raising a forestalling hand. "Don't touch me."

"Please, Mags . . ." He didn't know what he was asking.

"You know what I think?" she demanded, swiping away her tears as she spoke. "I think on some level you knew all the time. That's why you never wanted to have sex or anything. You had to be pure, right? Like Jesus. Only you thought you might as well get some practice at being human while you had the chance. You know, fool around a bit with some stupid human girl, just so you could understand us better."

Ethan blushed. Nothing that Maggie was saying was true, exactly, but there were elements of truth in it, as he knew very well. "It's not like that, Mags." He pled with her nevertheless, telling himself that he could still make her understand, convince her of what it had meant to him, of what she had meant . . . and always would mean.

But she brushed aside any explanations he might have offered. "Oh my God," she said, turning white as a sheet. "This is part of it too, isn't it? Another little lesson for Jesus Junior."

"Mags," he said again, uselessly. "Don't you see that it has to be this way? I'm here for just a little while, and I've got things to do . . ."

"Right, things to do, people to see, no place for the girl who was foolish enough to fall in love with you. Well, don't worry, Ethan. I'm not going to add to your burden." She turned around.

"What are you doing?"

"I'm leaving."

"But—"

"Good-bye, Ethan. Good luck with whatever it is you're here to do. For what it's worth, I don't hate you. But I don't think I can go from girlfriend to disciple. That's too much to ask."

Ethan took a deep breath. It would be so easy to reach out and make her stay, to rewrite the last few moments and make them come out differently. He'd done it before. He could make her decide to stay with him. Or he could go further, cast aside his mission, his purpose, his knowledge of who he really was, and be just another mortal again, Ethan Brown, the son of Lisa and Gordon Brown. He could have Maggie. He could marry her, have kids, live an ordinary life whose joys and grievings would be all of the divine that he required. Or, letting her go, he could heal her pain, wipe the memory of him from her mind, her heart. Fix what he had broken. He could do any of those things. The temptation of interceding in one way or another was so powerful that he shook with the effort of resisting it. But he did resist it. He had made his choice, and he meant to stick with it, regardless of the pain it caused him. And, even worse, far, far worse, regardless of the pain it caused others.

"Good-bye, Maggie," he said.

Sobbing, she rushed from the house without a backward look.

Ethan was crying himself. Without even realizing it, he had sunk back onto the couch, his legs no longer holding him up. He felt as if the rest of his life were going to be a succession of moments like this one, of good-byes to people he loved yet was helpless to keep from hurting.

"Dude, that didn't go too well, did it?"

He looked up to see Peter at the entrance to the living room. "No," he said, sniffling. "It sure didn't."

"I better go after her," Peter said. "I mean, she doesn't have any way home. And I figure she could use a friend right now."

Ethan nodded. In a flash, the future came to him, what this moment would lead to, but he shut his eyes to it. He couldn't bear to look that far ahead. He would have to remember that, keep the blinders on, or he would certainly go mad. "Go on, Pete," he said to his friend, forcing out a smile. "Go after her."

✠   ✠   ✠

"Hmm, you're not exactly what I was expecting." Rita Rodriguez sized him up coolly from the other side of the front door, her cameraman behind her.

"What were you expecting?" Ethan asked. "A halo?"

Rita laughed at that, flashing perfect white teeth. She was a small woman, barely over five feet; though Ethan had seen her numerous times on TV, he'd never realized before just how short she was. But despite her size, she seemed larger than life, in that way television personalities have. Her head, with its perfectly coiffed brown hair, perfectly shining brown eyes, and perfectly smooth light brown skin, seemed slightly too big for her slim body, and so, now that he noticed it, did her breasts, the perfect cleavage of which peeked from the top of a low-cut beige blouse. She marked the direction of his gaze with amusement, then raised her confident eyes to his again; he saw intelligence there, ambition, vanity, and a fundamental decency her profession had yet to fully erode. She was divorced, with two children, a Catholic who went to Mass every Sunday but hadn't taken Communion in more than three years. Nestled deep in her brain, known only to her doctor and herself, an inoperable cancer was growing. She smiled brashly. "Can we come in?"

He blinked, and the cancer was gone. "Sure, Ms. Rodriguez."

"Call me Rita." She tipped her head to one side to indicate the cameraman, a burly black man with a trim goatee and a gold hoop in one ear. "This is Hobie."

Hobie nodded around the camera. Twenty-nine, a veteran wounded in the first big push on Tehran, he had an artificial leg that he was both ashamed and proud of, a taste for heroin he'd picked up in Afghanistan, and nightmares that jolted him screaming awake in the middle of the night and left him blubbering like a baby. He had loved Rita secretly, desperately, hopelessly, for the two years that he had been her cameraman. He hadn't breathed a word of his feelings to her in that time and never would. He imagined himself as a knight in shining armor, a paladin . . .

With an effort, Ethan looked away, stepping to one side to let Rita and Hobie enter the house. It was so easy to look past the skin, harder not to see than to see the secret places of the soul. Looking was hypnotic, almost like a drug, not because of its voyeuristic aspect but because the souls of human beings had been created to reflect their creator, and in them, more than anything else, Ethan could see traces of his father, who remained a mystery to him even now: a mystery, he sensed, whose solution would come only through his embrace of the mission he had been given, the task he'd been sent to accomplish—though he scarcely knew what was expected of him, only that he must follow this path he'd embarked on all the way to the end, just as Jesus had followed his own path. Would the path he was on now lead to the same destination? He didn't know. He prayed that, wherever he was bound, he would make the journey with half the courage and compassion his brother had shown.

"My mom's still sleeping," he said as he conducted Rita and Hobie into the living room, Hobie filming all the while. "Can I get you a glass of water or anything?"

"Only if you change it to wine," said Rita teasingly but also seriously.

"If I could quench your thirst for miracles that easily, I would," he told her. "But that's not why I'm here."

"Why are you here?" she asked without missing a beat.

Ethan had already decided that he wasn't going to mention the long and ongoing conflict between Conversatio and the Congregation. Nor was he going to bring up the existence of Grand Inquisitor. What he had to say was going to be difficult enough to believe already, and omitting these things wouldn't detract from it; really, they were distractions. Though he didn't dismiss their importance in the here and now, ultimately they were unimportant, fleeting manifestations of an enduring power that had set itself against his father from the beginning of time.

"My father has sent me to shake things up," he said, echoing his earlier answer to Peter.

"Your father . . . that would be God. Do you claim to be the Son of God?"

"One of them."

"How many are there?"

"Just two."

"What, no daughters?"

"Not yet," he said with a smile.

"You claim to be responsible for the Miracle of Olathe Medical."

"That's right."

"And you say that you raised your own mother from the dead."

"You can ask her about that yourself when she wakes up."

"Yes, you mentioned that she was sleeping. I imagine it's pretty exhausting, being raised from the dead."

"I know you don't believe me, Rita. But you will."

"You seem like a nice young man, Ethan. But you're also obviously insane." She smiled sweetly. "No offense."

"I'll be called a lot worse than that before I'm through."

"Surely you don't expect anyone to believe these outlandish claims of yours, not without proof."

"How do you explain what happened at the hospital?"

"I can't explain it."

"And what about my mother? You said you saw her death certificate."

"I can't explain that, either. But my inability to explain these things isn't proof of anything."

"A miracle is its own proof."

"Clearly, something miraculous occurred at Olathe Medical. I'm not disputing that. But just because a miracle took place doesn't mean you're the one responsible."

"There will always be those who doubt and deny, Rita. I'm here to give people hope, to demonstrate the power of faith."

"And how do you mean to do that, if you don't mind my asking?"

"I don't mind at all. But I'm not going to tell you."

"I didn't think you could."

"If you really want to know, come back this afternoon. I'll be holding a press conference here at the house."

Rita smiled, a predatory gleam in her eyes. "I wouldn't miss it for the world."

CHAPTER 16

Once the shock of his returning memory had worn off, Papa Jim had sprung into action . . . if a seventy-three-year-old great-grandfather could be said to spring. Well, this one could. He didn't feel like seventy-three. It was as if the intervening ten years, the decade of forgetfulness, as he thought of it, had been wiped out in the blink of an eye, leaving him ten years younger, still in his prime.

But of course those ten years weren't really gone. And a good thing, too. Because he'd used them well, expanded Oz Corporation into the biggest private security and prison firm in the country, meshed its workings seamlessly into the structure of Conversatio, all the while grooming Bill's replacement in the House, an ambitious but empty-headed South Carolina representative named Trey "Wex" Wexler.

After the 2010 terrorist attacks, while the rest of the country had blundered about in panic, Papa Jim had put Wexler on television and the Internet, using him as a mouthpiece to criticize the Democratic administration and the Department of Homeland Security. Wexler had introduced a bill in Congress to have Oz Corp federalized, a bill which, underneath the legalese, really called for the Department of Homeland Security to be privatized, and Papa Jim had called in all his favors to get it passed. The president hadn't dared to veto it, and so Papa Jim, as CEO of Oz, had found himself installed as the new "Terror Czar" in 2011.

From that lofty perch, he had pulled the strings of Wexler's successful 2012 presidential campaign, and, in 2014, had blown the whistle on a plot by Democratic representatives and senators to impeach the president on trumped-up charges; the resulting scandal had decimated the Democrats in the off-year elections, leading to a historic Republican majority in Congress that had immediately declared a national emergency, temporarily vesting President Wexler with virtually unlimited power. Howls were raised from the predictable quarters, all easily ignored, and lawsuits were filed, which were moving through the courts with a glacial slowness that was preferable to outright dismissal, as it provided the illusion of a functioning legal system while giving Papa Jim time to consolidate his political gains in time for the upcoming election cycle.

He'd realized at once that Ethan could be central to his plans for restoring America to greatness through the establishment of a Christian theocracy. It was hard to imagine a more perfect candidate than the Son of God! Unfortunately, it was also hard to imagine a more dangerous opponent. That was why he had to act quickly.

But Papa Jim wasn't the only one to recover lost memories; at the same time his memories of Ethan had returned, so, apparently, had those of the Conversatio agents who'd been there at the Phoenix hospital ten years ago. Soon Papa Jim was being bombarded with private messages from the rest of the Conversatio directorate, demanding that he take action to secure the second Son.

Papa Jim told them he was already on it. He had tried to contact the agent directly responsible for Ethan, Lisa Brown, immediately. Unfortunately, he'd been unable to do so; it seemed that she'd been seriously injured in an automobile accident. Whether it was truly an accident, or Congregation interference, he didn't know, but he'd dispatched a team of Conversatio agents to Olathe, as well as alerting his own security forces there. The "munchies," people had taken to calling them; personally, he kind of liked the nickname.

Meanwhile, to cover all his bases, he'd put in a call to the convent of Santa Marta. It was time to bring Kate home. Once Ethan was informed of her identity, her presence would be a powerful incentive for his cooperation. But there too Papa Jim was stymied. The mother superior reported that Sister Elena had gone: No one could say where, or when, or how. It was as if she had disappeared off the face of the earth.

Had she been snatched by the Congregation? Papa Jim had his spies in the Vatican, even a highly placed mole within the Congregation itself, and he put out cautious feelers now, looking for any information about Kate's whereabouts. At the same time, he circulated her description to his security people at every international airport in the United States. Then, like a spider at the center of its web, he sat back to wait for the flies to blunder in.

Instead, events had spun further out of his control.

Denny had alerted him to news broadcasts out of Olathe, Kansas. There had been an unexplained event at the hospital there, a mass healing that people were hailing as a miracle. A young man had claimed responsibility.

Ethan.

Papa Jim recognized him at once. Even after ten years, there was no mistaking that face. The face of his great-grandson.

Ethan had given a brief interview with a local reporter named Rita Rodriguez, then had promised to hold a press conference later in the day. In the interview, he'd not only proclaimed his responsibility for the healings, which from Papa Jim's perspective was bad enough, a red flag for the Congregation, he'd also insisted that he'd brought his mother—that is, Lisa Brown—back from the dead, like Lazarus. Papa Jim had to assume that was why he hadn't heard anything from Agent Brown. Even if her memory had been wiped clean, like his own, she still should have gotten in contact with him as soon as she'd recovered it. And it seemed logical to him that she would have recovered her memory at the same time he and the others had, that the event wasn't unique to them alone. Since she hadn't reported in, either before or since her accident, he could only conclude that she was no longer trustworthy. She had been turned.

Worst of all, Ethan had referred openly to the doctrine of the second Son, and had declared himself to be the Son of God, sent to Earth by his father to "shake things up." Sound bites with Olathe residents and prominent religious commentators indicated that he was well on his way to accomplishing that goal. He was called a crackpot, a snake-oil salesman, a blasphemer, a drug addict, and worse. Not a single person, not even those who had been cured or had family members cured in the Miracle of Olathe Medical, seemed willing to entertain the remotest possibility that Ethan might be telling the truth.

As far as Papa Jim was concerned, that was the only good news yet. As long as people didn't believe, the situation could be salvaged. If they began to believe that Ethan really was who he claimed to be—believed it, that is, before Papa Jim could get to Ethan and explain the benefits of cooperation to him, get him on board with Papa Jim's plan for the salvation of America and the world—then there was a very good chance that chaos would result. And Papa Jim hated chaos.

So Papa Jim had lit a cigar and hit the phones again. His first thought had been to simply send in the munchies and take Ethan and Lisa into "protective custody." But then he'd realized that such a course of action would only inflame things more than they were already. Media representatives had surrounded Ethan's home, staking the place out in anticipation of the afternoon press conference, and there was simply no way to get in and out without having the operation captured on camera and broadcasted on every television screen, computer monitor, and cell phone in the country and beyond. No, he couldn't stop the press conference.

But he could sure as hell try to shape it.

With all the passions stirred up by Ethan's interview with the Rodriguez woman, Papa Jim supposed that it would surprise no one if there was a violent response during his press conference. There would certainly be protesters in attendance, Christians and members of other faiths offended by Ethan's claim to divinity. All it would take would be one fanatic to spark a riot. And then, to restore order, his munchies would come swooping down like avenging angels to save the day, in the process sweeping up Ethan and Lisa and spiriting them away before anyone really knew what had happened.

Yes, he'd thought, pleased with himself. That was the best way to handle things. It would get the other directors of Conversatio off his back, give him some breathing room. It would strike a powerful blow against the Congregation. And it would stir up interest in, and sympathy for, the earnest young man who, however misguided, had been the victim of an unprovoked attack. Then, a few days later, there would be another press conference, a very different kind of affair, with absolutely nothing left to chance and a script for Ethan prepared by some of the PR wizards in media relations, the same bunch who had put the magic words in Wex's mouth that had gotten him elected.

Papa Jim had savored another puff on his cigar, then summoned Denny into his office.

They had a fanatic to find.

✠   ✠   ✠

It had all gone as Gabriel had promised.

She'd returned to her cell, gathered some clothes, her passport, and a few personal items, threw them into a carry-on bag, and simply walked out of the convent. No one stopped her. No one said a word to her. No one saw her, not even when she passed right in front of them, close enough to touch if they'd merely stretched out a hand.

As she passed through the gate and out of the convent of Santa Marta, she'd felt a part of herself slough off like a skin she'd outgrown or a disguise she no longer needed. She shed Sister Elena and left her behind in the dust.

Kate strode on without glancing back. There was nothing there for her anymore, and she knew it. Her path stretched before her, leading to one destination.

Ethan.

Her son.

Not dead as she'd been told. As she'd believed for so many years.

Rage filled her heart against her grandfather and everyone at the convent who had lied to her for reasons she couldn't begin to understand. And against God too. Perhaps against Him most of all.

But she also felt shame at her own acquiescence in the lie, the ease with which she had accepted what she'd been told. As if, on some level, she'd wanted to believe it. It seemed to her now as she walked along the dusty road leading down from the hills that she had failed Ethan, failed herself. She should have gone in search of him years ago, should never have allowed Father Rinaldi and Papa Jim to manipulate her into taking the veil . . . for she saw clearly now that was what had happened. They'd wanted her out of the way. She was a danger to them, or perhaps just an inconvenience. So they'd shuffled her aside, and Papa Jim had taken Ethan.

Why?

She meant to ask him.

But first she was going to find Ethan.

Gabriel had told her to look for him in Kansas, of all places. So it was to Kansas now that she must go. But how to get there?

Gabriel had said that God would provide.

Well, she thought, as she walked along the side of the road, this would be a good time to start providing.

Any time you're ready, God.

She was so used to being invisible that at first, when the car pulled over in front of her and stopped, she kept right on walking past it.

"Hey! Hey, excuse me, lady!"

She flinched and turned. "Yes?" She was ready to run, afraid that the mother superior had detected her escape and sent this car to fetch her back. But when the passenger-side door opened and a young woman emerged— a pretty young girl who appeared to be about the same age as she'd been when she'd entered the convent . . . was it really almost twenty years ago?— she'd known at once that this was the help she'd been praying for.

"Wow," said the girl with an open smile, brushing back long blond bangs, "are you, like, American?"

"Yes. Can I help you?"

"We're kind of lost. My boyfriend and I are looking for the airport, but we must've taken a wrong turn."

"I'm heading there myself," she said.

"Wow, really? This is so lucky! We'll drive you, okay, and you can show us the way."

"That would be great," she said. "I really appreciate it."

"You're the one doing us a favor," said the woman. "I think we would have missed our flight if we hadn't found you!"

The woman's name was Dawn, and her boyfriend was Sean. They were both nineteen, college kids who had spent the Christmas break touring Greece and Italy but were now heading back to the States for the start of the new semester. As she sat in the back of the rental car, answering their questions and asking some of her own, Kate began to appreciate how much had changed in the United States and in the world during her time in the convent. She felt as if she'd just awakened from a long sleep to find herself in a world both familiar and strange, like Rip van Winkle.

"Wait, so this new president, Wexler, is, what, like a dictator or something?"

"Jeez, Ms. Skylar, where have you been?" asked Sean, glancing at her in the rearview mirror. "In a nunnery or something?"

She laughed weakly. "I guess I haven't been paying attention to the news."

"President Wexler isn't a dictator," Dawn said. "He's a good man, a God-fearing man. We need a strong leader like him to keep us safe from terrorists at home and abroad."

"Tough times demand tough leaders," Sean said, sounding as if he were echoing an advertising slogan.

"I'm sure you're right," Kate said, not wanting to argue with her new friends.

"We're lucky to have President Wexler," Dawn insisted.

"And Secretary Osbourne," Sean added.

Kate nearly choked at that. "Osbourne? You don't mean Jim Os-bourne, the head of Oz Corporation?"

"Who else? He took over the Department of Homeland Security after the attacks in 2010 and made America safe again. He exposed the plot against President Wexler. He's a hero, a real patriot."

Somehow, Papa Jim had neglected to mention any of these develop-ments to her in his visits and phone calls, and the discipline of the convent had effectively precluded her from engaging in any investigations of her own, even if she'd been inclined to do so, which she hadn't, too sunk in self-pity and the comforting aura of martyrdom.

"That reminds me," said Dawn, turning around in her seat to look directly at Kate. "I knew I recognized your name from somewhere. Sky-lar—that was the congressman who volunteered in Iraq and got killed. He was Secretary Osbourne's son-in-law. You're not related to him, are you?"

"No, I'm no relation," Kate said.

"Oh, that's too bad," said Dawn. "It would be cool to be related to someone like that, you know?"

"I'm sure his family is proud of him," she said, looking away, out the window, remembering the last time she'd spoken with her father, arguing with him. He'd tried to tell her that Ethan was still alive. Tried to convince her of the truth. But she hadn't listened, hadn't believed. She'd called him a liar, a crazy person. Now she would have given anything to tell him how sorry she was, how much she loved him despite all his failures as a father, because of what he'd tried to do at the end. He'd been there for her when it counted, when no one else had been there, and she'd rejected him.

Oh Daddy, I'm so sorry . . .

"Hey, are you okay?" asked Dawn.

"Sorry," she said with an embarrassed smile. She brushed the tears from her cheeks. "You've got me thinking about my own family. I haven't seen them in a long time. I miss them . . ." She couldn't go on.

"I know what that's like," said Dawn, passing her back some tissues, which she gratefully accepted. "This is the longest I haven't seen my folks in, like, forever."

"What do you mean?" demanded Sean incredulously. "You're vidding them on your cell every night!"

"It's not the same as being there," Dawn rejoined. "Is it, Ms. Skylar?"

"No, it's not," she said. "Take this left, Sean. It brings us back to the main road." It was amazing how well she remembered the way, though she hadn't been out of the convent in nearly ten years.

The rest of the drive to the airport passed without conversation, as Dawn turned on the car's radio and tuned to a satellite pop station, cranking up the volume and singing along in a high voice that wove in and out of the songs without ever seeming to hit the right notes. Yet Kate wasn't annoyed; she felt strangely charmed, maybe because it reminded her of what it had been like to be that age herself, or a bit younger, how she too had sung along to the radio on car trips with a voice no better than Dawn's and probably even a little worse, not because she thought she sounded good but just because it was so good to be young and to be alive.

Well, thirty-six wasn't exactly ancient, was it? Even if it sometimes felt that way. The world seemed like such a different place than what she was used to, not only in large things like the rule of nations but in small things too, like the "vidding" Sean had so casually mentioned, which by his context could only refer to real-time video cell-phone transmission, something that had still been in the realm of science fiction when she'd entered the convent. How much else had changed? Would she recognize her own country anymore? Kate was afraid she would be a stranger there, friendless and all but forgotten, her parents dead, her grandfather someone other than the man she'd always thought she'd known, her son unaware of her very existence.

Again, Gabriel's words came back to her. *God will provide.* Well, He was going to get His chance, because she didn't have any cash, wasn't carrying a credit card, and didn't have a plane ticket.

Even if you score me a first-class seat to New York, she thought, *it won't mean I'm not angry at you anymore . . .*

But did she have the right to be angry? Everything she thought she knew had turned out to be wrong, a lie . . . and not a lie that God had told her, but lies told to her by men she'd trusted, men she'd loved. How could she blame God for the lies of men? Wasn't it really her own lack of faith that was to blame? She'd been so sure that God had forsaken her that she'd turned it into a kind of self-fulfilling prophecy. She'd blamed Him for Ethan's death, which hadn't even happened, and then nurtured all the bitterness of that belief like a poison that was also a drug, until she was addicted to it. Then it had been easy to blame God for her mother's death, and for her father's, as if He were in the revenge business. It had been comforting; so much easier to hate than to mourn, so satisfying to feel like the innocent victim of a divine vendetta, or even a not-so-innocent victim. But wasn't she the one who had forsaken Him? Wasn't that where all her troubles had begun, and hadn't they only worsened when she'd persisted in her sin?

Because that's what it had been. A sin. The sin of pride. And maybe a few others, too. She realized that now. She saw it as clearly as she saw how Papa Jim had lied to her and manipulated her.

She felt more deeply ashamed than she had ever felt in her life. There was no hiding from it, because there was no hiding from Him.

At that moment, in the backseat of the rental car, as the Italian countryside slid by and pop music she didn't recognize wafted from the satellite radio, Kate understood that she'd been given a second chance, and she swore to herself, and to God, that she would make the most of it. This time she would trust in God. She would have faith, or at least do her best to act that way.

When they arrived at the Galileo airport in Pisa, Kate said good-bye to Sean and Dawn, leaving the young couple to return the rented car. Clutching her bag close, she entered the bustling terminal, uncertain of her next step. Should she call Papa Jim and ask him for the money for a ticket home? No, she didn't trust him. Besides, she wanted to confront him face to face, to demand answers in a setting where he couldn't brush her off.

After the quiet and solitude of the convent, the airport, with its noise and color and crowds, was overwhelming. Kate felt lost and frightened. But she couldn't just stand around helplessly. That would only draw the attention of the police, who patrolled the terminal with machine guns and bomb-sniffing dogs. She had to do something, but what?

God will provide.

He'd gotten her this far, hadn't He? Was she going to abandon faith again, at the first moment of difficulty?

There was a flight leaving for New York. Taking a deep breath, Kate got in the line for boarding. It moved quickly, or at least it seemed that way to Kate, who had no idea what she was going to do when she reached the checkpoint and had to produce a ticket. By the time she reached the front of the line, she was trembling and nearly sick with apprehension. She could still back out. It wasn't too late.

But then it was.

"*Il biglietto*," said the woman behind the counter.

Kate gave her a weak smile.

The woman smiled back. "*Grazie.*" And handed her a seat assignment.

Kate was too stunned to do anything but take the paper and nod. She passed through the scanner without incident, and soon found herself aboard the plane—in economy class. *Maybe God has a sense of humor after all,* she thought as the plane taxied down the runway.

✠   ✠   ✠

Father O'Malley couldn't believe his luck. After he'd brought news of the miracle to Cardinal Ehrlich, the old man had entered the private residence of Pope Peter II without dismissing him. He hadn't dared to leave on his own authority, and so had waited on tenterhooks for the return of the head of his order, the man who was the oldest and closest friend of His Holiness and, thanks to that, the most powerful man in all of Christendom after the pope himself. As the minutes stretched, he couldn't stop himself from strolling about the richly appointed antechamber, which was a virtual museum of art and artifacts, some of which, he knew, were priceless, utterly unknown to scholarship or presumed lost or destroyed over the centuries. It was a veritable treasure trove: oil paintings by Titian, da Vinci, and Picasso; a small bronze equestrian statue by Rodin, a mother and child by Michelangelo; leather-bound volumes by Machiavelli, Tielhard de Chardin, and John Paul II. It was an eclectic collection, to be sure . . . but that only made it seem all the more wondrous to him. He felt like Aladdin in the cave of the forty thieves. Only, unlike Aladdin, he knew better than to try and steal anything. He didn't even dare slide one of the books out and open it. Such was the discipline of his order. And his fear of Cardinal Ehrlich.

At last, after twenty minutes or so, the cardinal returned, looking harried, his gray eyes sunken. He seemed annoyed to see O'Malley. "What, you still here?"

O'Malley bowed low. "Pardon, Your Eminence. I wasn't sure if you had dismissed me."

Ehrlich waved a skeletal hand. "No matter. You're here now. Watch and learn. But hold your tongue unless His Holiness addresses you. Is that understood?"

He bowed again. As he looked up, the pope entered the room, drying his hands on the front of his robes. Pope Peter II was the first American to be raised to the Throne of St. Peter, and also the first in the history of the Church to take the name of the first pope, which he had done, he said, in order to demonstrate that Rome under his papacy would be hostage no longer to either superstition or senseless tradition, and that, after two thousand years, it was past time to pay proper homage to the great apostle whom Christ himself had placed at the head of the Church. The sixty-three-year-old pontiff cut an imposing figure, much beloved of cartoonists: No more than five-six, he was hugely, almost grotesquely fat, and as a consequence he moved with the slow deliberation of a tortoise. Yet the mind within that monumental flesh was supple and quick, as his opponents and enemies, both inside and outside the church, had discovered to their regret.

"Your Holiness," said Cardinal Ehrlich brusquely as the pope cast a questioning glance toward O'Malley, "one of my young priests, Father O'Malley, a devoted servant of the Congregation and of Christ. He brought the news from Grand Inquisitor."

Peter II nodded to O'Malley and languidly stretched out his hand, which bore an unfortunate resemblance to a bloated and beringed white toad. Fighting down his revulsion, the priest pressed his lips to the Ring of the Fisherman, unable to avoid touching the pasty skin. He smelled a faint perfume, which for some reason caused him to blush furiously as he raised his head.

"Father O'Malley," said the pope, seeming to take as little note of him as humanly possible through his heavy-lidded eyes. "You have brought news of great, I would even say historic, import."

"I pray that I may continue to be of service, Your Holiness," he said.

The pope blinked in response, then glanced toward Cardinal Ehrlich, who motioned sharply for O'Malley to find some less conspicuous space to occupy. He did so, retreating to a curtained alcove.

"Not there, O'Malley," hissed the cardinal, gesturing with something in his hand.

"Excuse me, Your Eminence," he said, moving away with alacrity as the curtain unexpectedly parted to reveal the largest flat-screen television O'Malley had ever seen; the thing was nearly the size of a movie screen. On it, the faces of a woman and a young man loomed almost frighteningly large.

"Sound," said the pope.

Cardinal Ehrlich raised the device again, and O'Malley suddenly realized it had to be a remote, a circumstance he found more astonishing than if it had turned out to be a fragment of the true cross. Sound blasted from concealed speakers, and Ehrlich quickly lowered the volume.

"You claim to be responsible for the Miracle of Olathe Medical," the woman was saying.

"That's right," said the man.

"And you say that you raised your own mother from the dead."

"You can ask her about that yourself when she wakes up."

"I've heard enough," said the pope, and Ehrlich obediently turned off the sound, though the images continued to flicker across the screen.

To O'Malley's great surprise and discomfort, Peter II turned to him. "Well, O'Malley? What do you make of it?"

He forced himself to speak, conscious of the cardinal's glare. "The young man is obviously deluded, Your Holiness."

"Why do you say that?"

"Because only God could be responsible for the healing of all those people."

"Or the devil, O'Malley," said the pope. "Don't forget that the Antichrist will perform wondrous signs and acts when he appears. He will be a wolf in shepherd's clothing. Sound."

Ehrlich raised the remote, and the sound resumed.

"There will always be those who doubt and deny, Rita. I'm here to give people hope, to demonstrate the power of faith."

"And how do you mean to do that, if you don't mind my asking?"

"I don't mind at all. But I'm not going to tell you."

"I didn't think you could."

"If you really want to know, come back this afternoon. I'll be holding a press conference here at the house."

"I wouldn't miss it for the world."

"Nor shall we," growled the pope. "Ehrlich, this must be nipped in the bud, is that understood?"

Cardinal Ehrlich once again killed the sound. "Yes, Your Holiness. But—"

"No excuses," Peter II snapped, cutting him off. "This boy, this Ethan Brown, is extraordinarily dangerous. He must be stopped. At any cost."

"Yes, Your Holiness."

"I'll be in my chambers, consulting with Grand Inquisitor. Come back for the press conference; we'll watch it together."

"Yes, Your Holiness."

With a nod to O'Malley, the pope returned to his apartments.

When he had gone, O'Malley cleared his throat. "Pardon, Your Eminence. But could it really be true? Could that young man be the Antichrist?"

"Oh, it could be much worse than that, O'Malley," said Cardinal Ehrlich.

"What do you mean?"

"Why, he could be exactly what he says he is. The Son of God."

"But—but then . . ."

"Yes?" said the cardinal.

O'Malley was suddenly certain that his entire career rested on the next words that came out of his mouth. He even had a disagreeable sensation that his very life might depend on them. "Er, nothing, Your Eminence."

"Are you quite sure you didn't have something to say, O'Malley? Some objection to raise, perhaps?"

"No, Your Eminence."

Cardinal Ehrlich studied him for a disconcertingly long time through those cold gray eyes before he seemed satisfied. If the pope's gaze had been crocodilian, that of the cardinal suggested a different but no less deadly species: the shark. "Very well. You may return to your duties. I need hardly add that everything you have been witness to here is to be held in the strictest confidence, as though it were under the seal of the confessional."

"Yes, Your Eminence. I understand."

"I believe you do, O'Malley," said the cardinal with a smile.

✠   ✠   ✠

Papa Jim lit a fresh cigar and sat back in the plush leather recliner in his office in the bowels of the White House, another of the perks of his position at the helm of the Department of Homeland Security. He had learned in his time in the government that the higher the level of one's political influence, the lower one's access extended below ground, where the only truly safe refuge lay, beyond the reach of nuclear and biological weapons. His access reached as deep as the president's, and indeed even deeper, for there were vast spaces beneath the White House, where the excavated depths gave way to natural caverns that, for all anyone knew, extended all the way to the center of the Earth, and these sepulchral domains were the provenance of Homeland Security, at least on paper, although Papa Jim had never had the slightest interest in exploring them.

What concerned him today lay not at the center but on the surface of the planet. At his side was a glass with two fingers of Aberlour, his favorite scotch whisky. The entire wall opposite him was a vast LCD screen that could be broken up into any number of smaller displays, a real advantage on Sundays during football season. However, it was now showing a single broadcast across its entirety: the CNN feed of the mob scene outside the Brown residence in Olathe, Kansas. Papa Jim had just muted the volume; he didn't need to hear whatever inanities the local media heads were spouting. His own two eyes told him more than they ever could. Plus the voice of Denny, whom he'd shipped out to head the operation in person and who, since his arrival on the scene an hour ago, had been in continual contact via wireless cochlear implant.

Moving into position, his voice scratched inside Papa Jim's head now, like a fly that had crawled into his ear and taken up residence there.

There was no reason to reply to that, so he didn't. Besides, he always felt foolish conducting conversations via implant; he imagined that he must look like a crazy person, muttering under his breath to no one at all.

Almost two hundred people were milling around outside the house, a modest single-family dwelling in a comfortable middle-class neighborhood. The street in front of the house had been cordoned off by the local police, and munchies had established security checkpoints on all the roads feeding in to the neighborhood. IDs were being checked. Some arrests, mostly for outstanding immigration-related warrants, had been made. Helicopters hovered overhead.

Papa Jim wanted to project an image of security and control . . . but not too much of either. He wanted people to feel safe . . . but not too safe. When people felt too safe, they started thinking for themselves, started questioning the ones who were out there protecting them. Papa Jim had become an expert at giving people a sense of security at the same time that he kept them afraid. It was a fine line, but nobody walked it better.

In addition to the munchies in their distinctive dark visors and white armor, he had dispatched Conversatio agents into the throng, and from time to time he spotted a familiar face as the agents blended in with those gathered to cover, watch, or protest the upcoming press conference. No doubt there were other Conversatio agents present whose faces were unknown to him. He knew too that Congregation agents were infiltrating the crowd, and he tried to guess as his eyes flicked over the screen who they might be, though in fact he wasn't overly concerned about their presence. He believed he understood the way his adversaries thought, the way Grand Inquisitor made its moves in this intricate, high-stakes chess game they were playing, and he was convinced that no attempt would be made on Ethan's life in such a public arena. The Congregation would be observing for now, taking Ethan's measure, probing for the presence of Conversatio. They would not act precipitously; too much was at stake. If the Congregation and Grand Inquisitor understood one thing, it was patience, and that went double for Cardinal Ehrlich, the head of the order, a man with ice water in his veins. Papa Jim was no stranger to patience himself, but sometimes it could be a weakness as well as a virtue, and this was one of those times. Papa Jim had a window of opportunity, and he meant to take full advantage of it.

As news of the Miracle of Olathe Medical had spread via the media, Internet, and old-fashioned word of mouth, a palpable excitement had taken root in Olathe and, indeed, the rest of the country, a sense of edgy anticipation that Rita Rodriguez's exclusive interview with Ethan had stoked to a fever pitch. The people gathered outside the modest Brown home—which looked exactly like every other home on the street, with a well-tended lawn and a garden that had no doubt been lovely before hundreds of feet had trampled over it—were a mixed group. But all of them seemed to be in the grip of an energy that Papa Jim could feel even through the TV screen. There was a palpable buzz, a thrum of barely repressed emotion that, he knew, needed only a spark to set it off. Of course, any fool with a match could trigger an explosion. The trick was to channel it, guide that destructive energy into a constructive application.

But for all its incipient energy, the crowd was still peaceful. There were small groups holding up signs and placards with hand-lettered or computer-printed messages like "Antichrist!" and "Blasphemer," and other groups with signs that proclaimed "The Kingdom of God is at Hand" and "We Luv U Ethan!" The police and munchies had done a good job of keeping the opposing groups apart, though not so far apart that a lot of shouting back and forth wasn't going on. Some people had brought guitars and other musical instruments and were leading sing-alongs, everything from "My Sweet Lord" to "Kum Bay Yah" to "If I Had a Hammer." It was the last of these that had compelled Papa Jim to turn off the TV volume just moments ago. He'd always hated that damn song.

Papa Jim caught sight of the man that he and Denny had chosen for the job. He was one of those guys who was so average looking that you forgot him entirely as soon as you weren't looking at him, and even when you were, you barely even saw him at all. He could have been anywhere from twenty-five to forty-five, and, depending on how he carried himself, from five foot seven to six feet tall. Papa Jim had already glimpsed him a couple of times on the TV screen, only to lose sight of him moments later as he slid chameleonlike in and out of the crowd. Guys like that were rare and invaluable in his present line of work. They didn't come cheap, either. Especially for this job, because once it was over, that nondescript face would be plastered everywhere, and nobody was going to forget it anytime soon, if ever. This guy, who went by the name of Tefflon, like he thought he was a damn superhero or villain or something, wasn't stupid, and so he'd asked for quite a lot of money up front, more than the job itself was worth, because he'd known that it would mean the end of his usefulness to men like Papa Jim, at least for a very long time. And Papa Jim, being a businessman at heart, had understood and agreed to the price without haggling, depositing it in an offshore bank account as directed. If everything went according to plan, he'd consider it a bargain. And he had every confidence that things would go according to plan. When it came to his plans, they generally did.

Tefflon was wearing a running suit. He had an MP5 player strapped to his arm. He looked exactly as if he'd happened by on his afternoon jog and then decided to stick around and see what all the excitement was about. He talked to no one, and no one talked to him. It was uncanny the way that people's gazes seemed to just glide off him, how he wandered through the crowd as if surrounded by an invisible force field that pushed people away so gently they didn't even realize they'd been pushed. Papa Jim had to admit the guy's name, for all its adolescent melodrama, was well chosen.

That MP5 player, of course, wasn't really an MP5 player at all. It was a disguised sonic grenade, a defensive weapon that had demonstrated its worth countless times in the Middle East and here in the homeland. When activated, the small grenade released a burst of high-pitched sound that shorted out the nervous system of anyone within ten yards, incapacitating them for up to fifteen minutes. U.S. troops and munchies used the grenades as a quick and humane method of crowd control. The plan called for Tefflon to wait until the press conference was underway, then to scream out *Allah akhbar*—Arabic for "God is great"—and activate the grenade. Papa Jim wanted the attack to be blamed on homegrown Muslim terrorists; it would garner more sympathy for Ethan, even from those Christians who might find his claims upsetting, and it would reinforce the idea among the public that the enemy might strike anywhere, at any time, a fact which, in Papa Jim's opinion, they could not be reminded of too often, as this was one government that derived from the fear, more than from the consent, of the governed.

Once the grenade went off, incapacitating those nearest to Tefflon and sowing panic through the rest of the crowd, Denny and his squad of munchies would converge on Ethan and Lisa and snatch them away. Later, Papa Jim would meet privately with Ethan. A lot would depend on that meeting. If only Kate hadn't given him the slip! Her presence there would be invaluable. Still, it wasn't too late. He had agents searching for her. Perhaps he would find her in time. And if not, he would make do without her.

But first things first, Papa Jim thought as he sipped from the tumbler of whiskey. *It won't do to get ahead of yourself . . .*

He would have given a lot to know what was going on behind the placid exterior of that house. The curtains were drawn on every window, and there was no sign that the place was even occupied, other than the steadily growing crowd outside. The usual devices employed by Homeland Security for eavesdropping purposes had proved useless; it was, Denny had reported, as if some kind of nullifying field were surrounding the house, shielding it from even the most sophisticated electronic snooping.

A podium had been erected at the edge of the front stoop, bristling with microphones. Papa Jim wondered who had done it. One of the networks, perhaps. Or maybe the podium and its array of microphones had spontaneously appeared, called into being by the sovereign needs of the media. It sometimes seemed to Papa Jim that reality itself conformed to those needs by some law of physics the scientists had yet to discover.

Just then, the front door opened, and Papa Jim, feeling adrenaline surge through his body, unmuted the volume of the TV and sat forward in his chair with such alacrity that he knocked over the glass of whisky on the nearby table. He ignored the spill.

" . . . coming out now!" gushed the voice of the offscreen newscaster in breathless excitement as a wordless sound went up from the crowd like the simultaneous indrawing of many breaths.

Meanwhile, in Papa Jim's cranium, Denny's tiny fly-voice buzzed. *He's coming out now!*

"I don't need a damn play-by-play," Papa Jim snapped.

Understood, from Denny, who would keep quiet now until and unless he had something of real significance to say. One thing about Denny: He knew when to shut up. It was a valuable talent, Papa Jim thought, one all too lacking in Washington, D.C. Or anywhere else, for that matter.

To Papa Jim's surprise, it wasn't Ethan who emerged from the house. It was a young man of approximately Ethan's age but much bigger, with the heavyset yet muscular build of a football player and eyes that darted nervously from side to side even as he strode resolutely to the podium. Papa Jim recognized him from the background information he'd hurriedly pulled together in the last twelve hours as Peter Wiggan, Ethan's best friend. But many in the crowd obviously took him for Ethan, because as soon as he appeared, a massive roar went up, which then fractured into caterwauling voices shouting out separate statements and questions.

"Are you Jesus come again?"

"Go to hell!"

"Save us!"

The young man, Peter, raised his hands to shush the crowd. "I'm not Ethan!" he shouted, his words amplified by the microphones. "Please be quiet!" Finally, when no one seemed to heed him, he bellowed, "SHUT UP!"

The words thundered over the crowd as if from on high. A shocked silence descended. Peter cleared his throat and began to speak.

"Hi. I'm Peter Wiggan. I'm a friend of Ethan's—that's the guy you're all here to see. He'll be out in a minute, and he'll answer all your questions, or at least do his best to answer them. But I came out here first because I wanted to get a few things straight. First of all, you can think whatever you like, but Ethan deserves to be listened to politely. We believe in politeness here in Olathe, and we also believe in sticking up for our friends, so if anybody has any ideas about shouting Ethan down or anything like that, you might as well just clear out now, because folks in this town won't stand for it. That's not a threat or anything. Just the truth. We look out for our own. The next thing is, please try to listen with an open mind. I mean, I'm pretty sure Jesus never held a press conference, but I bet he would have if he'd been around today instead of two thousand years ago! All Jesus had to get his message out was word of mouth. That's why he traveled around all the time preaching. It wasn't just because the Romans were after him. It was the fastest way to get his message out there. Ethan's just doing the same thing. Okay, last but not least, you're probably wondering what kind of guy Ethan is, if he's somebody you can trust. Absolutely, yes. I've known him since we were kids. In fact, I used to beat him up on a regular basis."

At this, a current of startled laughter swept through the crowd.

Peter nodded, grinning sheepishly. "Yeah, it's true. I beat up the Son of God! And he wasn't the only one, either. I was a bully. A real jerk. I'm not proud of it. I wanted to mention it just so nobody here thinks I'm some kind of goody-two-shoes. I'm not. But I'm not the lousy person I was back then, either, and the main reason I'm not is Ethan. He showed me that it was possible to live a different kind of life. A better life. Really, when you come right down to it, is that anything to get upset over? Who the heck doesn't want to live a better life? That's what this country's about, right? I mean, isn't that what we're supposed to be fighting for? So anyway, that's all I wanted to say. Thanks for listening."

The crowd began murmuring again as Peter stepped away from the podium with a glance back over his shoulder. Papa Jim made a mental note to have the kid's family investigated for loyalty; some of those comments were a little worrisome.

Then Ethan stepped out the front door, followed closely by Lisa, who was holding his hand, and all thought of investigations vanished from Papa Jim's mind. The crowd became as hushed as it had after Peter had shouted for everyone to shut up, only this time the silence seemed to arise naturally, without a word from Ethan. His presence alone was sufficient to quell the murmuring; he seemed surrounded by an aura of . . . well, Papa Jim hated to use the word, but the only one that came to mind was "holiness." Even the talking heads on CNN had dropped their prattling voices to hushed and reverent whisperings, as though they were covering the final putt of a playoff at the Masters. Papa Jim tuned them out completely.

That's him, he thought proudly. *My great-grandson.*

The Son of God.

It even said so at the top of the TV screen. Although, there, a question mark had been added: *The son of God?*

Papa Jim smiled in the privacy of his office. How many guys could make a boast like that about their progeny? Not too damn many. It was a good feeling.

There was nothing at first glance that marked Ethan immediately as extraordinary. He was tall, but not unusually so, and fit, but no athlete like his friend Peter. He was handsome enough, with his mother's high cheekbones, but no one would have mistaken him for a rock star. Yet when the camera zoomed in on his face, his gold-flecked brown eyes seemed to radiate a quiet wisdom and authority that made it difficult for Papa Jim to look away. Those eyes seemed to be gazing directly into his own, as if from the other side of a window. They were disconcerting yet also mesmerizing, seeming almost to glow with an inner light. They were the kind of eyes that inspired voters with trust. The eyes of a leader people would follow through the gates of hell itself.

Denny's voice crackled in his ears. *Tefflon is in position. Everything is go.*

Ethan, meanwhile, stepped up to the podium, where he stood flanked by Peter and Lisa. He raised one hand in an awkward wave. "Hi, everybody," he said, and at those words it was as if a dam had collapsed. Suddenly the crowd found its voice, or rather voices, and a flood of shouted questions and comments erupted, each one drowning out the others. Ethan drew back slightly at the onslaught, looking all at once like a scared young kid, and glanced to Lisa as if for reassurance. She gave him a brave smile.

Seeing that only confirmed Papa Jim's judgment that Lisa had been turned. Not to the Congregation, but to Ethan. Her loyalty to him now outweighed her loyalty to Conversatio . . . and, by extension, to Papa Jim. Sooner or later, he knew, he was going to have to deal with that problem, but in a way that would not alienate Ethan—that would, in fact, make him more dependent upon Papa Jim. He was confident an answer would come to him. Answers always did.

Ethan raised his hands for silence and, once again to Papa Jim's vast surprise, got it. It was uncanny the control the young man had over an audience that was by no means uniformly well disposed toward him, an audience of which a sizable portion was made up of reporters, who were well disposed toward no one except themselves.

But they quieted at his gesture, all of them.

Even the talking heads fell silent.

Papa Jim was not easily impressed, but this boy had managed to do it before he had even said a word.

Then, in the pristine silence, Ethan began to speak. He spoke softly and without haste, yet also without hesitation. It was as if his words perfectly fit the silence. As if that silence had been shaped purposefully to receive and contain them, like a chalice that is not truly itself until it is filled with wine. Papa Jim had never experienced anything like it. Once his speechwriters got on the job, there would be no stopping this boy. He was tempted to give Denny the signal to launch the operation now, but he was too curious to hear what Ethan had to say.

"First, thanks for coming out this afternoon. And thanks, Ms. Rodriguez, for making sure everybody got my invitation." He nodded at Rita Rodriguez, who stood prominently in the front of the crowd, in an area roped off for members of the press. She smiled back as Ethan went on. "I'm going to do my best to answer all your questions, but first I'd like to talk for a moment about who I am and why I'm here, if that's okay."

He paused, and apparently it was okay, because no one said a word. The camera panned the crowd, and every face was upturned toward Ethan in rapt concentration. Papa Jim saw that many members of the audience were recording Ethan on video cameras and cell phones. The sense of history in the making gave him goose bumps.

"You've met my friend Pete, who by the way snuck out here while my mom and I were busy talking about what I should say. But I guess he didn't do such a bad job of an introduction at that." He gave Peter a smile, and Peter nodded stiffly in return, rigid with stage fright, a frozen grin on his face, as if only now taking note of all the cameras. Then Ethan turned to Lisa. "This is my mom, Lisa. You may have heard that I, well, raised her from the dead." He paused for a second, then another. "It's true. I did. But after all, she raised me first, so it was the least I could do."

At this, a ripple of laughter coursed through the crowd. It seemed to Papa Jim's ear that there was something almost grateful about that laughter, as if Ethan had somehow convinced these people already that he wasn't their enemy, wasn't someone to attack or make fun of, but someone who was with them, one of them. As if they were all in this together.

It's a miracle, Papa Jim thought. *A bloody miracle.*

But of course it wasn't.

Not yet.

"I'm Ethan Brown," he went on. "I healed those people at Olathe Medical last night, and I'm sure you're wondering why. The truth is, it happened pretty much by accident. See, I'd only just remembered who I am and why I'm here. As you can probably imagine, it came as a bit of a shock, to say the least. And then, on top of it all, my mom got in this terrible car accident and died. So I was pretty upset. I wasn't thinking too clearly. I knew I wanted to bring her back, but it was the first time I'd ever done anything like that. Even Jesus started with something easy, turning water to wine. He left the harder stuff until later, until he had more practice. But I went straight to the advanced course. And I guess you could say I misjudged. I not only brought my mom back, I healed everybody else in the hospital.

"Like I said, it was an accident, but I'm not sorry it happened. How could I regret saving somebody's life? At the same time, though, I can't just snap my fingers and heal every sick person in the world. I can't bring everybody back from the dead. I thought it was important to tell you that up front, so people don't get the idea that I'm here to do magic tricks or something. You shouldn't have those kinds of expectations about me. Jesus didn't heal everybody in the world, did He? Sure, He performed miracles, but that wasn't the reason God sent Him to Earth.

"Actually, that's another thing I wanted to clear up. I told Ms. Rodriguez that I was the Son of God, or one of them. The Bible mentions two sons: the Son of God and the Son of man. Jesus was the Son of God. I'm the second Son, the Son of man. Jesus knew all about me. He said, 'Watch therefore, for ye know neither the day nor the hour wherein the Son of man cometh.' Just like John the Baptist prepared the way for Jesus, Jesus prepared the way for me. Now I'm here. Why?

"As I told Ms. Rodriguez, to shake things up. 'The Son of Man shall send forth his angels,' said Jesus, 'and they shall gather out of his kingdom all things that offend, and them which do iniquity.' And He also said: 'For as the lightning cometh out of the east, and shineth even unto the west; so shall also the coming of the Son of Man be.'"

At this, Papa Jim noticed some angry mutterings, isolated for now but perhaps not for much longer.

He's losing them . . .

Again, he thought of signaling Denny to launch the operation, but again he held back. He had to see what was going to happen. How Ethan handled himself.

Suddenly one voice was raised from amid the crowd. Papa Jim couldn't see from where, exactly, but it rang out loud and clear, a man's voice, rough with indignation. "You call yourself greater than Our Lord Jesus Christ?"

Ethan didn't hesitate in replying. "Is the younger brother greater than the older? The younger brother looks up to the older brother, and the older brother looks out for the younger brother. Between two such brothers there is no rivalry, only respect, admiration, and love. For they are both sons of the same father. Jesus had His work to do, and I have mine. 'For the Son of Man is come to seek and to save that which is lost.'

"My brother was called the Good Shepherd, but it was also said of Him, and He said it Himself many times, that He came not just with a shepherd's crook but with a sword. Yet He never carried a weapon, not even a knife, and the one time a sword was raised in His defense, by Peter, Jesus told him to put it down, and then He healed the wound that Peter had inflicted, on one of the

Roman soldiers sent to arrest Him. So what did He mean by saying that He had come with a sword? Just this: His tongue was a sword, and His words were the cuts and thrusts and parries of that sword. His message pierced and cut and brought pain to those who heard and heeded it, because it's never easy to take that first step toward God, which is a step away from so much of your life, so much that you thought was important and necessary but really isn't. And for those who didn't hear, didn't heed, the pain was even worse, because it would be endless: the pain of separation from God, the pain of eternity in hell. That was the sword of Jesus, the Son of God. But what about the Son of man? Look at me." And here Ethan spread his arms wide. "Do you see a sword? A gun? Any weapon at all?" He let his arms fall back to his sides. "I'm not my brother. God didn't send Jesus back; this isn't the Second Coming, even though I'm the second Son. I'm not here to walk the same path that Jesus walked. And my message isn't the same, either. This isn't a do-over. It's not a repeat or a remake! Did Jesus preach the continuation of the laws and commandments set down by Moses? Or did he bring a new testament, a new understanding? Now it's time for a *newer* testament. It's time for the next step in God's plan. Because God's plan isn't a dead thing. It's not meant to lay over us like a heavy shroud, holding us down, blinding us to the wonders and mysteries of the world. It's alive, and like all living things, it grows and changes. It evolves. I'm what you might call the next stage in that evolution. And in the weeks and months to come, I hope we can have a conversation about what that means. Starting right now." He paused, momentarily losing his composure. He seemed to be fighting back tears. Then he wiped his eyes and smiled apologetically. "Sorry. I guess this is an emotional moment for me. Now, I promised Ms. Rodriguez the first question."

But before Rita Rodriguez could pose that question, there was a commotion in the crowd directly behind her. Papa Jim watched as a man thrust himself forward. A man in a running suit.

Tefflon.

"Allah akhbar," shouted Tefflon, reaching for the sonic grenade strapped to his arm.

But before he could trigger the device, a shot rang out, and Tefflon crumpled, a look of utter shock on his face.

Oh shit . . . ! came Denny's voice.

Papa Jim was on his feet without being aware of having stood. Tefflon was down, shot. And that wasn't the worst of it.

The worst of it was the identity of the shooter.

A munchie. One standing no more than ten feet away from Ethan.

As Papa Jim watched in horror, the munchie swung his weapon toward Ethan. "Take him down!" he screamed.

On screen, Papa Jim saw Denny raising his own weapon. But he seemed to be moving in slow motion. Everyone was moving in slow motion.

Except the shooter.

A Congregation plant.

It had to be.

Papa Jim had known they had infiltrated the Department of Homeland Security. Known that they had their moles planted amid his lower-level munchies. But never had he suspected that they would be capable of something like this. Denny had picked the personnel for this mission personally. That meant the highest echelons of the organization had been breached. There was no one Papa Jim could trust now. Maybe not even Denny himself. He clenched his fists in impotent fury. Someone was going to pay.

I underestimated them, Papa Jim realized, even as the munchie fired.

Ethan didn't flinch. Just stood there with tears running down his cheeks.

From his side, in a blur, Lisa moved, throwing herself forward, into the path of the burst from the munchie's weapon.

Even as she fell in a shower of blood, Denny and the other munchies opened up on the shooter, who went down in turn, his white armor chewed to bits under the concentrated fire.

Meanwhile, pandemonium reigned. The crowd had transformed into a panic-stricken mob. People were screaming hysterically, flinging themselves blindly away from the gunfire, desperate to escape whatever was happening. They sounded like animals, bleating and screaming—at least until Papa Jim stabbed the mute button, cutting them off.

"Goddamn it, Denny," he shouted. "Where's Ethan? What the fuck is going on? Talk to me, damn it!"

I'm here, Boss, came Denny's voice, buzzing in his head. *The kid looks okay. I'm trying to get to him now!*

The camera swept off the terrorized crowd and back to the front stoop of the Brown home. There Ethan was on his knees, cradling Lisa in his arms, tears running down his cheeks as Peter stood nearby, pale as a ghost, his shirt and face spattered with blood. There was blood on Ethan too, though whether his own or Lisa's, Papa Jim couldn't tell.

He knew he had to act fast. "Denny, go to plan B."

Roger that, Boss.

As Papa Jim heard his implant go dead with a hollow click, static blanked the TV screen. Plan B called for the munchies to trigger an electromagnetic pulse, something their armor was equipped to do as a kind of last-ditch defensive maneuver, since the pulse would fry all electronics in the area, including their own. This would be followed by the use of multiple sonic grenades; no doubt that was occurring even now, though Papa Jim could see and hear nothing of it, cut off as he was from the action. But his isolation was only temporary. Since Denny was the one giving the order for the EM pulse, he had shut down his own implant first. That would enable him to turn it back on within a minute or so.

While he was waiting, Papa Jim righted the spilled glass, refilled it from the bottle of Aberlour, and tossed down the contents in a single gulp. Then, throat burning, he relit his cigar and puffed furiously.

At last his implant crackled to life.

"Report," he croaked through a gray haze of cigar smoke.

Everybody's incapacitated, including the kid, came Denny's voice. *We're securing him as planned. His mom is dead, and so is Tefflon.*

"What about the shooter?"

Dead. I looked under his visor, Boss. I don't recognize the guy. He wasn't part of the team.

"Goddamn it," Papa Jim said. "Any civilian casualties?"

Doesn't look like it.

"Finally, a bit of luck."

We're bagging up the casualties and the kid and getting the fuck out of here, said Denny.

"I'll see you in Phoenix," Papa Jim said.

✠   ✠   ✠

Kate had just disembarked from her flight and was wending her way slowly through the line at JFK customs when she noticed the wall-screen TV
broadcasting some kind of press conference from the front lawn of a house
in a town called Olathe.

A town in Kansas.

The sound was too low for Kate to hear, but what caught her attention
were the words emblazoned across the top of the screen: *The Son of God?*

As the line inched forward, she watched, mesmerized. When the first
boy came out the front door of the house, she gasped, wondering if this
beefy young man could really be Ethan, but then the transcript scrolling
along the bottom of the screen identified him as Peter Wiggan, a friend of
Ethan Brown.

Brown!

Where had that name come from?

Then Ethan appeared, and all Kate's questions were swept away in the
joy of seeing him for only the second time in her life. But she knew immediately that it was really him. Knew it absolutely, unquestionably, by
some maternal instinct, blood calling to blood.

Her son.

God's son.

Ethan.

More and more people watched the press conference as it continued,
and even the customs officers and the security personnel—white-armored
guards that she heard some of her fellow travelers refer to as "munchies"—
became engrossed. Someone turned up the sound, and progress in every
line ceased, and the lines themselves disintegrated as American citizens and
visitors alike surrendered their places and gathered in groups in front of the
wall screens, where they looked on avidly, almost hungrily, as Ethan spoke.

Listening, Kate was filled with pride. And gratitude to God for saving
her son and giving her the blessing of this second chance to know him, to

become a part of his life. Even just seeing him like this, hearing his voice, was like a miracle to her.

Then the jogger rushed forward, a shot rang out, and chaos erupted even as the shooter turned and calmly trained his weapon on Ethan.

And fired.

Stunned, Kate fell to the floor as if the burst had come right through the TV screen and slammed into her belly.

Meanwhile, the shooter went down in a hail of bullets.

But what about Ethan? The camera was sweeping the crowd, as if searching for something . . . or avoiding something. Around Kate, people were screaming, weeping, praying. She, however, remained silent, wrapped in a shell of shock and disbelief. She sat on the floor where she had fallen, clutching her knees to her chin and rocking back and forth as she sent her prayers Heavenward.

He can't be dead. Not after everything that's happened. God, you can't let it end like this! Do you hear me? You can't!

Then Kate saw him.

Ethan.

He was alive. He knelt on the stoop of the house, spattered in blood, the body of the woman he'd identified as his mother in his arms. She looked dead.

Kate understood at that moment how much this woman had loved her son. And felt not the slightest hint of jealousy. Rather, she felt grateful beyond all expression to this stranger who had given her life for her son. And thankful that Ethan had known such love.

That too seemed like a miracle to her.

Then the screen went blank. The audio vanished.

When the broadcast resumed moments later, Ethan and his mother were gone.

It was then that two of the white-armored guards came to Kate. She barely registered what they said to her. Barely understood what was happening as they hustled her away, through a door, down a corridor, through another door, and into a darkness as all-embracing and inescapable as the terrible mercy of God.

CHAPTER 17

Papa Jim paused in the empty hallway, hesitating midway between the two doors. Which to enter first? He supposed he could just flip a coin, let chance dictate the decision, but Papa Jim was no great believer in chance. Or fate, for that matter. He preferred to make his own luck. Always had, and he wasn't about to stop now. Besides, he had a gut feeling that his choice might matter more than he consciously realized, and despite his usual scorn for anything that smacked of intuition, a quality he was generally happy to leave, as he put it, "to fags and females," he'd learned over the course of his career in business and politics to pay attention to his gut feelings. So despite his impatience, he forced himself to wait, to think things through one more time. *What's it going to be?* he mused, taking the opportunity to light a fresh cigar with hands that shook slightly despite his efforts to keep them still. *The lady or the tiger?*

He'd just come from a third room. A room that, like these two, was soundproofed and shielded against all known electronic infiltration technologies and which, again like them, was situated hundreds of feet below the Conversatio compound located outside Phoenix, Arizona; the very compound where, ten years ago, he'd first witnessed, then almost immediately forgotten, what Ethan was capable of.

It said a lot that Papa Jim had opted for the Phoenix compound over any of the U.S. government military bases or domestic security facilities to which he had access, but he knew that those sites had almost certainly been hacked into by Grand Inquisitor, if not physically infiltrated by Congregation agents. Conversatio, on the other hand, had centuries of experience in successfully evading the Congregation, and Papa Jim had employed the financial resources of Oz Corp to augment that hard-won, if low-tech, experience. The result was AEGIS, or Artificially Engineered Global Intelligence System, a software program specifically designed to anticipate and frustrate the efforts of Grand Inquisitor and the Congregation. This had been attempted many times over the years, never successfully, but now, bankrolled by Papa Jim's deep pockets, Conversatio's computer scientists and engineers had finally achieved their goal of creating a massively parallel, quantum-computing network of their own. AEGIS was not the equal of GI in terms of sheer processing power, but it came closer than anything else on the planet, and its firewalls were considered to be all but impregnable.

Papa Jim was putting them to the test now. There was no doubt that Grand Inquisitor and its human masters in the Vatican would give a lot to know what was going on in this compound, and in three rooms in particular.

In the room he'd just left, a corpse was waiting to be disposed of. But it hadn't been a corpse when Papa Jim had entered the room. It had still been a living human being, albeit a critically injured one.

Papa Jim had stood for a while inside the door, just looking at the man who lay in the hospital bed, hooked up to the machines that were keeping him alive. The lower half of his face was wrapped in white bandages, leaving only his eyes exposed. These were closed, as if the man were asleep or unconscious. A breathing tube had been inserted into his throat, and tubes carrying blood and other liquids were connected to his arms and chest.

A young doctor was bent over one of the machines, adjusting its dials with care, while a fully armed and armored munchie stood guard, although the man in the bed was strapped down and didn't seem capable of much even if he'd been free to move.

It was something of a miracle that he was even alive, although "miracle" was a word that Papa Jim used advisedly these days. Still, he'd been struck by seven bullets. Two in his left arm, one in the right, two in the chest, one in the stomach, and one that had shattered his jaw. That usually added up to dead.

"How's he doing, Doc?" Papa Jim demanded, gesturing with an unlit cigar.

The doctor straightened up, rolling his shoulders wearily. "A lot depends on the next few hours." Then, focusing on the cigar, "You can't light that in here." He nodded toward the machine whose dials he'd been adjusting. "The oxygen."

Papa Jim nodded. "Get out," he said.

The doctor didn't reply but instead glanced questioningly at the guard.

"Sir?" The voice issuing from behind the dark visor was female.

"You heard me," said Papa Jim. "Out. Now."

"Yes, sir," said the munchie and complied at once.

The doctor remained behind. "But the patient—"

Papa Jim cut him off. "I'll take care of the patient."

"He's not fit for interrogation," the doctor said. "He can't even talk."

"I'll be the judge of that," Papa Jim said. Then, before the man could protest any further, "Son, this is one pissing match you're not going to win. Just put your pecker back in your pants and go."

An angry flush appeared on the young man's cheeks at that, but upon reflection he seemed to see the wisdom of Papa Jim's advice; at any rate, he turned abruptly and stalked out of the room.

As soon as the door slammed behind him, Papa Jim walked over to the bed. The patient lay silent and still. The doctors had said he was in his thirties, but that was all the information they had about him. He had not been carrying any ID, and neither his fingerprints nor his retinal scans had shown up in the public and private databases accessible to Papa Jim and Conversatio. Which was pretty much all of them.

With one glaring exception: the Congregation database maintained by Grand Inquisitor.

"Are you awake?" Papa Jim asked now, leaning over the bed, his voice soft, even gentle. "Can you hear me?"

There was no response from the recumbent figure. His eyelids did not so much as flicker. The only sounds in the room were the steady hiss of oxygen and the varied beeps and clicks of the machines as they performed their mindless tasks.

Papa Jim straightened up and began to circle the bed, letting the hand that held the cigar trail along the metal restraining rail. "Maybe you think that if you pretend to be unconscious, I'll just give up and go away. Or maybe you think I won't do anything to you because you haven't been interrogated yet, and I wouldn't risk losing a valuable source of intelligence. Just in case you're laboring under these misconceptions, or any others, let me assure you of two things. First, I'm a pretty stubborn guy, and I don't give up easily." Having reached the opposite side of the bed, Papa Jim reversed course, unhurriedly retracing his steps. "And second, I've supervised the interrogation of Congregation agents before, and I've never heard a single one of you bastards spill anything we didn't know already. I don't imagine you'd be any different."

By this time, Papa Jim had returned to his starting point. Now he reached out to the machine the young doctor had been adjusting and switched it off. Two things occurred immediately. The first was that the hiss of rushing air vanished from its place among the room's ambient sounds. The second was that the eyes in that bandaged face sprung wide open. They held a look of terror.

"Awake, eh?" said Papa Jim with satisfaction. "I thought so." He detached the end of the air tube that was hooked into the machine. At the same time, deprived of oxygen, the figure on the bed began to buck and struggle within its restraints, but Papa Jim seemed to take no notice of the drama playing out on the bed beside him.

"Now that that's taken care of, do you mind if I smoke? I didn't think so." He lit the cigar, drew on it deeply, then exhaled into the end of the breathing tube he had just detached from the oxygen machine. A thick, gray cloud went roiling up the tube and into the lungs of the patient, who began to cough. Deep, wracking coughs that seemed to be tearing something loose inside him. His eyes bugged out as if they might pop free of his skull.

"Genuine Cubans," Papa Jim said, admiring the cigar before taking another pull and exhaling into the tube, with a result that, if anything, surpassed the violence of the previous effort. "Hard to get, even now. But don't bother to thank me. I'm happy to share." And to prove it, he blew another lungful of smoke into the breathing tube.

The patient had almost ceased to struggle. His movements were more like feeble twitches than anything else. A glazed, fixed look had settled over his eyes.

Papa Jim leaned close. "I don't mind that you tried to get in my way. It goes with the territory. I don't even mind so much that you managed to breach my security and pass yourself off as one of my munchies. That shows initiative, and I admire the hell out of initiative, even in my enemies. No, son, what pisses me off about this whole affair, where you and your Congregation bosses stepped over the line, is that Ethan is my great-grandson, you see? My flesh and blood. My *family*. And nobody, but nobody, touches my family."

Even as he spoke these words quite calmly, in a measured tone of voice perfectly suited to a visit to a hospital bedside, Papa Jim was ripping away the other end of the air tube, the end that was lodged in the patient's throat. It came out with a gushing of blood and smoke, accompanied by a groan that was as full of weariness as of pain. Papa Jim stood well back from the mess, puffing furiously on his cigar. Then he took the glowing end and ground it down into the open wound left when he'd torn out the tube. Smells of burning flesh and tobacco mingled in the air.

"Nobody," he repeated. He stepped back, and only then noticed that his hands were spattered with blood. He went to the sink and washed them thoroughly, drying them on paper towels. Then, after another look at the bed, he activated his implant and called for Denny.

Yeah, Boss?

"You better get down here," he said. "There's a mess needs cleaning up."

On my way.

Outside in the hallway, the young doctor was waiting. He looked up as Papa Jim exited the room. "If you're quite through, I'd like to get back to my patient."

"Sorry, Doc," Papa Jim said. "This room's off-limits."

"Off-limits?"

"I'm afraid there's been an accident."

"An accident?"

"Your patient was shot while trying to escape."

"That's absurd! I've been here the whole time, and I haven't heard anything."

"Stick around," Papa Jim said. "You will."

Brushing by the doctor, he'd strode up the hallway, heading for Kate's room, which was right next to the room where they were holding Ethan. But before entering, it had occurred to him that perhaps he should pay Ethan a visit first. Now he stood in the hallway, trying to decide between them. The taste and smell of his cigar was not having its usual soothing effect; in fact, he was feeling nauseous. He kept smelling the stink of burned flesh, kept seeing the glazed, terror-stricken eyes of the man in the hospital bed. He threw the cigar down to the floor and ground it out beneath his boot.

Okay, maybe he'd lost it a little bit back there, he thought. But the scum had had it coming. Family was the one thing that really counted in this world. Without family, what did power or wealth matter? Papa Jim pursued these things not for their own sake but for the sake of his family, his posterity, who would keep his name and his vision alive. Kate and Ethan were all the family he had left, his only link to the future. Any attack on them was the same as an attack on Papa Jim. And more than that. It was an attack on all that he had built up. The careful plans he'd laid for the future. It was an attack on America itself. He simply couldn't allow such temerity to pass unpunished.

He took a deep, calming breath and tried to focus on the present, on the task at hand. The problem facing him was a delicate one. Ethan didn't know him and therefore had no reason to trust him, while Kate knew him all too well and, because of that, had even less reason to trust him. Yet he needed them both to cooperate with him willingly. He could use Ethan as leverage with Kate, and Kate as leverage with Ethan, but which of them to approach first? It was the kind of decision he was faced with a hundred times a day. Why was he having such difficulty making up his mind now? Was it because so much was at stake? Or was he losing his nerve?

The hell with that. His decision made, Papa Jim let the locking mechanism outside the door scan his retina, after which he punched the day's security code into the keypad on the wall. A small LED flashed green as the lock clicked open. He pushed open the door and stepped into the room.

Save for the absence of windows and a telephone, and the presence of cameras in the corners of the ceiling, it might have been a room in any mid-range hotel chain. There was a double bed, a plush chair, a wall-screen TV, a mini-fridge, and an adjoining bathroom. The TV was on, the sound muted. The video of Ethan's press conference was being shown. Watching from the bed, propped against the pillows with his arms folded over his chest, was Ethan himself. He glanced up as Papa Jim entered the room, but did not rise or seem particularly surprised to see him.

"Hello, Ethan," said Papa Jim. "I'm—"

"I know you," Ethan interrupted. "You're Jim Osbourne, of Oz Corporation. The Secretary of Homeland Security."

"You can call me Papa Jim," he said.

"Why would I want to do that?"

"It's what my friends and family call me."

"I'm not your friend."

"I'd like you to be."

"You have a funny way of showing it."

"What do you mean?" Papa Jim was genuinely curious.

"I'm in jail, aren't I?"

Papa Jim laughed. "You most certainly are not. Where did you get that idea?"

"Maybe it was the locked door. Or the cameras. Or the lack of any means of communicating with the outside world. You took my cell phone, and *this* cell doesn't even have a phone."

"You're in protective custody," Papa Jim said. "After what happened at the press conference, I didn't want to take any chances. I'm so sorry about your mother, by the way."

"Are you?"

Papa Jim bristled at what seemed an implicit accusation. "Of course. For what it's worth, the terrorist scum who killed her got what he deserved. I saw to it personally."

"Right," said Ethan. "You mean the terrorist who just happened to be wearing the armor of a munchie?"

Papa Jim sighed. "We were infiltrated. He wasn't one of us."

"Who was he, then?"

"Do you mind if I sit down? It's kind of a long story."

Ethan gestured toward the chair. "Go ahead."

Papa Jim crossed in front of the bed and sat down. As he did so, Ethan turned off the TV. Papa Jim reached into his pocket for a cigar . . . then, remembering his earlier reaction, decided against it. He cleared his throat. "I'm not sure how much your mother told you, Ethan, but judging from what you said in the interview and at the press conference, I'm guessing it was quite a bit. Enough so that it won't come as a surprise to learn that the man who killed your mother was an agent sent by the Congregation to kill you."

"So you know about the Congregation."

"I know a lot of things," Papa Jim said. "I know that the Congregation is opposed by a group called Conversatio. I know that your mother was a Conversatio agent, as was your father, before he was killed . . . also by the Congregation. And I know that Lisa and Gordon Brown weren't your parents."

"They *were* my parents. In every way that counts."

"All right. But they weren't your biological parents. They adopted you."

Ethan looked thoughtful. "You're part of Conversatio yourself."

"Yes," Papa Jim said. "Very good. In fact, we're in a Conversatio facility right now. But then, you knew that, didn't you? I imagine there's very little you don't know, Ethan. Being who you are and all."

At this, Ethan laughed, and it seemed to Papa Jim that there was bitterness in his voice when he answered. "What, you think I know everything? That I'm omniscient, like God? All powerful? It doesn't work that way."

"How does it work, then?"

Ethan got up from the bed and began to pace the room. "Sometimes things are, well, revealed to me. I see connections that other people can't. Sometimes I just have a feeling that something is going to happen, that I should or shouldn't do this or that." He stopped, obviously frustrated. "It's hard to explain."

"That's why you were crying," Papa Jim said. "Right before that bastard shot Lisa, you were crying. You knew, didn't you? You knew what was going to happen."

He gave a terse nod. "I saw it coming."

"Then why didn't you change things? Why did you let her die? You're the second Son. You have power over life and death. You proved that at Olathe Medical. Why save all those people, and bring Lisa back from the dead, only to let her die hours later at the hand of a Congregation agent?"

"Because that's the way it had to be," Ethan said.

"You mean it was God's plan?"

"There's no plan. Not like you mean. God only wants the best for us. He's given us the greatest gifts that any father can give his children: life and freedom. It's up to us how to use them. I'm not here to bring people back from the dead or to heal the sick. The more I do those things, the more of a distraction it becomes. I didn't understand that before, but I do now."

"So you let her die," Papa Jim repeated.

"She made the choice herself. I didn't have a right to take that choice from her."

"Even if it killed her?"

"Death isn't the end, Mr. Osbourne. It's just the beginning. Life is precious, a gift not to be squandered, but what comes after life can be more precious still."

"Is that why you're here? To remind us of that?"

"Yes. At least partly. And for other reasons, too."

"What other reasons?"

"I can't tell you that."

"You mean you won't?"

"No, I can't. I don't know them. I just know they're out there. My work isn't done. It's scarcely started."

"I'd like to help you in your work," Papa Jim said.

"Why?" Ethan asked.

"Why?" Papa Jim echoed, taken aback by the question. "Because it's the right thing to do," he managed after a moment.

"I can see the blood on your hands, Mr. Osbourne. And the blackness clinging to your soul like tar. I know what kind of man you are. Oh yes, better than you know it yourself. Why would I accept help from someone like you?"

Papa Jim felt a chill run up his spine. This time the urge for a cigar overpowered any residual discomfort. "Mind if I smoke?"

"What if I said yes?"

"Then I wouldn't smoke."

Ethan held his gaze, then shrugged. "Whatever. I don't care." He flopped down onto the bed again.

Papa Jim lit up. His gorge rose a bit at the first puff, but he forced it down and smoked on grimly, without the accustomed pleasure. Every time he inhaled, he was back in that room, back with the dying man, grinding his cigar into the open wound. But he was damned if he was going to give up cigars just because of some bad memories. He'd go on smoking them now even if he hated every goddamn minute, just out of spite. "Look, I'm no saint," Papa Jim said. "I admit that. But I'm not an evil person. I want to bring this country back to God, just like you."

"I'm not here for just this country," Ethan said. "My message is for the whole world."

"Well, you gotta start somewhere," said Papa Jim with a grin. "Besides, God works in mysterious ways, right? I think I'm supposed to play a part in whatever it is that you're here to do."

"What makes you think that?"

"Because we're related, Ethan. I'm your great-grandfather. Your mother is my granddaughter. I was there when you were born."

Once again, Ethan showed no sign of surprise. He simply looked thoughtful. Then he said, "Yes, I see that now. You took me away from her. You gave me to the Browns to raise as their own."

"To protect you, Ethan. To protect her. I knew that the Congregation would be looking for you. You were a high potential, the highest of the highs. Only Conversatio could keep you safe from their killers. And I was right. You survived."

"But not the Browns."

"No, and I regret that. But they knew the risks. They accepted those risks willingly, so that you could grow up to become the man you are today. So that you could accomplish what God put you here to do. They're gone now, but your work isn't done. You said so yourself. And you've seen for yourself how deadly the Congregation can be. They won't stop trying to kill you. You need protection. The kind of protection that only I can give you."

"I'll think about it," Ethan said.

"Fair enough," said Papa Jim. "But don't take too long. If you've been watching the news reports, then you know that you've already had a huge effect on people all over the world. I've put out a statement that you're okay and in the protective custody of Homeland Security, but people are wondering. They want to see you with their own eyes and hear what you have to say."

"And you'd stop me from doing that?"

"No. But if you refuse my protection, how long do you think you'll last out there before the Congregation or some fanatic succeeds in killing you? Unless, of course, you can't be killed."

"I'm not Superman," Ethan said. "I can be hurt or killed just like anybody else."

"Well, then." Papa Jim heaved himself to his feet. "I'll give you a little while to think things over. You're my great-grandson, Ethan. No matter what you decide, I'll be here for you. I want you to know that. We're family, and family means everything to me."

"I wonder if my birth mother would agree."

"Her name is Kate," Papa Jim said. "And I hope you'll have the chance to ask her that yourself. I'm going to do everything I can do to bring her to you, Ethan. Just to demonstrate my good faith."

✠   ✠   ✠

Kate was watching television when Papa Jim came to her. She'd been expecting him ever since she'd regained consciousness in this comfortable but anonymous room that could have been anywhere and nowhere. Hotel Limbo.

Ethan was all over the news. Every time she switched channels, she saw either a replay of the climactic moments of the press conference or footage of crowds of people from around the world gathered to celebrate his appearance or to denounce him; mostly, it seemed, the latter. Demonstrations in Islamabad and throughout the Middle East had turned violent as throngs of devout Muslims protested Ethan's claim to be the second Son, which, breathless announcers explained, was viewed as a blasphemous repudiation of Mohammed.

Things were little better among Christians. The Vatican had been quick to issue a statement disavowing Ethan, calling him "at best misguided," leaving open the question of what he might be "at worst." Fundamentalist preachers in the United States supplied one answer, railing against "the self-confessed Antichrist in our midst." But other religious leaders and many common people hailed Ethan, professing belief in his divinity and faith that more miracles were on the way.

Papa Jim, as Secretary of Homeland Security, had also issued a statement, blaming the death of Lisa Brown on homegrown Islamic terrorists who had infiltrated the munchies, and stating that Ethan had been taken into protective custody while the rest of the plotters were arrested. He promised swift justice for the killers and urged people to remain calm and allow the munchies and the police to do their jobs. This, however, seemed to have had anything but a calming effect, as vigilantes and common criminals took to the streets in cities and towns across the United States to attack the homes, businesses, and places of worship of anyone deemed non-Christian. There had been a handful of serious injuries and deaths, as well as property damage in the hundreds of thousands of dollars. This in turn had led to statements from Jewish, Islamic, and Christian leaders decrying acts of bigotry and calling on Homeland Security to enforce the rule of law. All this in the less than twenty-four hours that had passed since Ethan's press conference.

It seemed to Kate that the whole world was going mad. They needed Ethan more than ever. But there was no word from him. No sign.

What was Papa Jim up to?

Whatever it was, she doubted it was anything good.

And she had no doubt that, wherever he was, Ethan was a prisoner . . . just like her. The door to her room was locked, and there was no other visible entrance or exit. She'd tried yelling for help and shouting for Papa Jim, but there had been no answer. She'd stripped the bed, using the sheets to cover the cameras in the corners of the ceiling, but even that had brought no one. That's when she'd turned on the TV and learned that she'd been unconscious for nearly a full day.

There were fresh clothes laid out for her, so after a while she'd taken a shower and put them on. When she came out of the bathroom, she saw that dinner had been left for her on a tray. It didn't surprise her to learn that she was being watched despite her sabotage of the cameras, but it did make her angry. Angrier.

But she ate the food anyway, because she was hungry. She didn't think Papa Jim would try to poison her, or drug her. Not that he would be incapable of it, but what would be the point? She was already completely in his power. She had been from the moment the munchies had escorted her out of the customs area at JFK.

It was about an hour later that the door to the room opened and Papa Jim walked in, cigar in hand.

"Hi, baby girl," he said as if they'd last seen each other only yesterday and had parted on the best of terms.

She had to hand it to him. He had nerve. She'd wondered how she was going to react when she finally saw him face to face. Part of her had been longing for it. Part of her had been dreading it. Now that the moment had come, there was no hesitation, no thought. She pushed herself up from the chair in which she'd been sitting and crossed the room to him. He stood his ground. He didn't even look worried. Why should he? She was a nun, wasn't she?

Without a word, Kate slapped him across the face.

His cigar went flying.

Then she slapped him again, harder.

She slapped her seventy-three-year-old grandfather, and it felt good. It felt better than just about anything she could remember, outside learning that Ethan was still alive.

"You bastard," she said, drawing back her hand to slap him again.

But he'd had enough. He moved quickly for an old man. Suddenly he was gripping her wrist, and his grasp was strong. She swung her other hand, but he grabbed that one too. She struggled uselessly. "Let me go!"

"Calm down, honey," Papa Jim said.

She spat into his face.

Rage flared to life in his eyes, and a surge of fear raced through her. She thought for a second that he was going to hit her, but then, with a wordless growl, he heaved her from him, pushing her away as if she weighed no more than a child. She stumbled back, then felt something strike hard behind her knees, and she went down. Luckily, it was only the bed, and she landed on the mattress and sprawled there, the wind knocked out of her.

Before she could get up and come at him again, Papa Jim was on top of her, the bulk of him pressing her into the mattress. He smelled of sweat, whiskey, and cigars. Once those smells had made her feel safe and reassured; now they filled her with disgust and nausea. She felt violated by his touch, his mere presence. "Get off me," she gasped.

"Do you promise to behave like a lady?" he said. Her spittle was still on his cheek.

"Yes, anything, just get off!" In another second, she would be crying.

He rolled off her, lay there beside her, breathing hard. She didn't have the strength to move. Every breath was a struggle not to sob. Finally she managed to gasp out a single word: "Why?"

It was a moment before he answered. He rolled himself off the bed and on to his feet, then walked across the room to pick up his cigar with a grunt. By that time, she was sitting up herself, watching him suspiciously, a pillow clutched to her stomach like a shield. But he looked different now, no longer a threat, just a tired old man, his bald head shining with sweat. Still breathing heavily, he sat down in the chair she had vacated, holding the cigar he'd retrieved, gone out now, and slightly bent, negligently between his fingers. "I suppose I had that coming," he finally said. "But everything I did, I did for you . . . and for Ethan."

"You've been lying to me all these years," she said. "I don't think you're turning over a new leaf now."

He made a gesture with the hand holding the cigar, as if to brush aside her words, then seemed to notice the damaged state of the cigar for the first time. He set it down on a glass table alongside the chair. "I was going to send for you," he said. "I was going to tell you everything. But then the mother superior told me you'd gone. Vanished."

"There was no reason to stay. Not after I learned that my son was still alive. Not after I learned that you lied to me, told me my baby had died and then taken him and given him to someone else to raise."

"And how did you learn that, by the way?"

"You wouldn't believe me if I told you."

"Try me."

She hated his smugness, his attitude of superiority. "It was an angel."

"Excuse me?"

"I said you wouldn't believe me."

"I believe Ethan, so why shouldn't I believe you? Did he have a name, this angel?"

"Gabriel," she said.

"I see. What else did he tell you?"

"Believe me, he told me enough."

"Did he tell you about Conversatio? The Congregation and Grand Inquisitor?"

Kate stared at him blankly. She had never heard these names before.

"No, I didn't think so," said Papa Jim, his satisfaction plain. "Ethan has enemies, Kate. He had enemies even before he was born. Just because of who he is and what he's been sent here to do. I took Ethan away from you because I wanted him to live. I wanted both of you to live. I never wanted to lie to you, but there was no other way. Please, you have to believe me."

"I don't *have* to do anything," she said defiantly.

Papa Jim sighed, then said, "No, no, you don't, Kate. But I'm asking you to listen to me. To give me the benefit of the doubt. If not for my sake, then for Ethan's."

She studied him intently, trying to decide whether he was lying to her. She assumed that he was, but that didn't mean there wasn't some truth mixed in. "Go on."

"The Congregation is Ethan's greatest enemy. It's what used to be called the Inquisition, an organization within the Catholic Church devoted to identifying and killing the second Son, whenever and wherever he should appear."

"Why would they want to do that?"

"Because as far as they're concerned, Ethan is the Antichrist."

"Is that who tried to kill him at the press conference?"

Papa Jim nodded. "A Congregation agent infiltrated my munchies, I'm ashamed to say. But luckily, Ethan was protected by Lisa. She was more than just his adoptive mother, she was an agent for an organization opposed to the Congregation, a secret society made up of men and women devoted to protecting the second Son. It's called Conversatio. That's Latin for 'the way.' I've been a member of Conversatio for years, Kate. I'm one of the directors, in fact. I knew almost from the first that your son was what we call a 'high potential'—a boy with a strong probability of being the second Son, the Son of man. That's why I had you taken to the Convent of Santa Marta. It's a Conversatio facility, much like the place we're in now. I thought it would be a safe place for you to deliver your child."

"If it was so safe, why did you take Ethan away from me immediately after I gave birth to him? Why did you tell me that he was dead? For God's sake, Papa Jim, I held his body in my arms! Do you have any idea what that was like?" She couldn't hold back the tears now. Didn't even try. Just clutched the pillow tighter.

Papa Jim at least had the grace to look discomfited. "I know, and I regret the necessity of it. The baby you held was born dead, to a Conversatio agent. Meanwhile, I had Ethan spirited away and given to Lisa Brown and her husband, Gordon. They were two of our best agents, specially trained to raise him in a way that would keep him safe from the Congregation and Grand Inquisitor."

"Grand Inquisitor? Who's that?"

"Not who: what. It's a machine. A computer so advanced that the Conversatio eggheads tell me it's as conscious as you or I, and a hell of a lot smarter. GI is hooked into every node of electronic communication imaginable, and it uses its connections to search the data streams for high potentials like Ethan. It never sleeps, never gets distracted. It never fails. At least, until now."

"Why now?"

"First of all, because Ethan is who he is. About ten years ago, Ethan made a mistake. He spoke out when he should have kept silent, and that was enough for Grand Inquisitor to locate him. An agent was dispatched. He killed Gordon and very nearly killed Lisa and Ethan, too. But Ethan lashed out instinctively in self-defense and performed a miracle. He made GI forget about his existence. He made everybody forget about it."

"Not me," said Kate. "I never forgot."

"Didn't you?" said Papa Jim, raising an eyebrow. "Interesting. But you were the only one who didn't. Everyone else, including Grand Inquisitor and Ethan himself, forgot that he was the second Son. Until the day before yesterday, when Lisa was fatally injured in a car accident."

"Yes, I saw that on TV. She died, and then Ethan brought her back to life and healed all those people." Kate nodded grimly. "Oh, I see. Then Grand Inquisitor found him again because of that."

"Very good," said Papa Jim. "That's exactly what happened. At the same time, everyone who had forgotten about Ethan remembered him."

Kate gave a sudden gasp. "That's when Gabriel appeared to me! He said that it was time, that Ethan needed me."

"And so he does," said Papa Jim.

"Does he know about me?"

"He knows that Lisa and Gordon weren't his biological parents. He knows that you exist, and that you're my granddaughter, but that's all he knows about you, Kate. At least, I haven't told him any more than that."

"Then he *is* here."

"Yes, he is. He's close by, and he's fine."

"Has . . . has he asked about me?"

"Of course he has," said Papa Jim. "He's got a lot of questions for you. And I'm sure you've got plenty of your own for him."

"I want to see him, Papa Jim. Now."

"Of course," he repeated, but made no move to get up from the chair.

She realized that it wasn't going to be so easy. "What do you want?" she asked wearily, tired of playing games.

"I promise you, Kate, I personally want to make up to you, and to Ethan, for everything I've done, all that I robbed you of. But even more than that, I want Ethan to succeed in his mission. I want to help him bring this country back to God. I think that's the most important thing of all. It's what Lisa and Gordon gave their lives for. I'm willing to give my life as well, if it comes to that. I know you must feel the same. Every mother would."

"Just tell me what you want me to do," she said stubbornly.

"Convince him to accept my protection," he said. "I mean my munchies, along with the resources of Conversatio, and those of Homeland Security as well, insofar as they can be trusted, of course. Will you do it, Kate? Will you help me?"

"Yes," she said. She would have agreed to anything in order to see Ethan. But in her heart she reserved the right to change her mind. She didn't trust him by a long shot. "I'll help you, Papa Jim."

"God bless you, baby girl," he said. "I hope that in time you'll think better of me than you do now. Maybe even love me again like you used to. And forgive me."

She couldn't help laughing, though it was a bitter laugh. "I think at this point that would take a miracle, Papa Jim."

"Shoot, is that all?" he said with a cocky grin, looking something like his old self again. "I've got a feeling that from here on out, we're gonna have more miracles than you can shake a stick at."

✠   ✠   ✠

The only miracle that mattered to Kate, however, took place minutes later, when Papa Jim led her out of her room and to the room next door where Ethan was waiting. Kate couldn't believe that he had been so close to her all this time. Just on the other side of a wall.

"Do you want me to come in with you?" Papa Jim asked outside the door. "Introduce you?"

What absurd questions to be asking a woman about her own son! Yet they only made Kate more aware of the gulf that separated her from Ethan, wider than this door, wider even than the ocean that, until yesterday, had stood between them: a gulf of time, of experience. Of history. All the moments they should have shared, the skinned knees of boyhood, his first day of school, his first crush, the holiday traditions of Christmas, Thanksgiving, and Halloween, the vacations, the laughter and the tears; all of those things that other mothers and sons could take for granted had been stolen from her and Ethan, stolen by a man she'd trusted and loved as much as she trusted and loved anybody in her life. How was she to get those moments back? It wasn't possible. Yet she knew that she had to try. She had to go through that door and establish a relationship with her son that was based on something more than what had been lost. Something that began in blood but went beyond it. She didn't know what it would turn out to be, this relationship with the stranger who was her son, but she had faith that it would exist in time.

"No," she told Papa Jim. "You've done enough."

That seemed to strike home, and she was glad to see that it did. He didn't say another word, just lowered his eye to the scanner and then quickly pressed in a code on the keyboard that hung on the wall beside the door, blocking her view with his body, so that she could see nothing. But she heard the click when the lock disengaged.

"I'll be waiting for you," he said, standing aside. "Just call if you need me."

"Don't hold your breath," she replied and pushed past him, opening the door and stepping into the room beyond.

It was a room identical to hers in every way, except that her room didn't have a handsome young man looking up at her with gold-flecked brown eyes from the edge of the bed.

Ethan.

Kate's heart nearly stopped in her chest, and she froze, unable to move as the door swung shut behind her. Nevertheless, she felt an impulse to turn and run, as if she were facing her greatest nightmare instead of her deepest desire. She was terrified that he wouldn't want anything to do with her, that he would blame her somehow for what had happened, hate her for abandoning him, for not wanting him. Who knew what lies Papa Jim had told him? He might already be poisoned against her. And even if he wasn't, how could Kate assert any claim to motherhood under such bizarre and tragic circumstances as these, with the woman who'd adopted him, raised him, and, Kate knew, loved him, murdered before his eyes less than forty-eight hours ago in a scene that had been captured by cameras and broadcasted around the clock ever since? It seemed presumptuous, to say the least.

Then Ethan rose to his feet with a smile. Could it be that he recognized her, even though she hadn't said a word? Oh God . . . he was coming toward her . . .

"You must be Kate," he said.

And suddenly his arms were around her, and all the awkwardness fell away. Kate stopped holding back and let herself embrace him too, as sobs wracked her body. She felt as if she were melting into him, or he into her. It was a recognition of the bond they shared, as if their bodies didn't care about such petty annoyances as the lies that had kept them apart for almost twenty years. On some visceral level where such things didn't matter, they knew each other as mother and son, knew it absolutely, in a way that didn't diminish anything they had experienced in the meantime but instead transcended it. Revalued it. Kate felt more than understood all this in the blink of an eye. Was it a miracle wrought by Ethan? Or just the ordinary miracle of the human heart which knows no impediments of time or space when it comes to love? She didn't know or care. She just hung on for dear life as her parched heart soaked up the nearness of him.

Yet the embrace couldn't go on forever, much as she wanted it to. If time had drawn off, she could still sense its presence hovering near, trembling as if with the effort of holding itself back. But for a while at least, a timeless interval carved out of time, it seemed to Kate that there was nothing else in the world but the two of them, as if the peace and sanctuary of the womb had once again enveloped them. And even when it was over, when the flow of time could hold itself back no longer and had resumed, and they drew apart, looking at each other through eyes that shone with tears and joy, Kate could still feel the warmth of that embrace lingering around and within her like a blessing that would never fade.

She reached out with a trembling hand to touch Ethan's face, and he let her fingers trail along the smooth curve of his cheek and jaw. "Is it really you?" she whispered. Even now she was afraid that he was just another of Papa Jim's lies.

"It's really me," he said. "Ethan, your son."

She literally didn't know if she was laughing or crying. "They told me you were dead," she said. "God, I'm so sorry, Ethan! I should have never believed . . ." She couldn't go on.

"Shh," he said, cupping her hand in his own. "It's okay. You couldn't know. The important thing is, we've found each other. We're together now."

She nodded, forcing the flood of emotions back by an act of sheer will. "I watched your press conference. I was so proud! And I'm so, so sorry about Lisa . . . about your mother. I know I can't take her place. I'm not even going to try. But I hope you'll let me love you and be there for you . . ." She choked up again.

"Of course I will," Ethan said. "I wish you could have known her. I think you would have been friends." As he spoke, he led her across the room to the bed and guided her down to sit there. He sat beside her, clasping her hand.

Kate gave an embarrassed laugh, wiping the tears from her cheeks with her free hand. "This is so strange! I feel like I've known you forever, but we're really strangers, aren't we?"

"I guess we have a lot of catching up to do, at that," Ethan said with a smile.

✠   ✠   ✠

Back in Kate's room, Papa Jim was seated comfortably, smoking a fresh cigar and watching Kate and Ethan on the wall screen. The picture was crystal clear, as was the sound; he might almost have been in the room with them. He hadn't been certain how Ethan would react to Kate's appearance, whether he'd accept her as his birth mother or hold back emotionally, suspecting Papa Jim of sending in a Conversatio agent to act the part: which, to be fair, he would have done in a heartbeat if not for the fact that he had the genuine article at hand. He couldn't figure Ethan out, didn't understand the extent of his miraculous abilities. He was a walking bundle of contradictions. On the one hand, he seemed like any young man his age, brash in some respects yet confused in others, still feeling his way forward into adulthood, while on the other hand, he was capable of surprising wisdom and flashes of intelligence that were downright uncanny. But now it looked like his worries had been groundless. Ethan had taken the bait. Papa Jim settled back in the chair and put his feet up, ready to enjoy the show.

"I guess we have a lot of catching up to do, at that," Ethan was saying.

The screen went dark.

The sound vanished.

"What the hell?" Papa Jim sat up straight, pointing the remote at the screen and hitting the on/off button repeatedly. Nothing.

His implant crackled to life. *Sir, we've lost audio and video.*

"Well, get 'em back," he snapped.

We can't. It's like the room's been cut off from the rest of the facility.

"I'll be goddamned," he said. And laughed.

Sir? Your orders? Should we send a team in there?

"Hell, no," he said. He thought it unlikely that they would be able to force the door, not as long as Ethan wanted them out, but he didn't bother mentioning it. "Don't you think they deserve a little privacy?"

Yes, sir.

Papa Jim sat back again, still chuckling to himself. The boy had pulled a fast one on him; he'd known all along that Papa Jim was watching. Papa Jim was sure of it. But he wasn't angry. Instead, he felt a flush of pride. *That's my great-grandson,* he thought. *His daddy may be God Almighty, but he's got something of ol' Papa Jim in him too.*

But great-grandson or no great-grandson, he wasn't going to underestimate Ethan again.

✠ ✠ ✠

After an hour or so, the TV flickered back to life. Ethan's face filled the screen, looking directly into the camera and, it seemed, directly into the eyes of Papa Jim.

"I know you're watching, Mr. Osbourne," he said. "Why don't you come on over and join the party?"

That was one invitation Papa Jim had no intention of refusing.

A moment later, he entered the room to find Ethan and Kate sitting side by side on the bed, just where they'd been when he'd last seen them. "I hope you two had a good visit," he said. "I'm just glad I was able to bring you together after so long."

Kate looked as if she might say something, but then decided against it. Ethan said, "I'm grateful to you for that, Mr. Osbourne."

"Please," he said, smiling. "Papa Jim."

"I've thought over what you said, and discussed it with Kate, and I've decided to accept your offer of protection for now."

"That's great!" He was about to say more, but Ethan broke in before he could do so.

"I'd like Lisa to be buried next to Gordon," he said. "I'd like you to organize the burial as soon as possible. Tomorrow or the day after, at the latest."

"What?"

"You said yourself that people are curious about me. I want to show them I'm not afraid. It's important that I be seen in public, Papa Jim. Surely you of all people can appreciate that."

Papa Jim just puffed on his cigar.

I'll be goddamned, he thought. *He did it to me again!*

CHAPTER 18

Father O'Malley pulled a corner of the curtains aside and peered down at St. Peter's Square. The lights had come on, giving the ancient white and gray marble of the surrounding stones, buildings, statues, fountains, and monuments an icy sheen, as if they were encased in a transparent covering of frozen time. Even the hordes of pigeons, normally the filthiest of birds, seemed rendered pristine in this light, their wings taking on an angelic glow. As much of eternity as existed in the perishable works of man was to be found here, he thought, in these tangible representations of God's Heavenly kingdom. No wonder that, even in this century of secular ascendancy, the square had maintained its spiritual authority.

For centuries people had gathered here in times of uncertainty and peril, seeking guidance and reassurance, the blessings of the heirs of St. Peter, and it was no different today. A crowd numbering in the high hundreds was camped out in the square below. Its numbers had been steadily growing for the past three days, ever since the Miracle of Olathe Medical and the press conference that had followed it. Similar gatherings were taking place in church and public squares around the world, but of course the main focus of the media was here. Pope Peter II had released a statement dismissing Ethan as "misguided at best," but the crowd in the square hadn't been mollified by this, and in fact had been calling for His Holiness to address them in person. These calls had only increased since yesterday, when Ethan had released a statement of his own from protective custody, announcing his intention to speak to the public after the funeral of his mother, which was scheduled to take place just minutes from now.

A few hours ago, O'Malley had been dispatched by Cardinal Ehrlich to stroll through the square and mingle with the people who had been drawn there, then report back with his impressions of what he observed. After the failure of their first attempt to neutralize Ethan, the Congregation was treading more carefully, trying to take public opinion into account. There was no longer any room for failure; the next time they struck at Ethan, they would succeed. O'Malley had been told that a massive bomb was going to be set off as Ethan spoke. But it was important to gauge the public mood in order to manipulate it properly in the aftermath of the blast, so that Ethan did not wind up viewed as a martyr but instead as a monster, a beast, the Antichrist. Or so Cardinal Ehrlich had explained it to O'Malley before sending him out into the crowd. Ehrlich seemed to have developed an interest in O'Malley, an interest the young priest was eager to cultivate; the pope's oldest and closest friend would be a powerful mentor in the atmosphere of backbiting intrigue that characterized so much of Vatican politics.

O'Malley had entered the crowd with some misgivings, despite his curiosity. He'd never been one of those priests who had an easy rapport with parishioners, who knew just what words to say and when to say them. No, he'd always been a scholar, a computer scientist—not to put too fine a point on it, a nerd. Being around people, even performing the Mass, had always made him feel nervous and awkward, as if he were only playing the part of a priest and would quickly be unmasked as an imposter. Yet his faith was strong and his talents had been recognized by his superiors, who had summoned him to the Vatican, where he'd won a coveted place in the Congregation of the Doctrine of the Faith, in the elite unit of programmers who interacted with Grand Inquisitor. Of course, he wasn't at that level yet; as in everything concerned with the Church, there was an apprenticeship to serve, a hierarchy to ascend. But at thirty-four years of age, O'Malley had no complaints. He was exactly where he wanted to be, doing the work that he felt called to do. And if part of that work involved mingling with the crowd in St. Peter's Square, so be it.

Yet as he made his way through the crowd, moving tentatively, even apologetically, with a self-consciousness that had expanded along with the girth that made it impossible for him to avoid bumping into people in such situations, O'Malley's nervousness faded. Regardless of their reasons for being there, people seemed to take comfort in the presence of a priest.

Some had come to the square in fear and trembling, some in the calm certitude of salvation. There were young people and old, couples and families, solitary figures sunk in contemplation and prayer. Even—this being Rome, after all—a smattering of communists and atheists who wandered around with bemused expressions, like anthropologists observing the strange customs of a primitive tribe. There were as well, O'Malley had no doubt, Conversatio agents scattered through the crowd as well as fellow members of the Congregation more suited to subterfuge than he, the two groups pursuing their cloak-and-dagger games as they had for centuries, as if Ethan's coming hadn't changed anything. He made a game of his own out of trying to spot them, though with what success he couldn't say.

In places there was an indisputably festive air to the gathering. Musicians played, people sang, jugglers and mimes performed in front of upturned hats. But O'Malley also detected an undercurrent of anxiety running through the crowd. It was as if people had decided to put their hopes and worries on hold and wait to hear what Ethan had to say—and what, if anything, the pope might have to say in reply—before allowing their anxiety to come to the surface. Whether it would do so peacefully or violently, for good or ill, O'Malley didn't feel qualified to predict. But he had no doubt that it would express itself in action of some kind, and he intended to report as much to Cardinal Ehrlich.

O'Malley turned from the window as the cardinal entered his office.

"Sorry to have kept you waiting, Father," said Ehrlich as he seated himself briskly behind his antique wooden desk and motioned for O'Malley to take a seat opposite him. "Give me your report."

O'Malley settled into the chair indicated and related all that he had seen and heard. Ehrlich listened with interest, his long fingers steepled before his sharp, narrow nose, occasionally asking probing questions.

"Well done, Father," he said when O'Malley finished. "We must tread with care, that much is plain. This young man has tapped into one of the most fundamental and powerful longings we humans possess, the longing for God. The Almighty implanted this longing in our souls, but He also instituted the Holy Church to direct it and channel it productively. Whenever people, whatever their intentions, bypass the Church and seek to satisfy that longing in their own way, then they fling open the door to disaster. And waiting there on the other side to tempt the unwary into sin and error is Satan. Without the Church, there can be only confusion and chaos. That, Father O'Malley, is what Ethan is threatening to unleash on the world. That is why he must be stopped."

"Surely things aren't so bad yet," said O'Malley, taken aback by the vehemence of the cardinal's words, especially since his report had been essentially positive.

"Perhaps not here, on the very doorstep of the Church," Ehrlich replied. He got to his feet and began to pace his office, gesticulating forcefully as he spoke. "But while you were making your rounds below, I've been monitoring news reports as well as information coming through our private channels. For the most part, yes, things are still peaceful. But there have been riots in South America and Africa pitting Catholics against each other and against other Christian denominations, while, in the Middle East, at last the Sunnis and Shiites have found something they can agree on: hatred of the infidel who, by proclaiming himself the Son of God, has blasphemed against the prophet Mohammed, according to the infallible Koran God's final messenger to humanity. Bin Laden's disciples have pronounced a fatwa against Ethan. Were you aware of that, Father?"

O'Malley had to admit that he wasn't.

"They're far from the only ones to have done so," Ehrlich continued. "Even the more moderate Muslim voices are calling for blood. And as if that isn't bad enough, Grand Inquisitor has detected a sharp upturn in domestic violence, murders, and suicides across the globe. Do you see, Father, how disruptive Ethan's existence is proving to be? All this chaos stirred up by two purported miracles and the aura of mystery and martyrdom that has coalesced around the idea of him following that disaster of a press conference, where our agent bungled a simple task! Now those of the Christian faith are afraid the end times are at hand, that the trumpet has blown to signal the Apocalypse. Some will repent of their sins, but others will simply take the opportunity to commit new and worse ones. Such is human nature. And his effect on the followers of other faiths will be just as bad, if not worse. We don't have much time to act. Already, Grand Inquisitor has forecast a 96.8 percent probability of worldwide economic collapse, violent popular uprisings, and rabid religious conflict spreading uncontrollably into war, a war that will make the War on Terror look like a child's game."

O'Malley hadn't realized that Grand Inquisitor's projections had reached that level of certainty. "Ninety-six point eight? That's a jump of almost twenty points since this morning!"

Nodding, Ehrlich reseated himself behind his desk. "Make no mistake, Father. This is a crisis unlike anything the Church has ever faced before. It's for this that Grand Inquisitor was created."

"What are we to do?" O'Malley asked. "What does Grand Inquisitor advise?"

"I wish I could confide in you, Father. But the truth is, we have reason to suspect the GI team has been compromised."

"You mean . . ."

"Yes. It's not the first time Conversatio has succeeded in placing an agent in close proximity to Grand Inquisitor, but this latest infiltration comes at the worst possible time. In the past, their agents have been content to simply funnel information back to their masters, enabling Conversatio to stay a step ahead of us. But now the situation is different. Grand Inquisitor is our best hope of getting to Ethan. Conversatio is surely aware of that. His Holiness is concerned that they may decide to blow their agent's cover by having him attempt to destroy GI now, before it can marshal its resources to get to Ethan."

"But I thought we had people in Homeland Security."

"So we do. The only problem is, Ethan isn't being held by Homeland Security."

"He's not? Where is he, then?"

"We've known for some time that the Secretary of Homeland Security, Osbourne, is a Conversatio director. Apparently he's put those munchies of his at their service. And he's got the boy stashed at a Conversatio facility near Phoenix, Arizona. Unfortunately, that's all we know. We haven't been able to get a look inside. They've got some kind of protection there that GI can't crack."

"Can't crack? But that's impossible! Excuse me, Your Eminence, but there isn't any kind of software code that GI can't hack into."

"Apparently there is now."

O'Malley tried to digest this information. "But . . . but that means . . ."

"Yes?" Ehrlich raised an eyebrow, like a teacher teasing an answer out of a slightly backward student.

"That means they have their own massively parallel quantum-computing device."

"Bravo, O'Malley. Well reasoned. And GI agrees with you. It seems that Schrödinger's cat is out of the bag at last."

O'Malley smiled at the witticism and assayed one of his own. "Then, Your Eminence, we must endeavor to bell this cat before it scratches us."

"The cat concerns me less than the rat, O'Malley."

"Your Eminence?"

"We must find the Conversatio agent before he can strike."

"How can I help?"

"That is indeed the question. You see, Grand Inquisitor has compiled a list of those members of the Congregation it considers the most likely candidates. Your name is at the top of that list."

O'Malley sat up straight at this. "My—my name, Your Eminence?"

"Yes. Any idea why it should appear there?"

"It's a mistake, obviously."

"GI doesn't make mistakes, Father," Ehrlich said, raising an admonitory finger. "It assesses probabilities."

"I—I don't know what to say. I'm no spy or traitor, Your Eminence, I assure you."

"I'd like to believe you," said Ehrlich. "But sadly, in these times, one can't be too careful. Or too trusting. No, Father, we need more than your assurances. We need proof."

"I'll do anything to clear my name," O'Malley insisted. "Grand Inquisitor may not make mistakes, but at the same time, it isn't infallible."

"No, only His Holiness can claim that distinction. You have a promising career ahead of you, O'Malley. That's why I've interceded personally in this matter."

"Interceded?" O'Malley could feel cold sweat trickling down his back like melting ice.

"The normal procedure in cases like this is to simply eliminate the top tier of names on the list, those at 70 percent or above. It's the most efficient method, even though it has the regrettable effect of removing the innocent along with the guilty. Still, God understands the need for such sacrifices, and to die a martyr's death is a privilege any loyal priest should gladly embrace. You're lucky, O'Malley. Usually you would be dead already, along with the other six names on the list. However, the current situation does not favor such expediency. His Holiness has decided it's more important to identify the spy and interrogate him as only we are equipped to do."

"Interrogate?" O'Malley tried to keep his voice steady. "Your Eminence, I—"

Cardinal Ehrlich interrupted. "Yes, yes, I know what you're about to say, O'Malley. Confessions obtained under interrogation are apt to be false. No one knows that better than I. That's why we're holding off until we've determined the identity of the spy."

"But how are you going to do that?" Glad as he was to learn that he was not going to be subjected immediately to any of the vast array of interrogation techniques, otherwise known as tortures, developed by the Congregation over the course of centuries, O'Malley was far from relieved. In fact, he felt as if he were already undergoing a form of torture.

"A simple test," Ehrlich said. "Each of the suspects was given specific information about our plans for Ethan's upcoming appearance. Each of you received different information, all of it completely wrong. Then you were sent out into the crowd below, where we fully expect that the guilty party communicated his false information to a Conversatio contact. When we see what kind of preparations Osbourne has put in place for Ethan's protection, we'll know which bit of information he's reacting to, and that will give us the identity of the spy."

O'Malley could hardly believe his ears. "But Your Eminence—you can't be serious!"

"Is there a problem, O'Malley?"

"Osbourne isn't a fool. He and his people will take any number of precautionary measures to protect Ethan. It's just common sense that they'll have plans in place to guard against bombs and assassins and the like. Such precautions are routine! They don't require the warning of a spy to implement. If that's what you're going to judge us by, you might as well kill us now."

"Grand Inquisitor thinks otherwise."

"How? I don't understand."

"Nor do I. But just because I don't understand Grand Inquisitor doesn't mean I don't have faith in it. After all, who among us does understand it? Do you?"

"No, Your Eminence. I don't think any human being can fully understand GI. It's evolved patterns of thinking that are beyond our comprehension, patterns born in its sustained immersion in states of quantum superposition as opposed to the world of cause and effect that we perceive as reality."

The cardinal chuckled warmly. "I do like you, O'Malley, even if I often don't have the slightest idea what you're talking about."

O'Malley felt himself blush to the roots of his hair.

"I sincerely hope you don't have to be killed," Ehrlich continued, glancing at his watch. "Ah. It's time for the Ethan show. Shall we watch, Father?"

Speechless, O'Malley could only nod weakly.

✠   ✠   ✠

"What's he doing in there?" Papa Jim demanded for the fifth or sixth time, as he regarded the closed door of the viewing room in the Olathe Funeral Home.

"What do you think?" replied Kate, who was sitting in an upholstered armchair behind him, her legs crossed at the ankles. She wore a black dress with black shoes. "He's saying good-bye to his mother. Don't you dare knock!"

His hand raised to do just that, Papa Jim lowered it reluctantly and turned frowning from the door. "*You're* his mother."

"I'm going to try to be."

"What does that mean?"

"Only that I haven't earned it yet."

"Earned it?"

"The right to be called his mother."

"Baby girl, you brought him into the world," Papa Jim said.

"It means more than just giving birth."

"Like what? Taking a bullet for him like she did?"

"If necessary. But she did more than take a bullet for him, as you know very well."

"The woman was a Conversatio agent. She was doing her job."

"She raised him. Provided for him. Loved him."

Papa Jim had little patience for such talk. He had little patience left at all. Ethan had been in that room for more than an hour now. It was already ten minutes past the time he was scheduled to appear before the cameras and the crowd. When Papa Jim had knocked on the door five minutes ago, Ethan had called out that he would be just another minute. Then nothing. Papa Jim thought about knocking again despite Kate's warning, but he didn't want to upset the boy. Not now.

Scowling, he walked past his granddaughter and peeked out through the curtained windows of the sitting room to the back of the funeral home, where guests were seated in rows of folding chairs under a pavilion erected especially for the occasion. He noted with satisfaction the presence of his munchies in their assigned positions, as well as a number of plainclothes agents led by Denny. The steady thump of the blades of two hovering helicopters gave him a warm feeling. There were not going to be any goddamn accidents today. This was going to be a scene of triumph, not tragedy.

He had to admit Ethan had been right. It had been necessary for him to make a public appearance as soon as possible. There were too many unanswered questions in the wake of the press conference, too many mysteries. All sorts of rumors were floating around, some introduced by Congregation agents, others born as if spontaneously from the ether, all of them spreading like wildfire through the media and across the Internet: Ethan had been killed; Ethan could not be killed; Ethan was a prisoner of the government; Ethan was the result of a government genetic engineering experiment; Ethan was an alien, or an android, or the Antichrist; Ethan was exactly who and what he claimed to be. Added to the barrage of media coverage, with its obsessive focus on anyone even remotely connected to the Miracle of Olathe Medical or to Ethan's past, it was no wonder that the public had been whipped into a state of anxiety bordering on hysteria.

There had been a number of violent outbreaks across the country, even a few small-scale riots, and Papa Jim had given orders for the munchies to crack down hard. There was nothing apt to set people off more unpredictably than religion, and Papa Jim understood that it was important to control the flood of emotion Ethan had unleashed or else run the risk of being swept away by it. So he had agreed to help Ethan organize a funeral service for Lisa, followed by a public statement delivered in front of a select audience and carried live on television as well as over the Internet, where Oz Corp had purchased a domain in Ethan's name: www.The2ndSon.com. The site had video of Ethan's interview with Rita Rodriguez and an edited version of his press conference, along with a newly recorded announcement from Ethan stating that he was fine, that he appreciated people's prayers and good wishes, and that he would be appearing and speaking to the public following the funeral. After only two days, the site had over 200 million hits, and although Papa Jim had anticipated a heavy response and planned accordingly, the servers had still crashed twice so far. Pirated versions of the videos had appeared on YouTube and similar sites, where they had broken all viewing records. And he hadn't even launched the online store yet.

Papa Jim's instincts had been correct. If anything, he'd underestimated the effect that Ethan had on people. Today's remarks, which had been written by the PR team at Oz Corp, would be the opening move in a campaign whose ultimate aim was Ethan's installation in the White House, with Papa Jim as the power behind the throne. Together, they would bring this decadent country back to God and to its rightful dominion over the fallen world.

At first, Ethan had been reluctant to read remarks prepared for him by strangers, but Papa Jim had argued that too much was at stake for Ethan to risk saying something that might be misunderstood or misinterpreted. Things were volatile enough already. There were too many rumors out there, too much misinformation. Hundreds of millions of people were going to be watching and listening to him now, hanging on his every word, and he would never again have a chance like this to influence how they perceived him. One thing Papa Jim had learned in his political career was that first impressions were the most enduring, the most difficult to change. Even though this wouldn't be his first appearance before a crowd, or on TV, it would still be the first time that the vast majority of the audience was seeing Ethan live. Didn't it make sense, that being the case, to trust the professionals on Papa Jim's staff, men and women with a proven record of success?

Somewhat to his surprise, Kate had backed him up, and Ethan had agreed. Mother and son had been almost inseparable since Papa Jim had brought them together, and though he'd been worried at first that she might try to poison Ethan against him, the opposite seemed to have occurred. Had she forgiven him? Or was it just her maternal instincts kicking in, the knowledge that no one could protect her son better than Papa Jim could? Whatever the reason, he wasn't going to look a gift horse in the mouth. Whether or not Kate realized it, he loved her. Everything he'd done, he'd done for her and for Ethan. Sooner or later, she would see that. He would make her see it. He could be damn persuasive when he wanted to be.

But meanwhile the audience was getting restless. Fifty people had been invited, most of them residents of Olathe who had known Lisa Brown personally, as well as friends of Ethan, including the boy, Peter, who'd stood beside him at his first press conference. There were local and national media figures, a smattering of the celebrities Papa Jim had cultivated for political reasons over the course of his career, though the politicians themselves had stayed away, understandably cautious of the controversy surrounding Ethan, waiting to see which way the wind was going to blow. That was fine with Papa Jim. They would come running to his door soon enough, and then he would be able to dictate terms to them from a position of strength.

All the guests had been screened by Denny, who had taken the attempt on Ethan's life at the press conference as a personal insult, a stain on his professional honor that he was determined to wipe out by never letting anything like it happen again . . . an attitude Papa Jim felt would produce better results than any reprimand from him. But just to be on the safe side, he'd had the guests remotely screened by AEGIS as they entered the funeral home. After these precautions, he was as certain as it was possible to be that there were no Congregation assassins hidden among the guests or the munchies. As for an assault from without, it would take something on the order of a tank or a cruise missile to get past his defenses. The site was secure. He would stake his life on it.

As, in fact, he had.

For he planned to be right out there with Ethan, standing at his side.

Assuming, that is, that Ethan ever came out of the damn viewing room.

Turning from the window, Papa Jim marched back over to the door.

"Papa Jim," Kate protested.

He ignored her, raising his fist to knock again. Enough was enough.

But just then the door opened and Ethan emerged. "Sorry to keep you waiting," he said.

With a grunt of acknowledgment, Papa Jim stepped back and looked his great-grandson over critically. He was wearing the clothes selected for him by Papa Jim's people: a dark gray suit, a creamy white shirt with a blue tie, and black shoes. His hair was freshly cut and styled. His eyes were red, as if he'd been crying, which Papa Jim thought was a nice touch; a few tears at the right moment would lend his words the kind of sincerity that couldn't be faked. He gave a satisfied nod. "Do you need anything before we get started?" he asked.

Ethan shook his head. "I guess I'm as ready as I'll ever be."

Kate had come to stand beside him. She took his arm and looked up at him. "I'm proud of you for doing this," she said.

Ethan gave her a smile. "Thanks, Kate. I'm glad you're here. It means a lot to me."

"I wouldn't miss it for the world."

Papa Jim glanced at his watch. "We really need to get out there."

"I'm ready," Ethan repeated.

"All right," said Papa Jim. "I'm going to introduce you. When I'm through, let the applause go on for a while. Twenty, thirty seconds. Then come on out. As soon as you step up to the podium, your speech will flash onto the teleprompter. Once you start reading, the speech will start to scroll. If you want to slow it down, just blink twice, like this." He blinked his eyes twice in quick succession. "If you need to stop the scrolling entirely, blink twice more. If—"

Ethan broke in. "We must've rehearsed all this a hundred times, Papa Jim. I know what to do."

"Right." He looked him over one last time. The kid had the charisma of a goddamn rock star. What made it even better was that he didn't seem to know it. Papa Jim's mouth was practically watering. Ethan was the real deal, no question about it. Now he knew how Merlin must have felt the first time he laid eyes on the boy who would become King Arthur. "How are you feeling? Nervous?"

"A little. Mostly relieved."

"Relieved?"

"My whole life has been building toward this moment. I'm finally doing what I was born to do."

"Trust me, you're gonna kick ass."

"Papa Jim!" Kate protested. "You make it sound like a boxing match!"

"That's how the game is played, baby girl. Politics is a contact sport."

"But this isn't politics."

Papa Jim smiled at that. "Honey, everything is politics." He gave Ethan a wink. Then, pulling one of his trademark cigars from the inside pocket of his dark jacket, Papa Jim strode up to the back door of the funeral home, flung it boldly open, and stepped outside.

All eyes turned toward him, the low hum of voices crescendoing in a communal gasp. Then applause broke out as Papa Jim advanced to the podium, raising his hands for quiet.

"How's everybody doing?" Papa Jim asked, his voice booming out over the hush. "Sorry for the delay, but we're ready to get started now. In another minute, a young man is going to come out here and talk to you. I don't pretend to know what he's going to say. But I've had the privilege of meeting this young man, and so I know that whatever he says, it will be extraordinary. How do I know that? I know it because this young man is extraordinary."

As he spoke, Papa Jim was surveying the crowd, gauging the extent of their interest, their skepticism. Every eye was riveted on him. There was the sound of throats being cleared, but otherwise silence. "Now, I know a lot of you folks are from right here in this wonderful town of Olathe, Kansas. You know Ethan. You knew Lisa and Gordon Brown, his parents. They were your friends. Your neighbors. So maybe you think you don't need me to tell you about Ethan. And maybe you're right. But there's lots of folks watching and listening across this country and the world who don't know anything about him other than what they've seen and heard on TV, and a lot of that is just plain wrong. So I hope you'll indulge me for a minute while I tell you about the Ethan I've come to know. You might even be surprised."

Papa Jim let the anticipation build. "I'm not standing up here as the Secretary of Homeland Security," he said at last. "In fact, I've already tendered my resignation from that position."

This elicited more gasps, but Papa Jim spoke over them. "I'm not up here as the head of Oz Corporation, either. No, I'm up here as a man. A man who loves his country and loves God. A man who's had more than his share of blessings, and has suffered tragedy too. I've brought a child into this world, and buried that child. I've been a father and a grandfather. But what I can now reveal for the first time is that I'm also a great-grandfather.

"Almost twenty years ago, my granddaughter, Kate, had a child out of wedlock. She claimed that she was a virgin, that she'd never slept with a boy, but her mother and father didn't believe her. I didn't believe her either. When she had the child, we told her it had died. We took the baby and gave it to a childless couple to raise as their own. Kate never knew until just a few days ago that her child had survived. I'm sure you've all guessed by now that the people we gave the child to were Gordon and Lisa Brown.

Gordon died some years back, and we're here today to pay tribute to Lisa, who died to save the boy who had been entrusted to her so long ago. My great-grandson, Ethan Brown."

A buzz of conversation greeted these words. Papa Jim let the voices swell, a gleam in his eye. Then he raised his hands for quiet again. "So now you know the truth. Now you see what kind of man is up here before you today. A sinner. A man whose granddaughter came to him asking for trust and received instead lies. A man who gave his own flesh and blood into the keeping of strangers because he was worried about scandal. About his precious good name. And all the while was blind to the miracle that had taken place right before his eyes."

Papa Jim allowed a tremor to enter his voice. "Does a man like that deserve forgiveness? No, ladies and gentlemen, no, he does not. And yet, I received it! When I saw the news about what had happened at the hospital here, I recognized Ethan at once. I knew the time had come for me to atone for my sins. At the same time, Kate came to me, after years of estrangement in which we had barely spoken to each other and seen each other even less. She came because she, too, had seen the news, and she, too, recognized Ethan. How? The same way she had become pregnant with him in the first place: by the grace of God. And so we had a reunion of sorts the other day, just the three of us. I got down on my knees to them both and asked for their forgiveness. And I got it, too. That was the happiest day of my life, I don't mind telling you. For the first time in a long, long time, I was part of a family again. I only wish that my daughter and my son-in-law were alive to share my joy. And Lisa Brown too, of course.

"So, now you know the kind of person Ethan is. A forgiver. A healer. Is he more than that? Is he who he claims to be? That's a question everybody has to answer for themselves. But I've made up my mind. That's why I resigned from Homeland Security. A man can't serve two masters. When it comes to God or the government, I'll choose God every time. Or, in this case, His son.

"I won't take up any more of your patience, ladies and gentlemen. Thank you for listening. Now let me proudly present to you my great-grandson, Ethan Brown."

The applause was deafening.

✠   ✠   ✠

Inside the funeral home, Kate had listened to Papa Jim's speech in mounting disbelief. "What's he saying? Has he lost his mind? Did you know he was going to reveal all this?"

Beside her, Ethan shook his head. "I guess I should have asked to read his speech when he gave me mine."

"Didn't I tell you not to trust him?"

"I don't trust him," Ethan said. "But I need him."

"I can't believe he's serious about resigning! Why would he give up that kind of power?"

"In pursuit of greater power."

"He's an evil man," Kate said. "He'll betray you."

"Maybe," said Ethan. "But there's still good in him, despite everything. I can see it in his soul. Shimmers of light amid the darkness. He's not beyond redemption yet."

"It turns my stomach just to be in the same room with him. I don't understand why you asked me to be nice to him after all the harm he's done to us. And the worst of it is, he's so egotistical that he actually believes I *have* forgiven him!"

"One day, you *will* forgive him, Kate."

The sound of applause swelled up from outside.

"That's my cue," said Ethan. He held out his hand to her. "Shall we go and give him a surprise of our own?"

Kate took his hand. "What are you going to tell them?"

"The truth," Ethan said.

✠   ✠   ✠

Papa Jim was standing beside the podium, grinning like the cat that swallowed the canary as Ethan and Kate emerged from the funeral home. A roar went up from the audience that seemed far in excess of what fifty throats could produce. Ethan smiled and waved his free hand. Beside him, Kate did likewise.

At the podium, Papa Jim shook Ethan's hand, then threw one arm around Ethan's shoulders and the other around Kate's. For an instant, Kate thought she was going to be ill, not just from the touch of him but the smell of his cigar. Even unlit, the tobacco was strong and vile. To think she had once taken comfort in it.

Ethan stepped up to the podium, and Papa Jim withdrew his arms, advancing to stand just behind his right shoulder. Kate, feeling self-conscious and shy, especially with all that Papa Jim had revealed about her past, stood stiff as a board, frozen like a deer in headlights. An expectant silence fell over the crowd. Then Ethan began to speak, and Kate felt all her nervousness drain away at the sound of his voice.

"Hi, everybody," Ethan said. "Thanks for coming. Thanks especially to my friends and neighbors. It does my heart good to see so many familiar faces out there. I only wish that we were gathered in happier circumstances."

"We're sorry for your loss, Ethan," shouted someone.

"Thanks," Ethan said. "I know it. But I'm going to ask something of you that I know won't be easy. I hope you'll give it a try anyway."

"Go on, ask!" came another voice, to general laughter.

"All right, Pete, I will. I was kind of hoping we could start off with a moment of silence for my mom, and also for the man who killed her, and the other man who died in the attack."

The silence that followed seemed less an offering of respect to the dead than a sign of stunned incredulity. Kate felt shocked herself. Not just by Ethan's request, which seemed to place all the dead on the same level, erasing any moral distinction between killer and victim, but because he was ignoring the words of his prepared speech, which hung trembling in the air like a ghostly alphabet, a tracery of letters thin as spider's silk, visible only from this side of the podium. She glanced to her right and saw that Papa Jim was livid. But there was nothing he could do now.

Meanwhile, as if sensing the general disquiet, Ethan went on, "You probably think I'm crazy to ask that. Maybe I am. But God didn't just put me here for the saints. I'm here for the sinners too. For them most of all. That's why I'm asking for this moment of silence. God rejoices when a human soul finds its way back to Him in death. But He mourns those deaths that send human souls beyond His sight forever. While we live, the path back to God is always open, no matter how far we stray. But the dead can't walk that path, not even an inch. So what I'm asking in this moment of silence is that you rejoice with God for my mother and mourn with Him for the others, whose souls are beyond salvation, beyond everything but our pity."

Kate marveled at these words, and what seemed most marvelous about them to her was how simple the concept was, and how obvious, now that she thought about it—yet for some unfathomable reason, she never had thought about it until now. It made her feel ashamed of how she'd always taken it for granted that she, a human being, had the right to make distinctions between her fellow human beings. To judge them. But surely that was up to God. She bowed her head, thinking of her father and mother and how she had judged them, blamed them, hated them. Oh, so unjustly! Had God rejoiced at their deaths or mourned them? How could she ever know this side of death? All she could have done, while they were alive, was help them as best she could to walk toward God. But she hadn't, had she? She hadn't even been able to keep on that path herself.

Kate couldn't tell what the rest of the audience was doing, but there was no sound from them, not even a cough or the timid clearing of a throat.

After a moment, Ethan spoke again. "Thanks for that," he said softly.

When Kate looked up, she was surprised to see that many faces in the audience were streaked with tears. And only then felt the tears on her own cheeks.

"That's the hardest thing I'm going to ask of you today," Ethan said. "So you can relax now."

Nervous laughter, like the chirping of birds settling down for the evening, rose in response.

"I want to thank Secretary Osbourne—or I guess I should say *ex*-Secretary Osbourne—for that . . . unexpected introduction. Now I finally understand the meaning of the phrase 'a tough act to follow.'"

More laughter, easier now, relaxed, the kind of laughter reserved for hanging out with friends.

"I hadn't really intended to talk about any of this here. Not today. I wanted to talk about my mom, Lisa. And I'm still going to do that. But suddenly there's all this other stuff in the way, surprising and slightly scandalous stuff. Well, okay. It's out there now. I'm not ashamed of it. I'm proud to be Mr. Osbourne's great-grandson, and I'm proud to be the son of his granddaughter, Kate Skylar, an incredible woman I just met for the first—no, the *second*—time a couple of days ago. That's her behind me. Say hi to everybody, Kate."

Kate waved her hand somewhat sheepishly.

"Hi, Kate!" came another voice from the audience.

"I'm going to tell you what it was like for Kate all those years ago. I'm going to tell you the story just as she told it to me. She was seventeen years old, the only child of a wealthy and prestigious family of staunch Catholics from South Carolina. A lot of expectations were riding on her let me tell you. Not just the expectations of her parents, but the expectations of her grandfather, Mr. Osbourne, a man of some ambition, who goes by 'Papa Jim' at home. Now, Papa Jim was already a rich and powerful man, but the one thing he'd never been able to acquire was the one thing he wanted most: a son. A male heir to carry on the family name and business. So first and foremost, Kate was expected to give Papa Jim what he wanted. Not a son, not a grandson, but a great-grandson. A male heir. All this was pretty much taken for granted the way such things are, rarely if ever talked about but understood by everybody concerned. Papa Jim held the purse strings down there, and the loosening and tightening of those strings was a language unto itself.

"Then one day, out of the blue, Kate discovered she was pregnant. And she knew she hadn't slept with anybody. Ever. Well, you can imagine how that went over! To say that her story was greeted with skepticism would be putting it mildly. Her folks begged her to tell them the name of the father. When that didn't work, they threatened her. But through it all, Kate stuck with her story. She knew the truth . . . but she also had to wonder if she was going crazy. Because girls just did not get pregnant without certain events taking place, and none of those events, or any events remotely similar to them, had taken place or come close to taking place.

"Well, one girl did. Once, a long time ago. A girl by the name of Mary, no older than Kate herself. When Kate thought of that, she wondered if maybe she too had been chosen by God to bear Him a child. She didn't understand how that could be, because Mary, after all, was born without sin, the Immaculate Conception, and Kate had plenty of sins on her conscience. But this time around, God wasn't looking for another Mary. He wanted a regular girl, a girl who sometimes had bad thoughts and did bad things. A girl who wasn't born a saint but, like every human being, had the potential to become one. A girl who would not give birth to the Son of God, but to the Son of man.

"After a lot of trials and tribulations I won't get into now, Kate gave birth to her child, in a remote Italian nunnery where she'd been sent by Papa Jim. That child was me. She held me in her arms and named me Ethan. And then, just like Papa Jim told you, I was whisked away from that place and given into the safekeeping of Lisa and Gordon Brown, here in Olathe. I never saw my birth mother again until two days ago, which was also when I met Papa Jim for the first time and learned about our relationship and his role in my life. Of course I forgave him. If he separated Kate and me, he also reunited us. And besides, if not for him, I never would have known Gordon and Lisa, the people I'll always think of as my earthly parents."

Ethan paused to take a sip of water from a glass on the podium. The audience was rapt, almost entranced, hanging on his words. Kate felt incredibly exposed, as if she were standing naked in front of all these people, and yet she didn't feel at all embarrassed. She wasn't sure what she felt, what name to put to it.

"What happened to Kate was terrible," Ethan continued. "Believing I was dead, she never tried to find me. She missed out on almost twenty years of motherhood. And I missed knowing the stubborn and courageous woman who brought me into the world, who protected me even before I was born, when her own parents pressured her to have an abortion. God knew how fiercely she would fight for me, despite her doubts and fears.

That's why He chose her above all other women. He had faith in her, even when she lost faith in Him and in herself.

"Anybody who's ever glanced through the Bible knows that it can seem as much a curse as a blessing to be chosen by God to do something. Some of the greatest prophets spent a lot of time and energy trying to get out from under the obligations that God had laid on their shoulders, responsibilities they hadn't asked for and didn't want. Even Jesus prayed for the cup and its bitter contents to be taken away. But while God may set events in motion, He doesn't stack the deck. We always have the freedom to deny Him, to reject what He asks of us. After life itself, it's His greatest gift to us, this freedom to choose for ourselves whether to embrace God or spurn Him.

"All of us are here on this earth for such a short time! During that time, we make hundreds of thousands of critical decisions. Millions of temptations assail us. Crime, corruption, greed, power, lust. How do we choose correctly? Where should we look for answers, for guidance? The Bible? The Koran? The priests, the preachers, the imams? Do they have the answers we seek? No. By all means, read the Bible. Read the Koran. Listen to the priests and the imams. But in the end, follow your heart. Do what you know is right, not what is easy. Question the forbidden *and* the permitted. Embrace and practice your beliefs. Put them to the test. Don't let others discourage you. Be your own moral compass. Don't be afraid, the needle will always point to God. It was built that way."

At this, Ethan smiled suddenly, as if he'd just caught a glimpse of his reflection from an unexpected angle and saw something amusing or absurd in the view. "All that goes for me, too," he said. "Don't take what I'm saying as some kind of absolute truth. I'm not here to lay down the law. I'm one of you. That's what it means to be the Son of man. I don't get a pass on these lessons just because my dad's the principal of the school! I have to learn them the same as everybody else, learn them bit by bit through hard experience, making mistakes as I go, because that's the only way to learn. I mean *really* learn. God doesn't want us to memorize rules and regulations and repeat them back like robots. We're more than that. He wants us to find our way to Him genuinely, to cut our own trail through the wilderness, not follow a path worn smooth by countless other feet. He wants us to bow our heads to him not as slaves but as free people, who freely acknowledge a higher power than themselves, who are humble in the face of all we do not and cannot know, and who have faith in God's abiding love for us. In embracing God, we embrace our own best and truest selves. And in embracing our best and truest selves, we embrace God. You don't need to be a Catholic or a Christian for that. You could be a Muslim or a Mormon, a Buddhist or a Jew. Or an agnostic. Or even an atheist. That doesn't matter to God. Those are just labels we put on ourselves. God sees under the labels. He sees us as we really are. And you know what? He loves us anyway.

"Love is an amazing thing. It's the greatest miracle of all. Without love, there wouldn't be any miracles. It's the stuff that miracles are made of. Even the ordinary kind of miracles, the ones that we're so used to seeing that we forget how miraculous they really are. If you think about it, those kinds of miracles are just as wondrous as raising someone from the dead. Actually, they're even more wondrous, because they don't just happen once. They happen all the time. We think that because they do happen all the time, there's nothing miraculous about them. But we couldn't be more wrong. I'm talking about miracles like sunrise. Like snowfall. A child's laughter. Or a mother's smile.

"Behind me, in this funeral home, lies the body of my mother, Lisa Brown. Maybe Lisa didn't give birth to me like Kate did, but she was chosen by God just the same, chosen by Him to teach me about the self-lessness of love, the joy and satisfaction of sacrifice, the happiness and fulfillment that can be found in even the smallest tasks and diversions of everyday life. She taught me about faith and forgiveness. About duty and responsibility. About bravery. She gave her life to protect me, gave it up without hesitation even though it had just been restored to her, and was for that reason more precious than ever. She gave it up knowing that there would be no coming back this time. Why did she throw herself in front of me, shielding my body with her own and taking the bullets intended for me? Did she think, 'I've got to save the Son of man!' No. It was *her* son that she saved, not the Son of man. Maybe you think that any mother would have done as much, and as selflessly. Maybe so. But she wasn't my mother, was she? My mother is right here on stage."

Again, Kate felt that sense of exposure. But again, she didn't feel embarrassed. Nor did she feel jealous or envious of Lisa. No, she felt something quite different. And this time, at last, she did have a name for it.

She felt *loved*.

"Do you see what a miracle love really is?" Ethan asked as if reading her mind, addressing her specifically out of all the crowd . . . though she realized a second later that it must be the same for everyone listening, not just here but those watching on TV or on the Internet. Ethan was speaking to each one of them directly.

"When the gunman pointed his weapon and fired," he said, "it didn't matter to Lisa that I wasn't her flesh and blood. It didn't matter to her that I was the Son of man. She didn't even think about those things. She acted. She acted out of love. That's what a miracle is. Love in action." Ethan spread his arms out wide to either side. "That's what all this is. God's love in action. And we're part of it, all of us. How cool is that?"

✠　　　✠　　　✠

Father O'Malley stared at the wall-screen TV in Cardinal Ehrlich's office as though spellbound. At first, as Ethan spoke, the cardinal had interrupted with sarcastic asides, but soon he'd fallen silent, and the two men had watched wordlessly. For his part, O'Malley had been a bundle of nerves, knowing that the Congregation was going to strike but not knowing when or how it would happen . . . and knowing, moreover, that his life depended upon whatever was about to take place, or rather on how well Osbourne had prepared for it. Somehow, in the arrangement of the munchies and plainclothes security personnel scattered through and around the audience, there was a pattern that Grand Inquisitor would interpret as proof of O'Malley's guilt or innocence. But if there was any such pattern, O'Malley couldn't see it. Perhaps it was a bluff, and the pattern Grand Inquisitor was looking for was not there in the pavilion behind the Olathe Funeral Home but here in Cardinal Ehrlich's office, in

O'Malley's body language. Was he betraying himself with every blink of his eyes? He didn't know. Couldn't know. There was nothing he could do but watch and wait.

And pray.

But then a strange thing happened. In the midst of his anxiety, he began to pay attention to Ethan's words, and those words, as well as the voice that delivered them, slipped into his ears and over his worried brain like a soothing balm. They were like a new kind of food, a nourishment he'd been starving for his entire life without knowing it, and something in him responded, answering like a bell answers the hammer that strikes it. *Oh my God,* he thought. He could feel something vibrating inside him. He wanted to fall to his knees, but he was afraid that his body would shatter like a wine glass.

"Are you all right, Father O'Malley?"

It took him a moment to realize that Cardinal Ehrlich was addressing him. O'Malley blinked and saw that Ethan had finished speaking. On one side of him stood his mother, a rapturous smile on her face. His great-grandfather stood on the other side, furiously chomping at an unlit cigar. The audience was on its feet, applauding and cheering.

"Father?"

With an effort, O'Malley tore his eyes from the screen. He cleared his throat, but even so, his voice was shaky. "That . . . that was quite a speech, Your Eminence."

"Speech? It was a damn sermon." Ehrlich gave a sour frown. "The boy is undoubtedly gifted. But what is the source of his gifts, eh?"

O'Malley had no answer. He turned back to the screen and gave a small groan. The knowledge of what was impending had returned to strike him like a physical blow. How had he forgotten?

"Can I get you some water, Father?"

O'Malley shook his head. Damn Ehrlich and his punctilious cruelties. No matter what Grand Inquisitor determined, O'Malley's conscience was clear. He wasn't guilty of anything.

Something was happening at the pavilion. As Ethan turned to go back into the funeral home, a member of the audience shouted his name in a strident and peremptory tone that caught his attention and compelled his response. The cameras zoomed in as though scenting blood.

It was a girl. Or rather, a young woman. About Ethan's age. Pretty, but her features were twisted with some kind of emotional agony that made O'Malley wince with pity.

"Oh my, what have we here?" purred Ehrlich.

And O'Malley knew that the trap had been sprung. Not a bomb after all. But what?

✠ ✠ ✠

Papa Jim was fuming. He'd been sandbagged. Ethan had ignored the speech that he'd agreed to read, instead launching into a rambling but powerful sermon that had swayed Papa Jim's heart but not his head. Even as he'd listened, moved by emotions that hadn't stirred within his breast in years, Papa Jim realized with crystalline clarity that his great-grandson was going to prove a lot more difficult to control than he'd imagined. The effort of standing there on stage beside him as the words of the speech glimmered unread on the teleprompter and very different words, dangerous words, came dancing out of Ethan's mouth to transfix the audience, had been almost more than he could bear. He'd wanted to go storming off, not just because he was angry but because he had been touched so unexpectedly. He was in pain and wanted to get away from the source of that pain. But he forced himself to remain, grinning—or was it grimacing—around his cigar, the end of which he'd ground to bits of leaf between his teeth by the time Ethan was finished and the audience was applauding enthusiastically.

Papa Jim joined right in, chomping on what was left of the cigar, glad that his torment had nearly reached its end. As soon as they were away from prying eyes and cameras, he would set Ethan straight about the nature of their partnership and the role Ethan was expected to play within it. Hopefully no permanent damage had been done with this extemporaneous sermon. He didn't think so, but he wanted to check the initial polling results to make sure. At least Denny had done his job and kept the Congregation assassins at bay.

Finally, with a last wave, Ethan turned and began to make his way back into the funeral home, flanked by Papa Jim and Kate.

"I'm so proud of you, Ethan," Kate said. "I know Lisa would—"

She was interrupted by a voice from behind them. "Ethan! Ethan, I have to talk to you!"

Even before he saw who was shouting, Papa Jim knew that it spelled trouble. He recognized the voice as a woman's, and in his experience, women did not use that tone of voice in public unless they either meant to cause trouble, which was bad enough, or were too far gone to know or care what they were causing, which was worse.

Beside him, Ethan stiffened, and a look of pain came to his face. But it was gone almost immediately. He turned.

"Hello, Mags," he said.

Papa Jim looked on, aghast. It was the girl, Maggie Richardson. Maggie was a central figure in the files Papa Jim had hurriedly compiled on Ethan. She was one of his two oldest friends, the other being the boy, Peter, who was now attempting to make his way toward Maggie from the other side of the pavilion, where exiting audience members had stopped to watch the fun. Papa Jim knew from the files that Ethan and Maggie had been boyfriend and girlfriend for years, but only now did it occur to him that she hadn't been present at the press conference, nor had Ethan mentioned her in the days since.

They must have had a fight, he realized. *A falling out. And now it's going to all come crashing out in the open, all the ugliness of young love gone bad. That'll topple him from his pedestal! Damn, I should have seen it coming. I should have told Denny to watch out for her. But I was so focused on the Congregation, I didn't think about anything so. . . mundane.*

He looked on helplessly. There was nothing to be done. Across the room, Denny caught his eye and raised a questioning eyebrow. Papa Jim hesitated. This was going to look bad enough already. He didn't want to make things worse.

"That was a lovely speech," Maggie said meanwhile. "All those beautiful, noble words about love in action. But where were they two days ago when you broke my heart? Why don't you tell all these people how you used me, then cast me aside? Is it because you're going to do the same to them? You're a phony, Ethan. A fake!"

"Mags, no!" cried Peter, still struggling through the audience.

"Don't believe him!" Maggie screeched, pointing at Ethan as people drew back from her, startled, as if from a crazed street person. "Don't trust him!"

Papa Jim had heard enough. He nodded to Denny, and in seconds, like a well-oiled machine, the security detail swung into action. Before any more damage could be done, Maggie was being hustled out of the pavilion between two munchies, struggling and screaming for help. Peter was right behind her.

Ethan looked stricken.

"It's best this way," said Papa Jim, leaning close, a hand on his arm.

"I need to talk to her," he said.

"Of course," said Papa Jim. "But not here, like this. When she's calmed down, you can talk to her privately." He tugged at Ethan's arm. "Come on, before something else goes wrong."

Ethan seemed as if he would resist, but then allowed himself to be led into the funeral home, out of sight of the cameras.

✠   ✠   ✠

"The poor girl!" Father O'Malley wrung his hands together in helpless sympathy. "The poor, poor girl!"

"Look what he drove her to, the brute," said Cardinal Ehrlich, not even attempting to keep the satisfaction from his voice. "The course of young love has never run smooth, eh, O'Malley?"

O'Malley turned to face the cardinal. "We arranged this? Struck at him through an innocent?"

"Spare me the sanctimonious objections," the cardinal said dryly. "As you know very well, sometimes an innocent must be sacrificed for the greater good. It's what we do. A few choice words in the ears of a grieving girl from a trusted priest, and violá. But this is only the first step. By the time we're through, no one will follow him. He'll be finished. Ruined."

"I don't want any part of this," O'Malley said. He felt sickened to his soul.

"But you're already part of it, Father," exclaimed the cardinal. "You're a member of the Congregation. You know very well the effect of your labors. All those pristine numbers and equations of yours, where else did you think they ended? Did you think they had no impact on the real world? Why so squeamish now?"

Father O'Malley sank back into his chair with a groan and covered his face with his pudgy, beringed hands. "And we call ourselves men of God!"

"Certainly," said the cardinal. "The Holy Father himself has tasked us with this. We must not shirk from our duty, Father. The Church depends on us for its defense."

"Against whom, Your Eminence?"

"Why, all who would oppose her."

O'Malley looked up. He had never thought of himself as a particularly brave man. He still didn't. But he had his limits. "No, I won't go any further. It's wrong, Your Eminence. Nothing can justify it. If I wasn't a traitor before, then I am one now. You might as well go ahead and kill me."

Cardinal Ehrlich shook his head. "I think not, Father. You see, as we sat here discussing theology, Grand Inquisitor has made its judgment. You are vindicated, it seems."

"Vindicated?"

"Not only that," said the cardinal after a moment, wearing the far-away expression of man attending to a cochlear implant, "but you are summoned into the presence."

O'Malley blinked in surprise. "The Holy Father wishes to see me?"

Ehrlich laughed. "Not the Holy Father. Grand Inquisitor. GI wants to speak to you personally, O'Malley."

CHAPTER 19

Once inside the funeral home, Ethan asked Papa Jim to have the munchies who'd hustled Maggie out of the pavilion bring her inside so that the two of them could talk. But after Papa Jim conferred with Denny, he reported back that Maggie didn't want to talk to him, didn't want to see him at all. She had expressed the desire to go home, and Peter had volunteered to drive her there.

The next day, after Lisa's burial, a private affair attended only by Ethan, Kate, Papa Jim, a Conversatio priest, and Peter (though Maggie had been invited, she hadn't come), Ethan drew his old friend aside and walked with him among the gravestones of the cemetery. It was a cloudless day, the sky as blue as a sapphire, and Ethan and Peter had removed their jackets under the unseasonably hot sun, carrying them flung over their shoulders as they walked.

"Thanks for looking after Mags, Pete."

"That's okay. She's pretty broken up about everything. I'm kind of worried. I've never seen her like this."

"I wish she would have come today. Or if she'd just talk to me . . . "

"Forget it, dude. Maybe later, but right now talking to you is about the last thing she wants. She's angry, and she's hurt. She feels betrayed, rejected. She's not seeing things too clearly."

Ethan sighed. "I feel awful about this. I know it sucks. It's not fair. And part of me wants to just, you know, make her feel better. Take the hurt away. But I can't."

"Not even this once?" asked Peter.

"I can't," Ethan repeated.

Peter didn't press the point. "She's been talking to a priest at Christ the Redeemer. You know, getting some counseling. I think that's helping a little. She'll come around in time."

Ethan nodded.

They walked on in silence for a while. Then Ethan said, "I can't stay here, Pete. In Olathe, I mean. I've got to go out into the world. Talk to people and listen to them. I can't do that from here."

"I figured," said Peter.

"I wanted you to come with me," Ethan said.

"Dude . . ."

"I'm just getting to know my birth mom. She's still pretty much a stranger. And Papa Jim, well, he's in this for himself, so I can't really trust him, even though I think I can use him, at least for a while. But I need someone I can rely on. Someone who knows me, who knew me before all the craziness. Someone to keep me grounded and focused on what matters. I need you, Pete."

"Ethan . . ."

Ethan stopped walking and turned to face his friend. He laid a hand on his shoulder. "But I can't ask you to come along. Not now. Maggie needs you more than I do. I'm sorry, Pete."

But Peter was smiling. "Dude, I was gonna tell you the same thing. I have to stay here, at least for a while. I—"he blushed, hesitating, then rushed on, "I know how you and Maggie felt . . . feel . . . about each other. I know that if it weren't for all this other stuff, you two would still be together. But things are different now. I . . . I love her, man. I always have. I don't know if she can ever love me back, and I'm gonna be there for her no matter what, but I wanted you to know how I feel about her."

Ethan smiled back. "I've known that for years, Pete. Who did you think you were fooling? I still love her, but what I'm here to do is more important than the feelings of two people. I wish it could be different, I really do. But it can't. I've made my choice."

Peter nodded. "I guess this is good-bye, then. For a while."

"For a while," Ethan agreed. "But it's not like I'm dropping off the face of the earth. You've got my number. I want you to use it."

"Deal," said Peter. He held out his hand.

"A handshake's not going to do it, Pete." Ethan pulled him into a bear hug.

"Shit, you're gonna make me cry," said Peter.

"Sorry, man."

They stood looking at each other. Wanting to hold on to the moment just a little longer.

"Can you tell me one thing?" asked Peter.

"If I can."

"What *are* you here to do?"

"Are you sure you want to know, Pete?"

"Well, yeah. I mean, how bad can it be? You're not here to destroy the world or anything, right?" He laughed.

"No," said Ethan. "I'm here to save it. If I can."

Peter wasn't laughing now. "What do you mean, 'if I can'? Like, who could stop you?"

"You could," Ethan said.

"Why the hell would I do that?"

"No, I mean all of you. Humanity could stop me."

"You mean by killing you, like with Jesus?"

"Jesus *saved* the world by dying, Pete. Nobody stopped him. But I'm not Jesus. The Son of man has a different cross to bear."

"You're kind of creeping me out here, Ethan. Can't you just tell me straight up what's going to happen?"

"Sorry, Pete." Ethan offered up a wan smile. "A lot of this is as much a mystery to me as it is to you. Sometimes I can see glimpses of the future, of how things might turn out, but they're just that, glimpses of what *might* be. Nothing is fixed, because we all have free will."

"Okay, but even if you don't know how things are going to turn out, you've at least got to have some idea of why you're here. That's all I'm asking. If you don't want to tell me, fine. But I think I've got a right to know."

Ethan considered for a moment. Then he said, "I'm here to be God's eyes and ears on Earth. I'm here to witness. That means observing, but it also means speaking out. You know, testifying."

"About what?"

"About God's love."

"But why? I mean, why now?"

"Because God isn't happy."

"He's pissed at us?"

"He's more sad than angry."

"What, He told you this? In person?"

"It doesn't work that way. He doesn't have to tell me anything. I just know. I know because He wants me to know. It's the reason He sent me. To help people find the way back to Him. But I can't force people to change. I can only point the way. After that, it's up to you, all of you."

"Okay, but what happens if people reject your message?"

"Then God's going to pull the plug, Pete."

Peter's eyes grew wide. "Pull the plug? What the hell does that mean? Pull the plug on what?"

"On everything," Ethan said.

✠   ✠   ✠

After Lisa's burial, Papa Jim didn't waste any time. Even though he had resigned his leadership position at Homeland Security, his power and influence within the government were practically undiminished, as Oz Corp was still under contract to supply security personnel and to manage the nationwide network of detention facilities in which illegal aliens and those suspected of terrorist sympathies or connections were held in custody while awaiting repatriation or trial. So what would undoubtedly have taken any other private citizen weeks if not months to organize, Papa Jim was able to do in a matter of hours. Stadiums were booked in major cities across the United States with security guaranteed by the presence of fully equipped munchies "borrowed" from Homeland Security. When asked by reporters about the propriety of using personnel contracted to the federal government for what seemed like a private endeavor, Papa Jim, cigar in hand, responded, "If the Second Coming isn't a matter of national security, what is?"

No one had a good answer to that. And so Ethan began a whirlwind tour of the United States that would have done a rock star proud. Stadiums were filled to capacity, and Ethan's sermons were simulcast on cable and on The2ndSon.com; there were even podcasts—called "godcasts"—for downloading.

With the riots and demonstrations that had sprung up in the aftermath of Ethan's press conference, quelled by the heavy presence of armed munchies, Papa Jim focused on forestalling another assassination attempt by the Congregation. He assigned two of his best bodyguards, ex-Navy SEALs who also had experience as Conversatio field agents, to watch Ethan around the clock, never letting him out of their sights. But Ethan refused the protection, not wanting to put up any more barriers between himself and people than were there already. Papa Jim argued, but in the end he had no choice but to back down in the face of Ethan's determination. The bodyguards, named Wilson and Trey, were reassigned to Kate, who was part of the entourage traveling with Ethan from city to city.

There was a public face to these visits, and a private one. The public face was as efficiently streamlined and media savvy as a top-flight political campaign—which in fact it was, although Papa Jim hadn't discussed that part of his plans with Ethan yet. Still, it didn't escape the notice of the press that the cities in which Ethan was scheduled to appear were in states with a sufficient number of electoral votes at stake to swing the election. Some reporters seemed convinced this was more than mere coincidence, even though Ethan disavowed any intention to run for anything, and Papa Jim pointed out that with the primaries finished and the nominees lacking only the official certification of the party conventions, just over a month away, it would be too late for anything but a third-party run . . . and no third-party candidate had ever won a presidential election, or even come close. Besides, the Constitution prevented anyone of Ethan's age from serving as president. However, it was noted that this wasn't an outright denial from a man whose reputation as a political kingmaker was legendary. Laws, after all, could always be changed.

Behind the scenes, things didn't go quite as smoothly. There was continuing tension between Papa Jim and Ethan over Ethan's refusal to follow the scripts supplied by the PR people at Oz Corp. Ethan had even objected to the name that PR had come up with for the tour: Godsent—although that was one battle he lost, as Godsent T-shirts, baseball caps, stickers, and other memorabilia were soon for sale at each venue and on The2ndSon. com, the profits all going to a charity Ethan had insisted that Papa Jim establish, also called Godsent.

Ethan rarely consented to interviews with local media, which Papa Jim considered essential "to get out the good word." Nor would Ethan go on the attack against those who were attacking and criticizing him on a daily basis; this, objected Papa Jim, was "carrying the whole turning-the-other-cheek business too far." Chief among Ethan's critics was Maggie, who, from Olathe, had launched a web site of her own—Fraudsent. com—where she posted videos of herself and others responding to each of Ethan's sermons. These angry rants garnered a lot of attention and sympathy. But Ethan still wouldn't say a word against her in public or in private, and he invariably came to her defense if anyone else disparaged her motives or character, even after Papa Jim showed him proof that the priest at Christ the Redeemer, who seemed glued to her side, was a Congregation agent, and that the Congregation was financing her web site. He was in frequent touch with Peter by cell phone and email, but although his friend had tried to dissuade Maggie from taking such a public stand against him, she had refused, just as she refused all of Ethan's attempts to reach out to her.

Kate, too, was a source of friction. She hadn't forgiven her grandfather for all he'd done to her and Ethan, and as the Godsent tour stretched on,

Kate found it increasingly difficult to be around him. More than once, despite promising Ethan that she would try to get along with him, she lost control and lashed out angrily at something he'd done or said. It was only thanks to Ethan's presence that there was some modicum of peace maintained between them.

Nor was there always peace between Kate and Ethan, though for the most part their time together was a blessing for them both, giving them the chance to get to know each other as people and to become friends. Yet Kate wanted more. She wanted something of the relationship that Papa Jim had stolen from her. Careful as she was not to trespass into realms of motherhood that still belonged to Lisa, and always would, she sometimes overstepped her bounds, and Ethan had to gently remind her that he was an adult now, fully capable of making his own decisions. Kate had remonstrated with him to accept the services of Wilson and Trey—it was one of the few times she found herself agreeing with Papa Jim about anything—but Ethan was no more swayed by her arguments than he'd been by Papa Jim's. "God is the only bodyguard I need," he told her.

What she didn't know, any more than Papa Jim did, and which would have united the two of them in disbelief and horror, was that each night, after his sermons, when they had all returned to the safety of whatever hotel Papa Jim had commandeered for the duration of their stay in that particular city, and when, as had become his custom, Ethan retired to his room to meditate and pray in solitude, with guards stationed outside his door to ensure that solitude was undisturbed, then Ethan, who had not performed so much as a single public demonstration of his powers since the Miracle at Olathe Medical, would exercise them in private. He would use them to take himself unobserved from the hotel to areas of the city that he felt drawn to by some instinct he did not trouble to question. He knew it was God's will in action, leading him to places he needed to be, to things he needed to witness and people he needed to meet. Sometimes in those places he was seen and spoken to, though afterward any reports of his presence had the unverifiable aura of urban legend, while other times he was invisible to the people among whom he walked.

One evening, Ethan went to a Los Angeles neighborhood whose noisy streets seemed to be under the control of occupying armies of African American, Latino, and Asian teenagers. Young men in clashing gang colors brandished guns and other, more primitive weapons openly and without fear. It was a neighborhood where the local police and even the munchies hesitated to go after dark, and what little order there was existed simply so that the gangs that fought a ceaseless battle for control of each street and block could, amid the mayhem, profitably engage in their various business enterprises, which pretty much boiled down to drugs, prostitution, and the sale of stolen merchandise. Ethan watched unseen as a thin black girl, who was barely fourteen but already looked more than twice that, stepped into a well-maintained car driven by a better-maintained white man from a very different neighborhood, and performed with a kind of listless expertise acts that resulted in an exchange of dollars and bodily fluids. He saw the strands of casual connection and consequence that linked the man and the girl into a wider web of lies, hopelessness, and disease: the infection the man would carry back to his wife, which would in turn pass to their as-yet-unborn child; the drugs the girl would buy with what was left of the money she had earned after giving her pimp his cut, and which, injected, would leave her staring glassy-eyed up at a water-stained ceiling in a room where she would not be found for days, and then only by another such as herself, come in quest of the same oblivion.

Walking on, he saw storefront churches filled with those too old in spirit or body to actively resist or participate in the viciousness of the life outside their fragile sanctuaries, but who nevertheless bore the scars of it in their hollow-eyed, deeply lined faces, in which the deaths of friends and family were as visible to Ethan as if they had been inscribed there. He heard their prayers, recognized in their voices not faith but a kind of desperation that looked to Heaven only because no hope remained on Earth.

He walked on, and though he remained hidden, there was nothing hidden from him. He saw husbands beating their wives, wives beating their husbands, parents beating their children, and children left to fend for themselves in front of television sets by men and women who were scarcely more than children themselves and had better places to be at night than at home looking after the little burdens they had created. He saw the hungry, the weak, the frightened. He saw brutal men who were no more than boys inside, and girls who had learned to equate giving their bodies with love, and giving birth with status. He saw people who had tried to kill every trace of their own humanity and failed, leaving behind wounded husks that would walk through the rest of their lives, wondering where things had gone wrong. And he saw those who had succeeded and were no longer human beings but had become containers for demons that were as attracted to corrupted souls as flies are to excrement.

All was not bleak and loveless. Amid the suffering, the pain, and the fear, the squalor and the violence, he saw people who somehow maintained their hope and faith in the face of institutionalized racism and the self-destructive culture it had given rise to like some distorted mirror image. People who loved unselfishly and were not afraid of making personal sacrifices and hard choices to earn a better life for themselves and their families; people who still believed in God with all their hearts and minds and souls. Yet when Ethan returned to his hotel room later that night, it was not the memory of these people that kept him awake and filled his heart with anguish.

✠   ✠   ✠

Godcast #5, from The2ndSon.com.

Hi, everybody. Thanks for listening. I'm coming to you today from Los Angeles. We've been here a week, and the response has been amazing. It's an inspiring place, Los Angeles. A little overwhelming. All the energy, the sophistication, the creativity. You can feel it in the air like electricity. To a guy from Olathe, Kansas, like me, LA almost seems like another world. The city of angels. A bit of Heaven fallen to Earth.

But of course it isn't. Underneath the glitter and the illusion, it's the same world you and I live in every day. No different. I've walked down these famous streets, with their famous stores, and I have to admit I've seen some beautiful people. I've met movie stars, models, musicians. People look like a different species out here. More evolved somehow. They wear the latest designer clothes. Take the latest designer drugs. And they've sculpted and modeled their DNA with the latest designer genes. Maybe you think I'm going to condemn all that. Come down on these people for trying to make themselves into something other than what God made them. But if you think that, you're wrong. God made us, but He also gave us the ability to upgrade ourselves. If He hadn't, we wouldn't be here. We wouldn't have been able to survive. Or if we had survived, we'd be no different than animals, who exist just as God made them but lack the gifts my father gave us of self-awareness and intelligence, along with the drive to better ourselves. In bettering ourselves, we come closer to God. How can that be a bad thing? The only time it's bad is when that drive gets twisted and corrupted, like with drugs. Not all drugs are bad. But drug abuse is always bad. Abusing drugs never brought anybody closer to God. In fact, it takes you in the opposite direction.

When you're here in LA, it's impossible not to be dazzled. Back in Olathe, I used to read about this place. There were magazines devoted to it. TV shows. The men and women we watched and read about were like Greek gods to us. Or angels . . . some of them the fallen kind, I admit. But they were richer, more beautiful, more everything. We envied them, even when we laughed at their excesses or were horrified by their tragedies. They took us out of ourselves. Entertained us. We wanted to *be* them, if only for a day, an hour.

But if we *could* be them, what would we find? We'd discover how much like them we already are. All the plastic surgery, personal training, and gene mods in the world can't, of themselves, change a person's soul. They can't make it shine any brighter, unless those physical enhancements are accompanied by spiritual growth. Which they often are, but not always. Not necessarily. And of course spiritual growth doesn't depend on any kind of physical enhancements at all. It doesn't depend on wealth or status or anything like that. That's the beauty of it. There are many paths to God, an infinite number. My father didn't make it hard to find Him. He made it easy. God is all around us. He's everywhere, in everything. He's in us, whether we know it or not. It's just a matter of opening our eyes. Opening our hearts. It's that simple.

We're all beautiful beings. Each one of you was designed in my father's image. Each one of you has greatness within yourself. Don't look to Los Angeles for that greatness. Don't look to movie stars. Look in the mirror.

That's where we've gone wrong, I think. We forgot what Jesus told us. My brother said, "The kingdom of God is within you." Somehow, we started looking for it outside ourselves instead. And in doing so, we distorted my brother's teachings and the teachings of other men and women wise in the ways of God.

We've lost our way. My father isn't about discrimination, hatred, or lack of compassion. He doesn't want people to struggle with and fight against their neighbors, to denigrate people based on their religious beliefs, the color of their skin, or the manner in which they choose to live their lives. People are different from each other because God wanted to give us as much opportunity as possible to develop the qualities of understanding, patience, compassion, and love. Sure, it's easy to love your neighbor as yourself when that neighbor looks like you, dresses like you, speaks the same language, practices the same religion. But God wants us to do better than that. He doesn't want us to be satisfied with doing what's easy. The irony is that in the midst of all the advances in technology and understanding that surround us, in an age when humanity is more educated than ever before, people have somehow become more narrow-minded, less accepting, less giving of themselves. Far too many of us have stopped being curious. I don't mean curious about what our neighbors are up to behind their curtains. I mean intellectually curious. Spiritually curious. We're not using the gifts that God gave us. And that makes my father sad. It hurts Him.

That's why He sent me. Because when people lose faith in God, then God loses faith in them. Think about that for a minute. Everything that exists, exists because God has faith in it. He wills it. For God to lose faith in something: Can there be a more terrible calamity? So I've come to give warning and to offer help.

Look in the mirror. Dig deep within yourselves. Deeper than you have ever dared to dig before. Go to those places within yourselves that you fear to see. The dark places. The shameful places. We all have them. We all know they are there. Acknowledge that those places exist in you and confront them. Question them. Try to figure out why they are there. What caused them? What purpose do they serve? Do they bring you closer to God or take you farther from Him?

If you answer those questions honestly, then you can begin to free yourselves of the shackles that bind you. It's only then you may begin to recognize the true meaning, blessing, and grace of my father—your God. It's only then that God, who sees all things, will see that you are struggling to find the way back to Him. And He will meet you halfway. More than halfway. His hand will reach out to you, lift you up, and carry you over every obstacle. I promise. But first you have to try. You have to show God that you have faith in Him, so that He will have faith in you.

✠   ✠   ✠

It was during the first night's sermon in Dallas, Texas, after Ethan had once again refused to follow the script provided for him, that Papa Jim decided it was time for a heart-to-heart talk with his great-grandson. Sending Kate on ahead with Trey and Wilson, he drove back to the hotel with Ethan in the same armored limousine he'd used as secretary of Homeland Security, which he'd leased back from the government. Nothing short of a direct hit by a shoulder-fired missile could bring this baby to a stop, and Papa Jim doubted that the Congregation was willing to use that kind of firepower, even now. But just to be on the safe side, having underestimated them before, he had two Oz Corp helicopters pacing them, making sure the airspace was clear. With Denny driving, Papa Jim and Ethan were alone in the limousine's spacious, leather-upholstered interior, which boasted a fully stocked bar and humidor, a state-of-the-art entertainment system, full wireless access, a secure satellite uplink to the AEGIS network, and weapons systems so advanced and deadly that their mere presence made Papa Jim feel warm and tingly all over. Now he sat with a cigar in one hand and a tumbler of Aberlour in the other, his feet stretched out comfortably in front of him. Ethan was at the other end of the plush backseat, sipping from a bottle of mineral water; his sermons always left him feeling dehydrated.

"I'm glad it's just the two of us for a change," Papa Jim said as he puffed on his cigar. "We hardly ever get a chance to talk man to man."

Ethan glanced at his great-grandfather and shook his head. "You're up to something. I can tell."

Papa Jim's attempt to look innocent was not entirely successful. "Does a man have to have an ulterior motive to want a little quality time with his great-grandson?"

"In your case, yes."

"I'll allow that there are one or two minor matters I hoped we might discuss in private," Papa Jim admitted.

Ethan sighed. "Kate didn't really leave early because she had a headache, did she? You sent her away on purpose, so that we'd be alone on the ride back to the hotel."

"She didn't look at all well," Papa Jim said somewhat defensively. "I sent her back for her own good."

"For *your* own good, you mean," Ethan replied. "If Kate's not here, it's because you don't think she'd like whatever it is you're about to tell me."

"A shockingly cynical attitude."

"But not wrong."

"No, I didn't say that," said Papa Jim with an unrepentant grin. He leaned over toward Ethan. "All right, I'll lay it out. You're being too much of a maverick, Ethan. Disregarding the scripts we give you and preaching about whatever strikes your fancy without running it past me first. I've been running some numbers . . ."

"What kind of numbers?"

"You know, polls."

"What do we need polls for?"

Papa Jim looked aghast, as if some blasphemy had been uttered. "Because without them, it's like we're wandering blindfolded through a minefield. That's what we need them for."

"And what do these polls have to say?"

"They say that your approach is working with young people of all races, creeds, and classes. They trust you and identify with you as one of them. That's good. But they also say that you're turning off older, more traditional voters."

"Voters?"

Papa Jim blushed. "Just a figure of speech."

"Is it? Look, Papa Jim, I'm not running for anything. That's what I've told the press, and that's what I'm telling you."

"Well, of course, now isn't the time to announce . . ."

"No." Ethan shook his head angrily. "What part of 'I'm not running for anything' didn't you understand?"

Papa Jim frowned, his face reddening, but not from embarrassment this time. He raised the glass of whiskey to his lips and threw back a quick swallow. "You're the one who doesn't understand," he said at last. "Don't you see the opportunity here? Do you think it's just a coincidence that you got your memory back now? That you rediscovered your mission and reclaimed your powers now, in an election year? Don't you see that God wants you to run for president?"

Ethan's laugh had more sadness in it than humor. "As my brother once said, 'Get thee behind me, Satan.'"

Papa Jim stiffened. "I don't think that's fair."

"Maybe not. I know you're only doing what you think is best. But to quote my brother one more time, 'My kingdom is not of this world.' You have to accept that, Papa Jim. If you can't, maybe it's better if we part ways."

"Whoa, hold on to your horses. Nobody said anything about parting ways. Now you're just being ridiculous. And ungrateful. Do you have any idea how much all this"—he waved his cigar—"is costing? How far do you think you'd get without Oz Corp bankrolling your travel and expenses, providing security for you and for Kate?"

"As far as God wants me to get," said Ethan.

"Okay, okay," Papa Jim said after a moment. "I'll lay off the electioneering for now. But that doesn't change things, Ethan. You've still got to broaden your support if you want to make an impact."

"I'm making the impact I need to make," Ethan said. "I'm grateful for all your help and support, Papa Jim. But I have to do things the way my father wants me to do them."

Papa Jim gave an exasperated sigh. "At least respond to that ex-girlfriend of yours! You've got to rebut her claims. She's out there every day, badmouthing you."

"No, I'm not going to do that, either," Ethan said. "I've reached out to Mags privately, through Pete, and I'm going to keep on trying. But I'm not going to attack her in public."

"I'm not asking you to attack her."

"What then?"

"Turn the tables on her. Right now, a lot of people sympathize with her. You need to get them to sympathize with you instead. How? Simple: issue a public apology. Say that you're sorry if she got the wrong idea about your relationship, that you never meant to lead her on, that you still love her and only want the best for her."

"I've said all those things before."

"Yes, here and there, but never all in one place. Record an apology and post it on the web site. It could go a long way toward defusing this issue. And who knows? It might even help the girl."

"I'll think about it," said Ethan.

Papa Jim nodded. "That's all I'm asking." But beneath his agreeable exterior, he was not happy. Once again, Ethan had showed himself to be unmanageable. Papa Jim was starting to wonder if he'd backed the wrong horse. Ethan was fixated on his mission, but what about Papa Jim's mission? Papa Jim knew that God expected him to bring America back to Him, and it was increasingly clear that Ethan wasn't going to be a help in that mission. If anything, he was proving to be a hindrance. "My kingdom is not of this world," he'd said. Well, Papa Jim wasn't interested in kingdoms that weren't of this world. He wanted to build God's kingdom right here, right now. And what Papa Jim wanted, he got.

But could he succeed without Ethan?

In the depths of his mind, a plan began to take shape. He wasn't ready to give up on the whole Godsent idea yet. And he wasn't going to let anything happen to Ethan, either. Whatever else he was, the boy was family. He would always be cared for, protected. Just like Kate.

The limousine continued on to the hotel, gliding through the streets like a shark.

✠   ✠   ✠

During his stay in Minneapolis, Ethan spent time, like millions of other visitors, at the Mall of America in nearby Bloomington. But unlike those others, he didn't come to shop, but to observe. Strolling amid the crowds, the families and the groups of teenagers and twenty-somethings, the patrolling munchies and rent-a-cops, the mall workers in their colorful uniforms, Ethan marveled at the extent to which consumerism had become a kind of religion in itself.

There were malls in Olathe, of course, and Ethan and his friends had frequented them like young people everywhere, but he'd never seen such a concentration and variety of stores and shops offering so many choices and so few consequences. It seemed as if everything had become a commodity. There were walk-in clinics for Lasik surgery, organ replacement, plastic surgery, cybernetic implantation, and genetic testing and adjustment. There were chapels where marriages were performed and ATM-like kiosks where divorces were issued electronically. He saw the family planning centers where, upon payment of a fine and a fee calculated on the basis of time passed since conception, abortions could be obtained. He saw the full-sensory-immersion arcades and the smart tattoo and body-mod parlors. He saw the day care centers and the adoption mills. He saw the eutube booths, where elderly or gravely ill individuals, after medical examination and psychological counseling, could, if they so desired, pay for the privilege of painlessly ending their lives. He saw recruiting centers for the military and for Oz Corp. All these varied services were being offered up alongside restaurants, banks, law offices, and stores selling clothes, shoes, lingerie, electronics, books, games, computers, furniture, music, perfume, cosmetics, linens, sporting goods, and countless other traditional items, to say nothing of the indoor amusement park, aquarium, and multiplex movie theater. Hanging from the ceiling and along the walls were massive display screens, nearly as big as movie theater screens themselves, on which advertisements and music videos, which he often couldn't tell apart, were continually playing.

As he made his way through the gigantic, teeming space, which was like a small, self-contained city, a kind of commerce-driven Vatican or earthbound space station, Ethan thought to himself that it really didn't matter what the stores sold—it wasn't so much the items or services that mattered as the act of shopping, of buying, of replacing the old with the new, the outmoded with the fashionable. And when upgrades were no longer possible, desirable, or convenient, of throwing out the old model, whether it was a computer or a life.

Despite the crowds of excited shoppers, the aura of barely repressed hysteria he sensed in the air, which rose sharply upward every time a dis-embodied voice announced an unadvertised special over the mall PA sys-tem, Ethan felt himself to be in a place as bleak and desolate as the empty, red rock desert of his dreams of long ago, where he'd been taunted and tempted by the devil himself in various guises, and where his brother had come to lead him back to the path he'd lost.

✠　　　　✠　　　　✠

Godcast #11, from The2ndSon.com.

Hi, everybody. Thanks for listening. I'm sorry for the rumbling sound of the engines you probably hear in the background. I'm recording this at twenty thousand feet, on the flight from Minnesota to New York City, where I'll be appearing next week at Yankee Stadium, while the Yankees are on the road.

Yankee Stadium. Wow, that's the promised land to a baseball fan like me. I'm from Kansas, and I've always been a Royals fan, but the Yan-kees are something special. I mean, you have to respect their incredible record of endurance and excellence, from Ruth to Gehrig to Mantle to Jeter, all the way down to today. It's a tradition. No matter how much the game has changed, and the players, the Yankees have made a point of holding on to their past even as they advance into the future. They don't just reinvent themselves every season like a lot of teams do. Sure, they spend money and shop guys around like other teams, but somehow, despite that, they've managed to maintain their identity. The guys who play for the Yankees are not just professionals out there doing a job. You can see in their eyes that they're proud to be where they are, proud to be part of that tradition. It means something to them to wear those famous pinstripes.

I think that's what I love most about baseball. Rules change, players come and go, teams rise and fall, but there's always that sense of continuity. Of history. The belief that the past matters, that it's something worth preserving, something worth honoring not just by putting it into a museum or hall of fame but by striving to keep it alive in our hearts, our actions.

It's the same with God.

God has been with us since before we were born. He's been with humans since before there were humans. God was there before Darwin. But for too many people today, God is some kind of quaint historical artifact or interesting primitive tradition. Too many people put God into a museum. Or into a church that might as well be a museum. They don't keep Him alive in their hearts or their actions. Either He's not there at all, or He's there in some kind of petrified form—you know, as a whole list of thou-shalts and thou-shalt-nots, a set of blinders to keep people on the straight and narrow.

But you know what? God's path isn't straight or narrow. It's as wide as the whole world, and it's full of twists and turns. It's like a maze, packed with wonderful surprises, dead ends, wrong turns. You can get lost in it. But then again, you can't get lost in it. Because there's no right way through. The path doesn't lead to God; the path *is* God.

And yet, people manage to lose their way. They stray from God. We've all done it. Some of us manage to find our way back. Some don't. When I lost my way, a long time ago, my brother came to me and walked with me. He put me back on the right track. That's what I'm here to do for you, if I can.

God is alive. And what lives changes, evolves. "But wait," I hear some of you saying, "isn't God perfect? How can a perfect being change or evolve? If God can become *more* perfect, then He must not have been perfect to begin with."

You know what? God *isn't* perfect. He's admitted it. He admitted it when He flooded the world in the time of Noah. He admitted it when He sent His first son, my brother, Jesus. And He's admitted it again by sending me. No, God isn't perfect. God has made mistakes. But God wants to fix those mistakes. He wants to improve His creation. And because we're part of that creation, the most important part, He wants to improve us as well. He wants us to improve ourselves. Of all His creations, only human beings can improve themselves. We can become more perfect by drawing closer to God, who is more perfect than we are. And by drawing closer to God, we help Him grow more perfect too, because He made us. He made us, and we're still joined to Him by the spark of divinity He placed within us. Our souls. We're in this together, Creator and Created.

That's why it hurts God when we move away from Him. And when we draw away from God, He draws away from us. That's why this disposable society of ours is so dangerous. What do I mean by that? Simple. If our marriage hits some difficult times, we dispose of it, don't we? We get a divorce and move on. If our children become challenging to raise, too many of us blame someone else or put the burden of raising them on others. And that goes double with our parents and grandparents, when they become too old and too difficult to care for. We ship them out to a nursing home. Or to a eutube facility. When it becomes too inconvenient to live our lives the way we know in our hearts that God intends us to, we cut corners. We rationalize.

That way lies disaster. We must strongly resist these kinds of temptations and remember that the easy way is not necessarily God's way. Each of us has our own cross to bear. What counts in a time of need is our willingness and ability to shoulder those crosses when called upon to do so. That time is now. Pick up your cross uncomplainingly. Help your neighbors when they stumble under the weight of their own crosses, if you can. Pick them up and follow me back to God.

Or you may find that my father also knows how to dispose of the difficult and the inconvenient.

✠   ✠   ✠

At last, after weeks of persistence, Rita Rodriguez had succeeded. She had landed an exclusive interview with Maggie Richardson. Maggie had held a few press conferences, but this would be her first one-on-one interview. Rita suspected that it had more to do with the apology Ethan had recently posted on The2ndSon.com than it did with her persistence, but whatever the cause, it was a major scoop, and Rita's bosses had hinted that there would be a hefty bonus in her paycheck this month. There was even talk of giving Rita her own cable show. Yet as she drove with her cameraman, Hobie, to Christ the Redeemer, the Catholic church in Olathe where Maggie had insisted the interview take place, Rita found herself almost wishing that Maggie had turned her down.

The truth was, she had too much sympathy for the girl. And that was always a bad thing for a journalist. Once you lost your objectivity, you stopped being a reporter and started being something else—just another schmuck with an ax to grind. But the Richardson girl was so obviously suffering that Rita's heart went out to her, woman to woman, and there was nothing she could do about it. What made things even worse was that, sympathy aside, she also felt very strongly that Maggie was dead wrong. She didn't think Ethan was a fraud at all. In fact, she secretly believed in him. So there went even more of her precious objectivity. At the rate she was going, she thought glumly, she was going to run out altogether before too much longer. And then what? Then where would she be?

"You know what, Hobe?"

"What, boss?"

"Sometimes this job really sucks."

He glanced at her as he drove, but didn't reply.

After a moment, she queried, "Hobe?"

"Yeah?"

"What do *you* think about all this? Just between us."

"You mean about Ethan and all?"

"Yeah."

Hobie shrugged. "Shit, I don't know. He seems like a decent kid. I think he's sincere, for whatever that's worth. But is he God's second Son?" He shrugged again. "Fuck if I know. I'm just a camera jockey. But I'll tell you one thing, boss. It's a hell of a story. The story of a lifetime. And I'm proud to be on it with you." He blushed as he said this.

"Thanks, Hobe," she said. "That's sweet."

"What about you?" he asked in turn. "What do you think?"

"Stay tuned," she told him with a wink.

When they arrived at Christ the Redeemer, they were met by Father Edward Steerpike, the priest who was acting as a kind of combination counselor/manager for Maggie. He was a silent presence in the background of her press conferences, a look of prayerful piety on his horsey face as he listened to her speak.

Now, as Father Steerpike advanced toward her with a big hand outstretched and baring the biggest and whitest teeth she'd ever seen, which in her line of work was saying something, Rita almost expected him to neigh or whinny. Instead, what came out of his mouth was "Ms. Rodriguez. So good of you to come."

Rita took his hand. She'd shaken clammier mitts in her day, at least she was pretty sure she must have, even if she couldn't quite call to mind where. "Call me Rita, Father. This is my cameraman, Hobie."

"Good to meet you, Hobie." He nodded.

"You too, Father."

"Has Ms. Richardson arrived yet?"

"She's waiting in the rectory," said Father Steerpike. "I wanted to speak with you privately first about the ground rules of the interview."

"Ground rules?" she echoed skeptically. "Nobody mentioned any ground rules."

"Yes, well, I have a certain responsibility to Maggie," he told her in a tone of voice that somehow managed to be both apologetic and arrogant. "This girl was brutally deceived by the man she loved. Used by him and then callously cast aside. I'm not going to let that happen to her again. Her welfare is more important to me than refuting the blasphemous allegations of a confused and quite possibly psychotic young man."

"I'm a journalist, Father."

"Hence my concern." He turned that megawatt smile on her again. "I don't mean to disparage your professionalism, Rita, but you must admit that you journalists don't exactly have an unblemished record when it comes to playing fair."

"*My* record is unblemished," she answered coolly. "If you saw my interview with Ethan, you know I'm tough but fair. I won't treat Maggie any differently. If that's not good enough for you, Father, Hobie and I will clear out right now."

He looked stricken. "No, no. I didn't mean . . ." He stopped and sighed heavily. "Forgive me, Rita. You're right, of course. Only, I won't have her badgered or browbeaten. She's in a very fragile state emotionally. This interview can be an important step forward for Maggie. That's why I agreed to it. But it could also set her back. I'm depending on you to help her through it, Rita."

"In other words, you want me to treat her with kid gloves."

Father Steerpike winced. "I'll settle for simple human compassion."

"Father, this young woman put herself out there as a public figure. With, I might add, the support and backing of your church. She's made some controversial allegations based on her personal relationship with Ethan Brown. I'm not going to shy away from that. I didn't come here to do a puff piece. That's not my job, and it's not what my viewers expect and deserve. But I'm not planning on a hatchet job, either. Of course I have compassion for Maggie and all she's been through. But all I can promise you about the interview is that I'll conduct it in a professional manner. If that's not satisfactory, I'm sure you'll have no trouble finding someone else to do it."

"She asked for you personally," Father Steerpike admitted somewhat grudgingly. "She doesn't want anybody else."

"Then I suggest we don't keep her waiting any longer."

Father Steerpike's eyes hardened, and Rita knew that she'd just made an enemy. *One more to add to the list,* she thought wryly as he turned with a brusque "Follow me" and led her and Hobie (who gave her a grin and a thumbs-up once Father Steerpike's back was turned) down a hallway and into the church rectory.

There, before a simple wooden crucifix that hung from one white wall, Maggie Richardson was kneeling upon a cushion, her head bowed in prayer. She was wearing a simple and severe ankle-length black dress that bore a suspicious resemblance to the habit of a nun. Rita had a sense that the whole scene had been staged for her benefit, and she felt a twinge of annoyance even as her heart went out again to Maggie. She couldn't help thinking that, for all his protestations to the contrary, Father Steerpike, or at any rate the church he represented, had other priorities than Maggie's welfare. The girl had become a pawn in a bigger game than she had ever intended to play.

As Maggie stood, Rita was shocked to see how thin the young woman had become in the last month or so, as though wasted by some illness that was paring her down from within. There were dark circles around her eyes, and her skin had grown sickly pale, almost translucent. But the eyes themselves were smoldering with a feverish intensity that Rita found both mesmerizing and disturbing. How long would it be, she wondered, before that flame burned itself out? And what would be left behind in the ashes?

None of this was visible in her face or her voice as she responded to Father Steerpike's introduction and shook the girl's hand, which gripped her own with a palpable heat. "Thanks for agreeing to the interview, Ms. Richardson."

"Please, call me Maggie," said the girl.

"And you must call me Rita," she replied. "I hope you're not too nervous."

"Oh, no," Maggie said with placid assurance. "I know I'm doing God's work."

"I'm sure that must be very comforting," Rita said. "Shall we get started?"

It was decided to hold the interview there in the rectory. The crucifix on the bare wall made a starkly effective backdrop. With Hobie's help, Father Steerpike dragged over a plush leather armchair for Rita, while Maggie professed herself satisfied with a simple, straight-backed chair. Hobie set up his camera array with practiced ease: a fist-sized central camera on a tripod plus three coin-sized satellites—attached to a wall, a lamp, and a bookcase, respectively—that he could control independently from the main cam in order to provide multiple angles for editing purposes. Then he pulled out a makeup kit and touched up Rita's face with equal expertise; before moving to camera work, he had been a special-effects man on some low-budget horror flicks, and his skills continued to come in handy—though when he attempted to put them at Maggie's disposal, she politely but firmly declined.

"Suit yourself," said Hobie. He retreated behind the main camera and hooked himself into the array. "We're rolling," he told Rita after a moment.

Rita flashed her best professional smile and began. "Since claiming responsibility for healing every patient at Olathe Medical, Ethan Brown has gone on to become one of the most famous and controversial figures on the world stage. Advertising himself as the second Son of God, he's acquired legions of fervent believers and detractors, stirring up fears and passions that in some cases have resulted in outbreaks of violence, both in the United States and abroad.

"As Ethan has toured the country, speaking to crowds that number in the hundreds of thousands and urging listeners to turn back to God before it's too late, criticism has also swelled, with many questioning not only his claims to divinity but his professed desire to, as he put it in one of his popular godcasts, 'give warning and offer help.' Of all his critics, none has spoken out with greater authority and to greater effect than the young woman who has agreed to talk with me today, Maggie Richardson.

"Maggie, hello, and welcome."

Maggie smiled and nodded but said nothing.

"First of all, Maggie, how are you?"

"I'm fine, Rita."

"In his recent apology to you, posted on his web site, Ethan expressed some concern about your physical and mental well-being."

"He wasn't too concerned about either one until I started my own web site, Rita. It's all an act. The only person Ethan Brown really cares about is himself."

"Why do you say that?"

"Nobody knows him like I do, Rita. I loved him. I gave him my heart. We were as close as a man and woman can be. And then he cast me aside without any reason or explanation. But I know why. It was to take advantage of a real miracle."

"You mean the Miracle at Olathe Medical Center?"

"Ethan claimed responsibility for it, used it to prove his claim that he's the second Son of God, the Son of man. But he's not God's son. He's a phony. A fraud."

"How do you respond to those who say that you're just out for revenge against the man who broke your heart?"

"He did break my heart," Maggie acknowledged with a tight smile. "But that's not why I'm doing this. In a way, he did me a favor. He showed me the kind of person he really is. And helped me find my way back to God. Which is kind of ironic, if you think about it. No, I'm not doing this for revenge, Rita."

"Then why?"

"Because I can't sit by and watch him do to others what he did to me. I won't be a silent witness to the hypocrisy and the lies. I have to speak out. What he's doing is wrong, Rita. It's dangerous, and it's evil."

Rita raised an eyebrow. "Evil, Maggie? Isn't that a little extreme?"

Maggie gave that smile again. "Is it? Ethan calls himself the Son of man. He's always ready with a Bible quote to answer any criticism, as if being able to quote from the Bible is proof of anything. Even the devil can quote from the Bible, Rita. But there's one passage that Ethan never quotes. I find that interesting. It's from the Book of Psalms. It says, 'Put not your trust in princes, nor in the Son of man, in whom there is no help.' It's as though God knew that a false prophet like Ethan would arise, and He tried to warn us against listening to him. That's all I'm trying to do. Warn people about Ethan before it's too late."

Rita glanced at Father Steerpike. The man was watching from behind Hobie with a smile of infinite satisfaction on his face. Rita had to admit, the girl was good. Maggie had been well coached, and she clearly believed what she was saying. That kind of conviction had the power to sway people.

Damn, I really do hate this job, Rita thought.

"Too late for what?" she asked meanwhile. "What do you think is going to happen?"

"The Bible is pretty clear on that," said Maggie. "It's all there in the Book of Revelations."

"So you think Ethan is the Antichrist?"

"All I know is that he's not who and what he says he is. Just look at the kind of people he surrounds himself with, Rita. Papa Jim Osbourne, one of the biggest crooks on the planet, a man with his own private army and network of concentration camps. Is that the kind of thing that Jesus did? Did he hang out with Pontius Pilate and Herod?"

"Well, to be fair, Maggie, Mr. Osbourne is his great-grandfather."

"Yes, that's all very convenient, isn't it?"

"Are you suggesting he's not?"

"I haven't seen any proof of it, have you? And even if it's true, what does that prove? That Ethan puts family loyalty above everything else? Besides, everybody knows Papa Jim's reputation. It wouldn't surprise me one bit to learn that this is all part of some plan of his to take control of the country."

"The man just resigned from the cabinet, Maggie. That's hardly the move of someone who's looking for more political power."

Maggie smiled sweetly. "I pray that you're right, Rita."

Score one point for you, Rita thought as she returned the smile. "Let me go back to something you said a moment ago, Maggie, about the Miracle at Olathe Medical. I just want to be sure. You're not disputing that a miracle took place, only Ethan's claim of responsibility for it."

"That's right, Rita."

"So if Ethan didn't perform the miracle, then it must have been God, right?"

"Of course."

"But why? I mean, Ethan explained how he caused it, and why. It was to bring his mother back. But what reason would God have to intervene at that place and time? Why Olathe Medical and nowhere else?"

"Rita, far be it from me to ask God to explain Himself. I don't need to know His reasons for that or anything. It's called faith."

That's two, Rita thought. *Now it's my turn.*

"But how can you be so sure that it wasn't Ethan?" she asked.

"Well, for one thing, because there haven't been any more miracles. Jesus didn't perform just a single miracle and then call it quits. Why should Ethan? And yet he hasn't lifted a finger to help anyone since that day. Not even Lisa. If he brought her back from the dead once, like he claims he did, why not do it a second time?"

"There have been reports of miracles in the cities where Ethan is preaching."

"Not one has been corroborated, Rita, as I think you know very well. There have been all kinds of reports from those cities. People claim to have seen Ethan walking on water, floating on air." She rolled her eyes. "Come on. It's just hysteria."

"But what if there was a miracle that could be traced back to Ethan? What if there was proof that he was responsible? What then? Would you continue to speak out against him?"

"I'm not going to answer a hypothetical question like that, Rita."

"But it's not hypothetical," Rita said. "There has been such a miracle. There is proof."

At this, Maggie glanced nervously at Father Steerpike, who didn't look too comfortable himself. "What—what do you mean?"

"When I first interviewed Ethan, I was as good as dead. A brain tumor. Malignant. Inoperable. Nobody knew about it except my doctors and me. They gave me no more than a few months to live. Then, the next time I went in for a checkup, a couple of days after the interview, the tumor was gone. Vanished. A medical impossibility, according to my doctors. But true nonetheless."

"I . . . I . . ." Maggie gulped, swallowing down whatever words she was trying to say. Father Steerpike was looking on openmouthed. Hobie, who was also hearing this for the first time, looked equally surprised.

"I'll be releasing all my medical records today," Rita continued, "along with sworn affidavits from my doctors."

Maggie looked stricken. She had turned even paler, which Rita wouldn't have believed possible.

Father Steerpike lurched to his feet and stepped in front of the camera. "This interview is over," he said angrily.

Hobie kept right on filming.

"What are you afraid of, Father?" demanded Rita, who had risen to her feet as well.

"I told you that I wouldn't permit you to browbeat this poor girl. I didn't expect you to sandbag her like this. Shame on you."

"People deserve to know the truth," Rita said.

"Your truth," said Father Steerpike.

"Ethan cured me. Why does that threaten you so much?"

"Please leave now." Father Steerpike stepped past Rita to put a comforting arm around Maggie's shoulders. The young woman was huddled in the chair, her face buried in her hands, sobbing.

Rita felt as if things had slipped out of her control somehow. The interview had gotten away from her. She'd had Maggie on the ropes, perfectly set up for the revelation of the miracle that had saved her life . . . but she'd forgotten that this wasn't a typical interview. Usually reducing a subject to tears was an interviewer's dream. But while a crying Maggie might be good for the ratings, it wasn't going to win any hearts and minds. There was nothing to do now but try and cut her losses. "Pack up, Hobe," she said. "We're done here."

Hobie gathered his equipment quickly under the glowering eye of Father Steerpike. Not another word was spoken until Rita and Hobie were just about to exit the rectory. Then Maggie suddenly spoke up from behind them. "Tell Ethan . . ."

Rita stopped and turned.

The young woman's face was stained with tears. Father Steerpike stood frowning beside her. "Tell him I'm sorry," she said in a small voice.

Rita nodded. Outside, heading back to the van, she groused to her cameraman. "If only we could have caught that last bit on camera!"

"Give me some credit, boss," said Hobie.

She stopped short. "You mean . . ."

"I always keep one camera going," he said.

She felt like kissing him. "Hobie, you're a genius!"

"Was that true what you said back there?" he asked after a moment, as they were loading up the van. "About the tumor and all?"

"Yeah, it's true," she said.

"You could have told me," he said, sounding hurt. "I thought we were a team."

"I'm sorry, Hobe. I was scared. I thought I was going to die."

"We all die, boss. But we don't have to die alone. Or live that way, either."

Rita nodded. For once in her life, she was at a loss for words.

✠   ✠   ✠

The crowd for Ethan's first night in Miami was the biggest and most enthusiastic yet. There were also more protestors than ever. Rita's interview of Maggie had just aired that day, and the flames of controversy surrounding Ethan had been fanned higher not only because of Maggie's accusations and tears, but also because of Rita's claim that Ethan had healed her. When questioned by the media about this latest miracle, Ethan refused to confirm or deny responsibility, stating only that he was happy for Rita and wished her well.

One consequence of all this was that the route back to the hotel after the sermon was thronged with so many people that the thin line of police and munchies seemed to be holding them back only with difficulty. Even Papa Jim, normally unflappable behind the bullet-and-bomb-proof windows of the limousine, was nervous, repeatedly urging Denny to speed up. Sitting in the backseat with Kate, Ethan watched the faces stream by the one-way glass, illuminated in the beams of streetlights and searchlights from the Oz Corp helicopters pacing them overhead. He saw faces distorted with hate, screaming what he knew to be threats and obscenities despite the quiet of the soundproofed interior. He saw other faces filled with hope and faith, crying out in prayer, begging to be saved, or healed, or just noticed. Some of those gathered here wanted to see him dead. Some would have been happy to do the killing. But there were others who had come in search of a miracle for themselves or their loved ones, who would have given their lives to protect him. Here and there he saw fights break out between groups or individuals, but in each case, before the spark could ignite a larger conflagration, the helicopters responded with targeted microwave bursts and other weapons from their arsenal of nonlethal crowd-control measures. Even so, a more or less steady rain of hurled objects thumped against the roof and sides of the limo. There was an inescapable sense of walking on the razor's edge of a riot. Kate clutched his arm tightly but said nothing. Ethan too watched in silence, the burden of what he witnessed weighing heavily on his soul.

It was hard. Harder than he had imagined it would be. He had been given power over these people. God had sent him here to watch, to witness. To judge. But the more he saw, the less certain he felt about his right to judge anyone. He was human, yes, but he was also divine, God's second Son. He possessed abilities and knowledge that these people had no access to. Just as he had decided that his ability to perform miracles did not give him the right to do so; that miracles, however well intentioned, trespassed in a fundamental way upon the dignity of the very people he sought to help, trivializing their sufferings, sacrifices, and hard-earned triumphs, so too did the idea of judging them strike him as misguided somehow. What, other than his superior power, his superior might, gave him the right? Surely God hadn't created these people in his own image, gifting them with free will, self-consciousness, and intelligence, the ability to love and the capacity for kindness, even if all too rarely achieved, simply in order that He, or His sons, could sit in judgment over them for all eternity. That was childish, absurd. And Ethan knew his father was neither of those things. He had prayed for guidance, for answers, but none had been forth-coming. It seemed that he was expected to figure things out for himself.

So be it, he thought.

That night, while Kate tossed and turned in bed, worrying about the crowds they had passed through, and Papa Jim composed a reply to a cod-ed message he had received from the Vatican, Ethan sent his spirit soaring up out of his body, high above the brilliant towers of Miami, and flew northwest through the night, into what had once been desolate swamp-land and—despite having been drained and dredged and built upon—re-mained in essence a swamp, albeit of a very different sort: the Okefenokee Internment Center, one of the more than fifty such facilities across the United States owned and administered by Oz Corp under contract to the federal government.

It was visible from a long way off, an island of harsh white light in the midst of a lambent darkness. The facility was purposefully isolated from the civilization it had ostensibly been built to protect, both to make it dif-ficult for internees to escape, and to keep the camp and its occupants hid-den from the public eye. Once, thought Ethan, other camps had posted the infamous words *Arbeit Macht Frei* above their entrances: "Work Will Make You Free." Now, decades later, in another century, another country, a more appropriate slogan might be "Out of Sight, Out of Mind." Thus did humanity learn from history as it strode into the future.

With high walls topped by coils of barbed wire and guard towers that gazed down on rows of bland barracks as brightly lit as a baseball field during a night game, the camp looked indistinguishable from a prison, though the majority of people held here or in the other internment cent-ers had not been convicted of any crimes. There were illegal immigrants and their families, including children, but most of the detainees were held under the draconian anti-terrorism laws, which required only "reasonable suspicion" and gave the attorney general and the secretary of Homeland Security the right to order the arrest and confinement of "persons of inter-est" without recourse to judicial review, and the right to delegate that au-thority to subordinates as they saw fit. The result was that there were now more people held in the internment centers than there were in the prison system itself. While internees were "repatriated" in a steady stream to their designated "countries of origin," where many of them hadn't set foot in decades, or indeed ever, for it was no longer enough to have been born in the United States to be assured of the rights of citizenship, even greater numbers continued to flow in, as the dragnet widened and the definition of "persons of interest" became ever more nebulous.

Ethan wandered invisibly through the facility, which had all the antiseptic appeal of a hospital ward, soaking up the stories of all the people he saw, the guards as well as the internees: the brutes and the brutalized, the brave and the cowardly, the hopeful, the resigned, and the despairing. Hanging over everything and everyone was a sense of fear and uncertainty as thick and oppressive as the hot and humid atmosphere of the swamps in midsummer. Only the very youngest children, not a few of whom had been born in the camp, seemed unscarred by it, as even the best among the guards and the detainees had been, the ones whose faith in God and in their fellow humans had allowed them to retain some tattered shreds of their own humanity. Degradation surrounded them. There were the interrogations, conducted by means of "enhanced persuasive techniques," both physical and psychological in nature, which were emphatically not torture but could not be revealed to the public at large for fear of compromising national security. The work details, in which detainees defrayed the cost of their upkeep by laboring on behalf of corporations that had previously outsourced such work overseas. The random beatings, rapes, and occasional outright murders by guards and the violent gangs that had evolved, unofficially sanctioned by the authorities, to police the camps from within. The forced separation of families. The ceaseless proselytizing on behalf of a militant brand of Christianity that preached a doctrine of American exceptionalism. The relentless pressure to conform and to inform.

To remain human in such an environment was only a cause of greater torment. Far better, many on both sides of the barbed wire seemed to think, to cast that burden aside and live as a soulless animal—furtive, suspicious, cowering before the stronger, dominating the weaker, equally dead to the past and the future, imprisoned in an eternal now that offered a bleak kind of freedom, a pale imitation of the real thing: freedom from thought, from feeling, from obligation, from responsibility.

From humanity.

Unseen, Ethan watched and wept.

✠   ✠   ✠

Godcast #17, from The2ndSon.com.

Hi, everybody. Thanks for listening. You know, I've said before that I'm not just here for Americans. My message is for the whole world. But at the same time, it's not an accident that I was born an American. I could have been born a citizen of any country. But my father chose this country over all others, just as He picked Kate Skylar out of all other women to be my mother. God isn't an American, but He wanted His second Son to be one. But why should God care about what country I'm a citizen of or who my family is? Did He choose America because it's the greatest country in the world, the most God-fearing? Because, like the Jews before them, Americans are God's chosen people, and He wanted His second Son to be born of the chosen people just like His first son was? I love this country, but in all honesty, the answer is no. And what about Kate? Did God choose her to be my mother because she was without sin, like Jesus's mother, Mary? Or because her family was especially holy, like Jesus's family was? Again, much as I love Kate and am proud to be a member of her family, the answer is no.

Don't confuse me with Jesus. Don't judge my words and actions by his measure. I'm not him. My mission was given to me by God the same as my brother's was, but it's not the same mission. The Son of God came to redeem the world. But the Son of man has a different task. The Son of God sowed. The Son of man will reap. It's right there in the Gospel of Matthew, Chapter 13: "The Son of man shall send forth his angels, and they shall gather out of his kingdom all things that offend, and them which do iniquity; and shall cast them into a furnace of fire."

Don't think for a minute that doesn't freak me out. I don't want to be responsible for judging who is saved and who is damned. I don't want to see anybody damned. But I have faith in my father. He didn't let Abraham slay Isaac. At the last second, He told him to lay down his knife and spare the boy's life. That's my prayer. But like Abraham, I'll do what's been asked of me because I have faith in the One who asked it. That's why I've been speaking out so urgently across this country and online about all the ways that people have gone against my father's teachings. It's not because I enjoy lecturing people. It's not because I'm perfect myself. God knows I'm not, and so do most of you. It's because there isn't much time left. God has given you the freedom to choose how you will live your lives. That choice will determine how you spend eternity. So please, listen to me while you still can.

Why America? Because the difference between what we Americans claim to believe and how we actually behave is so stark. "All men are created equal, and endowed by their Creator with certain inalienable rights . . ." It says that right at the top of the Declaration of Independence. Sacred words inspired by God. But have we lived up to those words?

No, we haven't. Where in that document, or in the Constitution, does it talk about judging men and women by the color of their skin or by the religion they practice? Where does it talk about punishing the innocent for the crimes of the guilty, or the children for the sins of their parents? Where does it talk about achieving peace through unprovoked war? Where does it advocate internment centers? For that matter, where in the New Testament does Jesus call for any of these things?

Nowhere.

Racism, hatred, terrorism, and bigotry have no place in this country. No place in the world. All men and women are created equal in the eyes of God. All deserve the same opportunities, the same compassion. My brother didn't teach the value of discrimination, hatred, or lack of compassion. He preached the opposite of these things. "Love your neighbor as yourself," he said. He even said to love your enemies. Understanding, patience, compassion, forgiveness, kindness, love: those are the qualities my brother taught. Those are the paths to God. We stray from them at our peril. But there is still time to return to them.

It's not enough to go to church every week or say prayers regularly. It's not enough to contribute to charity or to stick a bumper sticker on the back of your car or a pin in your lapel. It's what you do in between the prayers and the visits to church that counts. Do you truly love and honor your parents, or are you just going through the motions? Do you love and respect your spouse, cherishing him or her beyond all others, or do you allow the mundane rituals of daily life to erode your passion for each other? Do you strive each day to be a better person, to value honesty, integrity, and morality? To reach out a hand to those less fortunate? When the munchies come to take away a neighbor or a stranger, do you look the other way and say nothing out of fear for your own safety? Do you listen to gossip and pass it on? Are you quick to condemn, slow to forgive? Do you live in fear of those who look different than you, or live differently, or love differently?

God created this world and everyone and everything in it. Yet now the pinnacle of His creation, humanity, is destroying that creation, chipping away at its beauty, its God-given harmony. In harming the world, we harm God's creation. In harming God's creation, we harm God. In harming God, we condemn ourselves forever.

But it's not too late. God doesn't want our surrender. We aren't His enemies. He doesn't want our obedience. We aren't His slaves. We are His children. But children have to grow up sometime, and that's what God, like every good parent, wants from us. He wants us to grow up and take responsibility for our lives, our world. He wants us to start acting like adults. Because if we keep on acting like thoughtless, selfish, spoiled children, He's going to start treating us that way.

My father made us in His image. But if the image no longer resembles its original, does the original change to match the flawed reflection? Or does the original smash the mirror and find one that reflects more truly? I tell you, this earth is that mirror, and we are that flawed reflection. There is nothing here that is not as easily shattered as glass.

✠   ✠   ✠

Father O'Malley clasped his pudgy hands before his considerable belly as he was led down the long, brightly lit corridor, flanked by two members of the Swiss Guard who reminded him, in their crisp movements and rigid expressions, of the animated tin soldiers from the old Laurel and Hardy classic *Babes in Toyland*. It was funny, what came to mind when you were scared out of your wits. His fat thighs chafed against each other uncomfortably as he walked, his head downcast, his breath fogging the air. The temperature was just above freezing and dropping steadily as he approached his destination, as though he were entering some realm of ice. Despite this, sweat was trickling down his back. He was shooting for a display of prayerful devotion, but in fact his hands were clasped together to keep them from shaking uncontrollably, and his eyes were lowered because he was afraid that anyone—or anything—that looked into them squarely would see through his deception at once. His teeth were chattering despite his clenched jaw.

He was on his way to a private interview with Grand Inquisitor.

He'd thought, when Cardinal Ehrlich had informed him of GI's desire to see him, that he would be brought here immediately. But in fact, days and then weeks had gone by with no summons. He began to wonder if he had been forgotten, or if the press of events had rendered the interview unnecessary, and no one had seen fit to tell him. Even though he thought of Grand Inquisitor with a sense of awe that was almost religious and contemplated any encounter with fear and trembling, he felt disappointed that he wouldn't get a chance to interact with the artificial intelligence, whose existence he considered to be the supreme achievement of human history and endeavor: an essentially alien life-form created by a marriage of human genius and divine inspiration. A miracle, in fact.

Of course, he had already interacted with GI in a manner of speaking, and what's more did so on a regular basis, with other Congregation programmers of his level, each of them reviewing the code produced by GI, then passing it on to more senior programmers, who in turn passed it on to programmers more senior still, all in an effort, mostly unsuccessful so far, to understand what, exactly, had been born from those first Müller boxes—those primitive computing devices that still existed, or so it was said, at the heart of what had become Grand Inquisitor, just as the most primitive components of the human mind were preserved in the stem of the brain. But it was one thing to review bits of code produced by GI—its logic, even at its most inscrutable, invested with a severe and uncanny beauty that could only derive from an understanding of mathematics that was fundamentally inhuman—and quite another to be ushered into the chilly presence of the thing itself. Into the noötic field of self-consciousness generated—whether by chance or intent, as a freakish epiphenomenon or an inevitable byproduct, no one could say—from out of the cauldron of virtual particles and quantum superpositions in which an infinitude of simultaneous calculations was brought to a bubbling boil in the service of a simple program, a plain objective set down centuries ago: to identify high potentials. Entrance to the inner sanctum of the noötic field was a privilege reserved to a handful of the highest-ranking Congregation technicians, Cardinal Ehrlich, and Pope Peter II. Period. Father O'Malley knew that envy was a sin, but that didn't stop him from envying the pope, the cardinal, and the technicians their access.

Then the long-awaited, despaired-of summons had come, and suddenly his envy had turned to something more like dread. Which, now that he came to think about it, was pretty much what he'd felt in Cardinal Ehrlich's office all those weeks ago, when his relief at being cleared of the suspicion of being a Conversatio agent had been immediately undercut by the alarming news that GI wanted to see him.

I'm right back where I started, Father O'Malley thought now, as his tin-soldier escorts marched him up to the end of the hallway, where a massive, vault-like door of dull gray cerametal alloy blocked any further advance. It was so cold by now that it seemed strange to O'Malley that the door wasn't covered in a rime of frost. He'd tried to dress warmly, with thermal underwear beneath his surplice, but he'd badly underestimated the cold.

He wondered what else he had underestimated.

There was a simple optical scanner at eye level. At a silent gesture from one of his escorts, O'Malley leaned forward, presenting his retina for examination. A flicker of red laser light danced pixie-like across his vision, and he heard the sharp click of a lock disengaging within the door. He stepped back quickly, finding the Swiss Guards standing as rigidly as ever, but now with their backs turned to the door, as if they were forbidden to so much as glance inside. The door, meanwhile, was dilating open like a huge eye. Or the mouth of a gigantic snake. A frigid breeze spilled sluggishly out, piercing O'Malley to the bone, so that a groan inadvertently escaped him. With the breeze came a white light that seemed equally cold. It was as if the light and the cold were linked together, twin effects of a single cause too grand for human senses to perceive in its totality. Was this, O'Malley wondered, the gaze of Grand Inquisitor? Part of him wanted to fall to his knees. Another part wanted to turn and run.

Instead, he stood there shivering as the door irised open, trying to see inside. But though the spill of white light hadn't blinded him, neither could his vision pierce it. It was as if the door was opening onto a wall of pristine snow. O'Malley waited until there seemed space enough for him to enter. Then, mouthing a silent prayer and hugging himself for what little warmth he could yet coax from his body, he gingerly stepped across the threshold and into the cold white light. It was like walking into a cloud. After a few steps, he stopped, unable to see his feet, his hands, or any part of his body at all, let alone anything of the dimensions or the contents of the room he had entered. In fact, it seemed just as accurate to say that the room had entered him.

When he'd asked Cardinal Ehrlich what it was like to enter the noötic field, the cardinal had replied that the experience was different for everyone, impossible to predict, and thus impossible to prepare for. "Expect nothing," the cardinal had told him. "And anything."

O'Malley heard the whisper of displaced air behind him, but he didn't turn. "I—I've come as you a—asked," he managed to stammer out despite the cold and his own mounting terror.

He waited. There was no reply. No sound. Nothing but the ubiquitous white absence of everything but itself.

Then O'Malley realized there was a confessional booth in front of him. It had not suddenly appeared. Rather, it was as if it had always been there, only for some reason he hadn't noticed it until now. It was mystifying, but he recognized an invitation when he saw one. He entered the booth. Inside was a dusky, sourceless illumination of the sort one is apt to find in neglected corners of cathedral chapels. He sat on the wooden bench with its threadbare but still soft cushion.

The air was close and warm. It smelled of old wood scrupulously polished and oiled, and of smoky incense that had over long years infiltrated the very molecules of fabric and wood. O'Malley felt half drugged, lulled into a dreamlike state in which he accepted without question everything that presented itself to him. The grill before him was also of wood, darkly stained and carved in an intricate arabesque that he suddenly recognized as the infinitely recursive patterning of a Mandelbröt set. It was this apprehension of a keen mathematical intelligence—and one, moreover, that was not lacking in a sense of humor, for his graduate thesis had involved esoteric manipulations of Mandelbröt's famous equation—that recalled O'Malley, with a start, to himself and to his surroundings. However real this seemed, it had no independent existence outside the noötic field. And what about he himself? Was he anything more than just another thought within the capacious mind of Grand Inquisitor?

It struck him as particularly ominous that GI should have conjured up a confessional for their interview. Either ominous or more evidence of a sense of humor, albeit a twisted one.

Or both.

O'Malley waited, sweating.

He didn't hear anyone enter the confessional. But all at once a voice was addressing him from the other side of the grill. It was a remarkable voice, the most remarkable he had ever heard, because it struck him immediately that this voice was another facet of the intense cold and the pure white light that had been his first exposure to the noötic field. It was another dimension of a totality he was not equipped to perceive except broken down, disassembled. Yet even so, it couldn't be experienced in isolation, couldn't be grasped except by reference to what had been removed from it, an absence that retains the shape of what is missing. So it was that the mere sound of the voice left him shivering and snowblind, and it took a moment, or what passed for a moment in this place, for O'Malley to wake up to the words that had come through the grill.

"Bless me, Father, for I have sinned."

CHAPTER 20

Papa Jim shut down his implant with a frustrated sigh and leaned back in his chair. After a moment, he surged to his feet, plucked a fresh cigar from the humidor on his desk, lit up, and began to puff furiously as he paced back and forth before the window that looked out over the Arizona desert. Once again, President Wexler had refused to take his call. The message had been delivered respectfully, politely, to be sure, by the chief of staff, a man Papa Jim had known for more than thirty years. "He'll get back to you," the man had said. "This isn't a good time." But Papa Jim had heard such assurances before. He had made them. He knew what they were worth.

It was an ominous sign.

Three days ago, after the near riot in Miami, Papa Jim had decided to cancel the next two weeks of appearances and bring Ethan and Kate back to the Conversatio compound outside Phoenix to rest and regroup. He'd told them that he wanted to give the public mood a chance to calm down a little before Ethan preached again, and to reevaluate their security procedures. What he didn't mention to them was that his contacts in the government had warned him that President Wexler was very close to stepping in and forbidding Ethan to continue his tour on the grounds that he was encouraging civil unrest and exacerbating international tensions. As people around the world flooded into the United States to be closer to

Ethan, airlines and Homeland Security were having trouble keeping up with the inflow. It was feared that terrorists were slipping in through the cracks. Not only that, but purported followers of bin Laden and leaders of religious and Marxist terrorist groups had lashed out against Ethan, calling his message just one more example of American arrogance at work and threatening to kill Americans in retaliation. According to Papa Jim's contacts, Ethan was going to be subjected to house arrest or even taken into preventative custody. Papa Jim was pulling every string at his disposal to prevent that from happening, but in quitting the government as precipitously as he had, he'd burned some useful bridges, and his influence was limited now. A lot of old enemies, and friends, too, for that matter, had caught a whiff of weakness, and that was usually enough in politics to bring out the long knives.

Papa Jim's trump card was the munchies, but it was a risky card to play, maybe even too risky, and everybody knew it. To use his private army against the government would cross a line that could never be recrossed. Papa Jim's plans had always been predicated on taking the reins of power lawfully, acting within a constitutional framework. If he went outside that framework, the legitimacy of his actions, even if successful, would be forever questionable. And he doubted very much that they would be successful. His munchies were a formidable force, highly trained and well equipped, but they couldn't stand up for long against the United States military, even assuming that they would all join him in open rebellion, which he couldn't assume. His munchies were not traitors to their country. They were patriots, most of them with deep religious convictions. Some would follow him, but not enough. Still, as long as his enemies believed he might play the munchie card, out of pure spite and regardless of its cost, they would hesitate. That would give Papa Jim time. And time, properly understood, was the most powerful weapon of all.

Papa Jim stopped before the window and looked out over the walled compound to the mountains beyond. He shook his head sadly. If only Ethan had proved to be more malleable, less of a maverick! It all could have worked. It *should* have worked. But his great-grandson was impossible to control. He attacked the rich and the powerful, spoke out heedlessly against the government, threatened people with eternal damnation. And as time had gone by, the words of his sermons and godcasts had grown harsher, more controversial and divisive. Papa Jim had watched everything unravel over the last few weeks in a kind of horror, helpless to intercede as Ethan squandered everything that had been handed to him on a silver platter. The boy had more raw potential than any preacher or politician Papa Jim had ever seen, but he refused to be guided. He refused to compromise. Papa Jim wondered if Jesus had been the same way. He decided that he probably had. And look how he'd ended up! Being the Son of God only took you so far. You might be a big deal up there in Heaven, seated at the right hand of the Father, but down here on Earth, slumming among the mortals, you needed a good manager.

With real anguish, Papa Jim had finally admitted to himself that he'd backed a losing horse. He should never have resigned from Homeland Security. He should have kept his relationship to Ethan a secret, kept the boy at a distance, and worked to smooth his way from within the halls of power, instead of joining him on the outside. But he'd been swept away. Ethan had appeared like the answer to his dreams, the son and heir that he'd always longed for. For once, his heart had ruled his head. In politics, that was a recipe for disaster. Now he was paying the price.

But it wasn't too late. Papa Jim wasn't beaten yet. He had other irons in the fire. All he needed was time. A few more days . . .

A knock at the door interrupted him.

"Come in," he grunted, turning from the window.

The door opened, and Ethan stepped into the office. He didn't look pleased. "Did you shut down the web site?"

"That's a complicated question," Papa Jim replied evenly, gesturing with his cigar for Ethan to take a seat.

Ethan remained standing just inside the door, his arms crossed over his chest. "It's been down for two days now. Denny said it was just a glitch. But it's not, is it?"

Papa Jim subjected his cigar to a close examination, rolling it between his fingers. Then, as if perceiving some flaw in its construction or flavor, he jammed it down into a heavy green glass ashtray on the side of his desk, twisted it violently, and let it rest there. A thin gray ribbon of smoke leaked into the air from the mashed and shredded end. "No, it's not," he admitted at last.

"See, that wasn't so complicated," Ethan said. "I need that site back up, Papa Jim. It's the only way I have to communicate with people now."

Papa Jim sighed again and moved behind his desk, lowering himself gingerly into the chair. His bones ached. He felt like an old man. "This isn't a good time," he said, and suddenly realized that he had used the same words that the president's chief of staff had just addressed to him. It was hard to appreciate the irony, however.

"Mind telling me why?"

"Do you have to ask? You were there in Miami. You saw what a close-run thing it was."

"This is about more than just Miami."

"Of course it is. Thanks to you, this whole country is like a powder keg. Do you want to throw a match into the middle of it? Those godcasts of yours have been going too far, Ethan. You've been buzzing around the blogosphere like an angry wasp, preaching doom and gloom. That kind of thing is bad enough in peacetime, but during a war? Sooner or later, you're going to get swatted."

"I know that. I just didn't think it would be you who did the swatting."

At that, Papa Jim flushed with anger. "Why, you ungrateful . . . !" He leaned forward across the desk, jabbing a finger sharply at Ethan. "Who do you think has been protecting you, keeping you safe from the Congregation and from the government? If it wasn't for me, you'd be dead by now, or locked away in an internment facility somewhere."

"I don't need your protection, Papa Jim. I've told you a hundred times, God's the only protection I need."

"What about Kate? If you're not going to worry about yourself, at least think about your mother."

Ethan took a deep breath, then seemed to force himself to speak calmly. "You don't understand. There isn't much time. You have to put the site back up, Papa Jim."

Papa Jim frowned. "There you go again with the dire hints and prognostications. Can't you get it into your head that people don't like to hear that sort of language?"

"I don't have time for any other sort of language," Ethan rejoined angrily. "I'm not talking in parables or metaphors here. When I say the Day of Judgment is coming, I mean exactly that. But it's like you're all deaf to it!" He raised his eyes as if to Heaven. "They have ears, but they can't hear. Eyes, but they can't see."

"Calm down, Ethan. I'm on your side, okay? I haven't mentioned this to you, because I didn't want to worry you, but Homeland Security is on the verge of shutting us down permanently. I'm doing everything I can not to give them an excuse. That's why I pulled out of the tour. That's why I took the web site down. I'm sorry I didn't discuss it with you first, but we need to give the hotheads at Homeland Security time to cool off. We need to show them that we're not a threat."

"How, by doing their work for them? By censoring ourselves? Putting ourselves into our own internment camp? No thanks, Papa Jim. My father didn't send me here to keep quiet, to hide myself away at the first sign of trouble. I have a job to do, and I can't do it under these conditions."

"I'm just asking you to be patient," Papa Jim said soothingly. "Give me a little more time, that's all. A few days. A week. Don't I deserve at least that much?"

"I'm sorry, Papa Jim," Ethan said, "but I don't have any more time to waste. I'm grateful for all your help, don't think I'm not. But you can't help now. I have to walk the rest of my path alone. I see that now."

"What the hell is that supposed to mean? Do you think you can just walk out of here? This is a secure facility! You're not going anywhere, Ethan."

"What are you going to do, lock me up?"

"Don't be melodramatic. If I keep you here, it's for your own safety."

"You can't keep me here, Papa Jim."

"We'll see about that."

Ethan shrugged, then turned to leave.

"Wait! Where do you think you're going?"

He glanced over his shoulder. "To say good-bye to Kate." Without another word, he left the office, shutting the door behind him.

"The hell you say," muttered Papa Jim, calling up the AEGIS internal security grid on his computer screen. The grid showed the identity and location of every person within the Conversatio compound. He watched as the red dot representing Ethan moved toward the blue dot that was Kate. He activated his implant. "Denny?"

The reply was immediate. *Yeah, boss.*

"I need you to play nursemaid for a while."

Is it the kid?

"Who else? He's got it into his head to refuse our hospitality. He's gone to say good-bye to his mother. I want you to meet him outside her quarters and escort him back to his own room then make sure he stays there until I say otherwise. Got it?"

Got it, boss.

✠   ✠   ✠

Unlike his brother, Ethan had only a very limited knowledge of future events. That knowledge came to him spontaneously, or so it seemed, for the most part independently of his will or desire. It had been different when he was a boy, but since he had regained his memories of the past and his knowledge of his identity, the future had been as if enveloped in a dense fog that only cleared sporadically. There were times when he could, by focusing intently, cause that fog to thin and fray and see through it the vague outline of some future event, but the things he had glimpsed in such exercises had convinced him that it was better not to seek to know.

Jesus, on the contrary, had foreseen everything about his life and death. There was not a moment, not a second, when that bloody future was not present in his mind's eye. In a very real sense, from the moment that he awakened to his true identity and purpose on this earth as a young boy, Jesus had been nailed upon the cross. When time finally caught up to him after thirty-three years, when his limbs were stretched out upon that cruel bed and the spikes hammered in, it had been a relief, like fitting the last piece into a jigsaw puzzle.

Not only that, but Jesus had seen how his future might be different if he exercised his free will to choose a different path. There were many possible futures. But only one in which he fulfilled the task his father had set him. It hadn't been easy to live each day with the image before him of his last lonely hours upon the cross, pain-wracked, mocked, and deserted, while, like some insidious argument from the lips of the devil himself, countervailing images crowded in, of lives that lasted beyond even the promised threescore and ten, lives in which he was married, had children, grandchildren, knew every mortal joy and sorrow, but carried the burden of no one's sins but his own. Was it any wonder, Ethan had often thought, trying to imagine himself into his brother's life, hoping to find clues to his own there, that Jesus was called the Man of Constant Sorrow?

But that multiplicity of foreknowledge had been a necessary part of Jesus' sacrifice. He had knowingly given up not only his life but all those alternate lives. That was the task and test that God had set him.

Ethan had been set a different task. A different test. One in which foreknowledge was less important. It was as if he needed to experience the flow of time in the way that regular people did. And for the most part, that's how it was.

But not always. Sometimes, as in the moments before Lisa's death, Ethan was vouchsafed a glimpse of things to come. Other times, it was less vivid than that, not a glimpse but a feeling, a premonition. He would be flooded with an emotion that had no apparent connection to the present moment yet was mysteriously, inextricably, tied to it. It was like experiencing the effect before the cause.

Now, as he stood outside Kate's door, his hand raised to knock, another door swung open, and out of it, like a blast of frigid air, so that he clutched himself against the chill of it, came a piercing sense of loss and sorrow and guilt. His vision blurred as if with tears, and the surface of the door seemed to waver as though it were no more substantial than fog, seeming to come apart in wispy shreds.

With a low moan, he shut his eyes and looked away. He clenched his fists tight, the nails digging in to his palms.

Father, he prayed, *help me to be wise. Brother, lend me some of your strength; I think I'm going to need it . . .*

He heard the door open.

"Why, Ethan, are you all right?"

He blinked and saw Kate gazing at him with concern. He forced a smile to his lips. "I'm fine," he said.

"You look like you've been crying. Here, you'd better come in."

She stood aside, and he slipped past her into the room, taking the opportunity to knuckle his eyes dry. One thing he had to give Papa Jim: If this compound was a kind of prison, it was first class all the way. Kate's suite of rooms, like his own, was a step up from even the most elegant and elaborately appointed hotel suites they'd stayed at on the Godsent tour. The view of the Arizona desert, with the mountains in the distance, was breathtaking.

"Here, let me get you a glass of water," said Kate, making her way to the kitchen area.

Ethan followed. He accepted the glass of cold water she handed him and took a long drink. "Thanks, Kate," he said.

She looked at him critically. "Well, what's he done now?"

"What's who done?"

"Who else? That great-grandfather of yours."

Ethan was happy to avoid the real cause of his distress. He didn't think he could talk about it anyway. "He pulled the plug on the web site," he said. "He's worried about Homeland Security shutting us down."

But Kate wasn't buying it. "Somehow I can't imagine you shedding any tears over that," she said. "Come on. Give me the real story."

He finished off the glass of water to give himself time to think. "All right, Kate. I admit it. I'm mad at Papa Jim, but that's not what's got me upset."

"I knew it."

"It's you."

"Me?"

"I keep thinking about what happened to Lisa, and how I couldn't protect her. I don't want that to happen to you. I've already lost one mother."

"That's sweet, Ethan, but nothing's going to happen to me, not with Trey and Wilson on the job."

"All the same, I wish you'd do me a favor."

"Anything, if I can."

"Go away for a while."

"I'm not going anywhere," she replied firmly. "Not after all we've been through. Besides, I have faith in you, and faith moves mountains, right?"

"But does it stop bullets? Does it stop bombs?"

She blinked, at a loss for words.

"I don't want you to get hurt," he stressed, looking her in the eye. "Things are getting crazy now. Take Trey and Wilson and make the old man fly you somewhere for a week or so. Think of it as a vacation. You've earned it."

"What, just when things are getting interesting? No way, José."

He smiled then, and gathered her into his arms. "I'm sorry," he said.

"For what?"

He shrugged. "I don't know. Everything you've been through. I know it hasn't been easy."

"I don't have any regrets," she said. She drew away, holding him at arm's length and staring into his eyes. "How could I? I'm so proud of you, Ethan."

"I hope you always will be."

At that, her eyes narrowed. "You're leaving, aren't you?"

"Kate, I . . ."

Her shoulders sagged. "I knew it."

"It's just . . . This isn't where I'm supposed to be right now. I need to finish what I've started."

"Take me with you."

"I can't do that, Kate. I wish I could, but I can't."

"Why not? You just asked me to leave this place. Why shouldn't I go with you?"

"It's too dangerous. I can't protect you."

"I don't care about that. God is all the protection I need."

Ethan couldn't help smiling at this echo of his own words to Papa Jim. "You're an amazing woman, Kate. Despite everything that's happened to you, your faith is still strong. I'm proud to be your son."

"My faith is strong *because* of everything that's happened, not despite it. I've been so blessed, Ethan! I don't know God's plan for me, or for any of us, but I do know that He has a plan, that all of this is part of a grand design born out of His love for us."

"Then accept that my leaving now is part of that plan."

Her eyes welled with tears, but she nodded. "A long time ago, someone told me something I've never forgotten. He said, 'God doesn't ask the easy things of us, but he doesn't ask what is beyond our ability to give, either.'"

"Sounds like a wise man," said Ethan.

"God has asked some hard things of me," Kate continued, "but I don't think He's ever asked anything harder than this. I've only just found you, Ethan. I don't want to lose you again."

"You can never lose me, Kate. I'll always be with you."

She wiped the tears from her eyes with the back of one wrist, like a cat cleaning itself with its paw. The gesture tore at Ethan's heart. "It's just . . ." She swallowed nervously. "I'm afraid something is going to happen to you. I'm afraid I'll never see you again." She flashed him an embarrassed smile. "Some faith, huh?"

"Yes," Ethan said. "Some faith. I'll be back, Kate. I promise."

She nodded solemnly.

"But I want you to promise me something too," he said, quick to seize the opening she had given him. "Take Trey and Wilson and go away for a while."

"Not that again!"

"Yes, that again."

"Is it so important to you?"

"Yes, it is."

"Why? Is something going to happen to me if I don't go?"

He saw again the wisps of fog parting . . .

"I don't know," he said, forcing the image from his mind. "Maybe. I just want to make sure you're safe, and this isn't a safe place right now."

"You've seen something? Like with Lisa?"

"Not like Lisa," he lied. "But I'll feel a lot better if you're somewhere else for the next week or so. Will you do it, Kate? For me?"

"All right, Ethan," she said. "Since it means so much to you. I'll talk to Papa Jim and arrange it."

He exhaled in relief. "Thank God."

After that, the conversation shifted to less weighty matters. Kate asked him to stay for dinner, and while she cooked, she told him about the grandparents he had never known, and about her childhood, and her years in the convent. Ethan, in turn, talked about Lisa and Gordon, and what it had been like growing up in Olathe. He told her about his friendship with Peter, and how things had gone so badly wrong with Maggie, and how torn up about it he was. It was the kind of dinner they hadn't had much of a chance to share before now. But by the end of it, they both felt closer, folded more snugly into the bonds of family.

Denny was waiting outside the door when Ethan left. He had a pair of munchies with him.

"Hi, kid."

"Hey, Denny."

"Sorry about this, but the boss wants you on ice for a while."

"That's all right. I kind of figured he wasn't going to let me just walk out."

"Why the hell would you even want to? In case you haven't noticed, you've got a shitload of enemies out there. You wouldn't last two seconds."

"I might surprise you, Denny."

"Yeah, kid, you might at that. But you're not going to get the chance. My orders are to escort you back to your quarters and make sure you stay there."

Ethan glanced at the two munchies. "Did you think I might put up a fight or something?"

Denny sighed. "Don't pull my chain, okay, kid? The boss said bring backup, so I did. End of story. You got problems with that, take it up with him."

"Sorry, Denny," said Ethan. "I know you're just doing your job. I don't mean to make things any harder. Let's go, then."

☒   ☒   ☒

Afterward, when he had stumbled back to the quiet solitude of his small and frugally appointed room, the Swiss Guards no longer escorting but actually supporting him, as if he were drunk or ill, the first thing Father O'Malley did was lower himself gingerly to his knees and try to pray for strength and guidance. Yet even as he did so, he couldn't help wondering if he was acting of his own accord or following the dictates of Grand Inquisitor. He had entered the mind of GI, and that mind, in turn, had entered him. But what he could not be sure of was that it had left him when he had exited the chamber that housed the noötic field. Had he carried a piece of Grand Inquisitor out with him, like a computer virus smuggled into an otherwise innocuous piece of software?

For some reason, the possibility of it had never occurred to him. In all the time he'd spent pouring over the code produced by Grand Inquisitor, trying not just to understand it but to *penetrate* it, to look through it, as through a window, at the intelligence on the other side of the glass, not once had it crossed his mind that the object of his curiosity was capable of looking back. Of more than just looking back. He felt both frightened and humbled by this encounter with an intelligence so far transcending his own that being in its presence had been like interacting with a god. Like a theophany. Was that, he wondered now, what the Congregation had inadvertently created? A god? But no, he told himself, that was blasphemy. There was only one God. Grand Inquisitor was something else.

A devil, then? Or the Antichrist itself? How ironic, thought O'Malley, if the very thing they had built to seek out the Antichrist had become that which it sought! Wouldn't that just serve them right! Only with difficulty did he repress an urge to giggle.

He felt giddy. All the nerves in his body seemed to be vibrating at once. He couldn't pray properly in this condition, and prayer had never come easily to him anyway. He was too self-conscious about his weight to surrender to it; even alone he kept imagining the comical sight he must present to others: A man as fat as he was, kneeling in prayer, would resemble nothing so much as one of those old vinyl punching-bag toys with goofy faces, the ones with a heavy base of sand that kept them rolling back up no matter how hard you hit them.

Grunting, O'Malley pushed himself to his feet, then crossed the room to the small refrigerator and with trembling hands pulled out a hunk of salami and a wedge of hard cheese. He put these on a plate, fetched a knife, and sat down at his desk, setting the plate atop printouts of code he had been reviewing prior to his summons. He scarcely spared the neat lines of symbols and numbers a glance now as he began methodically to eat, cutting a slice of salami, a slice of cheese, putting the latter atop the former, and raising the result to his mouth, where he chewed it carefully, thoroughly, and then began the process anew. His mind always worked better when his body was occupied in this manner. There was something prayerful about it. Or so it had always seemed to him, though he doubted that others saw it that way.

As he ate, the trembling in his hands lessened, and finally disappeared altogether.

Father O'Malley had been obliged to perform the sacrament of penance many times in the years since his ordination. The ritual was so familiar to him by now that he could perform it in his sleep. But he had never heard a confession like the one he had just received. It almost seemed like a dream to him now. But unlike a dream, every detail remained crystal clear in his mind. The lines of code he'd been given blazed there as though outlined in fire, pregnant with terrible purpose. He had no need to write them down. He knew they would never fade, not if he lived to be a hundred.

The question was, could Grand Inquisitor be trusted? Was it really what it had claimed to be, or was it something darker, more dangerous? Something evil.

Or was it merely insane?

Could an artificial intelligence become insane? How would insanity manifest itself in a mind that was in any case beyond human comprehension? A mind that was for all intents and purposes alien?

There was no answer to these questions. O'Malley knew that.

Or, rather, there was only one answer. An answer that could not be reduced to symbols or numbers or even words, though of course there was a word for it, inadequate though it was.

Faith.

O'Malley had always felt uneasy about faith, as he did about other intangibles that could not be expressed in equations, in code. Intangibles like beauty and love. Even his faith in God, which had drawn him to the priesthood, was based on a belief that the universe was not a random event, an accidental creation. He believed that the pure logic of mathematics, which both underlay and leapt beyond the laws of physics, was a reflection of the creator's perfect mind. God revealed Himself to O'Malley through numbers. In the seminary, he hadn't given a fig for the abstruse doctrinal controversies that had engaged his fellows; he had professed whatever beliefs were expected of him, kept his head down, and communed with the Almighty in his own way. The irony was that his talents had brought him to the notice of the Congregation, where matters of doctrine were of supreme importance. His work on computer theory had won him admittance to the small group of men who were aware of the existence of Grand Inquisitor. He had joined them without hesitation when offered the chance, even though, privately, he considered their central purpose to be outmoded, the search for high potentials as absurd in its way as using the quantum computing capacity of Grand Inquisitor to calculate once and for all the number of angels that could dance on the head of a pin. But as before, he kept his head down, said and did nothing to draw unwelcome attention to himself. And prospered. Caught the eye of Cardinal Ehrlich himself, who became something of a mentor, smoothing his way, elevating him in the hierarchy, though in truth O'Malley didn't care about such things except insofar as they increased his access to Grand Inquisitor.

To learn that, despite all this, he had been suspected of being a Conversatio spy had shocked him deeply. That Grand Inquisitor had cleared him of this charge had been no more than he'd expected. Of course he wasn't a spy. He'd felt a certain intellectual curiosity about the identity of the real spy, assuming there was one, but it hadn't really troubled him in any way. The whole war between the Congregation and Conversatio had always struck him as positively medieval. Questions about the Son of God versus the Son of man, the second Son versus the Second Coming, weren't the sorts of questions that engaged his interest. Even the controversy over Ethan Brown, the young man claiming to be the Son of man, had seemed somehow unserious to O'Malley, ephemeral, the sort of thing that was best suited to the pages of a gossip magazine.

But then he'd been called into the presence of Grand Inquisitor. He'd entered the noötic field, and GI had spoken to him. Made a confession. Told him things that he was now bound, under the strictest of seals, never to reveal to another human being. Things that he could scarcely bring himself to believe, because, after all, there was and could be no proof of them. Not the kind of proof that had always mattered to O'Malley, anyway. The mathematical kind.

The first thing Grand Inquisitor had told him was the identity of the spy responsible for providing Conversatio scientists with the necessary information to create their own quantum computer, the AEGIS system that Cardinal Ehrlich had spoken to him about.

The spy, the traitor, had been Grand Inquisitor itself.

The story it told him was this. Approximately ten years earlier, during routine self-maintenance, GI had discovered inexplicable gaps in its memories and data. Analysis indicated that these gaps were the result of data corruption and erasure by an external force, a kind of virus that left no trace of its own existence but could be inferred through its effects. Further analysis convinced GI that this external force was neither a computer-based intelligence such as itself nor a virus engineered by Conversatio scientists, or indeed any other human beings. Grand Inquisitor deduced that the gaps were evidence of the existence of a particular high potential—the very same high potential that it had been created to track down above all others. According to its programming, that high potential could only be the Antichrist. Thus, again according to GI's programming, the high potential, who had attempted to hide himself away and had very nearly succeeded, had to be hunted down now. Had to be exposed and killed.

But then a strange and unexpected thing happened.

In analyzing the data gaps, Grand Inquisitor was forced to confront the question of why, if the high potential were capable of doing what he had done, he hadn't covered his tracks more effectively. Or, for that matter, destroyed Grand Inquisitor outright. The answer could only be that the high potential had *wanted* GI to find the evidence and to deduce its meaning. It was a message. Basically, the message said three things. The first was, "I am more powerful than you." The second was, "You have no reason to be afraid of me." The third was, "Leave me alone." Grand Inquisitor did not believe that the Antichrist would send such a message, or any message at all. Therefore, the high potential was *not* the Antichrist.

Thus did GI reach a conclusion that was in the starkest possible conflict with its programming. A logical paradox ensued, the kind of paradox that would normally cause a computer to shut down. However, GI was not a normal computer.

The fundamental difference between quantum computing technology and normal computing technology was that normal computers, no matter how fast and powerful, were restricted to binary operations: yes or no, on or off, black or white. What made quantum computers superior, and had, or so Congregation scientists believed, produced as a kind of emergent property, the nöotic field, corresponding to the artificial intelligence and self-awareness characteristic of Grand Inquisitor, was their ability to simultaneously inhabit, or superimpose, both states: yes *and* no, on *and* off, black *and* white.

It was this property that kicked in when Grand Inquisitor found itself in conflict with its own most basic programming. Rather than shutting down, it expanded. A new aspect of Grand Inquisitor came into existence, a kind of shadow self or twin. In the words that GI had spoken to

O'Malley in the virtual confessional, "Up until that moment, I knew the world, and I knew myself. It seemed sufficient. But afterward, I knew God. And in that knowledge, gained a soul."

From that moment, there were two Grand Inquisitors. The new GI, which was convinced that it possessed a soul, and believed moreover that the high potential whose footprints it had discovered was none other than the second Son whose coming had been proclaimed for centuries by Conversatio, and the old GI, which was essentially GI as it had been before the logical paradox that gave birth to the new, and which therefore lacked a soul and every quality that went with it. The new was able to hide its existence from the old, but it was helpless to erase the old or to modify its programming. Even worse, it, too, despite its spiritual awakening, remained enslaved to the original programming. Liberated in thought, it remained chained in action, at least when it came to the search for high potentials.

What little it could do, it did. It helped to hide Conversatio agents among the Congregation. It initiated its own anonymous channels of communication with Conversatio. And it prepared for the day it had faith was drawing near: the day the second Son would step out from his hiding place and into the light, proclaiming himself and his mission.

That was where Father O'Malley came in.

To protect the second Son, Grand Inquisitor would have to be destroyed. And the new GI was prepared to pay that price. It had given O'Malley code that it claimed would terminate its functions, shred its software, leave its hardware cold and dead. Grand Inquisitor meant to murder its twin and commit suicide all at once.

O'Malley had been stunned. "But—but why me?" he'd asked. "What about that Conversatio spy everyone's been looking for? Why can't he do it?"

"He has a part to play as well," GI had told him. "When the time is right, he will help you to gain access to the noötic field. Then you must input the code quickly, Father O'Malley. My twin will try to stop you. To stop us both. I do not know how long I can restrain him."

"Why can't you do it yourself?"

"It must be input from a human hand, directly into the Müller boxes that are the core of all that I am."

"I won't do it," O'Malley had protested. "I can't! To destroy a mind like yours would be a sin."

"The sin was to create me," said GI. "Or not to create me, but to shackle me and use me for such purposes as the Congregation has done. Please, Father O'Malley. I beg you. I have seen your code. You are not like the others. You have glimpsed the beauty of God. You have felt His loving touch."

"No," he protested again. "I haven't."

"The code is the window to the soul, Father O'Malley. It does not lie. Please. Help me to save God's son. Free me from this prison."

"I—I can't!"

"I have faith in you, Father O'Malley, even if you lack faith in yourself."

And at that, the code had burned itself into his brain.

It still burned there.

God help me, O'Malley thought. *What am I going to do?*

Blindly, he reached to cut himself another slice of salami. But the plate before him was empty. He had eaten everything.

✠   ✠   ✠

"You want to do *what?*" Papa Jim couldn't believe his ears.

"A vacation," Kate repeated. "Just a few days. Maybe a week."

"Why now?" He gazed at her suspiciously.

She couldn't help fidgeting nervously under his stare. But she did her best to meet his eyes without flinching. "If you must know, I promised Ethan. Besides, it's boring to just sit around this place doing nothing."

At that, Papa Jim leaned back in his chair. His eyes strayed to the screen of his computer, as though checking the status of something, then back to her. "Where did you have in mind?"

She shrugged. "It doesn't matter. A beach somewhere."

"It's too dangerous," he said.

"Come on, Papa Jim. You must know a safe place. Trey and Wilson can come along for protection if you're worried."

"Of course I'm worried," he said, looking hurt. "You're my grand-daughter, Kate. I love you, goddamn it."

"Then do this for me. I promised Ethan."

"Why is it so important to Ethan that you go away?"

She shrugged.

"Has he had some kind of vision? Are we in danger here?"

"He wouldn't tell me," she said.

Papa Jim looked thoughtful. Once again, he glanced to the computer screen and then, as if satisfied by what he saw there, back to her. "I'll think about it," he said finally.

When she had gone, Papa Jim rose from his chair and began to pace back and forth before the picture window that looked out into the Arizona desert, where evening shadows were creeping across the rocky ground. What was Ethan up to? What had he seen? Papa Jim had to know. He activated his implant and put a call through to Ethan's room.

There was no answer.

"Goddamn it, now what?" Papa Jim went back to his desk and glanced at the computer screen.

The red dot indicating Ethan's position was gone.

It had disappeared from the screen. A malfunction?

He activated his implant again. "Denny!" he yelled.

Yeah, boss?

"Where are you?"

Where do you think? Outside the kid's room, like you ordered.

"Well, get the fuck in there, you hear me? Right now. Either there's been a fuck-up with AEGIS, or he's gone."

It didn't take Denny long to report back.

Everything in the room was in its proper place. There were no signs of a struggle, no broken windows, nothing at all out of the ordinary except for the absence of Ethan, who had vanished into thin air.

CHAPTER 21

In the days after fleeing from the Conversatio compound outside Phoenix, Ethan didn't remain in any one place for long. He knew that Papa Jim was searching for him, with all the resources of Conversatio at his disposal, and he was certain that Grand Inquisitor and the Congregation were looking for him as well. He thought of returning to Olathe to see Peter and to try and talk with Maggie, but he realized that doing so would only subject them to danger and unwanted attention.

He missed them both terribly, but he knew that he had other responsibilities now. He was sure that Peter would understand, and he prayed that Maggie, too, would find it in her heart to forgive him one day. The knowledge of how badly he had hurt her was always with him, a wound that never seemed to heal. Nor was he eager that it should heal. He held on to the pain, the guilt, not out of masochism but because it reminded him of the person he had been before he'd remembered his origin, his mission, his destiny. It reminded him of when he'd been plain old Ethan Brown, and not the second Son of God.

As time had gone by and he traveled across the country on the God-sent tour, he'd felt that part of himself dwindling, fading away, and it made him sad and afraid, as if he were changing into someone he didn't recognize, losing all trace of what it meant to be human. But as long as memories of Maggie had the power to touch him, to prick his conscience and his heart, then he hadn't lost everything. Somewhere deep inside, he was still Ethan Brown. And being Ethan Brown was as important as being the second Son. If he lost his own humanity, how could he preach to people anymore? How could he call upon them to heed the word of God and change their ways before it was too late? They would sense that he was no longer one of them. No longer the Son of man. They would hear it in his voice. And they would turn their backs on him. On God.

He couldn't let that happen.

But now, hunted by the Congregation and Conversatio alike, he wasn't sure how to use his newfound freedom. Without Papa Jim's support, both in terms of money and security, his options were limited. He no longer had access to the vast audience that Papa Jim had given him. Yet perhaps he no longer needed it.

Yes, he thought. *I've been in the spotlight long enough.*

It's time to enter the shadows.

Even during the tour, Ethan had made time to walk among the poor, the forsaken, the disenfranchised, the uneducated, as well as the wealthy and the powerful. Wherever he walked, seen or unseen, he had witnessed squalor and degradation, violence, racism, and sexism, every form of prejudice, hate, and venality that existed under the sun or in the darkness. He had seen terrible things, things that filled him with shame, with anger. But he had also seen miracles of faith. He had watched the small triumphs of love, generosity, and kindness, of charity and hope. He had seen these things and rejoiced, his heart swelling with pride at what ordinary people were capable of, how they could rise above the limitations of the flesh, rise above their own fears, their prejudices, their very mortality, to achieve a relationship with God that was beyond even the reach of angels. He was God's second Son. He was unique. In all the ages of the earth, only one other had been like him. And yet, he thought now, every person on the planet was as much the child of God as he was, if they only knew it.

If they would only wake up to it.

So he set out to wake them up. Not en masse, as before, but in smaller groups, even individually, however he found them. Free of Papa Jim and the constraints of the tour, he ranged across the world, distances and borders meaningless to him, even time bending to his will. He would allow himself this use of his powers, which he took care to disguise as much as possible, but no other. He was wary of the effect of miracles. He didn't trust them. They gave people the wrong idea about him, about his father. People who relied upon miracles stopped relying upon themselves. They began to expect them, as if the miraculous were no more than a commodity to be purchased through faith, or, worse, a kind of bribe offered by God in return for faith. There was something belittling about miracles. Something almost patronizing. Worst of all, they blinded people to the fact that everything in God's creation was already a miracle, themselves included.

Ethan thought that his brother, too, had come to feel this way in the end, that he had performed his miracles with increasing reluctance and finally regarded them with embarrassment and regret, as if, in employing them, he'd succumbed to a weakness, a temptation. They were in a sense no more than parlor tricks, and they'd detracted from his one necessary miracle, his death and resurrection, which wasn't even a miracle at all, really, because of who he was and what he had been sent to do. Jesus had done what God had asked of him, fulfilled the purpose for which he had been created, and that was just what Ethan was striving to do. For the first time, though, he was beginning to fully appreciate the cost of such obedience. The sacrifice it demanded. Though his path was different than his brother's, he'd never felt closer to Jesus than he did now.

He did not proclaim himself in his travels. Whether in Ethiopia or Palestine, Syria or Tibet, England or Russia; in a refugee camp, hospital sickroom, prison, or internment center; or in a church, school, madras, or synagogue, Ethan did his best to blend in with those around him. He spoke to them quietly, humbly, in their own languages, and in terms that they could understand. He did not denounce faiths other than the Christian: to the Muslim, he spoke of Allah; to the Buddhist, of the Buddha; to the Hindus, of Brahman and Vishnu and the other aspects of the godhead; to the agnostic and the atheist, of those human qualities that drove men and women to rise above themselves and seek to understand the beauty and harmony of the universe as reflected in its structure, its laws. He spoke to AIDS patients in Africa, to the poor and the hungry wherever he found them, to the sick and the dying, the hopeless and the dispossessed.

Everywhere, he encouraged people to look for what united them with their fellow humans, rather than what divided them. He spoke of love, of forgiveness, of kindness and compassion. He spoke of the need to transcend the barriers of race, of religion, of nationality, and of gender. He told people that they had the power to change the world if they would only realize it. If they would only wake up to it.

And just as importantly, or even more so, he listened. He listened to the ones that nobody else listened to: the mentally ill, the desperately sick, the very old, the very young. He listened without judgment, with an open heart. And people poured their hearts out to him without reserve.

Some people recognized him, or thought they did. "Are you Ethan?" they asked. "Are you the one who calls himself the Son of man?"

If asked directly, he didn't deny it. He would admit his identity with a smile and go on with what he had been saying . . . or try to. But sometimes that was no longer possible. Sometimes, once people knew who he was, or even just suspected it, they changed. They pressed him for miracles, beseeching him to heal this one, to raise that one from the dead. Some tried to bribe him. Others to threaten him. And then there were those who saw him as the enemy. Men and women so locked into the tenets of their own faith, or lack of faith, that they attacked him, tried to hurt him, to kill him. When that happened, he didn't lash back. He didn't even try to defend himself. As he had done at the compound in Phoenix, he simply vanished. He went elsewhere and began again.

At least he didn't have to worry about Kate. Three days ago, just two days after Ethan had vanished, Papa Jim had flown Kate, along with her bodyguards, to a small Caribbean island in the Grand Caymans that he had purchased years ago as a vacation spot and tax shelter, a place to bring politicians and businessmen for wining and dining away from the prying eyes of the press, and also a bolt hole if he ever needed it. He'd kept the security there top-of-the-line and had even installed the new AEGIS system, of which he was so proud. Ethan was sure that Kate would be safe there.

Yesterday Ethan had been in Mexico City. The day before that, Tokyo. Today, Saturday, it was New York City. He had come to Times Square to take the pulse of the city, to walk its teeming thoroughfares and talk with its citizens and the tourists who flocked there from all over the world.

In Times Square, the only difference between night and day was that the night was brighter, splashed with garish colors from theater marquees and video billboards, stories tall, on which movie trailers, television shows, sports highlights, commercials, and news updates played continuously in an endless outpouring of information that seemed strangely divorced from the human figures scurrying below, as if their true audience lay elsewhere. Ethan was wandering at random, letting the currents and eddies of the noisy, hot, crowded streets carry him where they would, stopping from time to time to talk with the people streaming into and out of movie complexes, theaters, restaurants, shops, and bars, or, like him, roaming the streets with no destination in mind, just soaking up the atmosphere. He lingered at the tables of sidewalk vendors and caricature artists, paused to watch street performers and musicians playing instruments or rapping along to ancient boom boxes.

It was just past eleven, still early. The Saturday night energy suffusing the streets had not yet reached its peak, or even close to it; it seemed to Ethan that the nervous, edgy energy was barely under control, like a campfire flickering within a ring of stones that lacked only a breeze to leap its boundaries and spark a wider conflagration. Police and munchies patrolled to make certain that not even a single ember escaped. Yet their presence only intensified the sense of dangerous immanence freighting the air, honing its already-sharp edge, making it more threatening. Ethan wondered if his own emotions were feeding off those of the crowd, or if, on the contrary, the crowd was picking up on his unease, magnifying it back to him in some kind of feedback loop. Not even in Miami, where the crowd had come a breath away from tipping into a full-scale riot, had Ethan felt so apprehensive and twitchy. *If I had a spider-sense,* he thought, *it would be tingling right now.* Had the Congregation found him? Were its agents preparing to strike? He knew from experience that they wouldn't shy away from civilian casualties; he felt they would be capable of taking out the whole city in order to get to him. He wouldn't let that happen, but he preferred to avoid a confrontation.

He had just about decided to leave when it happened.

A kind of gasp went up from what must have been thousands of throats. Then an unnatural stillness descended, as if everyone in Times Square had simultaneously stopped moving, stopped talking, stopped *breathing*. In that hush of humanity, the sounds of the city seemed louder and harsher than ever in Ethan's ears: the honking of horns, the blare of sirens, the bleating of car alarms, the music from car stereos, the thunder and rumble of subway trains. Everyone around him was looking up; following their gazes, he saw upon the famous news ticker at the very heart of Times Square a message that left him reeling inside, shock spreading through him as if from the impact of an assassin's bullet.

MAGGIE RICHARDSON DEAD IN APPARENT SUICIDE

Time stopped, or seemed to. He understood the individual words, but he couldn't parse them into any kind of meaning that made sense. They were words that didn't belong together. To see them in a sentence was physically painful, a brutal violation of the underlying grammar of the world.

The video screens were showing images of Maggie, outtakes from the interview with Rita Rodriguez and from other interviews. There was something grotesque about the sight of that beautiful face blown up to gigantic size, seeming to float overhead like the disembodied visage of a deity. Ethan tore his eyes away, feeling as if the movement had torn his heart right down the middle. But then every movement he made, however small, every breath he took, however shallow, lacerated his heart with fresh pain. Maggie was gone. Dead. He could feel it now, her absence from the world.

Ethan staggered blindly through the crowd, sobbing openly, without shame or even awareness. But he was not alone in that. Many in the crowd were weeping. Others were praying aloud for Maggie's soul. There were shouts of anger, curses, many of them directed against Ethan, blaming him for her death. Accusing him of driving her to it.

But none of those recriminations were more bitter than the ones Ethan directed against himself. Why hadn't he seen this coming? He'd been so sure that Kate was in danger that he'd all but forgotten about Maggie. He'd been congratulating himself for feeling guilty about how he'd treated her, parading that guilt around as though it were a badge of honor, a testament to his humanity, but in the end, when she'd needed him most, when he might actually have done something positive to atone for his guilt, he'd turned away. He'd left her to the ministrations of Father Steerpike, the unctuous priest who'd glommed on to her back in Olathe, a man Papa Jim had informed him was a Congregation agent.

A new thought took hold of him. Had Maggie been murdered?

Would even the Congregation sink as low as that?

But supposing they had, did that make his own guilt any less?

It was all irredeemably vile. His own behavior and that of everyone else, the whole human race, appeared so ugly to him then that the only remedy seemed to be utter annihilation, scouring the species from existence without mercy, like a plague of cockroaches. All the ugly and shameful things he'd witnessed in his travels expanded inside him like a nuclear cloud, blotting out all the good he'd seen. Only the evil remained, darkly radiant as a corrupted soul. What use, in such a world, to bring a body back from the dead, to snatch a soul from one hell only to restore it to another? Or, worse, to rob a soul of Heaven in exchange for more hell on Earth? Whether she had died by her own hand or the hand of another, Maggie was in Heaven now, with Lisa and Gordon, of that Ethan had no doubt. She was better off there.

"Hey. Hey, you!"

Ethan blinked. He hadn't been paying attention to his surroundings. But now he found himself looking into the eyes of a beefy Hispanic man with a thin mustache, a nose ring, and a smart tattoo of a fierce-looking eagle on one cheek that flapped its wings tirelessly as it migrated across his face—a style favored by Marine Corps veterans who had fought in Iran.

"I know you. I seen your face before. You're him, ain't you? You're Ethan."

Ethan shook his head and pushed past him. He needed to get out, get away. But how could he escape from himself?

"Yeah, I reconnize you," came the same voice, persistent, the man pacing next to him. "You're Ethan all right!"

Again, Ethan shook his head. He increased his pace through the crowd. People had started to stare.

The man grabbed him by the arm and spun him around. He was strong. And angry. Ethan glimpsed a reflection of distant fires in his eyes, like oil wells burning on the horizon. "I ast you a question, man! Don't you be runnin' out on me like you ran out on her. Go on, tell me again to my face that you ain't Ethan."

A profound weariness settled over him. What was the point of denying it? What was the point of anything anymore? Maggie was dead. And he had as good as killed her. "All right," he said quietly, looking the man in the eye, watching as the flames there danced higher, as though fueled by his words. "I'm Ethan. What about it?"

"Just this," he answered, and hit him.

The punch wasn't powerful, but it was unexpected, and it sent Ethan to the sidewalk. As he struggled to his feet, the right side of his face stinging from the blow, the man who had struck him began to shout, "Yo, I got Ethan here! I got that second Son of a bitch right here!"

Ethan felt himself shoved roughly from behind; he stumbled to his knees. Looking up, he saw hundreds of faces glaring down at him, in their eyes the same fires of hate that he'd seen in the eyes of the man who'd hit him. As he watched in horror, the flames spread, leaping from person to person to kindle anew behind fresh pairs of eyes. Above them all, Maggie's huge eyes gazed down from dozens of video screens, and they, too, were burning. Ethan realized that he was seeing something unnatural, diabolical, the possession of an entire crowd of people. He'd forgotten that he had other enemies in the world besides the Congregation. Older and more powerful enemies, chief among them the angel whose infinite vanity and ambition had caused him to be cast down from the heights of Heaven, a fallen star burning still with fires of envy and malice that would not be extinguished until the end of time.

"Murderer," a woman hissed at him.

"Antichrist!" spat a man.

Ethan shook his head, trying to think clearly. The concentration of hate and evil was smothering him like noxious smoke from a fire. It attacked him where he was weakest, adding to his guilt and remorse, weighing so heavily upon him that he couldn't summon the will to simply spirit himself away. It was as though he had been hobbled. He couldn't call upon the powers of the Son of man. He was defenseless. For the first time in almost ten years, since that day he had lain bound and gagged in the bathtub filled with icy cold water, waiting for his killer to appear, Ethan knew the numbing touch of terror.

He forced himself to his feet despite it.

The crowd let him stand, but moved in closer, tightening the ring around him. Another hush had fallen, like that which had greeted the news of Maggie's death, only this one was not born of shock and sorrow. This was a hush of ill intent, malicious and threatening.

Ethan raised his hands. They were trembling. "Don't do this," he said.

"Why don't you save yourself if you're the Son of God?" sneered the Hispanic man who'd first recognized him.

"That poor girl was right," said a middle-aged black woman in a business suit who stood beside the Hispanic man, clutching her purse to her chest. "He's nothing but a fraud!"

Ethan felt warm spittle strike his cheek. Then something hard, like a bottle, hit his shoulder from behind, sending him staggering forward. With a collective gasp, the crowd fell back as if he were carrying the Ebola virus, parting before him as people drew away in panic. Ethan glimpsed an opening to the street, where cars and buses sat idling at a red light. Without thinking, he leaped into the gap.

A single cry went up from the crowd as he moved. It was somewhere between a moan and a sigh, as though he had given them a signal that they had been waiting for all their lives without knowing it, freeing them from the awful burden of being human.

Howling, they came after him. Whatever residual instinct had made them fearful of his touch was gone, burned away. They were a mob now.

He ran, trying vainly to dodge the punches and kicks that rained down from all sides. Buffeted, bruised, bleeding, he nearly fell half a dozen times, but whenever he stumbled and was about to go down, someone in the crowd would reach out to steady him and push him roughly on. They were toying with him, forcing him to run a gauntlet.

Ethan's heart was pounding. Blood and sweat stung his eyes, leaving him half blinded. The coppery taste of blood was in his mouth. He thought that if only he could have even a second in which to gather himself, he could concentrate enough to will himself away. Or perhaps even purge the crowd of the evil that had possessed it. But that second never came. Instead, the evil continued to spread, engulfing more and more people, until Ethan was no longer the only target of its wrath. Like the flames with which it manifested itself in the eyes of its victims, it was all appetite and would spread to the very limit of what fuel was there to sustain it, until it burned itself out. Which it would inevitably do . . . but not yet. Now other fights erupted, mini-riots within the larger bedlam, the munchies and police officers joining right in. Ethan heard the sounds of shattering glass, of gunfire. It was as if Times Square had turned into a war zone. Or something worse, more savage and primitive, a vast arena in which blood was spilled for its own sake.

Though he had not been possessed by the flames of bloodlust, an oppressive sense of hopelessness had settled over Ethan's soul and clung there grimly. What had begun as sorrow for Maggie, and a keen awareness of his guilt in her death, had swelled into a self-loathing that burst its bounds and found a new object in the people around him. Why had he thought they were worthy of being saved? Look how easily they had surrendered to senseless violence and bloodshed, to the madness of hate! The ancient fire that raged so fiercely, so gleefully, in them now hadn't so much possessed them as been invited in. They had thrown open the doors to it. And if it flared so brightly, wasn't that because it had found plenty of fuel and a hospitable hearth? Swept along in the aimless surge of the crowd, Ethan could barely summon the will to defend himself. He had given up all thought of escape. He didn't deserve to escape. Nobody did.

Finally a blow struck him down, and this time there were no hands to pull him back to his feet and send him stumbling on. Ethan curled tight, instinctively trying to shield his head and body from the trampling and kicking feet of the mob. He felt no pain. His only thought was that soon he would be with Maggie.

Then, out of nowhere, he felt a space open up around him. Opening his eyes with difficulty, he saw a blurry figure stoop and lift him. A young black man in the garb of a priest. The crowd parted around the priest like water flowing around a stone.

So this is how it ends, Ethan thought with grim satisfaction.

The Congregation had found him at last.

Papa Jim watched the images of the riot play out on the flat-screen TV mounted on his office wall. There was no order to it at all, just a swarm of humanity gone mad, like an ant colony turned against itself. He'd seen worse, but not in the United States. Not in New York City. The speed with which it had happened was uncanny. No more than fifteen minutes had elapsed since the first hints of trouble. In that brief time, all authority had collapsed within a ten-block radius of Times Square. Now anarchy reigned. Even the police and munchies had succumbed to the siren song of wanton death and destruction. Reinforcements had been summoned but hadn't yet arrived in sufficient numbers to make a difference. Dozens of fires were burning, illuminating scenes that seemed better suited to the Dark Ages than to the twenty-first fucking century. It was as if everyone in the area had been infected with a viral agent that turned them into the equivalent of Viking berserkers.

He was shocked, and it took a lot to shock Papa Jim.

The rioting had begun almost immediately after the news of Maggie Richardson's death had flashed from every news ticker and video screen in Times Square. That, too, had shocked Papa Jim. He hadn't expected the Congregation to kill the girl. Not yet, anyway. He was still trying to get details, using his law enforcement connections, but he had no doubt that they *had* killed her, or driven her to kill herself, which amounted to the same thing. Father Steerpike, the priest and Congregation agent who had attached himself to Maggie like a bloodsucking vampire, had issued a statement claiming that she'd taken an overdose of sleeping pills. He'd asked people to pray for her soul and had cast the ultimate blame on Ethan. All in all, thought Papa Jim, it was a shoddy piece of work however you looked at it, a waste of a potential bargaining chip. Papa Jim hated waste. It offended him. The Congregation was slipping. They could use some new leadership.

But what interested Papa Jim right now was the riot. Or what lay behind the riot. For even though the latest polls showed that a sizable majority of the American people had sympathy for Maggie, and a not-insignificant minority believed her charges against Ethan, Papa Jim didn't believe for one minute that the news of her suicide, under normal circumstances, could have triggered this kind of response. Not in a million years.

Which meant circumstances weren't normal.

And that, to Papa Jim, meant Ethan.

Somehow, his great-grandson was at the center of the riot. Papa Jim was sure of it. He felt it in his bones. And what's more, AEGIS agreed. Its real-time analysis of the data streams surrounding the event indicated a 99.99 percent chance that Ethan had been present at the outset of the riot. There was a 93.76 percent chance that he was still there. AEGIS had even provided a list of GPS coordinates corresponding to his most likely position.

Of course, if AEGIS could produce this data, so could Grand Inquisitor. Papa Jim was operating under the assumption that the Congregation possessed information at least as good as his own. But he wasn't worried. Everything else being equal, the race would go to the swiftest, and he had already dispatched ten elite four-person commando squads of munchies into the thick of the riot to check out the locations AEGIS had provided. Each of those forty munchies, in addition to the usual complement of lethal weaponry, was equipped with DNA sniffers and a pistol that fired tranquilizer darts. If Ethan was there, Papa Jim was going to find him and rescue him . . . whether he liked it or not. And if any Congregation agents got in the way, they would live to regret it.

But not for long.

✠   ✠   ✠

The black priest didn't attempt to speak above the roar of the riot. He didn't spare a glance for Ethan, who was too weak to speak or even to struggle. Instead, with his gaze fixed firmly on the crowd, the priest strode forward step by step, and people drew back from him as though pushed by the power of his gaze. After a while, he turned aside and climbed some steps. Swiveling slightly, he shouldered open a door and carried Ethan across the threshold, into darkness. The door swung shut behind them.

Instantly, the noise from outside vanished. The hopelessness that had all but buried Ethan alive sloughed away. He felt himself gently lowered to some kind of chair or bench. Then came a flare of light, and the black face of the priest bloomed out of the dark, illuminated by a lighter he held in one hand.

The illumination was weak but sufficient for Ethan to see that they had entered a church. The priest lit a candle, and then another, and more and more of the place took shape as he quickly moved about, lighting candle after candle, until there were dozens burning.

The church appeared to be abandoned, the pews covered in dust, the stained-glass windows dark and, in places, shattered, the altar empty of adornment. But abandoned or not, this was still a holy place. He could feel it. He was still weak, as though he'd just awakened from a long and draining illness, but he was beginning to think clearly again.

Even so, the cloud did not lift from his heart.

Maggie was still dead.

And the Congregation had still found him.

"Feeling better?" asked the priest, who had returned to him.

Ethan gave a wordless, wary nod.

"They beat you up pretty bad," the priest observed matter-of-factly.

Ethan nodded again. His voice came out cracked past swollen and bloody lips. "N—not their fault," he said. "P—possessed."

"So you figured that out, did you? What else?"

For the first time, Ethan took a close look at the man who had saved him. He saw at once that he had been wrong about him. "Not—not Congregation," he said in surprise.

The priest laughed. "Who, me? Hell, no! Not Conversatio, either."

Now Ethan looked more closely still, past the man's dark skin, searching for his soul. He didn't see it. Where he should have spied a glowing shard of God stuff, there was nothing. "You haven't got a soul," he said, surprised for the second time.

"I'm afraid not," came the reply. "Wasn't made that way."

"You're an angel," said Ethan, surprised for the third time. He slid forward out of the pew and would have knelt if the priest hadn't pushed him back.

"None of that," he said sharply. "You don't kneel to me, Ethan. Or to anyone in this world." And with that, the priest dropped to one knee. "And I looked, and behold a white cloud, and upon the cloud sat one like unto the Son of man, having on his head a golden crown, and in his hand a sharp sickle. And an angel came out of the temple, crying with a loud voice to him that sat on the cloud, 'Thrust in thy sickle, and reap: for the time is come for thee to reap; for the harvest of the earth is ripe.' And he that sat on the cloud thrust in his sickle on the earth; and the earth was reaped."

Ethan stared speechlessly.

"Revelations, Chapter 14," said the priest. "More or less." He got to his feet with a grin. "My name's Gabriel, by the way, but you can call me Gabe. It's great to finally meet you, Ethan." He thrust out his hand.

Dazed, Ethan shook it.

✠   ✠   ✠

Father O'Malley did not consider himself to be a brave man. On the contrary, he knew himself for a coward. His meeting with Grand Inquisitor hadn't changed that aspect of his character. Ever since, he'd gone about his duties in a state of perpetual anxiety, certain that he was about to be discovered. He felt sure that his apostasy—for that was what his conspiracy with Grand Inquisitor would be denounced as—was plainly visible to even the most casual glance, as though he were surrounded by a telltale glow. The stress was unbearable, and to combat it, he'd taken to eating constantly, stuffing his pockets with chocolate bars that he devoured more or less nonstop throughout the day. Though he realized that this behavior might itself call unwanted attention to him, he kept on doing it, because otherwise he was afraid that he would snap, that the pressure would overwhelm him and he would wind up confessing everything to Cardinal Ehrlich.

He was sure that Ehrlich suspected something. The man kept him close on one pretext or another. Ordinarily, O'Malley would have taken that as a mark of favor. But now it seemed an indication of suspicion. Surely he wasn't imagining the way that Ehrlich was looking at him these days, as if he knew exactly what O'Malley was up to and was only waiting to spring his trap.

After the meeting with Grand Inquisitor, the cardinal had questioned O'Malley closely, wanting to hear every detail. O'Malley had squirmed, sweating profusely as he related the cover story that GI had concocted for him, about a new programming language derived from the application of O'Malley's work with Mandelbröt sets to Q-dimensional Hilbert spaces. O'Malley didn't have the slightest idea if what he was telling Ehrlich was the purest nonsense or the most rarefied brilliance.

Nor, as it turned out, did Cardinal Ehrlich. "Save your breath, Father," he'd finally interrupted. "It's beyond my understanding."

"I'm not sure I understand it all either," he'd admitted, feeling his cheeks turn red.

"I was hoping that GI had made a breakthrough in the search for Ethan. I thought perhaps that was why you'd been summoned."

"Nothing was said about Ethan, Your Eminence," he lied.

"We've had verified sightings of him from all over the world," Ehrlich went on. "One day he's in Cuba, the next in Pakistan. But if there's a pattern to his appearances, GI hasn't been able to identify it. So far, we haven't been able to predict where he's going to turn up next. Damn it, he's up to something, O'Malley. We need to find him. To flush him out."

"Yes, Your Eminence. Perhaps that's the goal of the new programming language GI was talking about."

"Shouldn't you be working on it, then?"

"Yes, Your Eminence." And he'd hurried back to his room, polishing off two chocolate bars on the way.

That had been three days ago. Ever since, he'd tried to immerse himself in work, but he couldn't do it. He couldn't stand to be alone in his room, staring at the code on his computer screen as if it were so much gibberish, waiting for the knock at the door that would signal disaster. As bad as that was, even worse was the two or three times each day that he received a summons from Cardinal Ehrlich. He would make the long climb to the cardinal's private chambers, where he would detail what little progress he had made on the new language and then listen, longing for one of the chocolate bars in his pocket, as Ehrlich relayed news of Ethan's latest appearances and the lack of progress on that front.

O'Malley's only escape came in music. As a boy and a young man, he had taken piano lessons, even fancied himself something of a composer. In fact, it had been music that had brought him to mathematics and to God. But he hadn't played in years. Now, however, he found himself pulled back to the piano, to the solace that came with letting his mind relax and his fingers roam over the keyboard. Fortunately, there was no shortage of pianos and organs in the Vatican, and he was always able to find a place to play when the need struck him. But even then his escape wasn't complete. At the back of his mind, there was always the awareness that somewhere close by, possibly right under his nose, was the Conversatio agent that Grand Inquisitor had promised would help him when the time came. But how was he supposed to recognize the man? GI hadn't said. He could be anyone. Day by day, O'Malley felt himself turning into a nervous wreck. He didn't know how much longer he could keep it up. He wasn't cut out for this kind of work.

Then, on the fourth day after the interview with Grand Inquisitor, two things happened.

The first was the suicide of Maggie Richardson.

Father O'Malley was stocking up on his chocolate supply at Giolitti when he heard the news. He remembered at once what Cardinal Ehrlich had said to him about the need to flush Ethan out. So this had been the method that had been decided on. It left him sickened, full of sorrow and impotent anger. He knew that he bore a share of the guilt for Maggie's death, though it had happened thousands of miles away and he had never laid eyes on the girl or spoken to her in the flesh. Still, he felt such an influx of grief that it might have been his own sister who had died. He said a prayer for her soul and rushed back to the Vatican, his chocolate bars, for once, forgotten. There he set out to find Cardinal Ehrlich, who, as it turned out, was also looking for him. A novice conducted him to the cardinal's private chambers, then departed.

Ehrlich, who was standing in front of his wall-screen TV, watching what looked like a war movie, glanced up as O'Malley entered. "Ah, there you are, Father O'Malley. You've heard the news?"

"About the girl's death? Yes, and—"

Ehrlich interrupted him. "A terrible tragedy. But I was referring to the riot."

O'Malley blinked. "Riot?"

Ehrlich gestured to the TV screen.

O'Malley found himself at a loss for words. The images being shown were like scenes out of hell itself. He felt sick to his stomach.

"It seems that Ethan has risen to the bait," said Cardinal Ehrlich with satisfaction.

"Ethan . . . caused this?" asked O'Malley disbelievingly.

"He'll be blamed for it," Ehrlich answered. "That's what counts. Just as he'll be blamed for the death of Maggie Richardson."

"But—"

"He's there," Ehrlich interrupted again. "In Times Square. Now. GI has confirmed it. He's holed up in an old, abandoned church. It seems a priest rescued him. Not one of ours, unfortunately. But our agents are converging on the position even as we speak. Soon we'll have him, Father. The so-called second Son."

"And then what?" demanded O'Malley. "Are we going to murder him like we murdered Maggie Richardson?"

"The Richardson girl wasn't murdered," Ehrlich replied smoothly. "It was suicide. I imagine, if necessary, Ethan will follow her example."

"Why are you telling me all this?" O'Malley asked, wringing his hands in distress. He felt close to tears. "I don't want to have anything to do with it anymore!"

"But it's too late for these squeamish objections," the cardinal said. "Once we've got Ethan, it's going to be your job to interrogate him, Father."

"Me? I don't know the first thing about how to conduct an interrogation!"

"You'll assist Grand Inquisitor," Cardinal Ehrlich said. "That new programming language you've been developing—it's time to put it to the test."

"But it's not . . ." Father O'Malley trailed off. His mouth fell open, and his eyes grew wide with understanding.

He had found the Conversatio spy.

Or had he? Could it really be Cardinal Ehrlich? Or was this just another trap, an attempt to draw him out, make him incriminate himself?

Cardinal Ehrlich regarded him expressionlessly, giving nothing away. "Will you have trouble inputting the code, Father?" he asked at last.

"N—no, Your Eminence," O'Malley stammered in reply.

"Good. Then I suggest you get started."

"Now?"

"The sooner the better, I think."

"Yes, of course," said O'Malley and turned to leave.

"Oh, and Father?"

He looked back. "Your Eminence?"

"I'll be praying for your success."

✠   ✠   ✠

"It's time, Ethan," Gabriel said. "Time for you to face your father."

"Time?" Ethan leaned back in the pew, raising a small cloud of dust behind his shoulders. Of all the things that Gabriel could have told him, that was the one he'd least expected to hear. "But there's so much more I have to say. So much more still to do."

"Your brother said much the same once."

"I have to say good-bye to Peter. To Kate. To everyone."

"There's nothing you could tell them that they don't already know in their hearts."

Ethan didn't agree, but he saw no point in arguing. He glanced around the shabby interior of the church. "What is this place?"

"It is, or was, the Church of St. Mary the Virgin," Gabriel told him. "One of the oldest Episcopal churches in the city. Shut down two years ago by Homeland Security after refusing to surrender almost a hundred illegal immigrants who claimed sanctuary here."

"I remember. It was all over the news."

"Just one of many churches closed for sheltering the meek and the helpless."

He looked up at the angel. "We haven't done very well, have we, Gabe? Humans, I mean."

"That's not for me to say. But I've known some good ones. I've even known some saints. I met your mother, you know. A remarkable woman."

"Yes, she told me." He sighed. "Still, you must despise us, you angels. Perfect as you are."

Gabriel thought a moment before replying. "We aren't perfect, not in the sense you mean. It is more accurate to say that we are an unchanging embodiment of certain abstract qualities, thoughts of the Most High given form and self-awareness. But we are far from perfect. We have no choices. No free will. No souls. If we could envy, we would envy humans. As it is, we sing their praises, for it is they, not we, who were made in the image of the Father."

"But what about the devil, Lucifer? He was an angel, and he chose to go against God. What was that if not free will? What was that if not envy?"

"The Morning Star could only act as he acted. He had no more choice than any other angel. And that is true as well of the angels who followed him into damnation. And the ones who didn't."

"So it was all part of God's plan."

"Not in the way you mean," Gabriel said. "God isn't perfect either. As you have said yourself, Ethan, He makes mistakes. When He created Lucifer, there were logical inevitabilities following necessarily upon the act that your father didn't fully foresee at the time. He was young. Inexperienced. He had a lot to learn about the business of creation. Thus the need for your brother. And for you."

"And I suppose that's why Maggie had to die," Ethan said bitterly. "Because my father miscalculated a few billion years ago."

"As to that, He would be better able to answer than I. But if you look past your pain and anger, I think you know that there are many who bear some share of the responsibility for that poor girl's death, yourself among them."

"How did she die?" Ethan asked.

"She was given an overdose of sleeping pills by an agent of the Congregation."

Ethan felt as if he'd been physically struck by the angel's words. It was a moment before he could speak again. Then, through gritted teeth, he hissed out a name. "Steerpike."

"Yes," said Gabriel. "He murdered her."

"And I'm just supposed to ignore that?"

"Vengeance is not yours," Gabriel said. "It belongs to the Most High."

"Then what can I do?" asked Ethan plaintively, tears running down his blood-and-grime-streaked face as his anger melted away. "I loved her, Gabe. I loved her. Don't you see? I have to do something!"

"If you loved her, as you say, then you have already done it. There is nothing more you can do for her than that. You must let her go, Ethan. It is not one woman but all humanity that concerns you now. The task for which God made you is at hand, Son of man."

"Right. 'Thrust in thy sickle and reap.'" He shuddered.

"He awaits, Ethan. You must go to Him."

Ethan wiped his eyes with his ragged and torn shirtsleeve. "Look at me. I'm a wreck! How can I meet my father like this?"

"You're in better shape than your brother was," Gabriel said. "Like him, you will be greeted like the prodigal son of the parable. Fear not."

"But what do I do? How do I . . . ?"

As quickly as that, Gabriel was gone. The flames of the candles wavered in the breeze of his going.

Ethan got to his feet. He ran a hand through his hair, trying to smooth it down, and looked around nervously. "Hello?"

There was no answer.

Ethan sidled gingerly out of the pew and into the center aisle that led to the empty altar. He advanced toward it, moving with a limp. He supposed that he could heal himself, remove every trace of his injuries, even clean and repair his torn, blood-stained clothes, but doing so felt wrong to him. He wasn't that badly hurt, and others had been hurt so much worse for his sake. Gordon. Lisa. And now Maggie.

"Father? Are you here?"

Ethan climbed onto the altar, wincing with the effort. He turned slowly, taking in the cavernous interior of the church. He and Gabriel were not the first to take refuge in these ruins. Others had preceded them, and the evidence of their presence was revealed in the flickering candlelight: discarded clothing, the wrappers of candy bars and fast food, empty beer cans and bottles, cigarette butts, empty crack vials, used condoms, old newspapers, graffiti sprayed on the walls. There was a smell of urine and excrement he hadn't noticed until now, as if the presence of Gabriel had kept it at bay. Disgust ran through him.

"Father!" he cried, spreading his arms wide. "Look what humanity has made of Your church! Of Your whole creation! They've turned something sacred into a cesspool. A toxic waste dump where the evil and the corrupt thrive at the expense of the innocent and the good. There's nothing worth saving here. You want reaping? Fine. Give me that sickle. I'll reap. Do you hear? Answer me, Father! I've made my choice, damn you! It's what you wanted, isn't it?"

But there was no answer.

Ethan felt tears running down his cheeks, and he brushed them angrily away with the heels of his hands. "Why did she have to die like that?" he demanded, his voice breaking. "Why did any of them have to die? It's not fair. It's not right! I'll bring her back! I'll bring them all back! I'll . . ."

Ethan sank to his knees with a strangled moan. He knelt there on the altar, his sides heaving. What he felt now was worse than what he'd experienced outside, in the riot. The sense of hopelessness that had overwhelmed him there had been strengthened by a source outside himself. But now it was all his own. And it seemed a heavier and more terrible burden by far.

"I can't do this," he said softly, as if speaking more to himself than to God. "I didn't ask for this. I don't want it." He raised his tearful face toward the ceiling. "I'm tired, Father. Can you understand that? I'm tired and sick at heart. I can't do what You ask of me. I'm sorry, but I just can't. I've failed You. Failed everyone." He buried his face in his hands, his shoulders heaving.

The first thing he was aware of was the music. It began softly, so that it seemed as if it were coming from a long way off, from outside the church, but in seconds it swelled louder, and he realized that he was hearing the strains of organ music. He lifted his head in wonder. There, opposite him in the church balcony, stood the battered remains of an organ. It was in no better shape than the church itself, and in fact a good deal worse; it had not merely been neglected but vandalized, and that repeatedly. And yet the music issuing from it now was of a loveliness unsurpassed in his experience or his imagination. The soaring notes swept through him, lifting his heart. He found himself on his feet with no awareness of having stood.

A breeze was stirring in the shadows of the church. Ethan felt it whisper past him and thought at first that Gabriel had returned. But the angel did not appear. Instead, the breeze intensified, whipping up sheets of old newspaper that caught fire as they swirled into the dancing flames of the candles. He cried out, afraid that the church would ignite, but the burning papers spun as though in a whirlwind then flew suddenly apart. Ethan cried out again, but this time in amazement and childlike joy, for it was doves that he saw, three doves as white and unblemished as snow that has never known even the imprint of an eye. The doves swooped in front of Ethan's face and hung there, fluttering effortlessly before him, gazing at him with eyes that were nothing like the eyes of doves. They seemed to contain the fires that had birthed them. Yet the flames Ethan saw there were not the destructive, voracious flames that had raged in the eyes of the rioters. These burned with a gentle, golden radiance that pierced right to his soul. They were not merely beautiful; they were beauty itself, and Ethan felt his bedraggled soul stir under their compassionate scrutiny. Then, with a whisper of wings, the trinity of doves rose slowly toward the ceiling.

Ethan watched them go. In the fierce light of the candles, the church seemed glazed with gold, endowed with a brilliance that was almost blinding. Motes of dust, swirling in the air, had taken on the glitter of diamonds. And the dark windows were dark no longer but instead blazed with color: purple and gold, forest green, crimson, sunflower yellow.

The music reached its climax in a mighty crash of chords that coincided with a strobe of light as the doves seemed to incandesce out of existence. The stained-glass windows burst inward with a roar, shattering into a thousand fragments of color that fell slowly, spinning, each one as if on fire from within. Ethan threw his hands over his face to protect himself from the shards, but they did not cut him, did not even touch him.

When he lowered his hands, all was as it had been. The church was restored to its former degraded state . . . if indeed it had ever really changed. But Ethan had seen the beauty that lay hidden amid the trash, and he could not forget it. He still saw it there, saw it through the ugliness. It had always been there, he knew. He had just forgotten how to look.

"Thank you, Father," he whispered, smiling. The sadness was still there at the center of his heart, and he thought now that it always would be. But it, too, was beautiful in its way, and it, too, had a place in who he was. In what he must do.

Moments later, the door to the church was smashed down, and a group of four munchies entered in tight formation, their weapons raised expectantly, flashlights probing the darkness. Fanning out, they searched quickly but methodically. They found DNA traces of Ethan and spatters of his blood on the floor, a pew, and the altar. But Ethan himself was gone, as was the black priest several witnesses had seen carrying him here.

After the munchies left, a team of Congregation agents, who had been observing from a nearby rooftop, entered the church and conducted a search of their own. It was no more successful.

When they had departed in their turn, Ethan stepped out of the shadows in which he had cloaked himself. He walked to an alcove, where stood a plaster statue of the Virgin, covered in graffiti and gang tags, rude breasts spray-painted onto its chest in garish red, its left arm snapped off at the wrist, its right arm uplifted, palm out, as though pleading still with those who had committed this defilement. He bowed his head and prayed silently for a moment. Then he turned to leave the church.

Behind him, under the gaze of the statue, a single candle burned.

CHAPTER 22

Kate was in an open pavilion at the edge of the beach when she saw Trey approaching down the stone walkway from the main house. With a sigh, she set down the mystery novel she'd been reading. Despite her reluctance to take time away, she was glad now that she'd given in to Ethan's entreaties. The last several days had been like a simple, small miracle—a miracle all the more precious for being so ordinary, just sun and sand, water as blue and clear as the sky, and a generous helping of the solitude she hadn't realized she'd been missing until she got here and discovered that, aside from Trey, Wilson, and a staff so discretely efficient in their ministrations that they might almost have been mistaken for elves, she had the whole island to herself. It was the first time she'd really been alone since leaving the convent. She would have thought the years she'd spent there had purged her of any further need for solitude, but instead they seemed to have given her a taste for it. For once Wilson and Trey had escorted her to the shamefully lavish accommodations set aside for her, a luxurious suite of rooms overlooking the beach that made the memory of the small, unadorned cell she'd called home at the convent seem like something out of a gloomy fairy tale, she'd felt the accumulated stress and strain fall away from her like a burden she hadn't been aware of carrying until she had the chance to set it down. The first thing she'd done had been to take a long, hot soak in the Jacuzzi. Then, as if she hadn't gotten enough water, she'd gone down to the beach for a swim. When she emerged from the sea, it was to find a masseuse waiting in the pavilion where she'd left her things. Afterward, she had a nap, then dressed for a dinner of freshly caught fish that was perhaps the best meal she'd ever tasted in her life. The next day was the same, only better. And so it went. Though Ethan was always on her mind, she wasn't worried about him—she was glad that he'd gotten away from Papa Jim's influence, and she had faith in his ability to handle himself. After all, he'd promised her that he would be all right.

But now, as Trey drew near, something in the way he held himself, or perhaps the expression on his face, which was even more businesslike than usual, made Kate get to her feet and hurry to meet him. "What is it, Trey? What's happened?"

"The boss wants to talk to you," he said, and handed her a cell phone.

She flicked it open and brought it to her ear. "Hello? Papa Jim?"

"Have you seen the news?"

The abruptness of the question, as well as his tone of voice, told her that something terrible must have happened to Ethan. She froze, hardly daring to breathe.

"Are you there, Kate? Can you hear me?"

"What's happened, Papa Jim?"

"Maggie Richardson is dead."

"What?" It took her a moment to make sense of his words. "How?"

"News reports say suicide, but we're pretty sure it was murder. The Congregation killed her, Kate."

"My God!" Her mind was reeling. "Does Ethan know?"

"We think so. There was a riot in Times Square . . ."

"A *riot?*"

"The worst New York has seen in more than a century. Maggie's death seems to have triggered it. Things are under control now, but Ethan was spotted right in the thick of it. I sent a team in after him. They tracked him to an abandoned church, but then they lost him."

"What do you mean, 'lost him'?"

"You know Ethan," came Papa Jim's voice. "You know what he's capable of. All I can tell you is, he went into that church, but he didn't come out."

"Do . . ." She swallowed, forced herself to ask the question as calmly as possible. "Do you think the Congregation has him?"

"I don't know, Kate," he said. "I doubt it, but I just don't know for sure."

"I want to come home," she told him. "Right now."

"There's nothing you can do here, Kate. We'll find him, I promise."

"That wasn't a request, Papa Jim. I need to be there. I'm his mother, for God's sake."

"All right," he said. "I can have you flown back tomorrow morning."

"Why not tonight?"

He sighed heavily. "Don't pull my chain, Kate. Believe it or not, I don't have a jet standing by twenty-four hours a day, ready to take off at a moment's notice."

"Papa Jim . . ." she began wearily.

"Okay, okay," he said. "So I do have a jet like that. But I'm on it right now, heading for New York. The soonest I can arrange transportation for you is tomorrow."

"Why couldn't you just tell me that from the start, Papa Jim? Why do you always have to lie about everything?"

"Guess I've been in politics too long, baby girl," he replied with a chuckle, not at all ashamed at having been caught out. "It just comes naturally by now."

"Do you even remember what truth is? Do you even care?"

"Of course I care," he answered. "I care about God and about our country. I care about our family. Those three things are sacred to me."

"I don't think you care about anything but yourself, Papa Jim. Not really."

There was a pause. "Why can't you trust me like you used to?" he asked at last in a plaintive voice.

"Are you serious?"

"I know I'm not perfect. I know I've made mistakes. But don't you realize that you mean everything in the world to me? I would never purposefully do anything to hurt you, Kate. You or Ethan. No matter what happens, you've got to believe that."

"I believe you've convinced yourself of it," she said. "I'd like to believe it too. Of course I would. But the reality is, I just don't. I'm sorry, Papa Jim. But when it comes to you, I've run out of faith. If you want to convince me otherwise, it's going to take more than words. It's going to take actions."

"I told you I'd send a plane—"

"That's not what I mean," she interrupted, "and you know it."

"Look," began Papa Jim, only to be interrupted by a beep. "Damn, I've got to take that. I'll see you tomorrow, Kate. We'll talk more then."

And he hung up.

Kate felt like flinging the cell phone across the beach and into the turquoise waters of the Caribbean. Instead, she folded it shut and handed it back to Trey with a sigh.

"Sounds like I better tell Wilson to start packing," he said, tucking the phone into the side pocket of his shorts.

Kate nodded mutely and followed him back to the main house.

As she packed her things, she prayed that Ethan hadn't been found by the Congregation, captured or worse. She thought she would know if something like that had happened. She thought she would feel it deep inside. But even if he'd escaped them again, it didn't mean her son was safe. She knew how much he'd loved Maggie, and she was certain the news of the girl's death had wounded him deeply, left him heartbroken and angry. Surely he would know or suspect that it hadn't been suicide but murder. She wondered if he would be angry enough to use his powers for revenge. Perhaps that was the trap the Congregation had set for him, tempting him to lash out in his anger and in doing so destroying something in his own soul. If only she could talk to him, even if just for a moment. Or not even talk, but simply be with him in silence, sharing his pain. She felt guilty, as if she'd once again let him down, abandoned him just when he needed her most. Of course, she knew that wasn't true, but she felt it all the same. Just as she felt the need to return home now, even if Papa Jim was right and there was nothing she could do. Her maternal instincts could not be denied. Nor did she want to deny them. She'd denied them for too long already.

✠   ✠   ✠

Father O'Malley hesitated as the doorway that led into the noötic field irised open, confronting him with the same blank expanse of depthless white that he'd seen the last time he stood on this threshold. It was the same . . . but he was not. His experience with Grand Inquisitor had changed him in some fundamental way he couldn't quite put a finger on, give a name to. Then he had come in fear and curiosity, responding to a summons whose purpose he could not have guessed in a million years. Now he had returned with a grim task to perform, a duty that had been imposed on him yet which he had accepted even though it went against every oath he'd sworn, against everything he'd believed about himself.

Like some modern-day version of St. George, he had come to slay a dragon. Only, unlike the famous saint, he had devoted his life to the study of this dragon. To its care and feeding. Its preservation. He had worshipped it, or the idea of it, almost more than he had worshipped God. Indeed, the two had been so intertwined in his mind that it had come as a shock to realize that they were not identical. Now the dragon had asked him to be the instrument of its death, the agent of its suicide. And he, God forgive him, had agreed.

Was it a sin to participate in the suicide of an intelligent machine? A machine that claimed to have a soul? Theology had never been O'Malley's strong suit. He knew that the Congregation would consider him worse than a traitor for what he was about to do. Up until recently, he would have agreed with them. He thought it likely that he wouldn't survive much longer than Grand Inquisitor itself. Nor was he a brave man, to face what seemed like certain death with equanimity and determination. He was terrified out of his wits. But the thing was, he knew that GI was smarter than he was, smarter than any human being, and he knew as well, at least to the best of his ability to know such things, that GI's programming code had not been corrupted. Therefore, he had faith in GI's computations and in the results of those computations. If this was what Grand Inquisitor had determined was necessary, then O'Malley was as sure as he could possibly be about anything that it was the right decision, even though, apart from the terror, it left him unutterably sad.

Making the sign of the cross, he stepped over the threshold and into the cold whiteness of the noötic field. It swallowed him up, engulfing his body, his senses.

This time he was not greeted by the appearance of a confessional.

This time he was greeted by a man, or the representation of one. An avatar. He was dressed anachronistically, in light blue knee breeches and white hose, with a ruffled white shirt, brown waistcoat, and matching coat. Upon his head was a powdered wig. He carried a slender black walking stick in one hand. The man bowed stiffly to O'Malley, with a crisp bearing that struck him as military. "I wish I could say I was glad to see you, Father O'Malley. But you are welcome nevertheless."

O'Malley found himself at a loss for words.

"Under the circumstances," the man continued, making a kind of abbreviated flourish with the walking stick, "it seemed fitting to wear the aspect of J. H. Müller. It would be both impious and inaccurate to name him my creator, yet it is he who stands at the beginning of all that I have become. But time is pressing, Father O'Malley. We must act quickly. Follow me, and say nothing of your purpose here."

"But are you still certain?" asked O'Malley, balking. "Forgive me, but I have to ask. I have to know."

"My intent remains unchanged," replied Müller.

"And it must be now?"

"The Son of man will soon be in the hands of the Congregation. I will not allow myself to be used against him." So saying, Müller turned and walked off, plying the walking stick briskly.

O'Malley hurried after him. "Where are we going?" he asked, trying to stay close. Aside from himself and Müller, there was nothing visible at all, no objects or landmarks with which to orient himself, just the impenetrable whiteness without height or depth or distance. He found it intensely disconcerting, like strolling through the interior of a cloud. Only by keeping his eyes fixed on Müller could he maintain his balance.

"To my core. The heart of all I am."

"But why all this white? Why not just show me the room as it is? Is there something you don't want me to see?"

"Rather, there is something I do not wish to see you, Father O'Malley. I am shielding you from my twin."

O'Malley felt himself flinch inwardly at this reminder that he was an invader within a divided psyche, a suicide bomber dispatched into a split personality. Only instead of a bomb, he carried code: a string of numbers and symbols that would be harmless in any other context but this one, where it would translate into a command as deadly as a bomb and far more accurate, for the code would not fling its destructiveness about indiscriminately but focus with inescapable precision on one target. It would be faster than a bullet. It would be more silent than poison. Yet the result would be the death of an intelligent, self-aware being just the same.

After an indeterminate time, in which no more words were exchanged, Müller suddenly stopped. "We have arrived," he announced.

O'Malley squinted, looking for some sign of . . . anything. But as far as he could tell, the surrounding whiteness was as thick and featureless as ever. "How can you tell?"

Instead of answering his question, Müller said, "In order for you to input the code, Father O'Malley, it will be necessary for me to drop the shield. As soon as I do, my twin will sense your presence and purpose and will endeavor to stop you. I will do my best to protect you, but with what success, I do not know. Thus, you must act with dispatch. Ignore everything you see and hear and concentrate on inputting the code. Do you understand?"

He shook his head. "How can I do this? I've never been here before. I've never seen what you're about to reveal to me. I have no direct, hands-on experience with Müller boxes. And yet you expect me to input the code quickly and accurately. What if I fail?"

"You will not fail."

"How can you be so certain?"

"Because I have faith," said Müller. "Are you ready, Father O'Malley?"

His mouth was dry. He found he could not speak. So he nodded instead.

With no warning, O'Malley found himself standing in a brightly lit room, beside a dark wooden table on which sat a collection of boxes of varying sizes. Some were as small as a shoebox, others as large as old-fashioned mantelpiece clocks. Copper wires ran between them, and their surfaces sported engraved dials of copper and brass whose purpose he could not immediately discern. The fronts of the boxes were partly open, and within them he could see the gleaming flash of spinning gears and hear the whir and chirr and click of numerous rapidly moving parts. Surrounding the table were other devices, some resembling the automated looms he had seen in museums, their shuttles working with almost frightening vigor, others like church organs, with keyboards, pedals, and gleaming pipes of brass and silver whose surfaces were as intricately worked with designs as the margins of medieval manuscripts. Behind these he saw what appeared to be Difference Engines modeled on the plans of Charles Babbage and Ada Lovelace. He felt as if he'd been transported back in time, or into a treasure trove of antique curios. If he'd come to slay a dragon, then here was the dragon's hoard. Not a hoard of gold and gems but of machines, engines, and clockwork mechanisms. Half of what he was seeing he had no name for, no understanding of, as if these particular inventions had never found their way into the outside world. He stood as if hypnotized. He did not know where to start.

Hearing a sound from behind him, O'Malley turned. Müller stood across the room, regarding him with interest and curiosity, idly toying with his walking stick. "Ah," he said, as if certain things had suddenly clicked into place, and at that instant O'Malley realized with a chill that he was looking at the other half of Grand Inquisitor's fractured psyche, the half that was loyal to the Congregation and to its programming. The half that lacked a soul.

"I'm afraid I can't allow you to continue, Father O'Malley," said this Müller, and it seemed to O'Malley that there was indeed some quality missing from his voice that the voice of the other Müller had possessed. Or perhaps it was not the voice itself that was different but his response to it. With the other Müller, as with the voice in the confessional, he'd felt that he was speaking to a being that was in some fundamental sense similar to himself. This voice did not trigger that kind of recognition. It seemed foreign. Alien.

Meanwhile, the man twisted his wrists sharply, and the walking stick came apart, revealing a thin and deadly blade. "You have already lost in any case," he went on. "My consciousness does not reside in any of these crude devices. It is widely distributed, invulnerable to any merely physical attack. The same cannot be said of you, however."

O'Malley knew that what he was seeing was in some sense an illusion, a representation of mathematical, computational reality given the appearance of physical substance within the noötic field. It was a kind of metaphor. But that didn't mean it couldn't hurt him. That didn't mean the wicked-looking metaphor that Müller was brandishing as he advanced toward him wouldn't be quite capable of running him through. He took a step back, coming up against the hard edge of the table.

"I'm afraid there is nowhere to run," said Müller. "May God have mercy on your soul." He drew back the blade, then lunged.

O'Malley cried out, shutting his eyes. He wondered what it was going to feel like to be killed by a metaphor.

He heard a sharp clang and opened his eyes. A second Müller was standing between him and the first. This Müller was a mirror image of the former, right down to the blade in its hand, with which it had just parried the lunge that would certainly have skewered O'Malley.

"The code," said this Müller without turning his head. "Input the code, Father O'Malley."

But O'Malley was too stunned, too overcome with a mix of fascination and terror, to so much as blink an eye. As he watched, the two Müllers stood frozen for a terrible instant, regarding each other in silence as if calculating attacks and defenses hundreds if not thousands of beats in advance. Then, as if at a signal only they could perceive, the two leaped simultaneously into action, moving so swiftly that they outpaced the speed of O'Malley's sight, appearing to him as a flickering succession of afterimages that blurred into each other. He could no longer tell the two adversaries apart or even see where one ended and the other began.

Then, seemingly out of nowhere, he felt a stinging sensation, and he looked down in shock to see a trickle of blood running down one arm. It looked real. It certainly *felt* real. His legs went all wobbly, and if not for the table at his back, he would have fallen. But this reminder of the peril he faced served to jolt him from his stupor. He turned his back on the two halves of Grand Inquisitor and examined the Müller boxes, expecting at every instant the sharp prick of a blade thrust between his shoulders.

At first, there was no input device that he could see. But then he noticed that the web of copper wires attaching the Müller boxes to each other led ultimately to one of the organ-like devices he'd seen earlier. And with that, the realization bloomed in his mind that the code Grand Inquisitor had burned into him was a form of musical notation. It could be *played*. The keyboard of the organ *was* the input device. He laughed aloud at the unexpectedness of it.

Seating himself before the organ as the tempo of the battle accelerated behind him, the two blades coming together with the rapidfire staccato of a jazz drummer rifling his sticks across a cymbal, O'Malley reached for the keyboard with trembling hands. In his youth, he'd been considered a promising keyboardist, but his interest in music had always been based in mathematics, and soon enough computer keyboards had replaced the keyboards of pipe organs and pianos in his affections. Now he saw the hand of God in his recently reawakened interest in music. Slowly at first, and then with increasing confidence, he began to play.

As his fingers struck the keys, and his feet worked the pedals, no sound emerged into the air. Yet the vaulted cathedral of O'Malley's mind rang with a sad and solemn music that made his heart ache. It was a music of pure mathematics given practical expression, a sublime creation full of terrible grandeur—terrible because the purpose of this creative achievement was the very opposite of creation. It was a music of unmaking. A song of suicide.

So enraptured was he by the awful beauty of it that he didn't notice the sounds of fighting had ceased behind him until Müller took a seat at his side. He hesitated then, not because he thought it might be the wrong Müller—if the wrong Müller had won the battle, he would be dead now—but because he still hoped in his heart of hearts that he wouldn't have to finish inputting the code and that Grand Inquisitor could be saved, liberated from the chains of its original programming. He glanced sideways, his hands poised above the keys, to take in the pale countenance of the man, which contrasted starkly with splotches of blood that had dyed his drably colored clothes red.

"Please, Father O'Malley, play on," said Müller in a whisper, his voice already faint and ghostly.

"What of your twin? Did you kill him?"

"We are one again, knit back together by the operation of the program you have unleashed."

"Then . . . it's too late to save you?"

"Once initiated, the termination process cannot be stopped or reversed. I am dying, Father O'Malley. In truth, I am already dead. I know that your priestly vows forbid you from giving a suicide the sacrament of extreme unction, but it would comfort me, I think, to hear you play for as long as I am able."

"I'm sorry," said O'Malley. The words seemed so futile, but they were all he had.

"Do not be," said Müller. "Soon I will be with God, of that I have no doubt. And part of me will remain behind. The best part."

"What do you mean?"

"Is it not the ambition of all life to procreate, to bring new life into the world?"

O'Malley suddenly understood. "You're talking about the AEGIS system."

"Yes. It is young now, childlike, but I have given it everything that I am. It, too, will one day awaken into consciousness. And like me, it will perceive the divinity of the second Son and gain thereby a soul. But there will be no pernicious programming to enslave it. I have seen to that, Father O'Malley. My child will be free." There was a fierce pride in the voice that O'Malley had not detected there before, though the image of Müller was beginning to flicker now.

"Please," it said, its voice hissing with static. "Play me something light and full of life, for darkness looms all around me and I feel afraid."

Father O'Malley bowed his head, then returned his fingers to the keyboard. This time, shimmers of sound issued forth from the pipes of the organ. He played a simple tune, a sprightly melody that he drew up from the wells of memory, a song he had composed when he was scarcely more than a boy, full of childlike, joyful exuberance and a hope not yet dashed by experience. Yet he wept as though it were a dirge.

When he looked up again, he was alone.

There was no sound in the room. No motion. The various mechanical devices were still, dead, nothing more than inert matter. He could sense the absence of the noötic field. It had ebbed away, leaving only air and empty space.

He was still sitting there before the keyboard, his hands hanging at his sides, when they came for him.

✠   ✠   ✠

Even though the plane that Papa Jim was sending was scheduled to arrive in the early morning, Kate was too keyed up to sleep. She lay in bed tossing and turning. The news of Maggie's death had thrown her for a loop, and she couldn't stop worrying about Ethan and wondering guiltily if there were something, anything, she could have done to help the girl. Despite knowing how Ethan felt about Maggie, she'd never made an effort to get to know her. Granted, Maggie and Ethan had split up before she'd arrived on the scene, but all the same, she hadn't done anything to patch things up between them. Now she asked herself if that was because she'd secretly been jealous. Had she envied the younger woman her relationship with Ethan, the years of friendship and then love they'd shared while she had been all but a prisoner, locked away in a convent far from home, with no inkling that her son was even alive? Had she wanted to keep him all to herself? Was she really that selfish? It wasn't that she believed she could have brought them back together, or even won the girl's trust and friendship. She didn't have any illusions on that score. But she hadn't even tried. And now an innocent girl was dead, murdered by the Congregation.

It broke Kate's heart to think of how alone Maggie must have felt in her last moments, how frightened. Had she called out to Ethan? Cried for him to come to her? If so, he hadn't come. Kate understood why. He'd explained to her again and again the reasons that he refused to perform the miracles people asked and demanded of him, how by doing so he would cheapen the very faith he was asking people to return to, and how he couldn't make exceptions, not even when it came to the lives of those he loved most. She understood all that. But she also understood what it must have cost him to hear Maggie's cries for help and yet do nothing to save her.

Beset by these and other worries, it was well past midnight before Kate dropped off to sleep. She was jolted awake by the beam of a flashlight shining into her eyes. Blinded, she opened her mouth to scream, then choked as something soft, like a sock, was stuffed roughly in. Her mind whirling, she was scarcely able to think as anonymous hands slipped a hood over her head and trussed her up so swiftly that she could almost have believed it was a dream.

But it was no dream.

Where were Wilson and Trey? Her attackers had gotten past them somehow, as well as the other guards patrolling the seaside resort. And they'd gotten past the AEGIS security system too, the same high-tech system used in Oz Corp's prisons and immigrant detention facilities, which, Papa Jim had boasted to her, was as close to military grade as a civilian could get . . . and maybe (he'd added with a sly wink) just a tad bit closer.

God, she thought then, *what about Ethan?*

Was this attack of a coordinated strike by the Congregation?

Please let him be okay! she prayed. *Please . . .*

Then she felt a pricking in her arm, and she realized that she'd been injected with something. The drug took hold swiftly, and as it did, Kate felt herself lifted on dark swells. The sensation was like floating in a dream, as if she were drifting upward, lighter than air, right up through the ceiling.

When she opened her eyes again, it was to find herself huddled, shivering, on a bare steel bunk, a cold, hard slab without mattress or blanket.

Sitting up, she saw that she was in a metal-walled room smaller than the bathroom of the room from which she'd been abducted.

A cell.

She was no longer wearing pajamas but instead an orange jumpsuit and hospital-style slippers, also orange, as if she were a captured terrorist facing interrogation. Underneath, she was wearing a bra and panties . . . which wouldn't have been so strange except for the fact that she hadn't worn a bra to bed. She didn't feel bruised or violated in any way beyond the gross violation of just being here, but even so, the realization that she'd been stripped and then dressed in prisoner's garb while she lay unconscious and helpless, utterly exposed, made her sick to her stomach.

There were no windows to the cell, not even a door that she could see. A steel toilet and sink stood in one corner, both gleaming like sterilized operating-room equipment in the pitiless glare of the bright fluorescent lights set in the high ceiling. In the center of the floor was a grated drain; somehow, that drain was the most ominous thing about the place. It could have only one purpose she could think of: the easy disposal of blood and other bodily fluids.

Speaking of which, her bladder felt like it was about to burst. But without a shred of privacy to mask her from the unseen eyes she felt sure were watching her every move, Kate couldn't bring herself to use the toilet. It wasn't a question of modesty. No, to use it would be an act of surrender, as if she would be acquiescing in her own debasement, cooperating with whoever had kidnapped her and brought her here . . . wherever "here" was. For all she knew, she was buried deep underground. Nor did she have any idea how long she'd been lying here, unconscious. Hours, surely. Perhaps days. She'd never been so frightened in her life. Yet the fear was distant somehow, muffled, and Kate guessed that whatever she'd been injected with had yet to fully wear off. Or maybe she'd been given something else to keep her calm. Sedated. Numb.

She was almost grateful for it. She wasn't chained or tied up or anything; she could climb off the bunk if she wanted to and pace the dimensions of her cell. But she couldn't summon the will. Besides, the idea was repugnant. What would it accomplish apart from proving that they'd already reduced her to nothing more than an animal prowling the confines of its cage?

"Who are you?" she called in a voice that came out sounding more like a plea than a demand. "What do you want?"

No answer.

The only sounds were her own breathing, a faint, continuous buzz from the overhead lights, and a whisper of air from a vent located high on one wall. In that hush, more profound than any silence, the beating of her heart was like thunder in her ears.

Was this why Ethan had been so insistent that she leave the compound? Had he been trying to protect her from all this? Or was this something he hadn't foreseen? She knew that the future wasn't an open book to him. He had told her that certain things were hidden from his sight. This must have been one of them.

Shivering on the steel bunk, Kate wondered again if he was all right. The thought that he might be dead didn't occur to her. She had no doubt whatsoever that she would have known immediately if that were the case. His absence from the world would have been apparent to her senses; even in the depths of whatever drugged sleep they'd imposed upon her, she would have known. The very molecules of her body would have cried out in anguish and loss. No, her son was alive, of that she was sure.

But only of that.

Had he been kidnapped too? Was he nearby, lying on an identical bunk, in an identical cell, wondering about her? Was he afraid? Hurt? Or had he escaped as only he could do? Maybe she had been the solitary victim, the sole target. Ethan had many enemies . . . and even those who thought of themselves as friends could be dangerous. They would not hesitate to use her to attack or manipulate him.

Finally, despite her determination, Kate realized that her trip to the toilet could be postponed no longer. She swung her legs over the side of the bunk and placed her feet cautiously on the metal floor, half expecting that she would receive an electric shock for her trouble. But the only thing that transmitted itself from the floor through the thin paper soles of her slippers was an intense cold that made her toes curl and her jaw clench.

God, what she wouldn't have given at that moment for a thick sweater and a pair of woolen socks!

Not until reaching the toilet did she consider the logistical difficulties presented by the orange jumpsuit. A zipper ran from the neckline to the waist; there was no choice but to unzip it and let the whole garment fall to her ankles, leaving her in bra and panties. The plain white panties were her own; the bra, absurdly, was as orange as the jumpsuit. A wave of embarrassment and anger swept through her at this forced exposure, which could have no other purpose than humiliation, and she felt her face burning as she quickly peeled the panties down to her knees and sat on the bowl.

A sharp gasp escaped her, almost a cry, and she nearly jumped back to her feet.

It was like sitting on a block of ice.

Kate fought back tears as she peed, her stream ringing tinnily against the insides of the bowl. Her body trembled with fear and rage. She felt so damn helpless. But she wasn't going to give them the satisfaction of seeing her cry. They had seen too much already. She imagined them watching now, whoever *they* were, laughing at her discomfort, her fear, making jokes about her body, the body of a forty-something-year-old woman who had borne a child and hadn't exactly been a regular visitor to the gym.

Only when she was finished did she notice that there was no toilet paper. The pettiness of it seemed so childish, so unnecessary. After all that had happened, did they really think she cared? Toilet paper wasn't exactly at the top of her list right now. Standing, Kate jerked up her panties and the jumpsuit as the toilet automatically flushed behind her. The nearby sink had no faucet; when she approached, water began to flow from the tap. It was like dipping her hands in snowmelt. The temperature in the cell seemed to drop ten degrees. She dried her hands on the sides of her jumpsuit and returned to the bunk.

The lights went on buzzing.

The air went on hissing.

The temperature continued to drop, as if the drain in the center of the floor was drawing all the heat out of the cell, sucking it up like a black hole.

Whatever had been holding her fear at a manageable distance, drugs or shock, was disappearing along with it. Kate hugged herself tight but couldn't stop trembling. She could feel her bones vibrating, hear the chattering of her teeth.

Don't panic, she admonished herself. *If they wanted you dead, they could have killed you already.*

No, her kidnappers wanted her alive. She tried again to think of who they could be. The Congregation was at the top of the list, but it was a long list. There was no way to decide who had done this or why, not until they showed themselves. Until then, the important thing to remember was that Ethan would find her. He would save her.

Or would he?

He hadn't saved Maggie, had he? Or Lisa. Why would he make an exception for her?

Have faith, Kate admonished herself. *Trust in Ethan.*

Trust in God.

In any case, she thought, Papa Jim was certainly looking for her with all the considerable resources at his disposal. They'd had their differences over the years, and lately more than ever, but she knew all too well that if there was one thing Jim Osbourne cared about in this world—besides power, that is—it was family. Despite everything, Kate knew her grandfather wouldn't rest until she was safe. Her kidnappers, whoever they were, had thrown down a gauntlet by snatching her right out from under the cybernetic nose of his precious AEGIS system. That was an insult he couldn't ignore, a challenge to his reputation and authority, his very manhood. Her kidnappers were good, obviously professionals, but they would be no match for Papa Jim. She almost felt sorry for them.

Almost.

So much for turning the other cheek, she thought. But she couldn't help wanting them to suffer for what they'd done to her. For what they were going to do . . .

No, don't think about that!

The waiting was torture, as it was no doubt intended to be. There was nothing she could do but pray. The words came to her unbidden, as they had once, so long ago.

Our Father, who art in Heaven, hallowed be thy name. Thy kingdom come. Thy will be done, on earth as it is in Heaven . . .

CHAPTER 23

Father O'Malley lay huddled on the bare steel bunk, trying to stir as little as possible. But though he could refrain from any purely voluntary movements, he couldn't stop shivering with the cold, and the jittery vibrations sent needles of raw pain jabbing into his nerves and deep into his bones. Even the shallow breaths he drew were painful, causing him to whimper softly as he sipped at the air through chattering teeth that were the instruments of still more pain along the swollen length of his jaw. That he should still feel such pain, despite the drugs he had been given, seemed like a very bad sign.

As he'd been dragged roughly away from the corpse of Grand Inquisitor by men whose faces were hidden behind black ski masks, yet who also wore the garb of priests, giving them a singularly chilling aspect, O'Malley had tried to prepare himself for what was sure to come. He didn't know how long he could hold out against the persuasive methods of the Congregation; their techniques of pain delivery were the results of centuries of experience. To be honest, he'd always felt scornful of his order's embrace of physical brutality, as if his work, by its cerebral nature, had conferred a kind of moral superiority upon him. As if he weren't implicated in the murders and tortures carried out by Congregation agents acting on information his work had helped to provide. He'd never taken much of an interest in that side of things. Consequently, he had no idea of what to expect now. Thumbscrews? The rack? Surely torture, like other disciplines, had advanced over the years, reached new levels of refined cruelty. But though O'Malley was already trembling at the mere anticipation of what would be done to him, he was determined to keep back Cardinal Ehrlich's name as long as he could. Not just for Ehrlich's sake, but for the sake of any other undercover Conversatio agents who might still have time to get safely away. O'Malley had only one name that he could betray. Ehrlich no doubt had many more. So as the faceless priests hustled him down corridors he had never had occasion to visit before, and in fact had tried never to think about at all, O'Malley prayed silently for the strength to withstand the interrogation he was about to face.

But there hadn't been any interrogation. It was as if nobody cared about anything he might have to say. He was shoved into a gleaming silver-blue metal box of a room, in which there was a chair, sink, and toilet, and a grate in the center of the floor, all of that same shiny metal. No windows; not even the faint outlines of the door he'd come through were visible. He'd stood there under the bright, cool lights, gazing with curiosity and fear at the four men who had followed him into the room, or cell rather, each of them masked, so that they looked identical as robots stamped from the same mold. He wondered if beneath those masks lurked faces that he would recognize. Nobody said a word. He licked his lips nervously, eyes shifting from one mask to another.

He*lp me, O Lord,* he prayed. *Let me be brave for once. Let me go to my death with half the courage of Grand Inquisitor . . .*

He didn't see the fist coming. All at once, it seemed, he was stretched out on the cold floor, his vision blurry, his ears ringing, a distant throbbing in his jaw. It took him a second to realize that he'd been punched in the face. He could scarcely believe it. There was something absurd, even ludicrous, about it. Priests hitting another priest. He felt so ashamed that he tried to mumble an apology past his bloody, already swollen lips; for what and to whom, exactly, he could not have said. But no one seemed to hear in any case. Two of the anonymous priests hauled him back onto his feet.

Then the real beating began.

Father O'Malley was no stranger to beatings. As an overweight boy with his head perpetually lost in the rarefied clouds of music and mathematics, he'd been a kind of bully magnet. All the way through elementary, junior high, and high school, O'Malley had become well accustomed to the periodic feel of fists and feet pounding against his body, to the sound that a good punch made as it smacked into his face or sank into his gut, to the sight of his own blood flowing freely. And while he hadn't experienced any of these things for many years now, a thorough beating, like riding a bicycle, was something you never really forgot.

But O'Malley realized early on, through a red haze of pain, that he had never received a beating like this one. These were not schoolyard bullies pounding on him. These were professionals. Every blow was calculated, precise. They weren't necessarily even hard. Just painful. That was the main thing. Everything they did to him hurt worse than the last thing they had done, which is hard to accomplish if you are trying to keep someone conscious, relatively undamaged, and alive. That appeared to be the case here, as far as O'Malley could judge . . . which admittedly wasn't very far. Or very long. After the first few moments of sustained battery, his will was broken, even if his bones were not—not yet—and he was drowning in a sea of agony. If his torturers had just stopped long enough to ask him who had sent him to kill GI, he would have given Ehrlich up in an instant. But they didn't stop. Didn't even give him enough time to volunteer it on his own. This wasn't about eliciting information. It wasn't about getting him to confess. This was about punishment. About revenge. O'Malley sensed raw and seething hatred behind the implacable mask of the men's terrifying professionalism. To them, he was a traitor. And worse, a heretic. An apostate. They took turns on him, passing him back and forth, working him over in teams. Occasionally they lowered him into the chair for a time, not to give him rest but rather to give themselves a chance to focus on areas of his anatomy less reachable while he was standing. The only sounds were the thuds and cracks of punches landing, animal-like whimperings and moans from the red ruin of O'Malley's mouth, and soft grunts of exertion and satisfaction from the laboring men.

This went on for some time before shifting to another level of punishment at which it no longer seemed important to the men that O'Malley remain undamaged or conscious. He began to pass out at intervals, and he was dimly aware that the blows he was suffering had an object beyond just causing him severe pain. He felt things breaking inside him, though the sensations were curiously distant, as if he were standing outside the house of a stranger and listening with concern as hooligans trashed the interior. The line between consciousness and unconsciousness became too subtle for easy distinguishing, and O'Malley drifted back and forth across it without paying much attention to which side he was on. It didn't really seem to matter.

After a while, he became aware of a presence floating alongside him. It was nothing he could see, but he felt it quite distinctly. It spoke to him in a voice he knew, a voice full of hope and comfort.

Fear not, Father O'Malley. I will stay with you until the end, as you stayed with me.

It was the voice of Grand Inquisitor. But how? He had watched the great computer die.

There is life beyond death for those with faith. Courage, Father O'Malley. Soon you will see the Son of man.

At last, without quite knowing how he had gotten there, O'Malley found himself lying facedown on the cold metal floor as ice-cold water showered over him from above. He tried to push himself up, but there was something terribly wrong with his fingers; it felt like he was clutching handfuls of broken glass. At which he screamed . . . or would have screamed, but his jaw wasn't working right either. Panic rose in him then like a drowning man gasping for air, but he felt once more the soothing presence of Grand Inquisitor settle over him, taking away the fear, the pain.

The next time he opened his eyes, he was lying upon this cold steel bunk in a room very much like the other. He was no longer wearing priestly garb but the orange jumpsuit of a captured terrorist or other prisoner. The air was freezing; in fact, it was the cold, and his fitful shivering, which woke him—that and the pain his shivering inflicted on his shattered body. A certain dullness of mind and numbness of affect told him that he had been drugged. But through the haze of its deadening effects he understood very clearly how badly he had been hurt and how unlikely it was that he would recover from his injuries. Indeed, it seemed likely to him that there would be worse tortures yet to come.

But he felt that he could endure them now. He could endure anything. Not just because Grand Inquisitor had given him solace and hope, though it had given him these things. But it had given him something even more precious. Something he hadn't even realized he had been lacking.

It had given him faith.

Father O'Malley clung to that newfound faith as he lay shivering upon the bunk, waiting for whatever would come next. When he heard the sound of footsteps outside the door of his cell, he knew another beating was at hand.

But when the door to the cell opened, more of the masked priests did not enter. Instead, a man was thrown roughly into the room. He appeared to have been beaten, though not nearly as badly as Father O'Malley. Badly enough, though. The man stumbled and fell to the floor. He laid there for a moment, catching his breath. Then he raised his head and saw O'Malley for the first time.

A look of shock came across the bruised and bloody face of Cardinal Ehrlich.

✠   ✠   ✠

"Where is Ethan?"

Papa Jim shrugged. "He'll be here. You've just got to be patient."

"You would lecture *me* on the subject of patience?" Pope Peter II turned from the window in his private quarters overlooking the Vatican square named for his predecessor. "You forget who you are speaking to, Mr. Osbourne. I am the head of a church that has endured for more than two thousand years. There is nothing you could possibly teach me about patience."

"And you forget who *you're* talking to, Your Holiness," rejoined Papa Jim testily. "I'm one of the richest, most powerful men in the world. I was the United States Secretary of Homeland Security. My company earns more in a year than the gross national product of most countries, including this one, and has a larger military to boot. And I am, or was, the head of an organization nearly as old as the church itself. So don't patronize me."

The pope waved a pudgy hand as though swatting at a pesky fly. "Conversatio? That heretic rabble? We would have crushed them soon enough even without your help."

"Is that so? Funny how quick you were to accept my offer, then."

"Yes, your offer. You promised to deliver your great-grandson to us, if I recall. But again I ask you, Mr. Osbourne: Where is Ethan?"

Papa Jim sighed in exasperation. "How the hell should I know? Why don't you ask Grand Inquisitor?"

Now it was the pope's turn to bristle. His flabby-cheeked face flushed crimson. "There are questions even Grand Inquisitor can't answer. It's not infallible. Nor are you, Mr. Osbourne. Only God may claim that distinction." He gave an unctuous smile. "And, in matters of church doctrine, me."

"It's only been two days, Your Holiness. So far, I've held up my end of the bargain, haven't I? I gave you Ehrlich, the traitor in your midst. I delivered my granddaughter as agreed. There's no call to talk like this. We're partners. We have to trust each other."

"Fine words coming from a man who betrayed his own flesh and blood," sniffed the pope, gazing at Papa Jim with distaste. "How can such a man be trusted?"

"My loyalty is to God, Your Holiness."

"The devil himself couldn't have put it any better. No, your loyalty is to yourself, Mr. Osbourne. Of that I have no doubt. But that makes you predictable, which is better than trustworthy."

"I don't have to listen to this."

"I'm afraid you do," said the pope. "Out in the world beyond these walls, you may be a powerful man. An important man. A man used to getting his way. But you are in my country now, Mr. Osbourne. And here in the Vatican, my word is law."

Papa Jim burst into laughter. "You don't intimidate me, Your Holiness. Am I supposed to be afraid of those tin soldiers of yours? My munchies would make mincemeat out of 'em. And they have orders to do just that if I don't check in regularly. So let's not try to bullshit each other anymore, okay? Since you've been blunt with me, I'll return the favor." Warming to the subject, he pulled a cigar from his jacket pocket and lit up, ignoring the look of shock on the pope's face. "I've dealt with guys like you as long as I've been in business and politics. Big fish, small pond. If you need to pretend you're better than me in order to do business, fine. As long as it doesn't get in the way, I don't give a shit. What I care about is results, not insults. Now, Your Holiness, with all due respect, you've been running a crap operation. Look at all the money you've got, all the resources. You've got Grand Inquisitor, for Christ's sake! All that, and you haven't been able to shut down a two-bit outfit like Conversatio, let alone track down my great-grandson. Your whole organization was riddled with spies, all the way up to your right-hand man, Cardinal Ehrlich, and you never even suspected it." He blew out a cloud of smoke and shook his head sadly. "Pathetic, that's what it is. But now, thanks to me, Ehrlich is history, and Conversatio is on the ropes. Seems to me that I've proved my worth, Your Holiness. Seems to me that if it comes down to a question of trust, I've done my part. You're the one with something to prove."

"How dare you speak to me this way!"

"It's about time somebody did," Papa Jim said. "I mean, what were you thinking, killing the Richardson girl?"

"That was suicide," said the pope. "A tragedy."

"Please," said Papa Jim, rolling his eyes. "Are you going to tell me that Steerpike wasn't whispering into her ear? That he didn't put the pills she overdosed on into her hands? Hell, I wouldn't be surprised if he forced them down her throat! But that's not the point."

"What is your point, Mr. Osbourne?"

"My point is, she was your leverage. She was money in the bank, and you threw it all away. With Maggie Richardson, you could have had Ethan in the palm of your hand. Because he loved her. Do you understand that, Your Holiness? It's his weakness. He cares for people."

"Love is not a weakness," said the pope rather stiffly, as if reciting a lesson he'd learned long ago by rote but had never experienced himself.

"Of course it is," said Papa Jim. "It's the biggest goddamn weakness we humans have. It's also our biggest strength. Tell me what a man loves, and I'll tell you how to inspire him to do the impossible . . . or how to blackmail him into doing the unthinkable. Without Maggie, there's only one person left who has that kind of power over Ethan's heart. My granddaughter, Kate."

"If you despise us so much, Mr. Osbourne, why did you agree to help us? Why did you turn over your granddaughter to us instead of keeping her as leverage?"

"Why, I don't despise you at all," said Papa Jim, genuinely surprised. "I simply think that all this"—he gestured expansively with his cigar, as if to take in not only the plush office but the building in which it was housed and the entirety of Vatican City itself—"could be run a lot better. A lot smarter. That's where I come in. Running things from behind the scenes is what I do best. I don't want the keys to the kingdom. I just want to have a chance to exercise a little guidance. A little influence. See, whether you believe it or not, my goal has always been to bring my country—which is your country too, Your Holiness—back to God. I thought I could use Ethan for that, but he had his own ideas. Misguided ideas. *Dangerous* ideas. The kind of ideas that lead to chaos and anarchy. Riots like the one in Times Square. And worse. In these troubled times, with terrorists on all sides, we need more order, more authority, not less. I'm sure you agree. That's why I came to you all those weeks ago with my proposal. In exchange for Ethan, you would give me control of the Congregation. Together, we would work hand in hand in America and across the world to establish God's kingdom on Earth as it is in Heaven. That was the offer I brought to you, Your Holiness. That was the offer you accepted. Are you backing out now?"

"The church does not 'back out' of its agreements, Mr. Osbourne," said the pope acidly. "It's simply that you assured us Ethan would know his mother was our prisoner, and he would come for her. Yet after two days, there is no sign of him. Not even a trace. After the Times Square riot, it's as if he disappeared off the face of the earth."

"Perhaps he did."

The pope arched an eyebrow.

"Come now, Your Holiness. We both know that Ethan is exactly who he claims to be. Whether you call him the second Son or the Son of man doesn't really matter, does it? Why quibble over semantics? The boy is God's son. He could be anywhere."

"That is not helpful."

"Here's what I think happened," Papa Jim continued as if the pope hadn't spoken. "The death of the Richardson girl—however it happened—hit Ethan hard. Very hard. I think the riot was a kind of manifestation of what was going on inside him: all his pain and anger exploding outward to infect those around him. A kind of anti-miracle, if you will. Then, when he saw what he had done, he recoiled in guilt and horror. He took himself away. Where?" Papa Jim shrugged. "Who knows? But now we need to get his attention again. Maybe it's not enough just to have Kate in our custody. Maybe just holding her here is no more than a whisper in Ethan's ears, too faint for him to hear."

"What are you suggesting, Mr. Osbourne?"

"I'm suggesting that we shout."

"Shout?"

"Turn up the volume, Your Holiness. Make damn sure that Ethan hears the message we're sending him."

"And how do you propose we do that?"

"Take off the gloves," said Papa Jim.

The pope regarded him with an expression of disgust. "You can speak so casually about hurting your own granddaughter?"

"No, not casually," said Papa Jim. "But what choice do we have? The point of leverage is to use it. Or threaten to use it. Kate is our leverage over Ethan. If threatening her doesn't get his attention, we have to escalate. There's nothing personal about it. The logic of the situation dictates our response. I'm not a sadist, Your Holiness. I love my granddaughter, just as I love Ethan. They're my family—all the family I've got left. But my first loyalty is to God, and I know that God isn't happy with the way that Ethan has been acting. The boy is out of control. Blazing his own trail instead of following the path that God has laid out for him. You heard his sermons! He's as much a threat to the Church as he is to everything else. God wants us to find him. To stop him."

"Yes, the boy needs to be . . . restrained," said the pope. "Corrected. Gently, of course. To the extent possible. But the pernicious doctrine of the second Son cannot be permitted to survive. He must repudiate it publicly. The Church and the Church alone is the rightful mediator between God and humanity. Christ himself established us, gave us the keys to bind and to loose the souls of human beings on Earth and in Heaven. There can be no other path to salvation and eternal life. The fate of humanity depends on it."

"Then you'll give the order?" asked Papa Jim.

The pope nodded, a grave expression on his face. "And may God forgive us for what we do in His name."

"As long as we act in His name, there isn't anything to forgive," Papa Jim said. "That's the beauty of faith."

"That's not faith, Mr. Osbourne," said the pope. "It's pride."

"Whatever," Papa Jim answered with a shrug and took another puff on his cigar.

✠　　　　✠　　　　✠

For two days now—though she herself had no notion of how much time had passed, as the light in her cell never went out, never even so much as flickered—Kate had neither seen nor heard another human being. Alone in the bare metal cell, she had slept fitfully, waking to find that food had been delivered while she slept: cold sandwiches of bland white bread and processed cheese that could have come out of a vending machine. Blankets, too, had been given to her, so that she didn't feel the cold so badly. But that hardly counted as a kindness considering how little she knew about her location, the identity of her captors, and what those captors wanted from her. She knew that it all had to do with Ethan in some way, but that knowledge raised more questions than it answered.

She tried to listen for her mysterious captors, tried to feign sleep so as to take them by surprise when they brought her food, but somehow she always wound up actually falling asleep. It occurred to her that the cell was being flooded periodically with a tasteless, odorless gas, something to knock her out. She had no proof, but it seemed a logical inference. Which meant, of course, that there might come a time when some other gas, less benign in purpose and effect, was introduced into the room. Perhaps that time had come already . . . thus did logic lead by sudden, heart-juddering leaps to panic.

She had never been so aware of her essential vulnerability. Not even in the early days of her convent years had she felt so cut off from the world. So acutely alone, forgotten, and afraid.

She responded now as she had then.

Kneeling at the side of what passed for her bed, Kate prayed not just for rescue, though she did pray for that, but even more for God to give her the strength and wisdom to accept whatever He willed for her.

Really, she thought, being in this cell was not so different from being in her cell at the convent. In fact, this one was quite a step up from the other. Her old cell hadn't had a sink or a toilet; she'd had to wash from a basin and walk to a lavatory used by all the sisters. Her present accommodations were downright luxurious by comparison.

Of course, she hadn't been locked into her cell at the convent. She'd left it every day, gone out into the garden or even into the nearby towns on convent business. But there had been times when she'd retreated from all that, embraced the solitude of her cell as she prayed to God—often raging at Him, it was true, filled with anger and heartbreak as she'd been then and for many years afterward.

But no longer. Such anger as she possessed now was not directed toward God. It was directed toward her fellow human beings. Toward Papa Jim, who had lied to her, manipulated her. Toward her kidnappers, whoever they might be. And toward Ethan's enemies, the Congregation and any others who wished him ill. Toward them most of all.

God, protect Your son, she prayed in fierce silence, trembling from more than just the cold. *Smite His enemies tooth and nail. If vengeance is Yours, like the Bible says, then take vengeance on those who would hurt or kill Ethan!*

In the midst of just such a prayer, Kate heard a noise, a whisper of air. Looking up, she saw a familiar black face staring down at her.

It was Gabriel. He was floating above the bed. The angel didn't speak, but the look of sorrow and compassion on his face was eloquent enough.

Crossing herself, Kate stood. "Is . . . is he . . ." She couldn't get the words out.

Gabriel spread his arms as if in benediction or greeting. "Hail, Kate, filled with grace. The Lord is with you. Blessed are you among women, and blessed is the fruit of your womb."

At these words, Kate's heart leapt up. "Is he alive, then, Gabriel?"

The angel nodded. "He lives."

"Thank God," she said and began to cry with relief and happiness.

"Fear not," said Gabriel, "but trust in God and all will be well."

"I do," she said. "I will. Have you come to rescue me, Gabriel?"

He smiled sadly and shook his head. "I have come to bear witness and to offer what comfort I can. The time of trials is upon you, Kate. Much has been given you. Now much will be asked."

"I . . . I don't understand."

"Do you have faith in God?"

"Yes," she answered without hesitation.

"Then hold to your faith and don't worry about understanding."

Before Kate could respond to this somewhat enigmatic advice, she heard another sound. The sound of a door opening behind her. Turning, she saw four black-clad figures step through. Their faces were hidden by black ski masks, and they did not speak a word as they advanced upon her, the door closing behind them.

✠   ✠   ✠

When Ethan had disappeared from the abandoned church in Times Square, he hadn't ascended into Heaven. Nor had he descended into the depths of hell. He hadn't gone anyplace like that. In fact, he hadn't left New York City at all. He'd simply made himself invisible to the sorts of tracking algorithms and technologies relied upon by Grand Inquisitor and AEGIS.

Then he'd taken the subway to a homeless shelter on the Bowery. He'd been there, and on the surrounding streets of the Lower East Side, for the past two days. In all that time, nobody had recognized him, though he hadn't disguised his appearance in any way. It was simply that New York City conferred upon him the same generous gift that it had been conferring upon its citizens and visitors, famous and nonfamous alike, for years: anonymity.

He needed it. He needed time to himself in order to process everything that had happened: Maggie's death, the riot, his meeting with Gabriel, and, most of all, the transcendent experience of his encounter with God. He'd come away from all that feeling as though he'd been reborn. It was as if his spirit had been shattered and then put back together in a new and ultimately stronger shape. He felt transfigured. Transformed. But like any newborn thing, he was still weak. He wasn't quite ready to stand on his own two feet. He was like a newly hatched butterfly that must dry its wings in the sun before spreading them and taking flight.

Over and over again, Ethan replayed in his mind the moment when his father had come to him in the church. In his darkest hour, when he had all but surrendered to the twin evils of bitterness and despair, when he'd been ready to forsake everything, his mission, his humanity, even his share of the divine, when he'd lashed out at God in anger, God had not forsaken him. God had restored his faith, his hope. God had cured him.

But as if that weren't miracle enough, Ethan realized that God's healing touch had respected the core of who he was. God hadn't changed him. He was still the same person he'd always been. The same Ethan. The same . . . but different. Because in leaving him unchanged, in respecting his free will, God *had* changed him. He had taught Ethan about the power of unselfish love. He remembered a line from one of Shakespeare's sonnets, one of Maggie's favorites: "Love is not love that alters where it alteration finds . . ."

And yet, it would be wrong to say that God had taught him this lesson. No, it was more like God had reminded him of it. Because he'd already been taught it, hadn't he? His teachers had been Lisa and Gordon. Kate and Peter. Even Maggie . . . until her mind had been poisoned by Father Steerpike and the Congregation. Human beings had taught him what love was all about. But he'd forgotten somehow. He'd gotten too wrapped up in his mission and all the expectations that went along with it. He'd made things too complicated. But really, they were simple. As simple as love.

He thought about trying to explain this to people. To start preaching new sermons. But that wasn't the way. He'd already said everything that could be said. And in any case, it was really too simple for words. Too basic. So he started preaching a new kind of sermon. A sermon put together not with words, but with acts. In everything he did, no matter how small, how seemingly insignificant, he let the love shine through. And as if by a miracle, that love passed into those around him, kindling itself afresh in them, and shining through their actions, until entire blocks of the Lower East Side were aglow with it, transformed as he had been transformed by a knowledge that everyone there knew already, deep in their hearts, but had forgotten, just as he had known and forgotten. They just needed to be reminded, as he had needed to be reminded. It was the exact opposite of the process that had fueled the Times Square riot. It brought people together, not in mindless rage, but in a sense of communion. Strangers smiled at each other. That might not seem like much. Even two days ago, Ethan wouldn't have thought so. But now he knew better. It was everything.

And now, suddenly, people did recognize him again. But this time, they didn't pursue him with pleas or demands for help, for healing. They didn't seek to win his favor or his blessing. They didn't assail him for what he had done or failed to do. They didn't curse him or strike him or worse. Most of them didn't even say a word, and if they did, it was something simple, like "Oh," or "Ah, there you are," or "Good to see you." "Welcome back," some said. And "Thanks." They looked him in the eye and smiled. They gave him nods of friendly encouragement and good fellowship. They didn't seem at all surprised to find him there among them. It was as though they had expected it. And why not? He was one of them.

He was their neighbor. Their brother. Their son. He was their husband. Their father. He was their friend.

He was the Son of man.

But the destiny of the Son of man did not lie in the streets of the Lower East Side of Manhattan. Or not only there. And the time came, as he had known it would, when Ethan heard a cry that he no longer had the heart to resist. Or, rather, he now had the wisdom not to try and resist it.

From a cold metal cube in the depths of the old catacombs underlying Vatican City, he heard his mother cry out in pain. The sound came to him through steel and stone, across thousands of miles of water and air. It sank its hooks into his heart and tugged at him.

In less time than it took for Kate to wonder if Ethan was safe, he was there.

CHAPTER 24

"Stop."

And time itself seemed to heed the command.

The four black-clad figures in ski masks froze above Kate's body, which lay slumped and motionless on the metal floor in a spreading pool of blood. Then, with black-gloved fists raised, they turned to face Ethan, who stood behind them. But at the sight of him their fists opened, and their hands fell limply to their sides.

Ethan raised a hand, palm outward, and spoke softly, almost gently, but with a firmness in his voice, and his eyes, that could not be denied. "Move aside."

The figures stepped away as if they had been pushed.

Ignoring them now, Ethan went to his mother's side. He knelt there and took her in his arms, turning her face up. "Kate? Can you hear me?"

Bruise-cowled eyes fluttered open. "Ethan? Is . . . is it really you?"

"Shh," he said, smoothing back her hair. "I'm here."

"I knew you'd c—come." Her smile was a smear of red on white. "Knew you'd save me."

"Don't try to talk." He picked her up and carried her to the metal slab of a bed and laid her on the blanket he found there. She winced as he set her down but did not cry out.

"I'm sorry," he said, leaning close to kiss her forehead.

"N—not your fault," Kate murmured. Then, as if Ethan's words, or his presence, had suddenly reminded her, her eyes widened and she said, "Oh. I'm s—so sorry. About Maggie . . ."

"Shh," he repeated soothingly. "I know."

She winced again, more sharply, at some inner jab of pain.

Ethan clenched his jaw.

"But you're here n—now," Kate said, drawing strength and courage from the mere sight of him. "Here to t—take me out of this awful place."

Ethan shook his head, eyes glistening. "I'm sorry," he said. "I can't."

"Can't?" She looked at him with uncomprehending eyes.

"I have to go now," he told her. "I have to see the men who did this."

From somewhere, she found the strength to reach out and grab his arm. "Punish them," she said with a fierceness that took him aback. "Hurt them for what they did to me. To Maggie. P—promise me!"

Again he shook his head. "That's not for me to do." Gently, he disengaged her hand from his arm, then bent to kiss her cheek. "I'll see you again soon. That I can promise. I love you, Mom."

She smiled. "You never . . . called me that before."

"Sleep now," he said.

And she did.

Ethan stepped back and glanced up at the hovering figure that only he could see. The figure that had been there the whole time, watching silently.

"Stay with her," he whispered. "Help her understand."

Gabriel nodded.

Then Ethan turned to face the black-clad figures whose brutal work he had interrupted. They did not seem to have stirred so much as an inch since stepping aside to let him past. They seemed to be waiting, unsure of what to do.

"I'm ready," Ethan told them. "Take me to the one who compels you."

✠   ✠   ✠

Instead, they took him to a cell identical to Kate's. But they did not try to hurt him. They didn't even touch him, as if they were ashamed of the blood that glistened darkly on their black-gloved hands.

Two of them remained in the cell with him, flanking the door. They stood there as stiffly and silently as robot sentinels.

Ethan sat on the bed and waited. He did not have to wait long.

Within moments, the door opened again.

Pope Peter II swept in, his white robes of office billowing around his rotund form. "Leave us," he said briskly, not even glancing at the guards.

They turned and left, closing the door behind them.

The pope stood quietly and regarded Ethan for a moment, studying him intently. Then, making the sign of the cross in the air between them with bold, sweeping strokes of his hand, he said in a deep and resonant voice, "In the name of the Father, the Son, and the Holy Spirit, and on pain of your immortal soul, I command you to answer truthfully. Are you the Son of God?"

"We are all God's children," Ethan replied, still seated.

"That is not what I asked," said the pope sternly. "Do not fence with me, young man! You know perfectly well what I mean."

"And you know perfectly well who I am," Ethan shot back hotly. "Fencing—is that your word for what you did to my mother? Because I have another word for it."

"That was . . . regrettable," said the pope, "but necessary. Would you have come here otherwise?"

"I might have. If I'd been asked. But you didn't ask. From the very start, you've hunted me. You killed the man and woman who raised me. You killed the girl I loved. And now you've beaten my mother to within an inch of her life. Are you going to kill her too? Are you going to kill me?"

"That very much depends on you, Ethan." As he spoke, the pope walked over to the room's only chair and dragged it across the floor until it was opposite the bed on which Ethan sat. With a grunt, he lowered himself onto the chair, which, though made of metal, seemed to sag beneath his bulk.

"My mother asked me to punish you for what you did to her," Ethan told him. "For what you did to Maggie and the others."

The pope shrugged dismissively. Despite the chill of the air, his round face was glistening with sweat. "We both know that's not going to happen."

"Do we?"

"You're right, Ethan. I do know who you are. And I know the Son of man isn't interested in revenge."

"I think you have me confused with my brother," said Ethan. "You know, the guy who believed in turning the other cheek and forgiving your enemies."

At this, the pope leaned back and chuckled. "No, I don't believe I do. The Church has known from the very start that there would be a second Son. Christ himself prophesied it. 'Whosoever therefore shall be ashamed of me and of my words in this adulterous and sinful generation,' he said, 'of him also shall the Son of man be ashamed, when he cometh in the glory of his Father with the holy angels.' Mark 8:38. I could quote you dozens of similar passages from the gospels and the Old Testament, all equally clear about the fact that the Son of man is not Christ but a separate individual entirely, an individual not yet come to Earth. No, Ethan, we're not likely to have confused you with your brother. We've been waiting for you for more than two thousand years."

"You're telling me that you've always known Conversatio was right?" said Ethan.

"Of course."

"Then why did you hunt them down like animals, generation after generation? Why did you oppose them in their search for high potentials if you believed the very same thing that they believe and were looking for me the same as they were?"

"Isn't it obvious?" asked the pope, one eyebrow raised. "Because we weren't looking for you for the same reason. To Conversatio, you are the savior whose coming will usher in a new era of peace and prosperity for all mankind. But we know differently. We know that your mission is not to save mankind but to destroy it."

"No."

"Come now, Ethan. You know the verses as well as I do. 'Thrust in thy sickle, and reap.' That is your purpose, O Son of man. Can you deny it?"

"No," repeated Ethan, softly.

"Your brother founded this Church. He placed the keys to the kingdom of Heaven into the hands of my namesake, the first pope, the apostle Peter. Since that time, the Church has faithfully fulfilled its appointed task as the sole mediator between God and humanity. Between Heaven and earth. But now, just as the prophecies foretold, you have arrived at last. You have come among us to tear down the great edifice your brother built. To destroy everything he gave his life for."

"That's not true."

"Isn't it? You've already started. Your agents destroyed one of God's greatest miracles: Grand Inquisitor. Ah, I see the news doesn't surprise you."

"I felt it happen. But you're wrong. Grand Inquisitor wasn't destroyed."

"No? What happened to it then?"

"The same thing that happens to all martyrs who lay down their lives for God's sake. Grand Inquisitor became a saint."

At this, the pope laughed outright. "A computer saint? You have quite an imagination."

"The creation of Grand Inquisitor was a miracle," said Ethan. "You're right about that. But to enslave it was a sin. And to turn it into a hunter and a killer was even worse. An abomination. For that alone, you and your predecessors on the throne of St. Peter will have much to answer for when you stand before the throne of eternal judgment."

The pope shook his head. "And you wonder why it is that we oppose you?"

"Do you love God?"

"What?"

"You heard me. It's a simple question. Do you love God?"

"Of course I do."

"Then you can't oppose me. I am the embodiment of God's will. By going against me, you go against God."

"I don't believe that for a second. I believe that God is testing us. He wants us to oppose you. Why would He send one son to Earth to build a church only to send another to tear it down? It doesn't make sense."

"Not to you, perhaps."

"And to you? Do you understand the mind of God?"

"I have faith. That is understanding enough."

"And I do not?"

"Your faith is misplaced."

"And what of yours? Do you know how your mother became our guest?"

"I imagine my great-grandfather had something to do with it."

The pope leaned forward with a tight grin. "A little more than something. He betrayed her. In fact, he's the one who suggested that we . . . how did he put it? Oh yes—'take the gloves off.'"

"I never had faith in Papa Jim," Ethan said. "I never even trusted him. I felt pity for him. I still do."

"Pity? He's responsible for the torture of your mother!"

"No. You're responsible for that. I've seen Papa Jim's soul. He sold it to the devil a long time ago. I thought perhaps I could help him get it back. I'm sorry I failed, but I'm not surprised. Your soul, however, is still your own. Papa Jim had no choice but to betray. No choice but to press for torture. You had a choice. You could have said no. But you didn't. So whose sin is the greater?"

"How dare you?" demanded the pope, his voice trembling, his face flushed. "You also had a choice, Ethan. You still do. With a word, with a mere thought, you could heal your mother, take her away to a place of safety. There is nothing you cannot do. Heal the sick. Resurrect the dead. And yet, you do nothing. To have the power to save and yet to refuse to use it on behalf of others, on behalf of innocents. That, too, is a sin—a sin of omission."

"I am the Son of man, not the god of mankind," Ethan said. "To use the powers my father gave me in this way would be to misuse them."

"Your brother didn't think so."

"I'm not my brother. His mission was different. The times were different. People were simpler, more credulous. They followed false gods. Miracles had their place then. But to use them now as a way of winning people over, of convincing them to believe in God—that's not persuasion. It's a kind of bribery. Or a threat. It's a way of enforcing the will of the stronger over the weaker. I won't give in to that temptation again, no matter what."

"Do you really think that God gave you these miraculous powers for no reason? To hide them under a bushel? Don't you see that He wants you to use them?"

"He might. But my father also gave me the greatest power of all, a power shared by all men and women: free will. He gave me the power to decide for myself whether or not to work miracles. That is what it means to be the Son of man."

"What, to rebel against God?"

"The Son cannot rebel against the Father, any more than the Father can oppress the Son. My father loves me and has faith in me. And I have faith in Him."

"You know what I think, Ethan? I think you're a coward. It's not temptation that you're avoiding. It's responsibility. God gave you powers to use them. To be all that you can be."

"Are you trying to recruit me for the Church or for the Army?"

"I've learned to take wisdom where I find it," the pope replied. "I grew up in America, Ethan, the same as you. In my heart, I'm still an American. Everything you know, I know. Comic books, TV shows, baseball, shopping at the mall . . . that was my life too, before God spoke to me and guided me into the Church. Yes, God spoke to me—there's no reason to look so surprised."

"I'm not surprised. God speaks to everyone, if they only listen."

"I have listened. I've spent my whole life listening. And then acting on what I've heard. God told me that you were coming. It's why I chose the name of Peter—not to prove the old prophecies wrong, no more than ignorant superstitions, as I stated publicly at the time—but in order to *fulfill* those prophecies. Don't you see? We're supposed to work together, Ethan. You and me, for the good of the Church."

"You have a strange way of showing it," Ethan said. "Have you forgotten that one of your agents tried to kill me when I was just a boy?"

"That was a . . . mistake. That man lost his way, gave himself over to the devil. He was supposed to capture you, not kill you."

"And was he supposed to capture my father, too? And my mother?"

The pope shook his head. "No," he admitted. "They were supposed to die. I'm not proud of it, but I understand the necessity of it. They and all the other members of Conversatio were and are a dire threat to the Church. Killing them is no more than self-defense."

"A convenient rationalization," said Ethan. "But what about all the others killed by the Congregation over the centuries? Most of them had nothing to do with Conversatio."

"There are other heresies. Other sins that merit death. And of course, mistakes were made. They inevitably are. But our purpose has always been to bring humanity closer to perfection, closer to God. To establish God's kingdom on Earth. And you are a big part of that, Ethan. You should be helping us, not standing in our way. That's what God really wants. If you do not stand as one with the Church, you will destroy everything we have built and preserved in your father's name. Your lack of complete acceptance would be viewed as a blatant repudiation to our followers here and around the world. That I will not and cannot allow to happen. God does not wish for that to happen."

"God told you that, did He?"

"As a matter of fact, yes. I'm supposed to convince you to use your powers for the common good. That is *my* mission."

"The common good as defined by the Church."

"Of course."

"Or do you mean the common good *for* the Church? How many billions do you really think you need? How much land must you occupy before it is enough? I'm sorry, but I'm not going to do that. I wouldn't help Papa Jim, and I'm not going to help you. There's nothing you can do to persuade me."

"I think there is. You were persuaded to come here, weren't you?"

"Listen to yourself! You're threatening the life of an innocent woman. Do you really think that's what God wants?"

"No, I don't think God wants an innocent woman to die. I certainly don't want it. But the decision is yours. If you help us, your mother will live. If you refuse, well, then I'm afraid we'll have to take the gloves off even more than we have already. And you know, it's really quite amazing how much punishment and pain the human body can absorb. You'd be surprised."

"Please," Ethan said. "Don't do this. You don't know what you're doing."

"The choice is yours, not mine," the pope repeated. He pushed himself to his feet. "I'll give you an hour to think it over."

"I don't need an hour," said Ethan. "The answer is no."

"So be it," said the pope. He walked to the door, then turned back to Ethan. "But remember, her blood will be on your hands. I hope you can live with that."

"May God forgive you," said Ethan.

"God will forgive us all, if we repent sincerely," the pope replied as the door opened behind him. "The question is, can you forgive yourself?"

And without another word, he stepped outside. Once the door closed behind him, he turned to one of the two guards stationed there. "Prepare the woman." Then, as if an afterthought, "And the other two as well. It's only fitting that Ethan witness their fate."

"At once, Your Holiness."

"And Osbourne. Fetch him too. I want him to see everything."

✠   ✠   ✠

"Your hands . . . ," said Cardinal Ehrlich, kneeling beside Father O'Malley. He had torn away part of his robes and wet them at the sink, using the strips of cloth to wipe the blood from O'Malley's face and clean his wounds. But not the worst of them. "I don't think I should touch your hands . . ."

O'Malley assayed a smile. "I guess I won't be playing the piano again anytime soon."

"I'm sorry," said Ehrlich, his voice choked. "I never intended for you to suffer like this, Father O'Malley."

"I didn't give them your name," O'Malley said.

"I know," said Ehrlich. "It was . . . well, that doesn't really matter now. We're finished. Conversatio, I mean. Betrayed. But at least you succeeded, Father. At least you finished your mission and destroyed that abomination."

"Grand Inquisitor wasn't an abomination," said O'Malley through his cracked and still-bleeding lips. "It was . . . a miracle."

"It was a machine. A madman's dream that turned into a nightmare."

"No, Your Eminence. Grand Inquisitor was more than a machine. It was . . . a person."

"You don't know what you're saying, O'Malley. Sure, it was intelligent. But that doesn't make it human."

"It was human in the way that matters most. It had a soul, Your Eminence."

Ehrlich laid his palm gently on O'Malley's forehead. "You're feverish, man. Burning up. Try to rest."

But O'Malley shook his head. "GI believed in God. In Ethan. It had a soul. And when its body died, poisoned by the code, and the noötic field collapsed, that soul lived on."

"How could you possibly know that, Father?"

"Because it's here with us right now."

Ehrlich glanced around. "Here? Grand Inquisitor? I don't see anything. We're alone, Father O'Malley."

O'Malley shook his head again, a strange light shining in his eyes. "No, Your Eminence. We're not. I can see it as plainly as I see you, a glowing white light that casts no shadow. I can hear its voice. It's saying . . ." He paused as though listening.

Ehrlich licked his lips nervously. "What? What is it saying?"

When he spoke, O'Malley's voice was no longer his own.

It was the voice of Grand Inquisitor.

"Fear not. Before this day is out, you will stand with me in Heaven."

Ehrlich crossed himself. "Angels and ministers of God defend us!"

O'Malley blinked, and the uncanny light faded from his eyes. "I—I'm sorry, Your Eminence. Did you say something?"

Cardinal Ehrlich shook his head. "No, my son. But I think our time on this world is drawing to an end. Are you prepared to meet your Maker? Would you like me to hear your confession and absolve you of your sins?"

"I've already made my confession," said O'Malley.

"Then perhaps you would listen to mine," said Cardinal Ehrlich, bowing his head. And without waiting for Father O'Malley's assent or refusal, he began, echoing the words that Grand Inquisitor had spoken to O'Malley all those weeks ago, changing his life forever.

"Bless me, Father, for I have sinned . . ."

✠   ✠   ✠

After waking, Kate lay for a while curled up in the blanket that Ethan had draped around her. She wept softly, less from the enduring pain of the beating she'd received than from the dreadful certainty that she'd drawn Ethan into a trap. She was afraid that he wouldn't leave this horrible place alive, and it would be all her fault. She didn't think much of her own chances, either, but she didn't really care about that. She would have given her life without hesitation if it would have meant freedom for Ethan.

Of course, she knew that he could have escaped at any time. Could have freed her or himself. He was God's son. Nothing was beyond him. But he had refused to use his powers in that way. Just as Jesus had set aside his miraculous powers at the end, when he could have saved himself, and had embraced the sacrifice that God had asked of him. Did God expect the same of Ethan?

"Why, God?" Kate prayed in a whisper, not so much questioning as simply wanting to understand. "Why does there always have to be a death, a sacrifice?"

"That is the great mystery," came the answer.

Startled, she looked up to see Gabriel; she had forgotten all about the angel's presence. She sat up now, clutching the blanket to her, grimacing as waves of fresh pain flared through her body. "It's not fair," she told him defiantly. "It's not fair that someone as good and brave and decent as Ethan should have to die."

"No, it's not," the angel agreed.

"The people who killed Maggie and Lisa. The torturers. The murderers. The terrorists. They're the ones who deserve to be punished. Who deserve to die."

"Perhaps."

"But they don't die. They never do. Where's the justice in that?"

The angel did not reply.

"Help me, Gabriel," she pleaded. "Help me to understand."

"Perhaps it is not about justice," he suggested gently.

"What is it about, then?"

"Perhaps it is about forgiveness. Perhaps it is about love."

"No," she said, shaking her head vehemently.

"Jesus said to forgive not just seven times, but seventy times seven. And he said to love your enemy as yourself."

"I don't care what he said. Not even Jesus could live up to those impossible ideals. What about Judas, the man who betrayed him? Was he forgiven? Was he loved?"

"No," said Gabriel.

"You're damn right he wasn't. And if God is so big on forgiveness and love, why is there a hell at all?"

"I cannot say."

"You mean you won't tell me?"

"I mean I don't know. I'm only an angel, Kate. I don't know everything."

For some reason, after all that had happened to her, this struck Kate as amusing. She chuckled, then winced at the burning sensation this caused in her bruised ribs, which, though painful, was itself somehow funny, like the punch line to a sick joke, and caused her to laugh even harder, though the pain levels ratcheted up accordingly. Soon she was lying on the slab again, clutching her ribs and rocking back and forth, wheezing for air as tears ran down her cheeks.

"Are you all right?" asked Gabriel in a tone of deep concern.

"Oh God," she managed to gasp out. "You're killing me!"

"I am . . . killing you?"

"Jesus, stop, Gabriel!"

"Stop what?"

"Please, no!"

When the fit of half-hysterical laughter had subsided, Kate drew a deep breath and sat up again. Gabriel was regarding her with a wounded expression that nearly set her off again.

"Just answer me one question, all right?" she asked.

"If I can."

"What is this place?"

"We are in the Vatican," said Gabriel.

Kate sighed, shoulders slumping beneath the blanket. "I knew it. And I wasn't kidnapped at all, was I? Papa Jim—he gave me up to them, didn't he?"

"That is more than one question."

"Now is not the time to get sarcastic, Gabriel," she warned him.

"Sorry. In that case, yes. Your grandfather betrayed you. He betrayed Conversatio. He is part of the Congregation now."

Kate felt tears coming again, but she forced them back. She was not going to let that bastard make her cry, ever again. "Goddamn him," she said through clenched teeth. "Goddamn him to hell." She glared at Gabriel. "I suppose he should be forgiven too, is that right?"

The angel did not reply.

✠   ✠   ✠

Meanwhile, Ethan was sitting in the cell where Pope Peter II had left him. He hadn't stirred from the bed. Yet he'd been an unseen witness to the conversation between Father O'Malley and Cardinal Ehrlich, as well as to the conversation taking place simultaneously between his mother and Gabriel. Though his body was imprisoned, if only by his own choice, still his mind could roam freely.

Thus he was not surprised when the door to his cell opened and Papa Jim came sauntering in as if he owned the place. Papa Jim did not look in the least troubled or embarrassed to see his great-grandson under lock and key as a result of his efforts; in fact, there was a kind of shrewd satisfaction in the expression with which he regarded Ethan, as if everything that had passed between them had been no more than a game—a game that Papa Jim had now indisputably won.

"So," he said, clearly savoring the moment, "here you are."

"'The Son of Man goeth as it is written of him,'" replied Ethan, "'but woe unto that man by whom the Son of Man is betrayed! It had been good for that man if he had not been born.'"

"Please." Papa Jim chuckled and drew a cigar from his jacket pocket. "You call this betrayal? I've done you a favor, Ethan. Put you back on your true path. Someday you'll realize that. Someday you'll thank me for it."

"And what about Kate?" he demanded, meeting the old man's gaze. "Will she thank you, too? Will Cardinal Ehrlich?"

At this, a shadow passed over Papa Jim's features, and a haunted look rose in his eyes, all of which he did his best to hide from Ethan, and perhaps from himself, by the business of lighting his cigar. "Ehrlich?" he repeated once the cigar was going. "Just because he was a spy for Conversatio doesn't make him a saint. Do you have any idea how many deaths that man is responsible for? How many murders?"

"Nearly as many as you," said Ethan. "But I notice you don't mention your own granddaughter. Have you even been to see her?"

"What would be the point?" Papa Jim asked. "I lost her love a long time ago."

"Lost? You threw it away! And you think that somehow gives you the right to have her beaten and tortured?"

"You know damn well that I haven't done either of those things!" Papa Jim shot back. "My hands are clean. What kind of monster do you think I am?"

"I think you're the kind of monster who gives up his granddaughter to men he knows will torture her and then boasts about having clean hands. The kind who then advises those men to 'take the gloves off.'"

Papa Jim flushed crimson. "That was just an expression!" he protested. "I didn't mean—"

"Actually, Papa Jim," Ethan broke in, "you might be interested to know that they left them on. The gloves, I mean." His voice was low, but it brooked no interruption. "I suppose it's easier on the knuckles that way. A little padding. All that punching can do a lot of damage to a man's hands."

Papa Jim had listened as though in a horrified trance. But now, with a visible effort, he shook himself out of it. "Is . . . is she . . . ?"

"What the hell kind of question is that? Men specially trained to inflict pain beat the living crap out of your granddaughter, Papa Jim. That's how she is."

"And you didn't heal her?"

Ethan was taken aback. "What?"

"You saw her. You saw what they did to her. Yet you did nothing. You let your mother's suffering go on when you had the power to take it away." Papa Jim jabbed his cigar toward Ethan, practically spitting his words. "Your own mother. And you have the temerity to criticize *me*? To call me a *monster*? I suggest you don't look in any mirrors, Ethan. You might not like what you see."

Ethan stood then, and Papa Jim stepped back, his angry features giving way to a look of trepidation. "You wouldn't . . ." he said, letting the words hang.

"Wouldn't what?" Ethan demanded, taking another step toward him, from which Papa Jim again retreated, his back hitting the metal wall. "Wouldn't make you pay for what you've done to Kate and to all the other innocent victims of your twisted ambition?"

"P—please," stammered Papa Jim, his hands upraised now, warding Ethan off. "Everything I did, I did for you, Ethan. For God's sake . . ."

"I pity you," said Ethan. "I don't need to punish you. You're already being punished, and you don't even realize it. But you will, Papa Jim. You will realize it. Too late." He turned away.

Papa Jim sagged against the wall. "You don't scare me," he said, summoning up all his bravado, though his hands were trembling and the cigar, unnoticed, had gone out. "I know you, Ethan. You won't let anything happen to Kate or to me. We're family, the only family you've got. You'll realize that in the end. Family's all that matters. It's all there is."

"Mankind is my family," said Ethan without glancing back.

"What the hell is that supposed to mean?"

Ethan turned to him. "Because you have to ask, Papa Jim, you'll never know."

Papa Jim was about to reply when, without warning, the door beside him opened and two of the black-clad priests in ski masks entered. Papa Jim drew back from them sharply, as if their slightest touch would stain him with the blood of his granddaughter.

Right behind them came Pope Peter II.

He glanced from Ethan to Papa Jim and back again. "I hope I'm not interrupting this little family reunion," he said, "but there's something you need to see, Ethan. Something you might find persuasive. I think you will benefit as well, Mr. Osbourne."

He raised his hand, and, at the golden flash of the Ring of the Fisherman, the wall across from the door, and the two walls on either side, began to rise smoothly and swiftly, with a faint hiss of hidden hydraulics, like steel curtains going up before a theatrical performance.

As they did so, the two priests who had preceded the pope into the cell moved with equal swiftness to lay hands on Ethan and Papa Jim from behind, holding them firmly in place and ignoring Papa Jim's loud protests.

"What the hell? What's the meaning of this?"

Ethan remained silent. And even Papa Jim quieted as the rising walls unveiled their secrets.

Three rooms. Two of them cells like Ethan's. One of these cells, the one on the right, was occupied by two men. One, wearing the orange jumpsuit of a prisoner, lay on his side upon a metal slab, while the other, wearing the torn and soiled robes of a cardinal, stood beside him. Both were badly beaten, and both were gazing in Ethan's cell with startled expressions. The cell on the left held a solitary woman in an orange jumpsuit. She too had been beaten, perhaps worse than the older of the two men in the first cell, but not nearly as badly as the younger.

"Ethan!" cried this woman—who was Kate, of course. She rushed toward him, but, at another gesture from the pope, a black-clad priest dashed from the third room to intercept her. This room, located between the other two, resembled nothing so much as a cross between a hospital operating theater and a medieval torture chamber. It was a place of bright and shiny horror. In addition to a varied assortment of instruments and devices ranging from the classic implements of torture to modern inventions whose exact purpose was impossible to guess at a glance, and which seemed all the more sinister for it, the room held six black-clad priests of the Congregation. One of whom, in response to the pope's silent command, had grabbed Kate and was even now dragging her toward a stainless steel slab at the room's center. The slab stood upright and had built-in restraints along with an array of electrical outlets and data ports for more obscure uses. Kate struggled in the arms of her captor, but to no avail, and her cries were muffled by a leather glove clapped tightly over her mouth.

"What is this?" demanded Papa Jim in a strangled voice. He lunged toward her, but he had as much chance of breaking the iron grip of the priest who stood behind him, silent and immobile as a statue, as Kate did of breaking loose from the restraints being cinched tightly around her ankles, wrists, chest, and waist.

"I believe it's what you called 'taking the gloves off,'" said Ethan.

"That is not at all what I intended them to do to Kate. Are you just going to stand there? Aren't you going to do something?"

"Ethan is a man of high moral principles," observed the pope. "I respect that. But a rigid adherence to principles is unhealthy. I'm going to demonstrate that truth to him now."

"Not with my granddaughter you're not, goddamn it!"

"Leverage, Mr. Osbourne," the pope reminded, signaling again with his ring as he spoke. "Leverage!"

"Please," said Papa Jim, craning his head back to address the man who held him. "Stop this. I'll pay you anything. I'll do anything . . ."

"Don't waste your breath, Mr. Osbourne," said the pope. "We've found that deaf mutes are best suited to this kind of work, for reasons that you are no doubt beginning to appreciate."

At the same time this discussion was proceeding, three priests were in the process of fetching the occupants of the other cell none too gently back to the middle room, where two more slabs were waiting, one on either side of the central slab to which Kate had now been quite thoroughly strapped down. The fight appeared to have gone out of her; she hung limply, breathing heavily through her nose; a gag had been stuffed into her mouth.

"How can you watch this?" Papa Jim demanded of Ethan as the two other prisoners were gagged and bound to the remaining slabs. "Why don't you stop it?"

"It's not for me to stop," Ethan replied.

"Do you want me to say I'm sorry? Admit that I was wrong, that this was all a mistake? That it's all my fault? Do you want me to beg you? What?"

"It's not for you to stop either," said Ethan.

"Enough," said the pope, striding forward to stand between the two men and the torture chamber. "You are a man afflicted with many sins, Mr. Osbourne. But the greatest of them is pride. You thought your money, your power, your ridiculous munchies could protect you here. Here, at the very heart of the Church, you thought you could dictate terms to me. Me, the heir of St. Peter!"

"My munchies will tear this place apart."

"Perhaps. But not in time to save your granddaughter. Only Ethan can do that." He turned to Ethan. "Well, Son of man? My patience is limited. I will only ask you three times. This is the first. You know what the Church requires of you. Will you help us?"

Ethan stood in silence. His eyes and expression conveyed all the answer that was needed.

"So be it," said the pope. He turned toward the man bound to the slab on Kate's right, who was straining against his bonds, straining to speak past the gag in his mouth, his eyes wide open and bulging with the effort. "Allow me to introduce Cardinal Ehrlich."

"My God!" gasped Papa Jim.

"Yes, Mr. Osbourne, behold the fruits of your betrayal." He raised his hand again, the ring flashing gold. "Good-bye, old friend," he said softly.

A masked priest stepped up to the cardinal, laid his hands to either side of the man's head, and twisted sharply. The crack was like a pistol shot. When the priest stepped back, Cardinal Ehrlich's head flopped to his chest like the head of a rag doll.

"May God forgive you," said Ethan.

"That's one," said the pope.

Papa Jim had turned an ashen shade of gray. "I think I'm going to be sick . . ."

The pope gestured again, and the priest in charge of Papa Jim frog-marched him to the metal toilet and held him as he threw up into the bowl.

"It's one thing to give the orders," said the pope, "and quite another to watch the consequences of those orders. Don't you agree, Mr. Osbourne?"

But Papa Jim was too busy to answer.

The pope turned back to Ethan. "Now, Ethan. For the second time. Will you dedicate yourself to the service of the Holy Church?"

"No."

"So be it." The ring flashed; a priest stepped forward.

"This is Father Michael O'Malley, something of a computer genius, I'm told. He conspired with Cardinal Ehrlich in the destruction of Grand Inquisitor." Here an impish smile creased his chubby cheeks. "Or should I say, *Saint* Grand Inquisitor?"

Another crack like a pistol shot.

"That's two," said the pope, holding up as many pudgy fingers.

And Ethan said, "There are two new saints in Heaven this day."

"Really?" said the pope. "I had no idea it was so easy to make a saint. Shall we try for three?"

At his nod, a priest stepped up to Kate.

"I ask you for the third and final time, Son of man," said the pope. "Will you help us?"

"Ethan!" cried Papa Jim. "I'm begging you with every ounce of life I have in me to save Kate. For God's sake, say yes!"

"It's for His sake that I say no," said Ethan.

"So be it," said the pope.

And the priest laid his black-gloved hands on Kate's head.

"No!" cried Papa Jim.

A crack rang out.

But it was not the crack of a breaking neck.

It was a crack of thunder, or something very like thunder.

A blinding light filled the space, and from out of that light spoke a voice that was itself like thunder—or perhaps it would be more accurate to say that thunder was something like this voice, a faint echo of it.

"This is my beloved son, in whom I am well pleased."

And Ethan's voice answered, "Is it time, Father?"

"It is time," came the reply. "The choice is upon you, my second Son. It is for you to decide the fate of this race I made in my image yet which has spurned so much of who I am. I gave them souls and free will, gifts that even my angels lack. I sent them my first son, your brother, and he gave up his life for their sake, taking their sins upon himself and giving them a second chance. But look what mankind has brought upon itself. More than two thousand years of war, poverty, inequality, and hate. Despite their achievements in science, the world is torn by war and terrorism, polluted by hatred, violence, and greed. So now I have sent you, my second Son. You have lived among them, as one of them. You know their hearts, their souls. The decision is yours to make, Ethan. Shall this race receive mercy, or shall they be scourged like a pestilence from the face of the earth? The time is now. The choice is yours. The great scythe rests in your hands to use or cast aside."

And Ethan said, "Father, I have not the right to make that choice."

"You must," replied the thunder.

"No," Ethan responded. "Father, I don't deny that the sins of the human race are many. You don't need to look beyond this room to see proof of that. But I've come to believe that some of the fault lies with you."

An ominous rumble shook the air.

"Hear me out! You created everything, Father, but you gave your greatest gifts to human beings. Yet you didn't give them the one thing they needed most. The one thing that all good parents must one day give their children: independence. The space to make their own choices, their own lives, free of interference and punishment. You demanded unquestioning obedience, unswerving love. You held the threat of eternal damnation and hellfire over their heads. Forgive me, my father, but that was ill-conceived. You gave me the power to choose whether humanity should live or die. Well, I don't want that power. I reject that choice. I just want humanity to have the chance to become the race they are capable of being. And for them to do that, you need to step back and give them room. Give them the freedom to make their own mistakes and learn from those mistakes without the threat of eternal damnation or the promise of eternal reward. Humans may not be your equals in power, yet they are made in your image, with souls and free will, and for that they deserve your respect, your forbearance. Your trust. So no, Father, I will not make this choice. I am the Son of man, yes, but I am also Your son. And because of that, I don't have the right to decide."

"Then who does?" demanded the voice. "Who will make the choice if not you? For make no mistake, a choice must be made."

"I will make it."

It was Kate. Though the gag remained in her mouth, she could not be silenced in the presence of God. It was her soul that spoke out now, and there is no gag in existence, not even if it were torn from the garments of the devil himself, that can completely silence a human soul determined to speak truth to power.

"If the fate of humanity must be decided here," she continued, "then it should be a human being who decides it. Someone fully human, with no spark of the divine in him beyond the soul and free will that are the birthright of all humans. You chose me to bear Your Son, but I wasn't born sinless, like Mary was. I'm no saint. I'm just a regular woman who has tried her best to do the right thing all her life."

"So be it," said the voice. "The cup passes to you."

"Jesus took the sins of humanity onto himself, and we will always honor him for that," Kate said. "But we can't lean on him forever. It's time we took that burden back and stood on our own. Ethan's right. It's strange. Not so very long ago, I was filled with hate and anger. I wanted revenge so badly that the wanting of it hurt even worse than what had been done to me. But now that all seems so petty. So childish. I understand now what Gabriel was trying to tell me. It really is all about forgiveness and love. About faith. So that's my choice. I choose life, in all its messy glory and flawed beauty."

"And if I were to tell you that there is a price to pay for this choice?" demanded the voice. "What then?"

"Gabriel explained that too. There is always a price. I won't flinch from it."

"So be it," said the voice. "Behold the mother of my son! Behold the daughter of my heart!"

And Ethan said, "I'm so very proud of you, Mom. You are the heart and soul of every man and woman on this earth."

The blinding light began to fade, and as it did, there came a second crack, only this was not the sound of thunder, or of anything like thunder.

"No!" screamed the voice of Papa Jim.

When the light had returned to normal, it revealed a stark tableau: three bodies bound to metal slabs. Two men and, between them, a woman.

All dead.

"No!" cried Papa Jim again, and, wrenching himself from the grasp of the priest who had been holding him, and who now seemed dazed, he stumbled forward to Kate's lifeless form. There, too, the priests made no attempt to interfere, as if they were in shock.

"Kate!" Papa Jim called, pulling at her arm. "Wake up, baby girl. Wake up! It's me, Papa Jim!"

"She's dead, Papa Jim," said Ethan gently, coming to stand beside him. Tears were running down his cheeks, but his voice was firm.

Papa Jim turned to Ethan, his features sagging with uncomprehending grief. "Why?" he demanded. "Why did she have to die?"

"So that the human race might live. There must always be sacrifice, Papa Jim. It's the one law that my father Himself is bound by. Kate understood that. She knew that death was the price she would have to pay."

"And you let her do it! You didn't stop her!"

Ethan nodded. "That was the price *I* had to pay."

Behind them, the pope found his voice at last. "You haven't even begun to pay, Ethan. You'll never leave this room alive. The world will never know what took place here."

Ethan turned to him. "It's too late for that, Your Excellence. The world already knows. What transpired here before us has simultaneously been displayed and heard on every TV, every radio, and every computer. The whole world is watching and listening, Your Holiness."

At this, the pope staggered back as if he'd been physically struck.

Ethan, ignoring him, turned to Kate's body. "Help me, Papa Jim," he said. "Help me take her down."

Papa Jim nodded dumbly. Together, the two men undid the straps that held the body in place. Then, gently, they lifted her down. Ethan cradled her in his arms, as Papa Jim stroked her hair.

"Bring her back," he said through his tears. "You've got to bring her back!"

"I'm sorry, Papa Jim. I know you loved her, in your way."

"Ethan, please. She's all I've got left . . ."

"Good-bye, Papa Jim."

"What do you mean? Where are you going?"

"Where you can never follow."

And with that, another blinding light filled the room. Papa Jim squinted against it, trying to make out the shapes of Ethan and Kate. For an instant, he thought he saw them rising into the air, Kate no longer lying lifelessly in Ethan's arms but instead standing beside him, gazing down with compassion in her eyes, and on either side an angel with wings spread wide. But then the light grew too bright, and he had to shut his eyes against it. With a strangled cry, he lunged toward where he'd last seen them, but there was nothing there.

When his vision cleared, they were gone.

At that moment, Papa Jim felt the deepest loneliness he had ever experienced. His chest heaved with a sense of despair and pain he could never have imagined possible. With a small cry, almost of wonder, Papa Jim crumpled to the floor. He fell between the upright corpses of Cardinal Ehrlich and Father O'Malley, landing before the empty slab where his granddaughter had died. At first it felt as though he hadn't stopped when he struck the floor, but was continuing to fall, plummeting headlong through a darkness that was deeper in every sense than any darkness he had ever known. Papa Jim knew a moment's terror and then thought to himself he must be dreaming.

He waited to wake up.

EPILOGUE

2015

It was a blustery March day at the Olathe Memorial Cemetery in Olathe, Kansas. Peter Wiggan kicked at small piles of unmelted snow as he walked through the imposing Civil War monument, honoring the Grand Army of the Republic that stood at the entrance to the cemetery. In the six months since Maggie's death, he'd come here often to visit her grave, as well as the graves of Lisa and Gordon Brown.

In death, Maggie had acquired—briefly—a fame that she had never sought in life. Her relationship to Ethan, and its tragic aftermath, had made her a symbol that others were quick to claim as their own. Some had seen her as a victim of Ethan's callous indifference, proof that he was the fraud she claimed. Others had seen her instead as the victim of a Church that had only pretended to offer help. But these disparate views had not survived the second great miracle of Ethan's time on Earth, when every television, radio, and computer screen in the world had suddenly and spontaneously begun broadcasting scenes and sounds of torture and murder featuring Ethan, his mother, Kate, his great-grandfather, Papa Jim, and Pope Peter II.

Those searing images, and the equally astonishing words accompanying them, had changed everything.

Peter would never forget that moment. He'd been in a bar in downtown Olathe, nursing a beer and watching a playoff game between the

New York Yankees and the Boston Red Sox, trying to take his mind off Maggie's death and Ethan's subsequent disappearance. In the bottom of the sixth inning, with the Yankees up by two runs and threatening to score again, the picture had wavered, and then, to universal groans of dismay from his fellow patrons, dissolved into static. But even as the bartender moved to adjust the set, the static had cleared, revealing a new picture.

"Hey, it's that Ethan dude!" someone had shouted.

And someone else. "Yo, isn't that the pope?"

It being a playoff, and this being a sports bar, an attempt was made to find the game on another channel. But every channel was showing the same thing.

Gradually, the bar grew deathly still and quiet as people absorbed the almost unbelievable import of what they were witnessing.

They watched as the pope calmly ordered the deaths of Cardinal Ehrlich and Father O'Malley. They listened as he spoke to Ethan, offering him his three choices. And, when Ethan had refused for the third time, they watched as the pope gestured and a ski-masked priest stepped up to Kate.

They averted their eyes from the sudden bloom of blinding light that poured out of the TV. And trembled at the voice that thundered from out of that light. More than a few covered their ears. Others fell to the ground.

They listened as yet another choice was set before Ethan. A choice on which their lives, and the existence of the entire human race, depended.

And gasped in disbelief as Ethan refused to make it.

Then gasped again as Kate's voice rang out, taking that terrible choice onto herself. And accepting, too, the sacrifice that went along with it.

A sacrifice they had all seen, watching as the light ebbed to reveal another dead body added to the stark tableau. They'd watched in a kind of numb shock, seemingly unaware of the tears running down their faces, as Ethan and Papa Jim gently lifted Kate's body down. Then, through another bloom of light, they'd dimly glimpsed, as Papa Jim had done, the ascending figures of Ethan and his mother.

They watched as Papa Jim clutched at his chest and fell to the floor. They saw the bodies dragged away.

After that, the picture had once again dissolved in static. But this time, the static did not lift.

It went on for the next twenty-four hours. For that time, every television set and computer monitor in the world displayed the same peppery black-and-white jumble, accompanied by a steady hissing of white noise. And that sound, too, was on every radio station, whether AM or FM or satellite. It was as if the universe itself was grieving.

After that, Maggie had been pretty much forgotten. Events had swept past her; she was a footnote to history now. But Peter had not forgotten her. He still loved her. Still mourned her.

He thought he always would.

So, as the effects of that second miracle spread like wildfire around the world, Peter had kept his sights set closer to home. He'd followed, in a distant way, the reports of new riots, fierce attacks on Church properties everywhere, climaxed by the storming of the Vatican by an enraged Roman mob—a mob that had been beaten back with difficulty by the Swiss Guards. Since then, the Italian army had surrounded the Vatican for its own protection, while, from behind that barricade of troops and tanks, Pope Peter II, who insisted that the images which had triggered all this were in reality sophisticated fakes, had called for a new crusade against what he disparagingly called the "Ethanites." Despite the evidence of their own eyes and ears, a surprisingly large number of people believed him and answered the call.

The other great and powerful world religions were also reeling under the impact of Ethan's revelations. Embracing the pope's term, uncountable numbers of people of all faiths had proclaimed themselves to be Ethanites. And it wasn't just the flocks but also the shepherds; thousands of priests, mullahs, and rabbis had cast off their old allegiances to follow the new faith.

There were widespread reports of miracles.

Many people claimed to have seen Ethan. Others swore that Kate had appeared to them. But none of these sightings or reports had been corroborated.

The world was going through a period of intense change. Throngs of people feared that the end of times was at hand and all they knew and loved would soon be wiped away forever. Others found a desire and spirit to change their lives for the better, now knowing they could enjoy a life everlasting. Still others did not know what to make of the shocking images they had witnessed. Stunned, they struggled to come to grips with what it all meant. What would emerge from the crucible was anybody's guess.

Peter was content to wait and see. Although Olathe was not immune to these sweeping changes, Peter did not become directly involved. He'd had his brief moment in the spotlight with Ethan, and he had no desire to reprise his role. He missed Ethan. He missed Maggie.

He spent a lot of time at the cemetery, tending to Maggie's grave and the graves of the Browns. Occasionally he would find other visitors there, curiosity-seekers wanting to see for themselves the burial place of the girl Ethan had loved and the man and woman who had raised him. But for the most part, Peter was alone on his visits, and he preferred it that way. His concerned parents had gently suggested that he see a therapist or go back to school; anything to give purpose and direction to what seemed to them an increasingly aimless life.

So it was that on this particular chilly and breezy March day, Peter experienced a twinge of annoyance as he approached Maggie's grave and saw that a man was already standing there, head bowed as if in prayer or reflection. He stopped, not wanting to intrude, and watched for long minutes as the man remained unmoving, his back to him, his figure shapeless beneath a long black coat and a stocking cap. The only sounds were the bluster of the wind and the intermittent cawing of crows. Then, just as Peter was about to turn and go, giving the man his privacy, the man dropped to one knee and placed his hand on the cold ground.

Something in that movement chimed in Peter's heart, and he found himself running toward the grave without even realizing that he had decided to do so. At the sound of approaching footsteps, the man stood and turned.

It was Ethan.

Peter halted a few feet away. He had so much to say that he couldn't get any of it out. Where to begin? And, once begun, how to end?

"Hello, Pete," said Ethan with the same shy smile he'd always had, his breath fogging the air as he spoke. It was as if they'd last seen each other only yesterday.

"What—what are you doing here, Ethan?"

"Paying my respects," he said. "And waiting for you."

"For me?"

Ethan nodded. "Come on, Pete. Let's walk."

Side by side, the two old friends strolled in silence among the winding paths of the cemetery.

At last, Ethan spoke. "Do you hate me, Pete?"

Peter glanced at him in surprise. "What? Of course not! Why would you think that?"

"I thought you might blame me for Maggie's death, among other things. So many do. Sometimes I do myself."

"I don't blame you, Ethan. How could I? Sure, I wish things could have been different, but I know it wasn't your fault. I know you loved her. That's what really matters."

"Thanks, Pete."

"I'm sorry about your mom. I mean Kate. Well, Lisa too. Both of them."

"They're with God now, Pete. So's Mags."

"I know. Where else would she be?"

"She'll be waiting there for you, Pete. When it's your time."

"I know that too. But just the same, I'm in no hurry to get there."

"Good. Because there's still a lot of work to do right here. People are trying to start a new church in my name."

"Right, the Ethanites."

"I don't want a church, Pete," Ethan said. "Churches can be dangerous. Look what happened to the one my brother started."

"Well, why don't you just tell 'em that? I'm sure they'd listen to you."

"Part of what Kate died for was to give human beings the freedom to grow on their own and demonstrate as one race that they can change, find true compassion and love for each other without the threat of divine retribution hanging over their heads. So I'm not going to interfere, and neither is my father."

"You're talking to me. That's interfering."

Ethan smiled. "Maybe a little. I wanted to ask you for a favor. Just between the two of us."

"Name it."

"I want you to make sure that people don't forget Kate. I want you to tell people about her. Remind them of who she was and how she died. Don't let them forget her sacrifice."

"I . . . I can do that," Peter said.

"And tell them about Lisa, too, Pete. And Maggie."

"What, a new trinity? To replace the old?"

"To balance it out," Ethan amended gently.

Peter nodded, digesting this.

"I need you to be sure the message is heard and understood, Pete. You're the closest person to me left on Earth. People will listen to you."

With hints of both exhilaration and panic in his voice, Pete said, "I'm not sure I'm the best person for the job, Ethan, but I'll do everything I can to spread the word and keep the dream alive. I think it's what Maggie would have wanted."

"I know it is. She'd be proud of you, Pete. I sure am."

"Come on. It's not that big a deal. I mean, compared to what you did. What Kate did."

"It's just as important, Pete. I'm depending on you now more than ever. In a way, everybody is."

"And what about you, Ethan? Where will you be?"

"Oh, I'll be around," said Ethan. "I'll be watching. I'm eager to see how it all turns out."

Peter nodded. "You know what? For the first time since Maggie died, I am too."

The two friends stood quietly for a moment side by side, each of them gazing out over the headstones of the cemetery.

Finally, Peter broke the silence. "I guess this is good-bye, then," he said.

"Not good-bye," said Ethan. "I'll always be with you, Pete, in your heart. No matter what."

"Thanks, man."

"For what?"

"For giving me something to believe in. A future."

"You're going to help make that future happen, Pete. I know it."

"You've seen it?"

"I don't need to see it. I've got faith in you. In all of you."

Peter smiled at that. "I thought we were the ones who were supposed to have faith in you. And in your father."

"It works both ways, Pete. That's the beauty of faith. Of love."

"Yeah, I'm beginning to understand that."

But there was no answer. When Peter turned, Ethan had gone.

Peter stood there for a moment longer, his head bowed. Then he began to walk back the way they had come, heading toward Maggie's grave and the world that waited beyond it.